"SIR, WE'RE UNDER ATTACK. MISSILES APPROACHING . . ."

"What?"

Eyes locked on the sky, Torin tongued the implant again. "Sir, I repeat, we're under attack."

The VTA slid sideways as Captain Daniels slapped the controls. The *Secure All* sounded. "Where are you going, Staff?"

"Back to my platoon, sir."

Torin was through the hatch and had it dogged shut behind her before she could answer. The civilian compartment was complete chaos. The ship twisted. A Rakva slammed into her, clutching desperately at her shoulders. "What is it? This one wants to know what is happening!" She threw him toward his seat, snapping, "Strap in, damn it!"

The three sergeants had keyed in an acknowledgment of the situation. There wasn't anything she could do for the platoon that they weren't doing. Someone had to take charge here.

"Staff?"

She could barely hear Lieutenant Jarret over the noise. "Sir, am securing civilians."

The VTA s[illegible] would have fallen had the Dor[illegible]ed one huge arm a[illegible]nst his stomach fu[illegible]nt," he said. "But [illegible]

Struggling [illegible]aws dig into the deck plating.

Impact.

I don't want to die with civilians. . . .

TANYA HUFF's Fantasy Novels available from DAW Books:

SING THE FOUR QUARTERS
FIFTH QUARTER
NO QUARTER
THE QUARTERED SEA

* * *

BLOOD PRICE (#1)
BLOOD TRAIL (#2)
BLOOD LINES (#3)
BLOOD PACT (#4)
BLOOD DEBT(#5)

* * *

SUMMON THE KEEPER

* * *

THE FIRE'S STONE

* * *

GATE OF DARKNESS, CIRCLE OF LIGHT

* * *

WIZARD OF THE GROVE

VALOR'S CHOICE

Tanya Huff

DAW BOOKS, INC.
DONALD A. WOLLHEIM, FOUNDER
375 Hudson Street, New York, NY 10014
ELIZABETH R. WOLLHEIM
SHEILA E. GILBERT
PUBLISHERS

Cover art by Jody Lee.
For color prints of Jody Lee's paintings,
please contact:
The Cerridwen Enterprise
P.O. Box 10161
Kansas City, MO 64111
Phone: 1-800-825-1281

DAW Book Collectors No. 1148.

DAW Books are distributed by Penguin Putnam Inc.

First Printing, April 2000
1 2 3 4 5 6 7 8 9

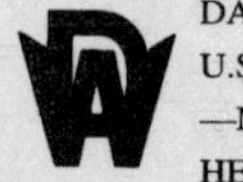

This one's for Sheila, 'cause she was willing to take a chance.

And for Gord Rose and David Sutton and Leslie Dicker and all the other men and women who actually do the work in military organizations worldwide.

Also for my father who, during the Korean War, made Chief Petty Officer. Twice.

PROLOGUE

A writer and philosopher of the late twentieth century once said, "*Space is big.*" There are three well-known corollaries to this. The first is that the number of planets where biological accidents occurred in the correct order to create life is small. The second is that the number of planets where life managed to overcome the odds and achieve sentience is smaller still. And the third is that many of these sentient life-forms blow themselves into extinction before they ever make it off their planet of origin.

If space is big and mostly uninhabited, it should be safe to assume that any life-forms who really didn't get along could avoid spending time in each other's company.

Unfortunately, the fact that said life-forms *could* avoid each other doesn't necessarily mean that they would.

When the Others attacked systems on the borders of Confederation territory, Parliament sent out a team of negotiators to point out that expansion in any other direction would be more practical as it would not result in conflict. The negotiators were returned in a number of very small pieces, their ship cleverly rigged to explode when it would do the most damage.

The Confederation found itself at a disadvantage. Its member races had achieved an interstellar presence only after they'd overcome the urge to destroy themselves or any strangers they ran into. Evidence suggested the Others had flung themselves into space without reaching this level of maturity. Clearly, in order to survive, the Confederation would have to recruit some more aggressive members.

Humans had a bare-bones space station and a shaky toehold on Mars when the Confederation ships appeared. Some fairly basic technology by Confederation standards, combined with the information that the Others were heading Earth's way, convinced humanity to throw its military apparatus into space where they took to interstellar warfare the way the H'san took to cheese.

Some one and a half centuries of intermittent war later, borders had shifted, and Humans had been joined by first the Taykan and then the Krai. Much of the military terminology introduced into the Confederation's common tongue remained Human although, as the three races became increasingly more integrated, Taykan and Krai words began creeping in. The Krai, for example, had sixteen useful adjectives describing the impact of an antipersonnel weapon on a soft target.

Although the induction of younger and more aggressive species had undeniably solved the problem presented by the Others, it had also irrevocably changed the face of the Confederation. Feeling just a little overwhelmed, many of the original species spent their spare time sighing and reminiscing about the good old days.

ONE

Reveillie was not the best thing to have reverberating through one's skull after a night of too much and too little in various combinations. Making a mental note to change the program to something less painfully intrusive, Torin tongued the implant and tried to remember how to open her eyes during the five blessed seconds of silence before the first of her messages came in.

At the chime, it will be 0530.

The chime set up interesting patterns on the inside of her lids. What *had* she been drinking?

Your liberty will be over at 0600.

Which might be a problem, considering how much trouble she was having with basic bodily functions. Groping for the panel beside the bed, she applied what she hoped was enough pressure for dim lighting and cautiously cracked an eye. From the little she could see, these were not her quarters. The less than state-of-the-art wall utility suggested station guest quarters—for a not particularly important guest.

Finally managing to sort current sensation from

memory, she turned her head toward the warm body pressed up against her side. The di'Taykan's short lilac hair swayed gently in response to her exhalation, the pointed tip of an ear covered and uncovered by the moving strands.

A di'Taykan.

That explained things. It wasn't a hangover, she had pheromone head.

Sliding out from under the blanket, Torin stood, stretched carefully, and filled her lungs with air that hadn't been warmed by the di'Taykan's body heat. As memories returned, she smiled. Not only did Humans find the Taykan incredibly attractive but a Taykan in the di' phase was one of the most indiscriminately enthusiastic life-forms in the Galaxy and offered the perfect and uncomplicated way to chase the memories of that last, horrible planetfall right back to the galactic core.

Captain Rose wants to see you in his office at 0800.

There were two piles of clothing on the room's one chair, both folded into neatly squared-off piles. *He must've been raised by one strict* sheshan, Torin thought, grabbing her service uniform and ducking into the bathroom. It had taken most of her nine years in the Corps to achieve that precise a fold, regardless of distraction.

When she emerged a few moments later, fully dressed, all she could see of her companion was a lithe lump under the blanket and a moving fringe of uncovered hair. Relieved, she moved silently toward the door, pausing only long enough to turn off the lights. A di'Taykan considered, *"Once more before breakfast?"* to be a reasonable substitute for *"Good morning."* and, with no time to spare, she was just as happy not to have to test her willpower.

Outside in the corridor, the familiar "something's leaking somewhere" smell of the station's recycled air drove the last of the pheromone-induced haze from her head.

0547 her implant announced when she prodded. Thirteen minutes before her liberty ended and her flasher came back up on screen. Thirteen minutes to get to a part of the station that wouldn't incite prurient speculation among the duty staff.

"I should've reset wake-up for five. What was I *thinking?"* she muttered, diving into the vertical—fortunately empty at this hour—and free-falling two levels. Grabbing a handhold, she swung out onto the lock level. Easy answer, actually. She'd been thinking that she needed to forget the carnage, forget those they lost limping back to the station on a ship that had won its battle but nearly lost its own little slice of the war, forget the messages she'd sent to family and friends, and forget that new faces, always new faces, would soon be arriving to replace those they'd lost.

And she had been able to forget. For a while.

A di'Taykan wouldn't feel used. She didn't think they could.

Considering the time, it was a good thing station guest quarters were on the same side of the core as the barracks. Another vertical, another lock, and she was in NCO country.

0600.

Heading for her own quarters, Staff Sergeant Torin Kerr had her implant scan the night's reports for any of the names she kept flagged. Apparently, no one had died and no one had gotten arrested.

Things hadn't fallen apart while she was gone.

No harm done, and it wasn't as if she'd ever see that particular di'Taykan again. . . .

At 0758, showered, changed, and carrying her slate, Torin approached the captain's door, turning over the possible reasons he'd moved their morning meeting up an hour. As senior surviving NCO, she'd been his acting First Sergeant since the battered remnant of Sh'quo Company had arrived back at the station. Clearly that wasn't going to last, but it was unlikely Battalion HQ would send out a new First before the recruits needed to bring the company up to strength—unlikely but possible, she admitted after a moment's reflection. Battalion HQ had shown what could only be called *unique* leadership in the past.

It was also possible that they were promoting her and the captain needed to tell her in time for her to make the 1000 shuttle. With a war on, it didn't take long to make sergeant, but after that, promotions tended to slow down, common wisdom suggesting that by the time a grunt got that third chevron, they'd learned to duck. Still, with the company losing their First, there'd be a Gunny moving up and that'd leave room for her.

She'd have rather had First Sergeant Chigma

back. The few Krai who went into the Marines usually opted for armored platoons or air support—their feet just weren't built for infantry—so those few who not only chose to be grunts but rose in the ranks left big shoes to fill in more than merely the literal sense. Unfortunately, since Chigma had ended up on the wrong end of an enemy projectile weapon their last planetfall . . .

0759.

Maybe Med-op had scheduled the captain for new treatments at nine.

Look at the bright side, she reminded herself, laying her palm against the sensor pad centered in the door, *we're in no condition to be sent back out.*

The presence of a two star general in the captain's office did not come as a pleasant surprise. In Torin's experience, when generals ignored the chain of command to speak directly to sergeants, it was never good news. And smiling generals were the worst kind.

"You must be Staff Sergeant Kerr."

She nodded as he stepped forward. "Sir."

"Staff, this is General Morris." The regeneration tank around the lower half of his left leg kept Captain Rose from standing, but his voice, unexpectedly deep from such a small man, was enough to stop the general's advance. "He has new orders for you."

"Say rather an opportunity. But don't let me interrupt." He gestured at the slate under Torin's arm.

"I understand you've been acting First. We'll talk once you've finished your morning report."

"Sir." Her face expressionless under the general's smiling regard, she crossed to the desk and downloaded the relevant files. Right now, with no more information to go on than his smile and two dozen words delivered in an annoying *we're-all-in-this-together* tone, she'd be willing to bet that, first of all, General Morris had never seen combat and, second, that Captain Rose liked him even less than she did. As the captain appeared to know what was going on, her sense of impending disaster strengthened.

"Doctorow's no longer critical?"

"Regained consciousness at 0300. Woke up and demanded to know what . . ." Given the general's presence, she rephrased the quote. ". . . idiot had taken his implant off line."

"Good news." Quickly scanning the rest of the report, the captain looked up, brows rising. "No one got arrested?"

"Apparently some vacuum jockeys off the *Redoubt* got into a disagreement with some of our air support in Haligan's, and betting on the fight provided a sufficient diversion."

"Wait a minute," the general interrupted, one hand raised as if to physically stop further discussion. "Am I to understand that you expected your people to get arrested?"

Together, Torin and the captain turned, Torin shifting position slightly, unable to move to the captain's side but making it quite clear where she stood as he answered. "I'm sure I don't need to tell the general what kind of planetfall we had. After something like that, I expect my people to need to blow off."

The general's broad cheeks flushed nearly maroon. "You've been on station for six days."

"Half of us have. Sir." Like many combat officers, Captain Rose had come up through the ranks and he'd retained the NCO's ability to place inflection on that final *sir*.

The two men locked eyes.

General Morris looked away first. "They say another company wouldn't have got that many out," he admitted.

"I have good people, sir. And I lost good people." The quiet reminder drew Torin's gaze down to the captain's face, and she frowned slightly. He looked tired; his fair skin had developed a grayish cast, and there were dark circles under his eyes. Had they been alone, she'd have asked how the regeneration was going; as it was, she made a mental note to check his condition with Med-op as soon as possible. As acting First, he was as much her concern as the company.

"Yes. Good people." General Morris straightened and cleared his throat. "Which leads us nicely into what I'm here for."

Oh, shit. Here it comes. Torin braced herself as he aimed that *I'm looking for someone to get their tail shot off* smile directly at her.

"I need a platoon for a special duty, shipping out ASAP."

"I haven't got a platoon, sir."

He looked momentarily nonplussed, then the smile returned. "Of course, I see. I should have said, I need you to put together a platoon out of the available Marines."

"Out of what's left of Sh'quo Company, sir?"

"Yes."

"Out of the survivors, sir?"

"Yes." The general's smile had begun to tighten.

Torin figured she'd gotten as much satisfaction from that line of inquiry as she was likely to. "A lot of them have leave coming, sir, but we should have new recruits arriving shortly."

"No. Even if I had time to wait for new recruits, I couldn't use them." Folding his hands behind his back in what Torin thought she recognized as parade ground rest—it had been a *long* time since she'd seen a parade ground—the general fixed her with an imposing stare. "I'm fully aware of your situation, Staff Sergeant Kerr, yours and Sh'quo Company's, and I wouldn't be canceling leaves if it wasn't absolutely necessary. The problem, Sergeant, is this; I'm putting together a very important diplomatic mission intended to convince a new race, the Silsviss, to join the Confederation and I need an honor guard. A military escort is absolutely essential because the political leadership of the Silsviss is dominated by a powerful warrior caste that we most certainly do not want to insult. After careful consideration, I've decided that Sh'quo Company is the best available unit."

"As an honor guard?" Torin glanced from the general to her captain—who looked so noncommittal that the hope it was some kind of a joke died unborn—and back to the general again. "We're ground combat, sir, not a ceremonial unit."

"You'll do fine. All you have to do, Sergeant, is have the troops apply a little spit and polish and then stand around and look menacing. You'll see new worlds, meet new life-forms, and not shoot at them for a change." He paused for laugher that never came, then continued gruffly. "It's a win/win situation. I won't have to pull a company out of their rotation for planetfall—which means Sh'quo Company won't be rotated in before it's their turn. As there's no need for heavy artillery, company equipment can still get the overhaul it requires."

"A full platoon makes quite an honor guard, sir."

"It's essential we make a strong impression, Sergeant." For less than an instant, an honest emotion showed in the general's eyes, but before Torin could identify it, he added, "Besides, it'll give you a chance to break in your new second lieutenant."

"My new . . ." Unable to think of anything to say to the general that wouldn't get her court-martialed, she turned to Captain Rose. "Sir?"

"He arrived yesterday afternoon. I asked him to meet us here at 0900. The general thought you should receive your orders first and then he could give the lieutenant the overview."

Officers handled the big picture, NCOs handled the minutia. Part of a staff sergeant's minutia was handling new officers in charge of their first platoon. This would be Torin's third, staff sergeants having a slightly longer life expectancy than second lieutenants.

The captain's door announced an arrival just as her implant proclaimed 0900.

"Open."

The door slid back into the wall and a di'Taykan wearing the uniform of a second lieutenant, Confederation Marine Corps, walked into the office, pheromone masker prominently displayed at his throat. It could have been any di'Taykan; Torin was no better than most Humans at telling them apart. Male and female, they were all tall, slender, and pointy and, even when heavily armed, moved like they were dancing. Their hair, which wasn't really hair but a protein based sensor array, grew a uniform three inches long so they all looked as if they went to the same barber, and with their somewhat eclectic taste in clothing removed by the Corps . . .

It *could* have been any di'Taykan, but it wasn't.

The lilac eyes, exactly one shade darker than his hair, widened slightly when he saw her and slightly more when he spotted the general. "Second Lieutenant di'Ka Jarret reporting as ordered, Captain."

"Welcome to Sh'quo Company, Lieutenant. General Morris will begin your briefing in a moment, but in the meantime, I'd like you to meet Staff Sergeant Kerr. She'll be your senior NCO."

The corners of the wide mouth curled slightly. "Staff."

"Sir." There were a number of things Torin figured she should be thinking about now, but all that came to mind was, *so that explains why he folded his clothes so neatly,* which wasn't even remotely relevant. She only hoped she'd managed to control her expression by the time Captain Rose turned his too perceptive attention her way.

"Sergeant, if you could start forming that platoon . . . see if you can do it without splitting up any fireteams. The three of us . . ."

She had to admire how that *us* definitively excluded the general.

". . . will go over what you've got this afternoon."

"Yes, sir." Turning toward General Morris, she stiffened not quite to attention. "Begging the general's pardon, but if I'm to cancel liberties, I need to know exactly how soon ASAP is."

"Forty-eight hours."

She should've known—a desk jockey's version of *as soon as possible,* or in other words, no real rush. "Thank you, sir." Retrieving her slate from the captain's desk, she nodded at all three officers, turned on her heel, and left the room.

The general's hearty voice followed her out into the corridor.

"Lieutenant, I've got a proposal, I think you'll . . ."

Then she stepped beyond the proximity grid and the door slid shut.

"Figures," Torin sighed. "Officers get a proposal and the rest of us just get screwed."

Technically, she could've worked at the First's desk in the small office right next to the captain's. All Chigma's personal files had been deleted, every trace of his occupancy removed—it was just a desk. Smarter than any other she'd have access to, but still, just a desk. Which was why she didn't want to use it. Sometimes it was just too depressing to contemplate how quickly the Corps moved on.

The verticals were crowded at this hour of the morning, so she grabbed the first available loop for the descent down to C deck, exchanging a disgusted look with a Navy Warrant one loop over; both of them in full agreement that their careful progress represented an irritating waste of time. By the time she finally swung out onto the deck, Torin was ready to kill the idiot in station programming who'd decided to inflict insipid music on trapped personnel.

"'Morning, Staff."

The cheerful greeting brought her up short, and she turned toward the Marine kneeling by the edges of the lock with a degrimer, turquoise hair flattened by the vibrations. The grooves could have been scrubbed automatically, but on a station designed to house thousands of Marines, manual labor became a useful discipline. "Maintenance duties again, Haysole?"

The di'Taykan grinned. "I was only cutting across the core. I figured I'd be there and back before anyone noticed I wasn't wearing my masker."

"You crossed the core on a Fivesday evening unmasked—and you're only on maintenance?"

"I kept moving, it wasn't too bad." Turquoise eyes sparkled. "Unfortunately, Sergeant Glicksohn was also crossing the core. Uh, Staff . . ." He paused while a pair of Human engineers came through the lock, waiting until they'd moved beyond their ability to overhear. ". . . I heard you were seeing stars in the captain's office."

Torin folded her arms around her slate. Many di'Taykan worked in Intelligence—most species had to make a conscious effort not to confide in them. She had no idea how need-to-know General Morris had intended to keep the status of his visit, but it was irrelevant now. "What else have you heard, Haysole?"

He grinned, taking her lack of denial for confirmation. "I've heard that the general's looking for a chance to be, oh, let's say more than he is."

"A promotion?"

"No one used that exact word, but . . ." His voice trailed off suggestively.

Torin ignored the suggestion. "That's it?"

"About the general. But I've also heard that the new *trilinshy* is a di'Ka."

She frowned, and his grin disappeared as he realized she'd translated *trilinshy* to something approximating its distinctly uncomplimentary meaning.

"That is," he corrected hastily, "the new second lieutenant is a di'Ka, Staff Sergeant. High family. Not going to be easy to work with."

"For me or for you?" Private First Class Haysole was a di'Stenjic. Five more letters in a Taykan family name made for a considerable difference in class.

"You know me, Staff . . ." His gesture suggested she could know him better any time it was convenient. ". . . I *try* to get along with everybody."

"Staff Sergeant Kerr?"

Torin started, suddenly aware she'd been staring

at nothing for a few moments too long, the implications of shepherding an aristocratic second lieutenant and a combat platoon through a planetfall where no one got to shoot anything suddenly sinking in. *And just in case that doesn't seem like enough fun, let's not forget you slept with said lieutenant.* The one bright light in her morning was that that particular little tidbit hadn't been picked up by the gossip net. "You missed a spot," she said, pointing, and left him to it.

The desire for stimulants following hard on the heels of sentience, coffee had been one of Earth's prime agricultural exports to the Confederation almost from the moment of contact. Most days, Torin appreciated the history of being able to drink exactly the same beverage that her several times great grandmother had back in the dark ages, but today she'd give her right arm for a cup of Krai *sah* and its highly illegal effect on the Human nervous system.

"Staff? I got that download you wanted on the Silsviss."

Resisting the urge to yawn, she leaned into the video pickup. "Thank you, Corporal. Send it to the desk."

"Sending," the tiny image of the Admin corporal acknowledged, and disappeared.

There wasn't much.

In an effort to secure a section of the front, the Confederation planned to lay a new pattern of defense satellites with the optimum pattern placing one satellite directly in the center of 7RG6 or what was now to be called the Silsviss System. Unfortunately, the Silsviss, a warm-blooded reptilian lifeform, had developed a limited intrasystem space travel. Both their moon and the nearest neighboring planet had been reached and they were in the process of building an orbiting space station—although Torin wondered how they'd found room for it given the number of weapons platforms already in orbit. Their technology, while crude by Confederation standards, was more than sufficient to destroy anything put into place without their cooperation—making it essential to get their cooperation.

"Thus the suck-up mission," Torin muttered, refilling her mug from the dispenser in the desk. She didn't know what General Morris had been drinking but spit and polish was not a high priority for a combat unit. If Haysole's sources were right—which they usually were—and the general intended this mission to push him toward promotion, the man was a bigger idiot than she'd first thought.

Unfortunately, he was a *two star* idiot.

Not counting Lieutenant Jarret and herself, she needed to find thirty-nine Marines—nine, four-person fireteams and three sergeants—who had not only been cleared by Med-op for planetfall but who wouldn't inadvertently turn a diplomatic mission into a bloodbath. Even had Sh'quo Company's three infantry platoons been at full strength, choosing nine from the twenty-seven fireteams wouldn't have been easy. Choosing from among the seventeen teams Med-op *had* cleared was a nearly impossible task.

It was a choice that didn't involve the kind of parameters a computer could handle.

First Sergeant Chigma would've called his three Staff Sergeants together. *To pick our brains,* Torin thought darkly. It wasn't a phrase she could say aloud, given the Krai's unfortunate taste for Human tissue. Unfortunately, with her acting as First that left only two platoon NCOs and Med-op had Greg Reghubir tanked for the foreseeable future. Down to one. After a moment's thought, she keyed Sergeant Sagarha's implant code into the desk. He'd taken over what was left of Reghubir's platoon. While it was likely he only knew the fireteams in his own squad, he was still the best source she had. Then she leaned around the edge of the dividing wall and into the next Staff cubicle.

"When you've got a moment, Amanda, I need you at my desk."

"You're running heavy on Humans here; there's got to be another di'Taykan or two available somewhere." Amanda tapped a fingertip against her screen until it protested. "What about Haysole?"

"I'm a little concerned about the class difference with our new lieutenant."

Sh'quo Company's other surviving staff sergeant raised an auburn brow. "You'd rather they worked it out in combat?"

"I'd rather they didn't work it out in front of a dozen diplomats and a species we're trying to impress." Leaning back in her chair, Torin turned toward the other person at the desk. "What do you think, Sagarha?"

Sergeant di'Garn Sagarha frowned thoughtfully. "Might be trouble if di'Ka wasn't an officer. Since he is, that shouldn't be a problem. I'll tell you what I would be concerned about, though; Haysole's a fuk-up. He's fine in combat, but the moment no one's shooting at him, he gets bored, and the next thing you know, he's got three days' latrine duty."

"Nothing wrong with clean toilets," Amanda pointed out.

"Is there anyone *else?*"

The three of them rechecked the lists.

"Not in a complete fireteam, no."

"Then I guess Haysole's going." Torin moved the di'Taykan's fireteam over to the platoon file. "If he gets too bored, I'll shoot at him myself."

"You're a little low on Krai."

"Only four of the six are available, and I'm taking one of them," she pointed out.

"Why not take Ressk?"

"I'd love to. It'd be nice to have a few more brains along on this trip." One of Sergeant Sagarha's squad, Ressk had been known to make secure military programming sit up and beg. Intelligence wanted him, but fortunately for the company, he didn't want Intelligence.

"You take Ressk, you also get Binti Mashona. I've recommended her for sniper school twice, but we keep shipping out before Admin clears the file."

"Like I said, I'd love to, but isn't their team leader still out?"

Sagarha checked his slate. "My Med-op download has Corporal Hollice cleared for duty in thirty-six hours."

"I wonder why mine doesn't," Torin muttered, tracing a path through the icons. "Some idiot probably sent it to the First's desk."

"Some idiot probably thought that's where you'd be," Amanda pointed out, adding, "I thought Hollice lost a thumb?"

"He did, but Ressk dropped it in a cold box, and the corpsmen had it reattached before we got back to the station."

"Bet Ressk was pissed at losing his snack," she snickered.

"Marines do not eat other Marines," Torin muttered absently. The eight teams they'd managed to come up with had used up all the "A" list and taken a few off the "B." Pickings were getting slim. Finally, she sighed. "I don't see any way around it. We're going to have to use Corporal Conn's team."

"No." Amanda shook her head. "I promised him some time to see his daughter. He's got leave coming."

"Point one, General Morris canceled all leaves. Point two, he's all we've got left. It can't be Algress, not with a reptilian life-form on the planet—not after Rarna IV."

"I thought Psych took care of that."

After a pregnant pause, the three NCOs snorted simultaneously.

"It'll have to be Conn," Torin repeated.

"But his daughter . . ."

With life expectancy at around a hundred and twenty old Earth years, most Human Marines put off having kids until they were either out of the Corps or had decided to make it a career. Corporal Grad Conn had fallen in love, applied for married quarters on station, and started a family. His daughter Myrna Troi had become Sh'quo Company's unofficial mascot and everyone took a turn at spoiling her. Even Torin, who usually found kids about as inexplicable as the H'san, thought she was pretty cute. And it was hard not to admire a four-year-old who could disassemble a hygiene unit into so many pieces it took three engineers most of a duty shift to put it back together.

"Extend his liberty until we assemble for boarding."

"On whose authority?"

"Mine."

Voice conspiratorially lowered, Amanda leaned toward the di'Taykan. "She's even beginning to sound like a First Sergeant."

"Very dominant," Sagarha agreed, smiling broadly.

"Very in charge of your butts," Torin reminded them.

"Crap." Amanda straightened, a sudden realization drawing her brows in over the bridge of her nose. "This means I'm going to be acting First while you're gone. If I find out you've volunteered for this mission to get out of processing those new recruits . . ."

"Shall I tell the captain you're volunteering to go in my place?"

"Not fukking likely."

"What about sergeants?" Sagarha wondered.

"Are you volunteering?"

He grinned. "Not fukking likely."

"I'd like to take Doctorow; he's a pain in the ass, but he's a socially apt pain in the ass and that could come in handy. Unfortunately, Med-op won't release him until Psych has a chance to go in and do some dirty work."

"You should tell them he's always like that."

"I did. They didn't listen. That said, I want Glicksohn, Chou, and Trey."

"Two humans and a di'Taykan?"

"The lieutenant's di'Taykan. We'll balance."

The three of them stared down at the final list of thirty-nine names. "You think the captain'll rubber stamp this?" Amanda asked.

"He'd better."

"Something I've always wondered . . . what's a rubber stamp?"

Torin shrugged, uploading the list into her slate. "Damned if I know."

A short visit to the armory turned into over an hour of listening to complaints. *I should've bailed when I heard "Hey, Kerr, aren't you acting First?" I can't believe Chig put up with that.*

Running late, Torin grabbed lunch at a species-neutral cantina in the core. Her day thus far called out for a big dish of poutine and a beer; unfortunately duty called out louder and she settled for a bowl of noodles garnished not very liberally with an indeterminate mix of greens and meat. *There are times,* she thought, deciding it might be best if the meat remained unidentified, *when I almost wish I'd stayed on the farm.*

"Can I join you?"

Then there were those times when there was no *almost* about it. "It's a public cantina, sir."

Pulling up a stool, Lieutenant Jarret rested his elbows on the table and smiled. "And if it wasn't?"

"Fraternization between the ranks is discouraged for a good reason, Lieutenant—di'Taykan with di'Taykan excepted, of course. It undermines the structure of command and it can lead to distorted judgment in life-and-death situations."

"Are you telling me last night—you and I—never happened?"

"No, sir, I'm telling you it won't happen again." She stared into her noodles. "Although it would certainly help my position with, oh, just about everyone, if we both pretend it never happened."

"Why?"

"Because every time I look at you I'm going to think of . . ." Lilac eyes glittered, and she smiled in spite of herself. "Yeah, all right, it's a pleasant memory, but . . ."

". . . you can't have every Human in the platoon thinking about it every time you pass on one of my orders." He returned the smile. "I understand the species parameters, Staff Sergeant Kerr, as regrettable as I may find them, which is what I actually sat down to tell you."

"Oh." A sudden burst of giggles from across the cantina gave Torin an excuse to move her attention to a small table overwhelmed by three Human teenagers.

"What is it?"

"You're being watched, sir."

He glanced over his shoulder at them, and, after a moment of stunned silence, one teen sighed, "Elves," while the other two just sighed.

The off-the-record reaction of the First Human Contact Team upon meeting the Taykan had been "Holy fuk, they're elves!" To the horror of right thinking xenoanthropologists everywhere, the name stuck. Once exposed to the mythology that had engendered the remark, the Taykan as a whole didn't seem to mind, and a number of the di'Taykan had embraced the lifestyle wholeheartedly. During basic training, Torin had actually met a di'Taykan who'd been named Celeborn after a character in an old Terran book.

The sighs turned to giggles.

"I think you may need to readjust your masker, sir."

"I think you've forgotten what it's like to be their age."

"And happy to have forgotten." She pushed the empty container into the recycling chute and stood. "It's 1340, sir. The captain wants to see us at 1400."

Lieutenant Jarret stood as well and nodded toward her slate as they crossed the cantina in step.

"Is there anything specific I should know about the people you've chosen?"

"They all would've preferred that I'd chosen someone else, but other than that, no." Torin considered it a good sign that the lieutenant was asking her for information. Too many officers came out of training thinking they were going to win the war single-handedly. Fortunately, that kind of officer usually didn't last long in front of a combat unit— sometimes the enemy even got a chance to remove them. She frowned thoughtfully as they took the stairs up a deck. "They're all good people to have at your side in a fight, sir, but I'm not sure how well they'll manage ceremonial duties."

"General Morris seemed to think that the Silsviss would be more impressed by your battle honors than by an ability to march in straight lines."

"Lucky for us."

"However, he did suggest that we run over some basic drill while in transit."

Torin snorted.

"You don't think it's necessary, Sergeant."

"Necessary? Yes, sir. Survivable?" She shrugged.

"The general seems to think that the platoon can consider this a sort of working leave."

"Does he, sir?"

"You don't?"

"Either we're working, or we're on leave. We can't logically do both."

"Good point, but the general thinks . . ."

Pausing outside the captain's door, Torin sighed and turned to face the lieutenant. It was easy to forget, given their maturity in other areas, that a di'Taykan second lieutenant was as young and inexperienced as a Human one. "Begging your pardon sir, but you'll be giving orders to this platoon, not to the general. It might be best if you think for yourself."

His ear points drooped slightly, but his tone showed none of the embarrassment he was clearly feeling. "I'll take that under consideration, Sergeant."

"Thank you, sir." She meant it sincerely and made it sound as much like *Thank you for listening.* as she could. Nobody liked to be patronized, second lieutenants uncertain of their own power least of all.

Lieutenant Jarret studied her face, then suddenly smiled. "You know the general also told me that a good Staff Sergeant is worth her weight in charge canisters."

"I suspect General Morris has never been in combat, sir."

"Why?"

"Because if that's all he's getting for a good staff sergeant, he's getting screwed . . ." Returning his smile, she stepped aside as the captain's door opened. ". . . sir."

Two

Is this all of them?"

"All but one, sir."

Lieutenant Jarret, who'd been studying the Marines milling about below him in the loading bay, turned to face his staff sergeant. "One?" he asked.

The emphasis made his actual question unmistakable. Torin, who'd been trying to avoid mentioning names, no longer had a choice. "Corporal Conn, sir."

"The man whose extended liberty you authorized?"

"Yes, sir."

"He does know we're leaving this morning?"

Torin winced at the deceptively mild tone. There was something about the way the di'Taykan used sarcasm that could cut through bulkheads. Before she could answer, an imperious voice demanding to be put down rose above the general noise, and she smiled. "That's him now, sir."

Jarret watched the big man lift a flame-haired

child off his shoulders and set her carefully on the deck. "He brought his daughter?"

"Yes, sir, Myrna Troi. She always comes to see the company off."

"I can't get over what Humans are willing to expose their children to," Jarret mused as the little girl ran about, accepting the homage of the platoon as her due. "Until they reach di' phase, Taykan are a lot more sheltered."

"We're a pretty flexible species, sir."

"And we're not?" Lilac hair lifted, adding entendre.

"Lieutenant . . ."

"Sorry." He grinned, clearly not at all sorry, and headed for the stairs. "Since Corporal Conn has decided to join us, let's get started."

"Probably I'll be bigger when you get back. Probably I'll be this big." Up on her toes, Myrna Troi waved her hand in the air as high as she could, which was just barely higher than the top of her crouching father's head. "Probably I gonna be a surgent," she told him sternly, russet brows drawn in over emerald eyes. "And then you gotta do what I say and then you gotta not leave."

"I'm sorry, sweetie. Daddy doesn't want to go, he has to."

She stared at him for a long moment, then leaned into his shoulder and sighed deeply. "I know."

"Take care of your mama while I'm gone."

"Probably Mama will cry. Mama says you shouldn't be a Marine no more. Mama says you should work on the station. Mama says probably Trisha got her boobs done."

Looking a little taken aback by the last confidence, Corporal Conn kissed the top of his daughter's head.

"You know what else? Probably my tooth will fall out when you're gone."

Torin moved past the two and went to stand by the huge double lock. *At least this time we know he'll be coming back to her,* she thought as she had the platoon fall in. And then, just so as not to tempt fate, she added a prudent *probably.*

Three days out from the station, the Marine package of living quarters, mess, gym, armory, and air support locked on to the Confederation Ship *Berganitan* bringing the diplomatic party from insector.

Moments after the all clear sounded, the entire ship folded into Susumi space and everyone but the plasma engineers settled in to wait. Time in Susumi space was pretty much irrelevant to everyone but those who spent it working out the calculations that would bring the ship back into real space at essentially the moment it left although a considerable number of light-years away.

"Good news. Second Lieutenant Jarret graduated in the middle of his class."

Several members of number one squad glanced up, and someone asked, "Why is that good news, Res?"

Bare feet up on one of the tables filling the area between the double row of bunks, Ressk stretched out his toes and grinned toothily up at Juan Checya, his fireteam's heavy gunner. "Top of the class would've made him an insufferable overachiever and bottom of the class would've made him a *chrick.*"

"Edible?"

"Edible."

Checya snorted and dropped onto his bunk. "What the fuk don't you consider edible?"

"Not much," Ressk admitted, fingers dancing over his slate. "Oh, my, this is interesting. One of the lieutenant's parental units was Admiral di'Ka Tereal, now ex-Admireal qui'Ka Tereal, and she tried to block his application to Ventris Station."

"Wanted him in the fukking Navy?"

"Wanted him out of the fighting entirely."

Corporal di'Merk Mysho tossed her brush into her locker and leaned over Ressk's shoulder. "It's a qui'Taykan thing," she explained. "There's nothing more conservative than a breeder. Aren't those restricted files?"

"Depends on what you mean by restricted."

"Not intended to be accessed by all and sundry."

"Which am I, all or sundry?"

She smacked him on the back of the head. "Didn't Staff Sergeant Kerr specifically tell you not to invade classified areas while we're on the *Berganitan?*"

"Technically, she told me not to invade classified

areas *of* the *Berganitan.* I'm in Division records; all Marine, no Navy, no problem."

"Unless you get caught."

He brought a cup of *sah* to his mouth with one foot and took a long swallow. "Do I ever?"

"Do you ever what? Regret not eating Hollice's thumb when you had the chance?" Pulling the cup from his toes, Binti Mashona, the fourth member of the fireteam, set it back on the table. "You know I hate it when you do that with food."

"You're just jealous my species has more opposable parts than yours."

"I'm just thinking that foot spent most of the day in boots doing drill."

"Speaking of opposable parts," Juan interrupted, leaning down from his bunk. "You get lucky with that service tech back on station?"

"Nah." Binti pulled a game biscuit out of her locker and slid it into the side of her slate. "She didn't want to get involved with someone from a combat unit."

"Involved? Fuk, I thought you just wanted to get laid."

"If you wanted to get laid, why didn't you ask a di'Taykan," Mysho wondered.

"Because once you pop your masker, I don't have a choice. Couldn't change my mind if I wanted to."

"But if you *wanted* sex . . ."

Ressk snorted. "It's a Human thing, Mysho, you wouldn't understand.

"Speaking of Human things, you guys hear what the staff is up to tonight?" Binti grinned, her teeth startlingly white against the rich mahogany of her skin. "Big fancy reception to meet these diplomats we're supposed to honor guard. Little tiny bits of food on platters, dress blacks, and polite conversation."

There was a moment of startled silence, then Juan slowly shook his head. "Staff's gonna fukking hate that."

"Anyone want to see how badly she hates it?" Ressk tapped his slate suggestively. "I can tap into the ship's security vids . . ." He let his voice trail off as the Marines gathered around the table exchanged speculative glances and then turned in unison toward Mysho.

"What?"

"You rank, Mysh."

"Oh, no, Conn got his second hook long before I did."

"Conn's off trying to rabbit something shiny for Myrna. Your decision."

She muttered something in her own language, then threw up her hands. "Why not. You're going to do it anyway, Ressk, so we might as well all get a look at it."

"Can one of you give me a hand with this? I can't get the jacket to hang straight."

Nearest the hatch separating the staff sergeant's quarters from the NCO Common, Sergeant Mike Glicksohn stood and beckoned Torin closer. "And aren't you just the picture of martial elegance."

"Aren't I just," she agreed handing him her belt. "I can't remember the last time I got this tarted up."

"When you made Staff?"

"No, that was a field promotion—I was covered in Staff Sergeant Guntah's guts and the only thing black on me was my fingernails where frostbite had started to set in."

"I remember." Anne Chou looked up from her slate. "Planet was barely habitable—we'd have ignored it if the Others hadn't tried to set up a mining base."

"So now *we* have a mining base there, and someday we'll have to go back to the frozen hole in the ass end of space to protect it."

"War is progress," Glicksohn muttered, stepping back. "That's got it."

"Thanks." Moving to the wall, Torin polarized the vid screen. "You think there's a reason they make these collars so uncomfortable?" she asked, checking her reflection. "Does it seem hot in here?" Working her shoulders under the black cloth, she wondered why she suddenly felt so . . . "Trey!"

The three Humans turned toward the other end of the room where the di'Taykan sergeant had just come through from the showers.

"Give me a break," she sighed, as she walked naked to her room. "What am I supposed to clip it to? Besides, you're Human, repression's good for you. And you," she continued, pausing to grin at Torin, "should thank me because before the Corps absorbed the di'Taykan, you would've had to wear a hat with that."

"Thank you," Torin told the closed door. "And thank *you,*" she added as Chou turned the air recyclers on high. "Speaking of maskers, anyone know where Haysole is? I've barely seen him since we locked."

"Zero gee bubble. He said something about trying to work his way through the *Berganitan*'s crew."

"Vacuum jockeys, too?"

"Not all of them." Glicksohn settled back in his chair and picked up the pouch of beer he'd discarded earlier. "I've got a game set up at 2130, and a few showed interest."

"Playing on neutral ground?"

"Close as you can get on this flying fish tank."

"Who's going with you in case the vjs get ugly?"

Glicksohn snorted. "Is there any other kind?"

"Mike . . ."

"Sam Austin's going and Esket from the aircrew. Happy?" When she nodded, he grinned. "You worry too much."

"It's my job. And speaking of my job, did either of you . . . any of you," she corrected as Trey came out of her quarters, "manage a species check on the diplomats?"

"Dornagain and Mictok," Trey told her dropping into a chair.

Glicksohn tossed her a beer. "I thought the Silsviss were reptilian; why not send Raszar or Niln? Let them know they're not the only lizards around before they join up."

"Or why not H'san?" Chou wondered. "Everybody likes the H'san."

"I'm guessing that they're not sending reptilians because they don't want to suggest competition." Torin flicked a bit of lint off her campaign ribbons. "And there was a H'san on the first contact team; the Silsviss kept remarking on how much it smelled like food."

"That's what I said, everybody likes the H'san."

"I know the Mictok are supposed to be these great diplomats," Glicksohn muttered, "but every time I see one, this little voice inside my head keeps screaming, *Get it off me! Get it off me!*"

Before she could answer, Torin's implant chimed.

Lieutenant Jarret is waiting for you in the corridor.

Before the di'Taykan, both the Marine Corps and the Navy had worn dress blues, but the induction of a race with pastel-colored hair and eyes had demanded a change. The Navy chose gray—dove gray for their pilots, slightly darker for the engineers who made Susumi space possible, and charcoal gray for everyone else. The Corps wore black. Regardless of trade or rank or designation, a Marine was first a Marine.

Fortunately, those with low tolerances for pastel over camouflage didn't tend to go into combat units.

Lieutenant Jarret was waiting for her by the ladder that connected the platoon to their air support, one deck up. The Corps prided itself on the flexibility of its packaging as well as its people and could snap together transportation units to match any configuration of troops. As Torin joined him, pilot and copilot slid down the ladder from above.

"Captain Fiona Daniels, Second Lieutenant Ghard, this is Staff Sergeant Torin Kerr. The sergeant will be joining us tonight at the request of Captain Carveg of the *Berganitan*.

"Glad to have you with us, Staff. The vjs are going to have us severely outnumbered."

Torin returned the captain's smile. "Happy to be providing backup, Captain." Fiona Daniels had the kind of rakish good looks that showed up on Human recruiting posters. Dark hair, green eyes, one deep dimple punctuating straight white teeth—only someone who'd seen Med-op reconstruction up close could tell from the slight difference in tone that the skin over the entire left side of her face had recently been replaced. She'd been one of the pilots who'd got Sh'quo Company off the ground after that last disastrous planetfall and if backup extended to smacking around a few vacuum jockeys for her, Torin would be more than happy to oblige.

On the other side of the lock, the walls changed to Navy colors and their implants simultaneously asked their destination.

Lieutenant Jarret's hair flattened slightly in irritation, but he answered politely. "Wardroom."

At the end of this passageway, take the vertical to deck seven. The wardroom is three doors from the vertical on the left. Please proceed.

"Don't let it bother you, Jarret," Captain Daniels advised as they began walking. "It's a Navy thing.

The vjs can't find their ass without a homing beacon."

"What's going on?"

"Ressk's tapping into that fancy party Staff's going to." Juan ducked as Binti swung at him. "Well, I'm not going to fukking lie."

Corporal Hollice shouldered in beside Mysho and leaned over the curve of the Krai's head. "Those are . . . okay, were . . . Navy security codes."

"He's in?" Someone at the back of the pack demanded.

"I'm in." Ressk reached out and very carefully shoved his slate into the port on the wall vid. The screen went black, then gray, then slowly focused.

Hollice sighed. "I'd just like to go on record as being out of the room the whole time this access was being forced."

"Seduced," Ressk corrected, fiddling with the contrast.

"Hey, look, Mictok."

The Humans present suppressed a racial shudder as a trio of Mictok accepted drinks from one of the commissariat.

The camera angle changed.

"I see Navy all over the fukking place," Juan complained. "Where's our team?"

"There, at the hatch."

As the two pilots led the way into the room, Torin glanced over at Jarret. Given the constant movement of his hair and the way he carried his weight forward on the balls of his feet, he was nervous. She didn't blame him. Most second lieutenants learned how to command with their platoon hidden in the midst of a battalion planetfall—not out in full view of a ceremonial mission. It couldn't help that every chest in the room but his and the diplomats carried a rainbow of campaign ribbons.

"Remember that the Navy's on our side, no matter how it sounds," she murmured as they crossed toward Captain Carveg. "We're sort of like siblings; bottom line, we stand together. As for the civilians, the older races think we're savages because we're willing to fight to maintain the Confederation, so the most rudimentary of social skills impresses them. Gracious manners'll knock them right back on their collective tails."

He half turned and his hair lifted slightly.

She shrugged. "Or spinnerets. Whatever."

When the officers had been introduced and greeted, Captain Carveg turned to Torin, smiling broadly. "The staff sergeant and I have met, although she was a sergeant at the time and I, a mere commander."

Although Torin could have picked the half-dozen Krai in Sh'quo Company out of a crowd, for the most part, they all looked alike to her. She knew it was speciesist but the facial ridges, so easily identifiable to another Krai, told her gender and nothing more. Skin tones never left the mid-range of Human norm, neither as dark as Binti Mashona nor as light as Captain Rose. The few bristles of hair around the base of the broad skull were no help at all. The di'Taykan, who used scent as much as appearance had a distinct advantage.

So, at least four years ago, she'd met a female commander named Carveg. . . .

"The *CS Charest*, leaving Sai Genist?"

The captain nodded. "I'm surprised you remember."

Torin grinned, careful not to show too much tooth. "You skipped a battle cruiser into the atmosphere and fried a fighting wedge of Other ships, saving at least a dozen of your pilots. From where I stood, it was an impressive light show."

"My captain had been killed in the attack, and this was the first battle where the Others had used the new cluster technology," Carveg explained to the listening officers. "I took a gamble that paid off, although considering the mess it made of the hull, I don't think the engineers ever forgave me. Meanwhile, dirtside, Sergeant Kerr and her squad pulled three of my downed pilots out of the wreckage of their escape pods and kept them alive at some risk to her squad until we cleared the system for medevac."

"What's so dangerous about carrying stretchers?" a di'Taykan naval officer wondered.

Lieutenant Jarret answered before Torin had a chance. "When you're carrying stretchers," he said, in a tone so pleasant the other di'Taykan's eyes lightened, "you can't use your weapon. Three stretchers meant a minimum of six Marines were defenseless and the strength of the squad almost halved. But we don't leave *anyone* behind to die."

The emphasis was a gentle, aristocratic chastisement.

Bet that's a di'Taykan with more than two letters in her name, Torin thought hiding a smile. The most junior officer in the room had been born into a family who'd been holding power from the beginning of their civilization. *He might be starting from scratch with the rest of us, but he can handle his own species just fine.*

"And never think we don't appreciate that," Captain Carveg told him, not bothering to mask her approval. "Come, let me make you known to the people you'll be accompanying."

"What's happening now?"

"More introductions."

On the screen, one of the Dornagain unfolded to his full height and bowed gravely.

"Fuk, those guys are big."

"That's likely why they're sending them, in case there's trouble."

"Nah, that's why they're sending us. The Dornagain don't fight."

"And even if they did, you ever seen one move fast enough to scratch his butt before the itch moved?"

"If they don't fight, whadda they use them fukking claws for?"

"Shellfish." The squad turned toward Hollice, who shrugged, "Don't you guys remember those 'Founders of the Confederation' vids we got in school?"

"All I remember is that the H'san sing every morning at sunrise. No matter what sun."

"No kidding? All I remember is that the H'san like cheese."

"Everyone remembers *that*."

"Lieutenant Jarret, Sergeant Kerr, this is Ambassador Krik'vir." Captain Carveg replaced the mandible clash in the middle of the name with a snap of her teeth Torin couldn't help but envy. Krai tooth enamel was so tough, bioengineers kept trying to replicate it as atmospheric shielding on the Confederation's vacuum-to-atmosphere vehicles.

The Mictok ambassador dipped her antennae in greeting. "We are very pleased to meet you both. We appreciate so many of you being able to accommodate us on such short notice."

Lieutenant Jarret inclined his head. "General Morris' orders, ma'am."

"Yes, of course." Amused, her outer mandibles clattered softly against the inner. "We forget you had no need to achieve consensus. We sometimes wish we had the same freedom. Allow us to introduce you to our staff; those you will also be guarding."

Get it off me! Get it off me! Torin had little success in putting Glicksohn's words out of her head as the next level of introductions were made. Although the beauty of Mictok art touched almost every known species and their diplomatic skills had been instrumental in creating the Confederation, Humans looked at them and saw giant spiders. Fortunately for Human/Mictok relations, the latter were almost impossible to insult.

Ambassador Krik'vir's staff consisted of only three other Mictok, a surprisingly small number for a communal species although one more than the minimum. Under the right conditions, three Mictok could begin a new nest, one becoming Queen, one a breeding male, and the third providing for the happy couple until the first eggs could hatch. If necessary, the male also became the incubator. Torin had often wondered how they chose but had never quite had the nerve to ask.

Introductions to the Dornagain ambassador, and his staff followed with much mutual bowing and exchanging of meaningless pleasantries. Dornagain names sounded strange to Human ears since they referred to personality traits or physical descriptions and changed several times over the course of a long life. The ambassador currently bore the apt although unwieldy name of Listens Wisely And Considers All.

Her rank, or rather lack of rank, exempting her from much of the social ritual, Torin was able to stand back and appreciate the way Lieutenant Jarret handled the situation. His hair had stilled as his apprehension had dissipated and he seemed to be enjoying himself. As a member of an ancient house, his background made him perfectly suited to do the pretty with their civilian charges, and she had to admit that, green though he might be in combat experience, he was the perfect choice to command this mission.

And he won't be quite so green by the time someone starts shooting at us. An officer who'd had command experience of any kind before going into combat created a win/win situation as far as Torin was concerned, and it helped her to think more kindly of General Morris—in spite of the stranglehold her dress uniform had achieved.

Parity with the Mictok necessitated that there be four Dornagain. Well aware that their size made them intimidating to smaller species—which, from their perspective, was just about everyone else in the Confederation—they moved slowly apart when the introductions were over.

The four Marines in tow, Captain Carveg interrupted an argument on cellular plasticity to make them known to Dr. Planton Leor . . .

". . . the environmental physician who'll be ensuring that you'll all remain healthy during your stay on Silsvah. He's predominantly a research physician," she added sotto voce as they moved away. "I'll be sending a couple of corpsmen down as well, just in case."

The rest of the civilian party consisted of the Charge d'Affaires and her two assistants, all three Rakva like the doctor.

"There was a Rakva had a canteen on station back when I was with the 9th," Ressk mused. "Great cook."

"Why would you care?" Binti wondered, looking up from her slate. "You'll eat anything you can wrestle down your throat two falls out of three."

"There's a difference between eat and enjoy," the Krai reminded her. "This guy could make a *juklae* so light you were convinced you were eating it in zero gee."

"Yeah? Too bad he's not here instead of this environmental physician guy." She snorted. "Like we never made a strange planetfall before." Shaking a finger in the air, she raised her voice into an approximation of a Rakva whistle. "Now don't touch that, we don't know where it's been."

"I, for one, am not looking a gift physician in the mouth."

Grinning, Binti glanced toward the dark rectangle of Corporal Hollice's bunk. "I don't think you *can* look a Rakva in the mouth, Hol, those beaky things aren't set up that way."

A hand appeared long enough to flash a very Human response. "Shortsighted. That's why you're still a private."

"You won't die. That's why I'm still a private."

"You're my reason to live."

"I'm honored."

"You should be. Now, shut up, I'm trying to sleep."

Still grinning, Binti turned her attention back to her slate.

The rest of the squad had gotten bored with watching diplomacy in action—even illegally obtained. Most had wandered off to the mess, but Ressk had stayed by the screen. As the introductions ended and Captain Carveg left the Marines by the refreshment table, he hastily reset the security vid parameters to follow the *Berganitan*'s captain.

"Now that's what I call a set of *amalork*," he murmured, settling back in his chair.

He could watch Staff Sergeant Kerr any time; female Krai in the infantry were few and far between.

Chewing on something vaguely kelplike, Torin watched Lieutenant Jarret work the crowd and wondered why he'd opted for combat when he was so good at . . . she supposed diplomacy was the politest thing to call it although the phrase "kissing butt" kept coming to mind. And why wasn't *he* being strangled by *his* dress uniform? She ran a finger under her collar, then reached for another kelp thing.

"We are pleased to welcome another reptilian species into the Confederation."

Torin hadn't heard the Mictok come up behind her, but there could be no mistaking the accent—mandibles were just not made to deal with the softer consonants. Forcing herself to turn slowly, she found herself face-to-essentially-face with the ambassador.

"The first contact team indicated that the Silsviss have a very vibrant and vital culture. We are looking forward to exploring it."

There didn't seem to be much to say to that, so Torin merely smiled and nodded. As it was a little disconcerting to see her reflection in the nearer of the ambassador's eyestalks, she dropped her gaze to the brilliant design painted onto the exoskeleton.

The eyestalk turned to follow her line of sight. "Do you like it, Staff Sergeant?"

"It's beautiful, ma'am."

"We think so, too, but we were not sure how it would appear to a biocular species." The foreleg with the least number of differentiated digits rose and tapped Torin's ribbon bar. "These are more than decoration, yes?"

"Yes, ma'am. They represent where I've been and what I've done." A barely remembered lecture on interspecies relations had suggested it was best to keep cultural explanations simple. She doubted she could make it much simpler than that.

"In reference to the fighting that you do?"

"Yes, ma'am."

The Mictok sighed—at least Torin assumed that's what the sound meant. "We do not understand why the Others insist on pushing into Confederation space. We do not like to think of sentient species having to die, even if it is the few dying to protect the many."

"We don't exactly like to think of it either, ma'am."

She made the noise again. "No, we don't suppose you do. We have often wondered why a smart weapon could not be created . . ."

"Begging your pardon, ma'am," Torin interrupted stiffly, "but you've got forty-two smart weapons on board right now. Forty-five, including our air support," she amended, hearing Captain Daniels' voice rise across the room. "You couldn't possibly program a computer to consider all the variables that can occur in combat."

"And when there is finally the development of a true A-I?"

"You'd just be sending a different sentient species to die."

Ambassador Krik'vir tapped Torin's ribbon bar again. "If one of these is not for debate, Staff Sergeant Kerr, we think it should be. Lieutenant Jarret wears no colors," she continued, not waiting for a response. "He is very new."

It wasn't a question, so Torin waited for the ambassador to make her point.

"He knows how important the Silsviss are to our defenses in this sector?"

"Yes, ma'am, he knows."

"We understand the Silsviss to be impressed by warriors. General Morris has made an interesting choice."

"General Morris knows what he's doing, ma'am." Personal opinion of the general aside, Torin wasn't about to have him criticized by a non-Marine. Besides, this evening's exercise had pretty much convinced her that Jarret had been chosen to deal with the diplomats, the *rest* of them had been chosen to impress the Silsviss. When the ambassador repeated her thought aloud, she was startled enough to actually meet the Mictok's eyes where eight reflections stared back at her in astonishment. Unable to avoid realizing that she looked like an idiot, she closed her mouth and the eight reflections closed theirs.

Ambassador Krik'vir's outer mandibles clattered

against the inner. "We do not read minds, Staff Sergeant, but it was not hard for us to guess your thoughts." The sweep of a foreleg indicated the rest of the room. "Here tonight there are four Marines as well as four Mictok, four Dornagain, and in order to be equal, four Rakva. It is, as you Humans say, appallingly politically correct. We think you will have an easier time fulfilling your commission than your lieutenant will fulfilling his. You, after all, have only one species to impress."

It might have been a warning. "And we will, ma'am."

"Good. We apologize for interrupting you while you were feeding, but we are pleased we had this opportunity to talk."

As the ambassador scuttled back into the crowd, Torin snagged a drink off a passing tray and took a long swallow. *Get it off me,* she sighed silently.

"I'm a little surprised you're coming back with us." Hand on the identity plate, Captain Daniels stood aside while the other three went through the lock, then followed and cycled it closed. "I'd have thought you'd have hooked up with another di'-Taykan and spent the night away."

"Actually, I was wondering what would happen if I unmasked around a Dornagain."

"A Dornagain?"

"Most sentient carbon-based mammals react."

"Are you out of your mind? The females have got to weigh close to two hundred kilos and the males aren't much smaller. If you weren't crushed, you'd be . . ." Then she caught sight of the expression on Jarret's face. "I can't believe I fell for that."

The grin broadened. "Fell for what?"

Trouble is, Torin mused, following along behind the three officers, *with a di'Taykan there's no way to be sure they're kidding.* Some of them, given the opportunity, would pop their maskers in front of a Dornagain just to see what would happen. Lieutenant Jarret didn't seem to be the type, but their previous contact certainly proved he could pop it off fast enough when a willing partner appeared. *And you're never going to think of that again,* she reminded herself, tonguing her implant for the duty report.

"What do you think, Staff?"

Attention abruptly switched back to her companions, she tongued her implant off and shrugged apologetically. "Sorry, sir. I wasn't listening."

"Checking on the children?" Jarret wondered.

"Yes, sir."

He nodded, satisfied. Torin was impressed. A great many junior officers took months to realize that no news was good news. Some of the more officious never caught on.

"I was wondering," Captain Daniels asked, catching her eye, "if you had an opinion on the evening."

Torin had overheard more conversations than she'd been a part of. Most of them had been amazingly inane. "A military opinion?"

"Please. I think we've all heard as many uninformed opinions on the state of the buffet, the other species present, and the new season of *All My Offspring* as we can stomach."

"There's nothing like having a Mictok overanalyze your favorite vid," Lieutenant Ghard sighed.

Nothing Torin could think of anyway. "The civilians seem concerned that the Silsviss come in on our side," she began, organizing her impressions as she spoke, "although the doctor isn't pleased about bringing a fourth aggressive species into the Confederation."

Representatives of the three other aggressive species snorted.

"The Navy seems concerned that the Others will figure out what we're doing and blow this new defensive array into atoms before it's up and running. And one of the vjs who took the first contact team in said we'd better recruit the Silsviss before the Others do because she wouldn't, and I quote, want to meet those s.o.bs in battle."

Jarret nodded. "I heard that, too. Good thing we're going in as friends."

"All right, people, the clock is running again; we're forty-nine hours to planetfall. You've all seen the vids on the Silsviss, you've heard how important it is to impress them enough so that they join the Confederation before the Others move in. Given that, over the next forty-nine hours we'll be practicing ceremonial drill morning, afternoon, and evening. Or the shipboard equivalent thereof."

"Aw, Staff, we've been drilling . . ."

"I know." Torin fixed Haysole with a basilisk smile. "I've seen you." She lifted her gaze to include the entire platoon. "I've seen all of you. And that's why you're doing *more* drill."

"I thought the Silsviss were supposed to be impressed by our military prowess," a Human voice muttered.

"I've got a better idea, Drake . . ."

The heavy gunner started, while those around him snickered at his discomfort.

". . . let's start by impressing them with how well you can tell your left foot from your right. All of you; flight deck, with your weapon, 0830. Dismissed."

She stepped back to stand by the lieutenant as the platoon moved muttering out of the mess.

"Do they really need more drill?" he asked quietly.

"Not really. Considering that none of them have done it since basic, they're surprisingly good."

"Then why?"

"You don't want them thinking too much before a planetfall."

"But this isn't like other planetfalls."

"None of them are, sir. None of them are."

THREE

"Not a bad looking place." Through the cloud cover, the orbital view of Silsvah showed two large land masses and half a dozen smaller ones. Although a little smaller than Terra with a little less ocean, Torin found the planet had a comfortable familiarity—even though she'd been born on Paradise, the first of the colony worlds, and had never personally seen the Human home world from space.

"Mind you," she muttered thoughtfully to no one in particular, "the fact that no one'll be trying to shoot us out of the sky as we land adds to the attraction."

As the *Berganitan* began passing over a storm that seemed to involve half the southern hemisphere, her implant chimed.

DIGNITARIES APPROACHING.

Wincing, she tongued the volume down and hurried across the flight deck to join Lieutenant Jarret. Sergeants and above had received the Silsviss translation program and the upload had scrambled her defaults, forcing her to reset almost every function.

Her next promotion would net her a new implant and she had to admit that, as little as she enjoyed the techs cracking her jaw, she was looking forward to the new hardware. Among other things, she'd gain direct access to the Navy net and power enough to reach any ship not in Susumi space should the company need to be pulled out. Her next promotion would also get her a few years away from combat and she had to admit she was looking forward to that as well.

"Did you hear, sir?"

Jarret grinned, lilac hair flicking back and forth. "I heard. Get them ready, Staff Sergeant."

"Yes, sir." She called the platoon to attention as the hatch cycled open. She'd intended to have them tucked safely away on the VTA before the civilians boarded but the lieutenant had wanted everyone to get a look at each other before they left the ship. It was a good idea—the fewer surprises dirtside, the better—although she'd been a little surprised that her brand new second lieutenant had been the one to have it.

The platoon looked good; not quite so dangerous as it did fully loaded, but good. And if there were a few nonregulation weapons tucked away in nonregulation places, well, these people were used to using every trick it took to stay alive, and she wasn't going to take that edge away.

The Mictok and the Rakva arrived at the top of the gangway before the four Dornagain had ambled across half the flight deck. Face expressionless, Torin amused herself by watching how every deliberate movement rippled new highlights through their thick fur. Then she amused herself by imagining them attempting to outrun enemy fire. Then she wasn't amused.

Captain Carveg should've sent them down an hour ago—then maybe we'd have left on schedule.

The Dornagain ambassador reached the bottom of the gangway.

Maybe two hours ago.

The ramp had been designed for loading—and off-loading—armored personnel carriers. After some discussion of weight ratios and stress factors, the Dornagain went up it in pairs.

Somehow I doubt the Honorable Listens Wisely And Considers All has considered what a pain in the ass this lack of speed is going to be for the rest of us.

When the last rippling highlight had disappeared into the forward compartment, Torin double-timed the platoon up into the belly of the beast, past the two APCs, past the armory, and into the troop compartment.

"Sergeants, sound off when squads are webbed in."

"Squad One, secure."

"Squad Two, secure."

"Haysole, secure your feet or I'll cut them off." Glicksohn growled as the di'Taykan kicked a strap free.

Turquoise eyes narrowed, hair flat against his head, Haysole retrieved the strap. "I don't like it when I can't move my feet, Sarge."

"What you like has crap all to do with life. Tie them down." Cinching his own webbing tight,

Glicksohn shot a "Why me?" look at Torin and snapped, "Squad Three, secure."

"Platoon secured for drop, sir."

Lieutenant Jarret had barely passed the information along to the pilot when the VTA dropped free of the *Berganitan*. "Making up for the Dornagain?" he wondered aloud as the platoon bounced against its webbing. "Or just trying to beat that storm in the southern hemisphere?"

"More likely force of habit," Torin told him. "General Morris, in his infinite two-starred wisdom, assigned a combat pilot to this mission—probably still trying to impress the Silsviss with our military might. Combat pilots flying VTA troop carriers hit dirt as quickly as possible in an attempt not to get themselves and their cargo blown out of the air on the way down."

"And in your experience, when they hit dirt, is their cargo able to walk away?"

"Yes, sir." She grinned, teeth together so as not to bite chunks off her tongue during a particularly vigorous bit of atmospheric buffering. "Most of the time." A quick check on the platoon showed everyone more or less enjoying the flight. "Whatever it is you're eating, Ressk, swallow it before we land."

"No problem, Staff."

"More like *whoever* he's eating," Binti muttered beside him.

"You ought to count your fingers," he suggested. "You're too *serley* stupid to notice one missing."

"Maybe you ought to *gren sa talamec to.*"

"That's enough people."

When the Confederation first started integrating the di'Taykan and the Krai into what was predominantly a Human military system, xenopsychologists among the elder races expected a number of problems. For the most part, those expectations fell short. After having dealt with the Mictok and the H'san, none of three younger races—all bipedal mammals—had any real difficulty with each other's appearance. Cultural differences were absorbed into the prevailing military culture and the remaining problems were dealt with in the age-old military tradition of learning to say "up yours" in the other races' languages. The "us against them" mentality of war made for strange bedfellows.

Conscious of Lieutenant Jarret webbed in close beside her, Torin shied away from that last thought. Not that sex with a di'Taykan could be considered anything but the default . . .

Is that going to keep cropping up during the entire mission, she wondered. *'Cause if it does, a therapeutic mind wipe is going to start looking pretty damned good.*

"We're over Shurlantec and have picked up an escort—they look like short range fighters from here. Ground in seventeen minutes."

Captain Daniels' announcement drew her attention back to the situation at hand. "Listen up, people, and I'll go over our dispersement pattern one last time. Squad One down to the ramp to the left, Two to the right, Three along both sides. When our civilians move out, Squad Three falls in behind, One and Two spread out enough to cover full flanking positions. Remember we're supposed to be a ceremonial guard, so weapons remain at parade rest. I don't care if the Silsviss come up and bite you on the ass, do *not* respond. We're here to make friends, and we do not blow away, blow up, or just generally put holes in our friends. Is that clear? What is it, Checya?"

The heavy gunner lifted a miserable gaze to her face. "I feel naked without my exoskeleton. I never fukking landed without it before."

Throughout the platoon, the other eight HGs nodded in agreement. "And thinkin' of Checya naked ain't helpin'," one muttered.

"I know how you feel, but orders say small arms only." She glanced aside at her own KC-7 and smothered a smile. Small was a relative term—the KC just happened to be the smallest weapon they carried, excluding knives, fists, boots, teeth, and brain. A Marine was expected to survive dropped naked into enemy territory and that expectation had kept a few alive. It had probably killed a few, too, Torin realized, but since the Others didn't take prisoners, it really came down to whether or not a person died trying.

And that's just cheerful enough to make thinking of sex with the lieutenant a preferred option.

Her implant chimed, and she hit the master webbing release. "We're down. Let's go."

Under cover of the resulting noise, Lieutenant Jarret leaned close and murmured, "I'm not questioning your decisions, Staff, but why such a complicated procedure? Why not just march them down and line them up."

"Two reasons, sir. First, the Silsviss are impressed

by military prowess, so we're showing them we have every intention of defending our civilians even though we won't have to. Second, if we leave this lot standing around for too long with nothing to do, it won't be pretty. I said, swallow it by landing, Ressk!" She sighed. "I did warn General Morris that we were a combat unit."

"You worry too much, Staff. This'll be a break for them."

The word *break* had occurred to her although not in that context. Break bones, break bottles, break up negotiations; yes. Enjoy standing around in a dress uniform while diplomats made decisions that eventually they'd have to risk their butts to enforce; no. But all she said was, "Yes, sir."

At the base of the ramp, the local version of concrete stretched off into the distance until it met with a wall of what looked like the same material. Except for the lack of burns and pitting—the place had obviously been resurfaced for their arrival—it could have been any friendly landing field in the Confederation.

Except for the giant lizards approaching at one o'clock, Torin amended. They were too far away for details, and she knew how the heavy gunners had felt about leaving their exoskeletons behind because she really missed her helmet. With its scanner, she could have counted the striations on each scale. Without it, she wasn't entirely certain they had scales although the claws protruding from each foot were uncomfortably large enough to see.

They didn't seem to be wearing much, but considering the damp heat that was hardly surprising.

The heat would make the Krai happy and was within Human tolerances, but she'd have to see that the di'Taykan got extra water.

A quick glance at Lieutenant Jarret showed his hair flat against his head and his nostrils flared. "When you can smell a planet over the landing fumes," he said stroking the temperature controls on his cuff down to their lowest setting, "you know it's going to be bad."

"Pity about the Human sense of smell, sir." The di'Taykan made no secret of how useless they considered Human noses.

He looked at her then. "Nobody likes a smartass, Staff."

"Very true, sir."

The Mictok were the first on the field, then the Rakva, then, to no one's surprise, the Dornagain. By the time the Dornagain had lumbered off the ramp and the Third Squad had fallen in behind, the Silsviss welcoming committee had taken up position between two brilliantly colored banners and a formation of their own soldiers, matching the Marines exactly in numbers and mirroring their position.

They knew how many of us were coming. . . . One painfully constricted heartbeat later, she remembered *this* time that wasn't a problem.

Off to one side of the soldiers, a small cluster of what could only be reporters recorded the moment for posterity. Their technology might be unfamiliar, but their attitude was unmistakable.

Beyond checking that her translation program was working properly, Torin didn't actually pay much attention to the opening exchange. Nothing of substance would be discussed on the landing field anyway so, after catching Ressk's eye and glaring at him until he brought his upper lip back down over his teeth, she used the time to size up their potential allies.

The Dornagain were still the biggest species on the ground by a considerable margin. The Silsviss present were about as tall as a tall Human or an average di'Taykan although Torin had no idea if this group was representative of the species as a whole. Maybe short Silsviss didn't go into the army or the civil service. It did seem, however, that larger Silsviss went into the army as only one or two of the civilians matched the size of the soldiers. They all had short muzzles, a little larger than those of the Krai, and thick necks with minor dorsal ridges. Like the two other reptilian species in the Confederation, they used their tongues a lot when they spoke, flicking it about an impressive array of teeth.

Those present were a mottled shade of grayish-green—slightly more monochrome on the front—but Torin expected that this was merely the local coloring. They'd be making another four regional stops before the "all Silsvah" meeting and, unless the Silsviss were truly unique in the galaxy, there'd be a number of variations on the theme.

Their tails were about as big around as their upper arms, not significantly larger at the base than the tip, and they never stopped moving. A number of the civilians wore bright metallic bands, and although the distance made it difficult to tell for certain, it seemed the soldiers wore duller bands not so much as decoration but to reinforce their tails as weapons.

Hand to hand to tail; good thing they're coming in on our side. One of the Other's subordinate species had been tailed, and old mind-sets had needed to be reworked when an attempt to save as much of the research station as possible led to close-quarters fighting. After half a dozen Marines had been taken down by what amounted to a smack upside the head with a rubber truncheon, they learned not to relax when they saw both hands raised in surrender.

The Silsviss had similar tails. Similar reinforced tails.

They had round eyes set wide apart that seemed to be as unrelieved a black as those of the Mictok although the Silsviss had the more standard two. Evolutionary science hadn't managed to come up with a good reason for it but sentience seemed to lean toward bi-structural development. Their hands were long fingered, and although they obviously had to have opposable digits, Torin wasn't close enough to see how they opposed.

Unable to identify any sexual characteristics, she had no way of telling if the placement of the minimal clothing was merely decorative or gender specific. Not even the soldiers were wearing much although the harnesses and the impressive amount of hardware clearly added up to uniform. Considering the heat and humidity that thickened the air almost to the consistency of soup, minimal clothing seemed wise. The exposed skin on her face and hands was already greasy with sweat.

She'd added, "Have sergeants remind the Humans in their squads to be careful about losing their grip on their weapons," to a mental list when she remembered General Morris' words: *"You'll see new worlds, meet new life-forms, and not shoot at them for a change."*

And that just feels wrong, she realized. *I really need to get out of combat for a while.*

". . . walk in parade ssso our people may sssee sssome of the many typesss of life the Galaxy offersss."

Walk in parade? Her gaze flicked over to the Dornagain and she wondered if there was a diplomatic way to say, "You've got to be fukking kidding."

Apparently, there was, and transportation was arranged.

Torin's translator insisted on calling the three vehicles flatbed trucks—or more specifically, trucksss—although they didn't look like any truck she'd ever seen. They looked a little like a cross between the sleds they used to move the heavy artillery and most of the farm machinery she'd left behind; functional and far from comfortable. Both military escorts were clearly expected to walk.

"I think the di'Taykan should ride as an honor guard for our diplomats, sir. They—you—don't handle this kind of heat well," she added when the lieutenant's hair rose in inquiry. "There's no need for any of us to be unnecessarily uncomfortable."

"You don't think the Silsviss will object?"

"I think the Silsviss will assume we're being cautious in a strange place and slap an equal number of their people on board."

With the Dornagain climbing into place surprisingly quickly, they didn't have time to discuss it.

"Very well, but I walk with the rest of the platoon."

She considered arguing but nodded instead. Rank had its responsibilities as well as its privileges. Besides, if he walked, the Silsviss wouldn't leap to the conclusion that the other di'Taykan were riding because they couldn't walk. It was something *she'd* suspect were their positions reversed, but with Lieutenant Jarret on the ground, the whole thing could be chalked up to weird alien ritual. *And if they plan on joining the Confederation, the Silsviss had best get used to dealing with that. . . .* Remembering the first time she'd ever seen the Krai sit down to a festival meal, she suppressed a shudder. She'd barely been able to stop herself from freeing the appetizers before they reached the table.

During the delicate diplomatic maneuvering of boarding the trucks—while both the Silsviss officials and the Confederation delegates worked out which aliens it would be in their best political interest to ride with—she made sure that all the di'Taykan had their temperature controls at the lowest possible setting. The Silsviss did indeed match the Confederation guards with their own and Torin exchanged a glance of recognition with the soldier arranging it. Senior NCOs shared a bond that went beyond species affiliation and could recognize an expression that said, *"Who the hell came up with this brilliant idea?"* on any arrangement of features.

Lieutenant Jarret and the Silsviss officer were

standing together off to one side, very probably being polite in that "we're above all this" way that officers had. The two were of a height, and di'-Taykan body language seemed to suggest there had been no determination of which was the superior force. Silsviss body language seemed to be saying the same thing, but Torin had long since learned not to jump to cross-species conclusions.

As she approached, reinforced bootheels stamping emphasis into the landing field, she saw her reptilian counterpart moving in on a parallel course. Fully aware of what the other was about to do, and under no obligation of rank to make nice, they ignored one another.

Torin stopped a body-length back of the officers in time to hear the Silsviss say, ". . . no fear of the crowdsss. The citizensss in and around Shurlantec are very much in favor of usss joining with the Confederation."

And did that mean, Torin wondered, *that citizens in other areas are less in favor?* When the lieutenant turned toward her, she stiffened to attention. "The platoon is in position, sir."

"Thank you, Staff Sergeant."

"Ret Assslar." The Silsviss NCO tapped the metal band near the end of his tail sharply against the pavement. "Our troopsss are likewissse posssitioned."

The translation program left names and titles alone but changed everything else to its closest Confederation equivalent. Torin didn't know why it had decided to maintain the elongated sibilants, but she suspected all that hissing was going to get old pretty damned quick.

Ret Aslar acknowledged the information, then turned back to Lieutenant Jarret. "We will, no doubt, have further opportunity to ssspeak at the Embasssy, Lieutenant." His tail hit the pavement much as his NCO's had. "Until then."

"He's definitely done diplomatic work before," Jarret murmured as they moved toward their position.

"He, sir?"

"Ret Aslar. You can only develop his skill with small talk crammed into a room full of strangers who've been told to be polite."

"How could you tell he was male, sir?"

"Smell. The big ones are male. All the soldiers are male."

Only a di'Taykan could scent the sex of species not even in the same phylum. Torin made a mental note to keep an eye on Haysole who seemed determined to be more di'Taykan than most.

"First impressions, Staff?"

It took her moment to realize he meant the Silsviss. "They look like they fought to get to where they are and have no intention of giving any of it up."

Lieutenant Jarret shot her a confused glance. "Any of what?"

"Of who and what they are."

"The Confederation never asks that."

"When was the last time you went out without your masker?" When he opened his mouth to answer, she added, "In an area not controlled by the di'Taykan. When you get right down to it, sir, the Confederation is essentially an agreement to compromise, and I don't get the impression the Silsviss play well with others."

"You got all that . . ." His nod somehow managed to take in both the civil servants and the soldiers. ". . . from watching this lot stand around for an hour?"

"Yes, sir."

His eyes lightened as he glanced down at her. "So staff sergeants really do have super powers?"

Torin *had* been about to explain that survivors learned from experience to recognize those species likely to follow up their first shot with a second and a third but decided instead just to answer his question, responding to his teasing smile with as bland an expression as she could manage.

"Yes, sir."

Outside the high walls of the landing field, huge, fernlike trees not only made it impossible to see more than a few meters from the road but explained why the city had been so difficult to spot from space. Torin only hoped that the defense satellites were as good as tech thought they were because should the Others break through, take Silsvah, and attempt to enslave the Silsviss, it would be a nasty job taking all these overgrown bits of it back.

Not that the Silsviss would be particularly easy to enslave, she acknowledged, listening to the soft rhythm of claws impacting with pavement.

They hadn't gone far when the burned concrete smell of the landing began to clear from her nose and Torin got her first unimpeded whiff of Silsvah. It reminded her of hot summer afternoons spent turning the compost pile, of anaerobic bacteria, and of scrubbing the algae out of the water troughs. It reminded her of one of the many reasons she'd left the farm.

The crowds lining the roads hissed and pointed and occasionally clusters of them would break into high-pitched ululating cries. It didn't sound friendly, but Torin was willing to allow that Ret Aslar knew his people better than she did—H'san cheering for the home team sounded like they were being skinned alive. Although some of the platoon were looking just a bit twitchy by the time the parade came to a stop at the edge of a wide plaza, they managed to form up without incident.

Taking her place at the rear, behind the three sergeants, Torin made a note of rigid shoulders and flattened hair and hoped that whatever was about to happen wouldn't take long.

They were facing an enormous colonnaded building set off from the plaza by a set of steps broad enough to be used as a graduated dais. The two groups of diplomats stood between their military escorts and the stairs. The media occupied the outer edges of the first two sections and standing on the top were those Silsviss too high ranking to be bothered with a trip to the landing field. A male and three females, judging by size alone, or a large male and three smaller males, or two smaller males and a female, or two females and a smaller male or . . . *Now* this *is a species that could use a little pink and blue.* The actual genders were of no immediate importance, Torin just liked to know. They wore robes—the first she'd seen—of some pale, diaphanous fabric that glittered in the sunlight and all four exuded nearly visible arrogance.

At least half the media seemed to be pointing their recording devices upward, and everyone seemed to be waiting for something to happen.

The big male at the top of the stairs stepped forward.

Inflated a brilliant yellow throat pouch.

And roared.

Shit! Torin couldn't hear anything over the pounding of her heart, but she saw at least three weapons snap up into firing position and her own muscles trembled with an instinctive need to respond. Lieutenant Jarret stepping forward brought her back to herself, and she marched around to take up his vacated position, thankful for the chance to move. This, at least, had been covered in the briefing.

"At some point in the ceremony we'll be asked for our battle honors." Lieutenant Jarret had gazed earnestly at his sergeants as he passed on the bare details of the day. *"Staff Sergeant Kerr will take the platoon while I answer."*

If it turned out that the lieutenant had known just what form that question would take and hadn't told her, Torin planned on kicking his aristocratic derriere right back to Ventris Station where he could repeat the course on keeping his NCOs informed.

Standing on the first step, he raised his head and began. "We are of Sh'quo Company . . ."

He clearly knew he couldn't match volume for volume so he played with tone, answering the heat of the Silsviss challenge with cold. As he detailed the company's history, his subtext clearly said: *We have nothing we need prove to you.* Torin was impressed. She could feel the mood of the platoon behind her change, until, when he finished speaking, the Silsviss were in the least amount of danger they'd been in since the Marines had landed.

Then he spun on one heel and walked back to his platoon.

At that moment, they *were* his.

Pity it won't last, Torin thought returning to her original position.

The rest of the ceremony maintained a more conventional tone. Two of the three high ranking females—or smaller males—gave speeches of welcome, the two ambassadors reciprocated, and finally the third of the smaller Silsviss at the top of the stairs announced they were giving over an entire wing of the Cirsarvas for the visitors to use while they were in Shurlantec.

Then the press moved in to take one final image of their leaders standing beside aliens from the stars.

"Well, that wasn't so bad," Ressk grunted, kicking off his boots and stretching his toes.

"Speak for yourself." Mysho pulled off her tunic

and threw it over a stool. "I feel like I've been cooked."

"Ready for seasoning and serving," one of the other di'Taykan groaned.

Stripped down to his masker hanging from a thong around his neck, Haysole fell back onto a bunk. "Look at the bright side, these mattresses are wide enough for two."

"Species with tails need more room," Corporal Hollice, said, coming in from the hall. "You should see the design of the crapper. It's not just the tail either," he went on, moving out of the way so the curious could go take a look, "they're up on their toes so their legs bend high, like the Dornagain's."

"You an' Kleers are gonna need a fukking stool," Juan snickered to Ressk when he returned. "Good thing there's so many of them around."

"Tails," Hollice said again, one hand absently rubbing Mysho's shoulder as he spoke. "You can't use a chair with a back when you've got a tail."

"So, corporal got-all-the-answers, how do you explain that the showers are bang on identical to the fukking showers back up on the vacuum pack?"

"They've never been used; I'd say someone sent down the specs and the Silsviss built them special for us."

"Must've smelled you coming, Juan." Grinning, Mysho stepped away from the heavy gunner's swing and backed right into Binti's arms.

The other woman inhaled deeply and her steadying hand moved slowly around the di'Taykan's waist. "I think you need to turn up your masker," she murmured, face buried in the moving strands of pale hair.

"Unfortunately, I think I need to take a cold shower." Sighing, she untangled herself. "It's the heat, I've got to bring my body temperature down, or I'll keep over-emitting."

Binti snorted and slapped Haysole on a bare thigh. "So how come the pheromone kid here isn't any more enticing than usual?" she asked over his protest.

"I don't know—maybe I'm from farther north, maybe the recruiting sergeant checked his psych profile and gave him an industrial strength masker, or maybe . . ." Her tone grew distinctly dry. ". . . becuase not all members of the same species react to heat the same way."

"Or maybe," Juan continued before anyone else could respond, "your climate controls are fukked." He held out his hand. "L'me look at your tunic while you shower."

"We're on duty."

"So get permission from the sergeant—just do it in your shirtsleeves so I can look at your tunic. It's not doin' you any fukking good and anyway, the regs say dress c's are uniform of the day unless on parade or on guard. What?" he added when everyone in earshot turned to stare. "You never read in the crapper?"

"Just great, if her climate controls go . . ."

"She'll be miserable, but she'll survive." Hands on her hips, Trey turned a slow circle in the middle of the small room assigned to the NCOs. "I can't get over how quiet everything sounds in here."

"Old building, thick walls," Torin told her shortly. "Power grids are all surface mounted, so this place is probably at least a hundred years old. And I wasn't thinking so much of Mysho but of the effect on the rest of the platoon."

"So *they'll* be miserable on duty and in the sack off duty, but they'll survive, too. Haysole'll probably consider it license to turn his masker off at every opportunity, but other than that I don't see much of a problem." Fuschia eyes narrowed. "You don't usually worry this much about the di'Taykan. This have something to do with the lieutenant?"

"Like what?" Torin asked, wondering if that last night of liberty was finally coming home to roost.

"Like a little sucking up to the species in charge."

Hoping the relief didn't show, Torin raised both brows. "In charge?" she repeated with heavy emphasis.

Trey grinned. "Good point. Anyway, I wouldn't worry about an overheated masker. Considering what we usually face eight hours into a planetfall, it's minor."

Torin grunted an agreement and dropped onto a stool, grabbing the edge of the desk just barely in time to stop herself from tipping over backward. Chairs with no backs, desks with no brains, and a climate that clung—all inconveniences that could be ignored under fire but under the current circumstances . . . "So is it a sign of pure intentions that this "embassy" is pretty much completely indefensible or have we deliberately been given the weaker position?"

"Or are you completely paranoid?"

"Just doing my job."

"Hey, Torin." One hand on the heavily carved and overly ornate wooden door, Mike Glicksohn leaned into the room. "Sled's finally here from the VTA."

"About time. Hold down the fort," she tossed over her shoulder at Trey as she headed out into the hall. "I'm going for my slate. And you," she threw at Glicksohn as she passed, "get a work detail together and get everything unloaded before the Silsviss offer to help."

The two sergeants exchanged a speaking glance as Torin's footsteps faded out toward the courtyard.

"Is she completely paranoid?" Glicksohn asked after a moment.

Trey shrugged. "Apparently, it's her job."

"Hey, did any of you guys notice that some of the Silsviss soldiers inflated those throat pouch things when that big guy on the step roared?"

"Not me." Ressk wrapped his feet around the bar at the end of his bunk, toe joints cracking. "I was too busy trying not to overload the moisture sensors in my uniform."

Frowning, Juan looked up from the sensor array exposed in the armpit seam of Mysho's tunic. "What the fuk does that mean?"

"It means he was trying not to piss himself," Binti explained from her bunk. "Me, I was just glad my brain came back on line before my finger squeezed the trigger." She reached up and stroked the stock of her KC. "And civilians wonder why we're not hard-wired into our weapons. Mama does like having her baby this close, though."

Each bunk had a weapons rack built in. Or what looked like a weapons rack. The platoon had decided, individually and collectively, that they didn't much care what the Silsviss used it for.

A sudden cheer from the dice game in the back corner drew everyone's attention.

Corporal Hollice ducked his head so that he could look through the line of bunks at the players. "Hey, Drake, you win back that fifty you owe me yet?"

"As if!"

"Then keep it down before one of the sergeants shows up."

A Human, his skin only a little lighter than Binti's rose up out of his crouch and flicked a good-natured finger in the corporal's direction. "Why don't I owe you this, too?" Then he froze. "Or not."

The Marines closer to the door turned to see what had caught his attention.

Sergeant Glicksohn smiled. "You're not gambling back there, are you, Drake?"

"Uh, no, Sarge."

"Glad to hear it. Outside, now. The sled's here from the VTA, and it needs unloading." His smile broadened. "Bring your friends. And if you . . ." A finger jabbed at Haysole. ". . . aren't back in uniform in three seconds and heading up to the sled, I'm coming over there to kick your bare butt. You're standing down, you're not off duty."

"But, Sarge, it's hot."

"So."

"The Silsviss aren't wearing clothes."

"Grow a tail and we'll talk." As the dice players filed past him, he frowned thoughtfully. "In the interests of expediency, you three . . ." The frown lit on Hollice, Juan, and Ressk. ". . . can join the detail, too."

"Aw, Sarge, I'm fixing Mysho's fukking tunic."

"What's wrong with it?"

"Cooling system's fukked. She's getting too warm for her masker to handle."

"That's just what we need. All right, Mashona, up top in his place."

Binti dropped off her bunk, muttering under her breath just low enough for the sergeant to ignore.

"What're we unloading, Sarge?" Ressk asked, shoving his boots back on.

"Personal effects and rations," Glicksohn told him. "Not that it matters, you'd be unloading it regardless."

"So you find out what the Silsviss drink for fun yet, Sarge?" Ressk asked as they started up the stairs to the courtyard, side by side.

"Beer. Local brewery supplies the army with its own brands. There's a light and a dark and a green."

"Green?"

Glicksohn grinned. "Maybe they're Irish."

"Irish?"

"Skip it. Alcohol content's low by our standards

and since there's nothing in any of it that'll hurt us, once we get used to the taste, we'll be able to drink the Silsviss under the table. Officers and ranking civilians'll be drinking a distilled, fruit liqueur that packs more of a punch but smells like socks after a month in combat boots and will build up toxins in both Human and di'Taykan. You Krai, as usual, can handle it."

Following close behind, Hollice and Binti exchanged an identical, questioning glance.

"We've only been here a few hours, and we spent most of that time playing toy soldiers. How did the sergeant find that stuff out so fast?"

Hollice shrugged. "It's a gift. Let's just hope he never uses it for evil."

"Half the time, I don't know what the hell you're talking about," Binti muttered, shaking her head.

Although the door was open, the lieutenant wasn't alone. Moving quietly across the wide hall—an action made more difficult by the steel-reinforced heels of her dress boots—Torin paused in the open door. Rank had gotten Lieutenant Jarret a pair of adjoining rooms on the upper floor. Out of the half dozen available, he chose two at the top of the central stairs and Torin had to admit she liked the symbolism. Enemies of the Confederation would have to go through him to get to the civilians.

She liked the symbolism of the doctor and the corpsmen setting up shop directly across the hall a little less.

The room the lieutenant had decided to use as his

headquarters was huge, painted a deep, under-the-canopy green, and mostly empty. It held what passed for a desk on Silsvah, a long, low table along one wall, a number of stools of varying heights, the lieutenant, and a Silsviss male. At least Torin assumed it was a male; it was difficult to tell the genders apart without either a size comparison or an inflated throat pouch.

He was standing with his back to her, facing the lieutenant across the desk. A pair of scars ran parallel across the dark gray of his right hip and another marked his right shoulder.

Left-handed, Torin thought. *Weaker on the right.*

He wore three narrow metal rings spaced evenly around the lower end of his tail and a military-style harness with about half the hardware that had been attached to the soldiers who'd met them at the landing field.

"Of coursse there'sss no intention of making thisss your permanent embasssy should we decide to join your Confederation." His voice, while still annoyingly sibilant, was deep and, allowing for the variables of translation, he spoke with a confidence Torin rather liked.

She cleared her throat.

The Silsviss reacted a fraction of second before the lieutenant but waited for his host to look up before he turned.

Retired officer, she decided. *One of the good ones.* Catching the lieutenant's eye she said, "Excuse me, sir, but you wanted to go over the duty roster."

Lieutenant Jarret had clearly forgotten he'd ever

given her such an order, but he recovered quickly and beckoned her into the room. "Yes, of course. Staff, I'd like you to meet Cri Sawyes, our Silsviss liaison. Cri Sawyes, Staff Sergeant Kerr."

"Ah, yes, your Rissstak." The flat black gaze weighed and measured. Whistling softly—it was a quieter version of the sound the crowd had been making, so Torin assumed he approved—Cri Sawyes turned back to the lieutenant. "Here we have a sssaying that a good Rissstak isss the equal of location *and* sssuperior numbersss."

"We have a similar saying."

"Sssoldiersss are sssoldiersss whatever their ssspeciesss." Tapping his tail lightly against the floor, Cri Sawyes moved toward the door. "I will leave you two to your dutiess. When you need me . . ." He indicated the squat, pale green box on the desk. ". . . you have only to call. A pleasure to meet you, Ssstaff Sssergeant."

"Sir." Torin waited until the sound of his claws faded, then leaned over the desk. "And this is?"

"A communications device." Lieutenant Jarret looked speculatively down at the pattern of slots. "It's set up for claws, but I expect I can make do with a stylus." He held out his hand for her slate. His fingers were warm where they brushed against hers—a quick glance at his cuff showed his climate controls still at the lowest setting. He couldn't be comfortable, but it didn't show. "You have fireteams with di'Taykan standing watch at night when it's cooler?"

"Yes, sir."

"Good." He downloaded the schedule into his own slate and handed hers back. "Everything looks in order. Let me know if you make any changes."

"Yes, sir."

"The desks are somewhat less than we're used to, aren't they?"

"Yes, sir."

He drummed his fingertips against the wood and sighed. "In fact, I'd have to say that, officially, they suck."

Torin smiled, more at his indignation than anything but he didn't need to know that. "Yes, sir, they most certainly do suck."

"The doctor says we're all on rations tonight until he finishes testing the local food, so I've had a reprieve."

"A reprieve?"

"The local versions of state dinners." Jarret dropped down onto a stool. "I'd rather be shot at."

"That's because you've never been shot at, sir."

His hair lifted. "And how many state dinners have you attended, Staff."

"None, sir."

"Then I'd say neither of us have a basis for comparison." Smiling up at her, he leaned back and caught himself just before he fell off the stool.

Four

The week in Shurlantec went remarkably quickly. To Torin's surprise, the entire platoon kept their off duty behavior within acceptable parameters—no one got arrested, eaten, or shot. She didn't want to know how Haysole's shoulders got gouged and since Sergeant Glicksohn assured her that both the di'Taykan and diplomatic relations were essentially unaffected, she didn't have to ask.

Although he had a tendency to make enthusiastic and inappropriate suggestions, Lieutenant Jarret allowed her to do her job without unnecessary interference. By the time they reboarded the modified VTA, Torin had to admit that, so far, she had no complaints. The lieutenant would make a fine addition to any Intelligence or Administration unit. Whether he could command a combat unit was still open to question.

With minor geographic differences, experiences at the next two cities on the Silsvah Marine Corps tour were much the same.

Daarges, the largest city in the Southern Hemisphere, took hot and humid up a notch to hot and raining. Cri Sawyes, now traveling with them, explained that the south was in the midst of their rainy season. During a discussion over a jar of green beer, one of the local NCOs shot a disgusted look at the sky and told Torin it didn't actually get much dryer.

"Agriculture down here, technology up north." He sorted through a bowl of small amphibians and tossed a pale yellow one into his mouth. "Not an entirely fair sssyssstem, but it worksss."

The citizens of Daarges were more green than gray, and both fingers and toes were webbed. Torin had never seen a species as good as the Silsviss at waterproofing; exposed metals were coated in an organic sealant and even hand weapons could be fired underwater. Once she got a look at some of the things that lived in the water, she understood why.

"In the old daysss in thisss part of the world, the young malesss went into the water with only a knife to prove themssselvesss against the *karn* and win the right to breed. Thisss hasss not been allowed for sssome time."

Torin looked where Cri Sawyes pointed and only just managed to stop herself from backing off the other side of the narrow boardwalk and right into the swamp.

"That's the biggest snake I've ever seen." Lieutenant Jarret's tone suggested polite interest—his hair, flattened to his head, suggested a slightly less sanguine reaction.

"That isss the more mobile sssection of the *karn*.

The greater part of itsss body isss buried in the mud."

The thought of going up against such a monster with only a knife drew both Torin's brows up almost to her hairline. A handheld missile launcher with soft target impact detonating charges, yes. A knife, no. The expression on the lieutenant's face indicated a similar thought.

"I can see why they put a stop to it," he murmured.

Cri Sawyes made a sound between a sigh and a hiss and his claws curled into the damp wood. "The *karn* isss now a protected ssspeciesss. One by one, our young lossse the challengesss that help them to mature."

Torin was impressed that the *karn* had needed protecting and, not for the first time, gave thanks that the Silsviss were coming in on the right side. The last thing she wanted was to face off against someone who went up against something the size of a *karn* with only a knife. Those kinds of crazy people were dead to reason and nearly impossible to stop.

The third city, Ra Navahsis, was a pleasant surprise. The temperature still hovered between uncomfortable and slow roast, but the air was dry and even the di'Taykan found it bearable. The city was inland and everything, including the Silsviss, was more gold than green.

Given to flashy colors and brilliant displays, the inhabitants kept everyone moving so quickly between ceremonies that Torin barely had a moment to call her own and at that, she had a significantly better time than the lieutenant. After his first Ra Navahsis banquet, he'd staggered into their temporary barracks, gazed glassily at his assembled NCOs and was suddenly, noisily, sick. Not at all sympathetic, Dr. Leor suggested he try eating perhaps half as much the next time.

"There wasn't actually a chance to turn anything down," Jarrett explained as Torin helped him back to his quarters after the doctor had done what he could. "They knew what local foods each of us could eat and they were determined to feed it to us. The Dornagain seemed to enjoy it—I think one of the ambassador's assistants changed her name to Well If You Insist Just One More—the Rakva can't eat enough of the local food to have a problem, Ambassador Krik'vir and her lot switched to external digestion and that got them off the hook, but it was up to me to uphold the honor of the Marines."

"The Marines appreciate it, sir."

"Don't patronize me, Staff, or I'll puke on your boots."

"Sorry, sir."

"Maybe I should deputize one of the Krai to eat in my place."

Torin eased him down onto his bed. "I'm not sure any of our Krai would be up to that kind of a ceremonial function."

"Ceremonial function, my brass. More like competitive gluttony."

"That, they'd be up to."

He belched, exhaling a breath redolent with Silsvah spices, and fell back against the ridge in the top of the mattress that passed for a pillow. "Don't think for a moment they weren't judging my abilities, throwing food at me until they knew exactly where I stood." One hand clutching his masker, he closed his eyes. "See if you can get them to shoot at me instead. I'm sure I'd feel a lot better if I'd just been shot."

"I stand by my theory that that's only because you've never been shot, sir."

"Fine. You shoot me."

Torin had no idea how the lieutenant managed to survive the continuing round of banquets his rank obligated him to attend, but the only shooting involved an elaborate display of military marksmanship where the visitors outscored the home team over two to one with their own weapons and then proved themselves laughingly inept with the Silsviss small arms.

The Silsviss, on the other hand, took to the KC like a H'san to cheese.

"Sorry, Staff." Ressk pulled his slate back from Torin's jaw and ruefully shook his head. "I can't get a clear enough interface with your implant. The data I'm getting's so scrambled, I can't find what needs fixing."

"So I'm stuck with the sibilants?"

"'Fraid so. Bottom line, you need an upgrade."

Her hand rose to protectively cup her left cheek. The tech team insisted that the installation was essentially painless, but Torin had found a lot of leeway within that qualifier. "There's an automatic upgrade coming with my next promotion. Can't it wait?"

He shrugged, a Krai adaptation of a Human gesture. "That depends."

"On?"

"Time frame. Your opstem's on the downward slide. Eventually, it'll degrade into piss and wind and even your primary programming won't run. Now, if it was up to me, I wouldn't wait for that piece of shit the techs'll put in; I'd get me a Bg347 with a direct cerebral uplink."

Torin snorted. "And if I could afford that, why would I be here, wasting my time with you lot?" She headed for the door without waiting for an answer. "Thanks for the diagnostic, Ressk."

"There'll be a little something added to my pay chit?"

"No." Pausing just inside the door's sensor range, she grinned back over her shoulder as it cycled. "But I'll ignore your little excursion up on the *Berganitan*."

"How did you . . . ?"

"I'm a staff sergeant. I know everything." She stepped over the hatch's raised edge and added, as the door cycled shut behind her, "And don't ever do it again."

"I told you she'd find out," Binti muttered, lightly smacking the back of his head as she passed behind him.

"No, you didn't."

"Yes, I did."

"Didn't."

"Did."

"Would you two shut your fukking holes." Arms stiff, Checya glared at them in mid push-up and jerked his chin toward Conn. "You think the poor bastard doesn't already miss his four-year-old? You two have to remind him of her?"

The corporal looked a little startled at suddenly being the center of attention. "Were you guys talking to me?" He held up his slate. "I was just writing to Myrna. Captain Daniels told me she'd squirt a letter up to the *Berganitan* when we land."

"Tell her I said hi." Stepping over the heavy gunner, Binti hung her tunic over the back of her assigned position and continued toward the hatch in the back of the troop compartment that led to the APCs.

"Where are you heading?"

"I thought I'd go play with the di'Taykan."

Corporal Hollice cracked one eye and glanced up at the board. "You've got half a standard hour before we're to strap back in."

"Plenty of time if we skip the small talk."

Hollice opened the other eye and glanced around the troop compartment, counting Marines. "There's four of them in there."

"So?"

"Hey, if you can march after that, more power to you, but you know the rules about other races joining in with the di'Taykan. No allowances made. You play, you pay. And your basic Human bits are just not . . ."

"All right, killjoy, I get it." Binti frowned, turned,

and dropped back into her seat. "Maybe I'll just play a level of Goopa Elite instead."

Hollice smiled and closed his eyes again. "Probably wise."

"I think it's time someone took his sergeant's exam," she muttered, shoving a game biscuit into her slate.

The Silsviss had asked that they stay within the atmosphere while traveling between cities so that as many people as possible could see the alien ship. As they were willing to provide the extra fuel it burned, Captain Daniels flew the fine line between too close to the ground and insulting their hosts.

Distances that could have been covered in a hop and skip out of the atmosphere took hours.

Torin had pulled the NCOs out of the troop compartment as soon as the VTA had reached its cruising altitude. Too much off duty time spent with the troops tended to turn even the most levelheaded sergeant into a playground supervisor—which left no one happy.

She'd have ignored the game in the armory, but the sight of a Rakva perched behind the ammo case they were using as a table pulled her in for a closer look.

"For the sake of our beginner here, we'll keep it simple." Mike dealt one card up and four down to all six players. "The game's five card draw. Jack bets."

The junior Rakva extended a slender digit and tapped the plastic square. "This is a jack?"

"That's a jack."

"Ah." He scooped up his other four cards and fluffed out his crest as he studied them. "This one thinks that this one understands but would like to know one small thing again."

Scratching his cheek where the follicle suppressant was beginning to wear off, Mike shrugged. "Anything."

"What is it that beats a pair of eights?"

Torin grinned as the sergeant tossed his hand down in disgust. The metal ammo case had reflected the cards far too fast for Human eyes but not for Rakva. "You're not gambling in here, are you, Sergeant Glicksohn?"

"Wouldn't think of it, Staff. We're just involving our feathered friend here in a cross-cultural exchange."

The Rakva's crest fell. "This one thought you were teaching him to play poker?"

Torin left him to explain.

Her rounds bringing her back into the civilian's seating behind the bridge, she straightened her tunic and put on her best company expression before stepping into the sensor field. Although about half the size of the troop compartment for significantly fewer people, the four Dornagain made the area seem cramped and overcrowded. Her nose twitched. And, in spite of the best efforts of the ventilation system, just a little rank.

The lieutenant was talking to the Dornagain ambassador, and she wondered how he was coping. Breathing through his mouth wouldn't help—the most sensitive scent receptors were along the edge of his soft pallet. Did he need rescuing?

Given the way the ends of his hair were flicking back and forth, she'd say that would be a yes.

Fortunately, Listens Well And Considers All spoke significantly faster than he moved, and at the first natural pause, Torin stepped forward. "Excuse me, Ambassador, Lieutenant. Sergeant Trey needs to speak to you at the APCs, sir."

"Thank you, Staff Sergeant." To have shown that much relief in his voice would have been rude, but Torin read it in the sudden stillness of his hair. "Excuse me, Ambassador, duty calls." He bowed and turned, and mouthed a second, silent *thank you* as he passed.

"Staff Sergeant Kerr."

"Yes, Ambassador?" She thought he was smiling at her, but she wasn't as familiar with Dornagain social cues as she should be. His ears were up, only his bottom teeth were showing, and he was resting back on his haunches—although that last bit was more an indication of the compartment height than any sort of mood.

"How are *you* finding the Silsviss thus far?"

I don't have to find them, they're all over the bloody place. "I think they'll make fine allies against the Others, sir."

"Ah, yes, the Others." Long claws dug absently at a tangle of his cream-colored fur. "You are aware that their ships have been seen approaching this sector?"

"Approaching? How close?" she demanded, then added a quick, "Sir."

"I am afraid I am not aware of their exact position, Staff Sergeant, only that the nearness of the enemy prods us to make our decisions based on expediency rather than what might be best for both the Confederation and the Silsviss."

Torin ran that through her translator one more time, just to be sure she understood. "You think we're letting the Silsviss into the Confederation too soon?"

"They are not as sociologically advanced as I would like."

"They're at about the same level Humans were, and you let us in."

"Because we required someone to fight our battles."

"Still do," Torin reminded him,.

"Yes." The Dornagain nodded slowly, smoothing his whiskers with the back of one hand. "I had much the same conversation with your lieutenant, only he used the di'Taykan as his example. So I will ask you what I asked him: Do you not think it would be better if we learned to fight our own battles?"

"It's a little too late for that, Ambassador. It's now our battle, too. On the other hand, we wouldn't say no if you wanted to help."

"Help?"

"Fight."

"Ah. Yes." Eyes half closed, he began grooming again. "I will have to think about that."

Hoping he hadn't considered it a personal invitation—while amateur soldiers weren't the last thing she wanted, they were low on the list—Torin bowed and left him to his deliberations.

As near as she could figure, the approaching Others were still a diplomatic situation, not yet a military one. With any luck, someone would let her know if that changed. Hopefully, *before* the shooting started.

The other three Dornagain appeared to be asleep, the doctor was studying his slate, the Charge d'Affaires and her remaining assistant were having a low-voiced discussion—hopefully not about their missing team member, now involved in Sergeant Glicksohn's cross-cultural exchange—and all four Mictok had webbed themselves into a corner. Torin didn't know what they were doing and she wasn't going to ask.

Carefully skirting one of the sleeping Dornagain and the surrounding musky atmosphere, she joined Cri Sawyes at the vid screen. It wasn't until they reached the edge of the forest that she realized the mottled green field they'd been flying over was actually the tops of trees. "We seem to be above a whole lot of nothing."

"One of the wildernesss pressservesss," the Silsviss explained. "Our governmentsss put large areasss asside to ensure our young malesss are properly challenged."

Torin knew better than to be drawn into a discussion of alien gender issues but she couldn't stop herself from asking, "Only your males?"

"We only have a sssurplusss of malesss."

"So challenged means . . ."

"Exactly what you think it meansss, Sssergeant. We have too many malesss not to weed out the weak."

They were passing over low hills. Something moved down in one of the valleys, something big, but they were by too quickly for Torin to see exactly what it was.

"Young malesss reach an age when their body chemissstry requiresss them to essstablish their posssition. They . . ." He glanced over at Torin and his tongue flicked out. "*We* will fight any other male we meet. It isss much easssier on sssociety if malesss during that time are placed where they can do the leassst damage."

"To everything but each other."

"Yesss. Within the pressservesss, we form packsss, continually challenging for the leadership. A good leader throwsss pack againssst pack, keeping hisss followersss too preoccupied to take him down. Eventually, chemissstry changesss again and the sssurvivorsss realize there isss more to life than fighting."

"Like sex?"

His tongue flicked out again. "Sssex is much like fighting for my people, Sssergeant, but if you mean reproduction, then yesss. And that requiresss a sssocial posssition you cannot gain by tooth and claw in the wildernesss."

"Your females don't fight?"

"Not without cause. Our malesss outnumber our

femalesss almossst twenty to one. There may have been a reason for such dissscrepancy once—I don't know, I'm not an anthropologissst—but technology overtook evolution and now we do what we mussst to maintain civilization."

"Which is why all your soldiers are male?"

"Yesss. It helpsss integrate the young malesss back into sssociety, maintaining the hierarchy ssstructure they're familiar with and teachesss them waysss to advance that don't involve biting off an oponent'sss tail and ssstrangling him with it."

"But armies are just bigger packs."

Cri Sawyes nodded and drummed his claw tips against the edge of the screen. "Thisss will be an interesssting transssition for my people. The arrival of your Confederation ssstopped a major war and half a dozen border actionsss. Thanksss to your Confederation, we are becoming one."

"It was much the same with my people," Torin admitted. "Well, not the gender differences," she amended as he turned to stare, "but the becoming one part."

"And was it difficult for Humans?"

She shrugged. "We're an us against them kind of species, Cri Sawyes. As far as I can tell, and I'm no more an anthropologist than you are, we just redefined us and them."

"I sssee." He turned to stare back down at the screen, muscles tensing as they passed over an area burned clear. "I think it will be harder for usss."

They'd been to three large cities, each run by a male and two or three females. Remembering the scars on the males, Torin wondered if the delegates were being given the tour of Silsvah while the overall leadership of the planet was being determined.

And then cleaned up after.

Not my species, not my problem.

On the screen, the wilderness was replaced by cultivated land.

There was a band at the landing field in Hahraas. At least, Torin assumed it was a band. Although she couldn't hear anything that might resemble a melodic line, there was a beat that could be marched to and she didn't actually ask for more than that.

Besides the band, there was a mirror image platoon, a number of civilian dignitaries matching theirs, a banner, and a new team. The landing field had been resurfaced for their visit.

Same old, same old, Torin thought as Mike took his squad down the ramp. It was amazing how quickly the strange became the familiar and how soon after that familiarity bred contempt. As she followed Squad Three out of the VTA, she made a mental note to try and keep her troublemakers too exhausted to make trouble.

"You wanted to see me, sir?"

Lieutenant Jarret glanced up from his slate and waved Torin into the room. "Captain Daniels is on her way in from the landing field with a message from the *Berganitan.*"

"Is there a problem with the link?" The captain had the access codes to both her slate and the lieutenant's—if there was a problem, her maintenance programs hadn't flagged it.

"No, no problem." He tossed his slate onto the desk and stood, rolling his shoulders forward and back. "We're not entirely certain our communications are secure, so she's bringing it personally."

Torin frowned, trying to remember all the contact she'd had with the aircrew since they'd landed. "You think the Silsviss have cracked our link?"

"Not really, no. But it doesn't hurt to be careful." Grinning, he grabbed his left elbow behind his back and stretched. "Actually, I suspect Captain Daniels is bored spitless and is taking advantage of a loophole in her orders to stay with the VTA." Switching elbows, he continued to stretch.

"Are you stiff, sir?" The words were barely out of her mouth before she realized what she'd said. *What a question to ask a di'Taykan! Especially one you've got a history with.* As his eyes brightened and his grin broadened, she raised a cautioning hand. "Not an invitation, sir. I was just asking about your back."

"My back?" For a moment, she thought he wouldn't let the innuendo go and then he smiled. "It's nothing, I've just been sitting in one position for too long."

"Should I get Dr. Leor?" she asked, when her imagination kept filling the silence with other suggestions. She was *not* going to offer to rub it.

The lieutenant looked confused. "For a stiff back?"

"Of course not. Sorry, sir." Clearly, the troops weren't the only ones getting restless. She needed something to do. Something real. Something physical. All this ceremonial standing around left her far too much free time. And if she felt that way, she'd better start keeping a closer eye on the troops. "Any idea what Captain Daniels' message is?"

"She didn't say." The sound of approaching bootheels ringing against the polished stone floor drew the lieutenant around to the front of his desk. "But I think we're about to find out."

"Captain Carveg sends her regrets, but the *Berganitan* was the closest ship."

"If long range sensors have detected a possibility of the Others near the edge of the sector, her responsibility is clearly to investigate." Lieutenant Jarret sounded as sincere as only a young officer with his first command could. "We're perfectly safe down here until they get back."

Torin wondered if considering that statement to be a fine example of famous last words made her unduly paranoid or just conscious of historical precedent.

"I hope your civilians take it as well."

"I don't think they'll be surprised," Torin offered, remembering her conversation with the Dornagain ambassador. "They knew the Others were approaching."

"If they're just making a recon flight, it's nothing the *Berganitan* can't handle."

If, Torin added silently.

Captain Daniels ran a hand back through thick, black hair, standing it up from her scalp in damp spikes. "Have these people never heard of air-conditioning?"

The lieutenant snorted. "Modern buildings have all the conveniences, but we keep getting billeted in these historic piles of stone. Not," he added afer a moment's reflection, "that the Silsviss are big on cooling things down at the best of times. You and your crew have it easy. All the comforts of home and you got to show off in that air show."

"Oh, yeah, that was fun. Flying a VTA in atmosphere is like wrestling a H'san—let your mind wander for an instant and you're eating dirt." The pilot wandered from window to window, peering down into the empty courtyard, and finally settled one thigh on the broad stone sill. "So, still managing to hold up under the weight of the ceremonial circuit?"

"Honestly?" Lieutenant Jarret dropped down onto a stool, caught himself with a practiced motion, and leaned carefully back against the wall. "I'm beginning to wish they'd sent me into battle instead."

"Be careful what you wish for." The captain waved a chiding finger and then turned to Torin. "And what about you, Staff? How're the troops holding up?"

"No casualties so far, sir. Which reminds me . . ." She nodded toward the lieutenant. ". . . I should go check on Haysole and tell the platoon about the *Berganitan*."

"How do you think they'll react?"

"To the navy buggering off and leaving them on

their own?" She grinned at the two officers. "Same old, same old."

"It sure is boring being a guard." Binti tossed her tunic across the end of her bunk and collapsed down onto the bag of heated sand the Silsviss in this part of the world used as a mattress. "And what the hell are we guarding against anyway? I thought the Silsviss were supposed to be our allies?"

Various forms of grunted assent answered her as Squad One filed into their temporary barracks and found their bunks.

"It's for fukking show," Juan grunted, carefully racking his weapon before dropping onto his own sandbag. "Lets them lizards see we're ready to fight if we have to be."

Ressk hissed through his teeth as he stretched out his toes. "Staff better not hear you calling them lizards."

"But they *are* fukking lizards."

"Who's fukking lizards?" Haysole asked, coming in from the shower. He shook his head to settle his hair back into place and glanced around at the bodies on the bunks. "Come on, who?"

"Besides you?" Binti snickered.

"It was an adjective, not a verb," Corporal Hollice interrupted. "Not that you morons would know what that means." A raised hand cut off the protests of his fireteam and those other squad members close enough to hear. "Don't bother proving it."

"This is a new low. We're arguing about grammar." Punching his sand into shape, Ressk settled back. "Me, I pray to all the gods of my *tarlige* that this will be over soon."

"Might not."

All heads turned toward Haysole.

"Staff came in as I finished the crappers, just before Squad Two headed out to replace you. The *Berganitan* has left orbit."

"What?"

"Sensors read Others at the edge of the sector and they took off."

"Leaving us here, ass-deep in ceremonial fukking duties?" Juan struggled up into a sitting position and glared at the di'Taykan. "You're fukking kidding, right?"

"Wish I was. Staff told me to let you guys know when you came in."

"You know what this means? This means we could be finished with this gig before they get back and we could be stuck here. This could just go on and on and on and on."

"What if they never come back?" someone muttered.

"Okay, that's it." Binti stood up and grabbed her tunic. "I can't stand it anymore, I'm out of here."

"Mess is right next door. Big change."

"I'm not going to the mess. I'm taking my souvenir Silsvah money in my souvenir Silsvah belt pouch—which appears to have been made from a souvenir Silsviss—and I'm going out for a drink and a little action."

Ressk's eyes snapped open. "You're what?"

"Look, we know they drink, we've had the beer,

and that means they have to have places they drink in."

"Maybe they drink alone."

"Did you pay no attention in school?" she demanded, smacking him on the side of the leg. "So far, only social species have achieved sentience . . ."

"Oh, yeah. Big achievement."

Binti ignored him. "The Silsviss are sentient, which makes them social, which means somewhere in this godforsaken town there's a bar."

"At the risk of sounding like the voice of reason," Hollice interrupted, "our orders are to stay put."

"No one's saying you have to come."

He snorted. "You think I'd let you run around without adult supervision?"

Ressk stared up at the corporal, then sighed and began putting his boots back on. "Come on, Juan. Looks like we're moving out."

"Praise the fukking lord."

"Anyone else want to come?"

The other Marines in the room declined. One or two expressed opinions about the wisdom of the trip, but no one raised any major objections. They all knew that someone had to be the first over the wall.

"Haysole?"

"I should get some sleep. My team's got the last watch."

"And your point is?"

"Give me a minute to get dressed."

It took very little more than a minute and then the five of them slipped to into the hall and past the mess, heading for the boiler room at the end of the corridor.

"Of course I know that door leads outside the compound," Haysole muttered when asked. "You think I was cleaning the crappers because I wanted to?"

"And where do you lot think you're going?"

Hearts in their throats, the five turned as one, falling instinctively into a defensive position, the heavy gunner out in front.

Mysho grinned at them. "From the spreading stain in Juan's crotch, I guess I've got that impersonation of Staff Sergeant Kerr down pat."

"Fukking *trilinshy*," Juan muttered, unable to stop himself from looking down.

"*Trilin*sha," Haysole corrected, scowling darkly over his head at the corporal. "Female tense. But other than that . . ."

"Name-calling; very mature. It's a good thing I'm going with you."

"You don't even know where we're going," Binti pointed out, shuffling impatiently from foot to foot.

"You're going out to find a bar and get stinking with the natives. I don't need to be a H'san to figure that out." Mysho's grin slipped, and she jerked her head back toward the mess. "If I have to spend another evening in there listening to Justin analyze old Earth entertainment, I'm going to deactivate my masker and give us all something more interesting to do."

"Hey, he makes some very good points about *Babylon Space Five*."

"Moron. It's *Deep Babylon Nine.*"

"Whatever."

A sudden noise from the mess moved them toward the boiler room again. Slipping single file past the storage tanks, they reached heavy metal door.

"Wonder what the fukking sign says." Juan flicked the painted letters with a finger.

"Keep out. Authorized personnel only."

In the silence that followed, five heads turned toward Ressk—only Haysole kept his attention on the lock.

"You read Silsvah?" Binti asked after a moment.

Ressk snorted. "Don't need to. That's what it always says on these sorts of doors."

"Okay, we're through." Haysole straightened, twisting a pair of connections together. "This is what gave me away the last time."

"Security system?"

"I think Staff said it was a fire alarm."

"You think?"

"Doesn't matter." He closed the door behind them, careful not to let the connections slip. "I've fixed it."

They were in a long corridor, wide enough to hold three Marines walking abreast. It appeared to be made of Silsvah's poreless concrete and it sloped gently up toward a blue light—the only source of illumination.

"The upper door leads out onto the street that runs behind the compound." Haysole murmured as they climbed. "It's mostly an access alley, so there's no windows overlooking it. Unfortunately, Sergeant

Glicksohn was standing there waiting for me, so I don't know where the road goes."

Binti reached the door first. "I'm assuming the letters on that light say exit—which reminds me, we have a small problem. No translation program."

"Not entirely accurate. And quit looking at me like that!" Ressk snapped as all six pairs of eyes turned toward him. He pulled his slate off his belt. "Staff's implant's acting up, so she asked me to have a look at her translation program. The data was too scrambled for me to fix the problem, but . . ." He finished keying in his entry and from the small speaker came an extended string of sibilants.

"And that means?" Binti demanded.

"I'll have whatever he's drinking."

She beamed down at him. "You know, for a short, hairless troll, you're pretty damned smart."

"I still say it wasn't very smart not to bring our fukking weapons," Juan muttered as Haysole worked on the door.

"We're going out for a drink, not to start a war," Hollice reminded him. "Besides—anyone who's not actually armed in some way, speak up now."

The silence stretched and lengthened, broken finally by Haysole standing and cracking open the door. The air that pushed in was significantly hotter than the air in the tunnel.

"It doesn't even fukking cool down here at night."

"Ra Navahsis was cool at night."

"And that would mean something if we were *in* Ra Navahsis."

Mouth slightly open, Mysho waved a hand vigorously in front of her face. "I really hate the way this place smells."

"What?" Juan demanded. "Your fukking nose plugs aren't working either?"

"They're working. But I still hate the smell."

One by one they slipped outside, the two di'Taykan, eyes at their darkest to utilize the minimal amount of light, on point.

As they rounded the first corner, two dark figures slipped out of the shadows and followed.

FIVE

Silsviss street lighting consisted of dim globes bulging out of the sides of concrete pillars, designed to imitate the phosphorescent fungus that grew on many of their trees. It shed a diffused green light that didn't so much pierce the swirling mist as it was absorbed and reemitted by it.

"Why are the streets so empty?" Binti asked as they hurried from pillar to pillar. "There aren't even any vehicles moving around out here."

"You don't think they put potentially dangerous aliens near where people live, do you?"

She reached out and lightly smacked the back of Ressk's head. "Who are you calling *potentially* dangerous?"

Maintaining defensive positions, they crossed a narrow parklike strip of short vegetation, every step disturbing a cloud of tiny insects that buzzed around their knees before settling back to the ground.

"Fukking bloodsuckers," Juan muttered and crushed one against his thigh.

"They're not sucking your blood," Hollice told

him, "so leave them alone. And since we're speaking of alone—Haysole! There's nothing out here. Where are we going?"

The di'Taykan pointed through a masking screen of giant ferns toward a cluster of low-lying buildings skirting what looked like the Silsviss version of a chain-link fence. The buildings behind the fence had the unmistakable appearance of barracks. "This is the direction the soldiers came from when we went through maneuvers today," Haysole explained. "And where you find soldiers, some enterprising sort has to have built . . ."

"A bar." Mysho finished.

"Do we really want to drink with Silsviss soldiers?" Ressk wondered.

"Would you rather drink with civilians?"

"Good point."

"Stop skulking." Hollice grabbed Juan's shirt and hauled him upright. "You skulk and you attract attention."

"So if I don't skulk, are they going to fukking ignore us?" he demanded, yanking the bunched fabric down.

"Probably not, but at least they won't think we're up to something."

"We're *not* up to something."

"The Silsviss don't know that."

"Binti's right," Ressk snickered. "It's time you took your sergeant's exam. That kind of paranoia isn't normal"

"Look, you walk like a tourist out seeing the sights, that's how you're treated. You walk like you're heading into enemy territory . . ." The corporal shrugged, his point clear.

As they emerged from the ferns and stepped out onto another road, the two di'Taykan slowed, allowing the rest of the group to bunch up at their backs. "We've been spotted," Mysho murmured. "A pair of soldiers, over against the end of that building."

"Officers?"

"No, their harnesses are too plain. They're just a couple of regular grunts."

"I wonder how *they* think we're walking?" Binti asked sarcastically.

"Here they come."

The six Marines split into three pairs and moved far enough apart to maneuver should it come to a fight.

One of the Silsviss soldiers spoke, and a moment later Ressk's slate demanded to know where they were going. Everyone looked at Hollice, who looked at Binti.

"Your idea," he reminded her.

She rolled her eyes and stepped closer to the Krai. "We're looking for the real Silsvah, not what the politicians decide to show us."

The soldier who'd spoken before snorted and no one needed the slate to translate, *fukking politicians.*

"Not likely," Binti snorted. "Probably catch something."

The translation program seemed up to the play on words and both Silsviss hissed appreciatively. After a quiet conversation the slate couldn't pick up, they came to an obvious agreement.

"We're heading to our *savara* . . ."

It took the slate an extra moment to translate the new word into the closest Confederation equivalent.

". . . frequently visited drinking establishment. You can come as our trophies."

"Trophies?" Hands dropped toward hidden weapons and Ressk's lips curled back.

The translation program tried again. "Guests."

Raising an eyebrow at Ressk, Binti accepted for all six. "Love to. Frequently visited drinking establishment?" she asked a moment later when names had been exchanged and the Marines had fallen in behind their new friends. "Trophies? What the hell is that all about?"

"I pulled the program out of Staff's head while doing a diagnostic. I may be missing a few variables. At least it's not hissing."

"You ever think that we're only hearing what the program wants us to hear?" Mysho mused. "I mean, when those oxymorons in Military Intelligence get through with it, how do we know that Silsviss doesn't go in one end and complete garbage comes out the other?"

"You sure you want to be a corporal?" Ressk asked Binti dryly. "It'll only make you paranoid."

"Mysho's got a point," Hollice objected.

"See?"

"We don't know what we're saying to them any more than we know what they're saying to us." Hollice lowered his voice further. "Look at their throat pouches."

Both pouches were slightly distended, the stretched skin startlingly pale in the darkness.

"They're fukking pleased with themselves, aren't they?"

"Hey, they're kids," Binti reminded them. "Remember the first time *you* met an alien up close and personal?"

The two di'Taykan exchanged a meaningful snicker.

"At the risk of being species specific," she muttered, "not quite what I meant."

They could hear the *savara* before they reached it, and even the Humans could smell it soon after that.

"Outside patio," the Silsviss who introduced himself as Sooton explained, leaning in close to the slate. "We'll wait here and Hairken can go around and give them some warning. The known fellow soldiers have been drinking—if they're startled, they might take a shot at you."

"Don't want that," Binti agreed. "Known fellow soldiers?" she sighed when Hairken had disappeared around the corner and Sooton had moved to a vantage point where he could watch both his friend and the Marines. "That sort of thing's going to get old fast."

"'Specially if you fukking repeat it every time," Juan muttered.

Hairken reappeared and waved. Sooton beckoned them forward.

"Once more into the breach, dear friends," Hollice declaimed quietly.

The other five turned to stare.

"It's a Human reference."

Juan snorted. Binti rolled her eyes.

Hollice sighed. "Just forget I said anything."

Taking a step toward them, Sooton hissed and beckoned impatiently. The Marines hurried to his side. "Look, all the fellow soldiers want to meet you, but there's six members of my *partizay* there—eight counting Hairken and me—I think we should join them. There are assurances of less violence in numbers."

"Safety in numbers?" Binti hazarded.

The translator hissed her question back at the Silsviss who nodded, "Yes."

Turning the corner onto the patio brought them under the scrutiny of between thirty and forty pairs of eyes. Only the four throwing steel darts at a dangling target ignored the new arrivals. The background music didn't quite fill in the sudden silence.

After a moment, about half of the staring Silsviss decided it was beneath them to seem impressed by the same aliens they saw daily on the parade square, and conversations started up again, defiantly loud. The remaining eyes tracked them as they moved single file through the gate in the simulated woodgrain plastic fencing and threaded a careful path through tails to a large round table off to one side.

A shuffling of stools gained everyone a space about the same time Hairken arrived from the service window with a tray of beer.

"Thanks." As his slate spat out the Silsviss translation, Ressk slid it out onto the table.

One of the soldiers stopped clawing an obscene sketch into the tabletop to poke it with a finger. "This will allow us to speak to each other?" he asked.

Ressk swallowed his first mouthful of beer with a happy sigh. "More or less," he acknowledged, wiping foam out of his lower nasal ridges. "But the program's set up for officers, so it'll probably add in a lot of bullshit."

The flickering tongues around the table spread throughout the room as those near enough to hear passed on the quip. Tension levels eased somewhat.

"Hey, *artras*!"

"You like *artras*?" a scarred soldier asked passing the platter so that the Marines could help themselves to the salty pastry. When the answer came back a solid affirmative, his tongue flickered out and he said, "Then you should try a *kritkar*. Yrs!" The smaller male beside him jerked erect so quickly he almost spilled his beer. "Go to the place in this building where the food is prepared . . ."

Hollice kicked Binti under the table before she could either repeat the phrase or roll her eyes and get them all eviscerated. Somehow he doubted that the damage to the side of the Silsviss' face was the only reason the big soldier appeared to be snarling.

". . . and get a big bowl of *kritkar* for our alien friends."

Clearly feeling responsible, Sooton and Hairken indulged in a brief shoving match. Sooton lost. "Wait a minute, Yrs." He turned to the scarred soldier. "You said it yourself, Plaskry, these are aliens. Why would they eat *kritkar*?"

"Why wouldn't they?" Plaskry's throat pouch inflated slightly. "Do they refuse my hospitality? Or do they not have the male equipment to eat soldiers food?"

Wondering what Plaskry had actually said before the translation program mangled it, Hollice touched Sooton lightly on one arm. "We can handle it," he said, then added more loudly, "bring on the *kritkar*."

Yrs continued to hesitate.

"What?" Plaskry demanded.

"*Kritkar's* expensive, Plas, and I got my pay chit docked for a moldy tail guard."

The snarl broadened. "I'll pay."

"Hey, it's his *partizay*, and he'll pay if he wants to," Hollice said brightly as the smaller Silsviss scurried away.

Everyone in ear shot turned to stare.

"Just fukking ignore him," Juan advised.

Moving between the pockets of deep shadow created by the dim street lighting, the pair of dark figures had followed the Marines from the embassy to the bar. There'd been a brief exchange when the six had met up with the two Silsviss soldiers, but they hadn't interfered. Seconds after the Marines had followed Sooton and Hairken onto the patio, they'd slipped into the *savara* by a side door. The taller of the two had pulled the proprietor aside for a hurried conversation and, after an official bit of hardware had been flashed, they'd been led along the edges of the room and up a flight of stairs to an empty loft overlooking the patio.

Down below, the Marines were waiting for the *kritkar* to arrive.

"I see why no one uses this place," Torin complained, pulling off the leather cap that had hidden her hair and reshaped her head to a vaguely Silsviss silhouette. "It's hotter than bloody blue blazes up here."

"How hot isss bloody blue blazesss?" Cri Sawyes wondered, settling himself at the edge of the loft.

"Not as hot as this. Are you sure they can't see you?"

He pulled his tail back into the shadows, "Posssitive. I would, however, be more concerned that they don't sssee you. I very much doubt that any of your lot would recognize me at this dissstance."

"The two di'Taykan might. They have a highly developed sense of smell."

"Even over thisss?" His gesture took in the nearly visible miasma of beer, greasy food, and heated bodies rising from the patio.

"Probably not." Torin made a note of both exits, then settled down beside him. "Should I be worried about the Silsviss we passed downstairs? One or two of them seemed to be giving me what I could only call a flat, unfriendly stare."

"We interrupted their drinking. Thossse inssside are not necesssarily here for a good time. They're the ssseriousss drinkerssss."

"From the scars, they looked like serious fighters."

"Yesss . . ." Cri Sawyes fingered the scar on his

hip. "They're the type who challenge and lossse and challenge and lossse—they can't win, but they can't ssstop challenging either. I expect it'sss why they drink. Pitiful really."

"And the boys on the patio?"

"I doubt there hasss ever been a sseriousss challenge made by any of them."

"How can you tell?"

"Few ssscarsss. And besssidesss . . ." His tongue flicked out. "I helped to ssselect the sssoldiersss who would guard the politiciansss who would meet with the aliensss."

"Ah." A quick glance over the railing showed Ressk had slaved his slate to Binti's. "It's not going to be hard to keep an eye on my lot, is it? Given sizes and colors, they stick out like half a dozen sore thumbs."

Cri Sawyes glanced down at his hand, looking more than a little puzzled. Then he shook his head, having clearly decided it didn't matter. "To be perfectly honessst, I'm amazed your Lieutenant Jarret allowed you to go through with thisss."

"Our orders state that we're to report on how the Marines and Silsviss interact. We can't do that unless we have some actual interaction." Torin nodded toward the patio. "Besides, there're three Humans, two di'Taykan, and a Krai down there, and if any one of them can't get along with your common Silsviss soldier—or vice versa—I want to know now. Not when we're facing the Others and it might cause a problem."

"And you don't think it will caussse a problem now?"

She shrugged. "It'll cause a bigger problem if it's accompanied by live ammunition."

"True. But sssuppossse the right combination of Marinesss hadn't decided to go over the wall?"

"I'd have sent them back until they got it right."

"Ssstaff Sssergeant . . ."

"All right, when it came down to it, this is essentially the group I expected to make the break. Everyone's rapidly reaching the point where they need to do something that doesn't involved standing guard at an unused door, but these six are a little closer to that point than the rest." Torin swiped at the sweat on her neck, then rubbed her hand dry against her hip. "It's also why four of them are in the same fireteam—complementary temperaments ensures they work well as a unit."

"And their copy of the transsslation program? You planned that asss well?"

"I made it available to Ressk. He did the rest."

"I sssee." Cri Sawyes sat quietly for a moment, tail tip twitching as he thought. "You know your people," he said at last.

Torin nodded. "They're *my* people."

The *kritkar* arrived in a covered dish. An expectant silence followed its path from the kitchen to the table as the Silsviss on the patio waited to see what these alien soldiers would do.

A few tongues flicked out as Plaskry elbowed Yrs out of the way the moment he'd set the dish down.

It was the bigger male's joke, after all, and he wanted to deliver the punch line.

"Help yourself," he said and lifted the lid.

A claw, about half an inch long, appeared over the edge of the bowl as the first of the *kritkar* attempted a last minute escape.

The tongue flickering grew more pronounced.

"Like this," Plaskry hissed, scooping up a handful of the tiny live crustaceans and popping them into his mouth.

"Oh, like *that*." Ressk looked around at the others as though he'd only been waiting for instruction. "Not one at a time . . ." He scooped an equally large handful out of the bowl. ". . . like this."

Plaskry stopped chewing to watch and forgot about chewing altogether when Ressk reached for seconds, thirds, fourths, and finally picked out and ate the last three. Suddenly conscious of everyone staring at him, the Krai flushed and stopped digging at a bit of shell caught between his teeth. "Oh. Sorry. Did the rest of you want some?"

The silence lasted another two heartbeats, then erupted. Sooton and Hairken thumped each other on the chest and whacked tails, triumphantly reminding each other that they'd brought the aliens to the *savara* in the first place. After a moment of pulling the loudest phrases from the air, the two slates now holding the program spat out mostly unintelligible congratulations and a few insults thrown toward Plaskry.

"Just once I'd like to go some place where they didn't try to gross us out with the local delicacy,"

Binti muttered under the noise. "So, what'd they taste like?"

Ressk shrugged. "*Chrick.* Crunchy—but then all seafood tastes the same to me."

"Pity you didn't leave enough to run past a slate," Hollice grunted. "We could've checked to see if they were poisonous to the rest of us."

"And you'd have eaten a handful?"

"Hey, I once ate two dozen raw oysters to impress my best friend's date and crunchy could only be an improvement over that phlegm on the half shell."

"You figure tall, tailed, and ugly over there is going to spring for another bowl?" Binti wondered.

On cue, Plaskry rounded the table and clamped one hand down on Ressk's shoulder. "Your little food eaten before the main meal . . ."

Binti snarled and hooked her slate back on her belt.

". . . cost me a third of my pay chit!"

Continuing to dig at the bit of shell, Ressk grinned. "Guess there's no chance of seconds, then."

The big Silsviss hissed, and his tail whacked Ressk's stool at the spot where a tail would usually have hung. "Seconds? You aliens have got more male equipment than a large carnivorous quadruped!"

Ressk snatched his slate to safety before Binti could edit the program with her fist. "Then I guess I owe you a beer. Yrs!"

Attention jerked away from his mournful examination of the empty bowl, Yrs looked first to the slate and then up at Ressk.

He tossed over his souvenir credit chit. "Beer for the *partizay* on me!"

"Deftly done," Cri Sawyes acknowledged as Yrs left the patio to renewed noise.

"It's an old shtick," Torin told him. "The Krai can eat almost anything on almost any world. They have the Galaxy's most efficient gut."

"I wasss referring more to the way they usssed that efficient gut to manipulate the sssituation. Only the Krai, who asss you sssay can eat anything, had to eat the *kritkar* and yet all the Marinesss benefit. They have been accepted by the sssoldiersss."

"So far," Torin agreed. "But don't forget they're also buying a round. That helped."

"True. You do realize that the sssoldiersss will now attempt to get your people drunk."

"I realize."

"And?"

"It should be interesting."

The high-pitched beeping cut through the ambient noise like a hot knife through field rations and fell right smack in the middle of the tonal range guaranteed to produce maximum irritation. Swearing in three languages, all six Marines dropped their attention to their slates.

"Mine," Sooton muttered, plucking a black rubber cylinder off his harness. He flicked out an antenna, opened his auditory ridge to insert a round knob and bent the rest of the cylinder around by his mouth. "Yeah . . . Just a minute, I'm getting interference from the buildings . . ." Pushing back his stool, he walked over to the edge of the patio, talking as he moved.

"You think they operate on fukking radio waves?" Juan wondered, eyes gleaming.

"That's always been the cheapest." Mŷsho waved her beer around at the Silsviss. "And they've got to be cheap. Almost everyone seems to have one."

"Low tech," he sneered. "They've only got audio."

"Give them a break, Juan. They'd barely got off the planet before the Confederation contacted them."

Grunting a reluctant agreement, Juan moved over beside Sooton when he returned to the table and asked if he could see the cylinder.

"Sure. It was Blarnic," he added to the table at large. "Wanted to know if anything was happening here tonight."

Tongues flickered.

Squinting down at the handset, Juan rubbed a finger over the rubberized controls. "How does it work?"

"You mean inside?"

"No, I mean how does it fukking break rocks. Yeah, I mean inside."

"No idea." Sooton looked around, then pointed. "But Hars over there is a tech. He should know."

Juan grabbed for his slate as he stood, but Ressk blocked his hand. "Not yet. I've only copied half the translation program."

"You haven't even started copyin' it onto Haysole's slate, and he seems to be fukking managin' without it."

They both looked over to a dark corner where the di'Taykan had gathered a small group of his own.

"He's probably playing I'll show you mine if you show me yours. I doubt he's talking much."

"Wonder if he's winning."

Ressk snickered.

"What isss the young male with the blue hair doing?"

"Plopping his pecker on the table, as near as I can tell from up here."

Cri Sawyes turned from the view below to stare at Torin. "I beg your pardon, Ssstaff Sssergeant."

"It's a di'Taykan thing. They like to know where they stand."

"He isss comparing the sssize of his reproductive organ to thossse of the sssoldiersss?"

"Yeah. Don't Silsviss do that?"

"Yesss, when we are young in the pressservesss but not usssually at thisss age."

"The di'Taykan can be pretty persuasive, and he's probably curious because nothing shows." Her gaze dropped. She didn't intend it to, but she couldn't help it.

Cri Sawyes' tongue flicked out. "I am *not* going to show you mine."

"No, sir." Ears burning, she returned her attention back to the patio.

". . . so we've got them pinned down in this small village, the civilians cleared out when they saw trouble coming so it's just them and a couple of nasty artillery pieces that don't seem to be running out of their powering medium any time soon, and those egg suckers with the most metal send us in to clear the place residence by residence!"

"Idiots!" Hollice slapped the table for emphasis. "Why didn't they just call in an air strike?"

Sooton hissed and smacked his hand down beside the corporal's. "That's what we wanted to know!"

Juan grabbed a small electrical component just before it rolled though a puddle of beer and tried to snap it back into Hars' headset. "So this goes here?"

"No." A somewhat unsteady claw tapped the rubber. "Here."

"That's what I fukking said, *here*."

Hars belched.

"But you're a mammal!"

Mysho's eyes lightened. "Your point?"

Binti's third dart hit the spinning target on the outer edge and during the instant between the cancellation of the old momentum and the application of the new, her fourth dart hit the black triangle in the middle.

"Harttag!" roared her partner, smacking her in the backs of the legs with his tail. He hissed, disappointment coloring his glee, and smacked her again. "How can we celebrate *harttag* when you have no tail!"

"I don't have a tail," Binti agreed, moving inside

the painful blows. "But I do have hips." Her answering blow lifted him over an empty stool and into the lap of a Silsviss who'd been watching the game.

After a moment's stunned silence, tongues began to flick.

With his own tongue flicking so fast he could hardly breathe, Binti had to help her fallen partner to his feet.

"Your people ssseem to be drinking in moderation."

"Moderation might be a bit of an overstatement." Torin tracked Mysho's path from the bar to the table and noted whom she unloaded the beer in front of. "But they're being careful." It helped that the Silsviss beer contained less alcohol than they were used to, but she saw no need to pass that information on. "It shouldn't be long now."

Cri Sawyes blew out his throat pouch impatiently. "What shouldn't?"

"See that group over in the corner? I'm guessing they're a different *partizay* than the group my lot hooked up with and that the two don't get along. Maybe one *partizay* feels like they've been pulling more crap duties than the other, maybe it's personal, it doesn't really matter—they've been glaring across the patio all night."

"Maybe they just don't like aliensss."

"No, they'd like aliens fine if those aliens were with them, but since they're not, they've become a convenient excuse."

"For a fight?"

"Yes."

His throat pouch inflated slightly as he studied the movements in the crowd below. "And the fight becomesss a ssstudy in the sssocial interplay between ssspeciesss."

Torin shrugged. "When something is inevitable, you might as well learn what you can from it."

"We are not Human, Ssstaff Sssergeant." He turned his golden gaze from the patio to her. "Nor are we Krai, nor are we di'Taykan."

"No, but you *are* a social species with a paid fighting force who share intoxicants in a social setting." She shrugged again. "If it walks like a duck . . ."

The movement of his inner eyelids made him look momentarily cross-eyed. "What," he demanded, "isss a duck?"

"A medium-sized water bird from Terra."

He opened his mouth, clearly thought better of what he was about to say, and shook his head. "You really are a most confusssing ssspeciesss."

Hollice felt something compact under his foot, wasted a second wondering where that something had come from as the floor had been clear when he'd started the step, and then suddenly realized what that something had to be.

"That was my tail!" A large Silsviss, nearly Plaskry's size, rose off his stool and spun around to face the Marine. "Clumsy alien, egg sucker," he snarled into the silence that had answered his first bellow. "Clumsy alien, tailless, egg sucker."

From the reactions around him, Hollice suspected the insults had lost a little in the translation. "Sorry. Didn't see it. Let me buy you a beer to take your mind off the pain."

"You think that is all my tail means to me!" The throat pouch began to distend. "I will rip your miserable alien heart out and eat it!"

He felt more than heard Binti move from the dart game into place behind him. The others were too far away to add much initial backup, and he couldn't see Haysole at all. "Look, I said I was sorry and I offered to buy you a beer. I don't know what else I can . . ." The blow glanced off his left shoulder. It threw him sideways without doing any real damage, and he came up smiling. First contact had been made.

His return blow took the Silsviss in the belly and would've had more impact had he not been avoiding a swinging tail when he made it.

The Silsviss' companions rose as one.

Hollice heard the high trill of a di'Taykan attack cry, saw Binti smash a tray into a Silsviss face, and then had time to notice nothing beyond his immediate survival.

"There, see! The us-against-them split isn't Silsviss, nonSilsviss. There." Torin pointed. "And there. Silsviss fighting beside Marines."

"Thisss isss what you wanted to sssee happen?"

"This is exactly what I wanted to see. The lieutenant will be pleased."

"Then if you have the information you need,

we'd bessst ssstop the fight before sssomeone isss . . . before sssomeone elssse isss . . ." Nostrils flaring, Cri Sawyes glared down at the battle. "When you sssaid the Krai would eat anything, I never assumed that included tailsss."

"Your boy bit him first." Torin watched a Silsviss who'd been thrown down onto the floor bring the claws on both feet into play and nodded thoughtfully. "But you're right, we should stop it before an outside authority arrives."

They turned together and came face-to-face with two of the uglier customers from the room below. A little surprised they'd been able to move into position so quietly, Torin ducked the fist blow.

The second connected.

Had the rail been an inch shorter, she'd have gone over it. As it was, she dropped, rolled, and came up holding a Silsviss tail in both hands. A yank and a kick toppled her attacker sideways, his claws barely tearing the fabric across her thigh.

He was fast, she acknowledged as she leaped into an answering kick.

Son of a . . . I should never have let go of that tail! Sucking a painful breath in through her teeth, she wondered if the ribs were broken.

The Silsviss responded to her pain by inflating his throat pouch and roaring.

Heart pounding, the taste of her own blood in her mouth, Torin scooped up her stool and smashed it into the side of his head.

He finished the roar on the way down, and it ended with impact.

"Well done, Ssstaff Sssergeant." Throat pouch still slightly extended, Cri Sawyes cleaned his claws against a bit of his opponent's harness. "You were certainly not what he expected."

"Oh?"

"A challenge isss alwaysss anssswered before the fight continuesss."

She poked the prone body with her foot until he moaned, reassuring her he was still alive. "I *answered* the challenge."

"In your own way, yesss. Are you hurt?"

Shallow gouge, bruises, one rib possibly cracked. "I'm fine. What about you?"

His tongue flicked out, and he tapped his fallen opponent lightly with his tail. "I told you, they challenge and lossse and challenge again."

Torin grinned. "Pitiful really."

"Indeed."

Which was when she noticed it had gotten very quiet down below. "Wonderful; looks like the authorities have arrived."

"Tarvar ssselk." After a moment, her translator came up with, "Military police."

"You, alien, tell me who issued challenge."

Hollice shifted his weight off his swelling right knee. "I didn't notice."

The Silsviss swept his gaze over the rest of the Marines. "And I suppose none of you other aliens noticed either?" When he received the expected negative chorus, he turned his attention to his own people. "Well?"

Wiping his claws off on his leg, Plaskry snarled, "Happened too fast."

"What about you, Yrs?"

"Didn't see nothing."

"Really?" The MP smacked his tail guard against the floor as he swept his gaze over the rest of the room. "Ranscur. Looks like you took a few hits. You wouldn't know who hit who first would you?"

The big Silsviss who'd made first contact gazed over the heads of his companions at the Marines then at the MP. "No idea."

"Don't give me that *ara srev crovmirs shartlerg*!"

All six slates hissed and sputtered but surrendered the attempt at a translation.

"Someone challenged first, and we're all going to stay right here until I find out who!"

Standing just off the patio, Torin watched Cri Sawyes walk over to the MP and show his credentials. Their discussion didn't last long. The MP wasn't happy, but Torin suspected his unhappiness didn't come close to how the Marines felt when they were escorted out of the *savara* and found their Staff Sergeant waiting.

Haysole finally broke the silence. "Did you know your leg is bleeding, Staff?"

"Yes. I know."

"Were you fighting?"

"I'd worry less about what I was doing, Private, and more about what you've been doing." Eyes narrowed, she very deliberately examined each of them. Injuries seemed minor although they'd all been marked by Silsviss claws.

"The military police officer tellsss me that none of your people will sssay who ssstarted the fight."

Torin looked past the Marines to Cri Sawyes and past him to the Silsviss standing quietly on the patio. "Is that true, Corporal Hollice?"

"Yes, Staff Sergeant."

"And do you know who started the fight?"

"It all happened so fast, Staff Sergeant."

She snapped her gaze down to meet Hollice's level stare—slightly less level than usual due to a rapidly spreading black eye—and smiled. "Of course it did, Corporal." Still holding his eyes with hers, she raised her voice. "Cri Sawyes, if you could please see that things are settled here, I'll take my people back where they belong."

"Of coursssse."

He caught up just before they reached the embassy. "The proprietor hasss been paid for damagesss, the military police officer hasss left—nothing will come of thisss adventure."

Torin grinned as a certain amount of tension left the shoulders of the six Marines marching in front of her. "Nothing will come of it from the Silsviss," she amended.

The shoulders tensed again.

She marched them to the west door, managed not to laugh at the faces of the two Marines on guard, and waved them through. "Lieutenant Jarret wants to speak with you."

"Now, Staff Sergeant?"

"Do any of you need to see the doctor immediately?"

"No, Staff Sergeant."

"Then the lieutenant would like to speak with you *now.*"

Just inside the door, she paused to watch them climb the stairs and note who was favoring what. Her own injuries had died to a dull throb, easy to ignore. As she followed, she realized she actually felt better than she had in days.

"You enjoyed that, didn't you?"

Torin glanced up at Cri Sawyes. He could be requesting information, but she suspected that he'd learned to read Human reactions fairly accurately during the last few weeks and was, in fact, asking only for confirmation. "Yes," she told him, trying not to smile as broadly as her mood demanded, "I did."

He nodded thoughtfully. "Remember how you told me you knew what would happen tonight becaussse you knew your people?"

"Yes."

His tongue flicked out. "I would say that your lieutenant knows *his* people, too."

SIX

"I would say that your lieutenant knows his people too."

Torin frowned as she limped up the stairs to Lieutenant Jarret's office. Their orders *had* wanted them to report on the interaction between the Marines and the Silsviss. To do that, they *had* needed interaction to occur but, more importantly, they'd needed to control the inevitable rebellion born of inactivity that was brewing in the platoon.

"Inevitable?" the lieutenant had repeated.

"Yes, sir. The Marines have trained these people to survive on the edge. It's what they're used to, and, after a while, it's what they'll go looking for. They need the rush that comes with facing the unknown."

"You think I should let them look for that rush."

"Yes, sir. I think you can use whatever they find to make field observations and to bleed off the excess energy before the whole system blows." She'd shifted her weight from foot to foot as she considered how much more she should say, then, finally, had added, "I told the general right from the beginning that this was no job for a combat unit."

"You don't think that sending a group of boredom-crazed Marines out among the Silsviss will set diplomatic relations back to square one?"

"No, sir. Not if we maintain control."

"So, you believe that since something's going to happen anyway, it shouldn't happen randomly?"

"Yes, sir."

Lieutenant Jarret had stared at her in silence for a few moments. "How do you suggest we control the situation?" he asked at last.

"When a group large enough to make observations valid goes out the lock, Cri Sawyes and I will follow them, observe them, and keep them out of trouble if need be."

"No. I don't think we should involve the Silsviss."

"I don't think we should let our people out without involving the Silsviss," Torin told him dryly. "And Cri Sawyes has the authority to stop anything that might start."

Although he clearly hadn't liked the idea, he reluctantly nodded. "All right. Cri Sawyes goes, but why you? Why not one of the sergeants?"

"The sergeants are specific to each squad, sir, and we can't be certain which squad will go over."

"Whereas you've put the fear of the gods into the whole platoon?"

"Yes, sir."

He'd stared at her a moment longer, lilac eyes dark. "I see."

At the time, Torin had considered his response nothing more than a noncommittal way to end the conversation. Now, though, she wondered what he'd seen. Had he seen past her reasoned arguments, noticing that the forced inactivity and the pointless ceremonial duties were driving her just as crazy as the six Marines now leading the way up the stairs? Had the night's adventure been as much for her to release pressure as for the platoon or for their orders?

Was he actually a good enough officer to see what she needed, or had that one unfortunate night together taught him more about her than he had any right to know?

Give it up. He's a di'Taykan. Sex may be a large part of their lives, but they keep it separate. Is it so hard to believe that he might actually be becoming a good officer?

It seemed a little early, but she supposed it was possible. It was always a difficult transition to begin thinking of second lieutenants as more than merely warm bodies in a uniform, to realize they were actually beginning to take command.

He's got a lot of bloody nerve trying to manipulate me. battled with *They grow up so fast.*

Her half-dozen malcontents/observational subjects were waiting in the hall outside Lieutenant Jarret's door. Torin walked through them, looking neither left nor right as they shuffled out of her way, and she knocked on the worn wood.

When the lieutenant's voice told them to enter, she turned to the Marines. "Form a line, single file, along the south wall under the row of high windows." Fortunately, the latch—its dimensions uncomfortable in human hands—gave her no trouble.

Few things undermined authority like public fumbling. "Private Mashona . . ."

Binti paused in the doorway and Ressk turned sideways to get around her.

". . . the gash on your shoulder is bleeding again. You should see the doctor immediately."

"What about your leg, Staff?"

"What about it?"

"It's bleeding again, too."

Torin looked down at her leg and up at Binti. The younger woman's expression was easy to read: *If you don't need to see the doctor immediately, neither do I, so I'm not abandoning my team. And besides, if I'm standing there bleeding on his floor, the lieutenant'll keep it short.*

There were just the two of them and the Silsviss in the hall now. Her own face expressionless, Torin moved out of the way. "Get in there, then."

When she turned to Cri Sawyes, he shook his head.

"Thisss isss no busssinesss of mine. I will wait and sspeak with the lieutenant later."

"Thank you for your help."

"You're very welcome, Ssstaff Sssergeant. It wasss not unenjoyable. I sssussspect I learned asss much about your people asss you did about mine." He slapped the floor with his tail.

Good thing you're on our side, then, Torin mused, entering the office, and taking her position to the right of the line.

The lieutenant's outer office was empty of everything except an unplugged and therefore inoperative vending machine the Silsviss had considered either too heavy or too unintrusive to move. Because the triple banks of lights buzzed continually, Lieutenant Jarret preferred to work in one of the inner rooms.

Almost immediately upon Torin taking her place, the door to the next room opened and the lieutenant emerged in full dress, gloves tucked into his belt.

"Shouldn't I be waiting for them?"

"No, sir. They wait for you. You don't wait for them."

He didn't look any more perceptive than he ever had—no matter how much circumstances seemed to support Cri Sawyes' observation.

"These are the six?"

"Yes, sir."

The ceiling was so high, the room so large and empty that their voices echoed slightly.

As Lieutenant Jarret walked slowly down the line, Torin was pleased to see that all eyes were locked on a position about six inches above his left shoulder—all eyes except for Corporal Hollice's shiner which had swollen shut. After a second pass, where he tersely told Haysole to adjust his masker, the lieutenant paused and said before he turned to face them, "I gave orders that no one was to leave our assigned area."

He pivoted on one heel, the ends of his hair flicking back and forth. "You six chose to disobey that order." A lilac gaze raked them up, down, and side to side. "What happened after is not my concern, but if the Silsviss chose to make an issue of it, I shall have no choice but to let them. Do you understand?"

"Yes, sir." The unison was a little ragged. Although the question was no doubt right out of the officer's handbook, Torin hoped he wouldn't ask any more—this lot was just as likely to start giving him answers he didn't expect.

"Three days' stoppage of pay. As your entire fireteam was involved, Corporal Hollice, you will all be standing night two until we leave Silsvah. Corporal di'Hern Mysho, you'll be using your off duty time to help the doctor scan his specimens. Private di'Stenjic Haysole, you may continue cleaning the sanitary facilities. When you're dismissed, you're all to go directly to the doctor. He's expecting you. You can dismiss them now, Staff."

"Yes, sir." Torin gave the one word order but watched the lieutenant as the Marines obeyed. Had she been close enough, she suspected she'd have been able to hear his hearts pounding. Fortunately, everyone else in the room had been focused over his left shoulder and on their own predicament, so they hadn't noticed how nervous he'd been. There was nothing like a discipline parade to make a junior officer realize the power he held over the forty-odd lives in his platoon.

It was also the place where a junior officer could abuse that power were he so inclined, and senior NCOs had learned to watch them closely at such times.

"Staff?"

"Yes, sir?" Torin shifted her weight back onto both legs and straightened.

"Do you think I . . ." He took a deep breath. His hair stilled. "How do you think it went?"

How did I do? They weren't the words he'd used, but it was the question he'd asked. She hid a smile. Her baby wasn't quite ready to leave the nest. "It went well, sir. You didn't waste time talking at them and at no point did you talk down to them. The punishments were fair, hard enough so they'll think twice about going out the lock again, not so hard they'll say 'fuk you' and go just to show you they can."

"We came up with punishments together."

"Yes, sir. But you *could* have overruled me."

Relief made him smile. "Really?"

Torin lifted a brow and said, in the dry tone her second lieutenant expected. "Not easily, sir."

"Thank you, Staff Sergeant. You'd better go see the doctor about your leg."

"Yes sir."

"Staff?"

"Sir?" She turned, sucking air through her teeth as the movement pulled the damaged muscle.

"Did we win?"

She paused, waiting until she was certain she wouldn't be overheard. "We kicked lizard butt, sir."

"Good work, Staff."

"Thank you, sir."

"Three days' loss of pay." Binti sighed and poked at her shoulder. "That sucks."

"We're stuck on this *serley* mudhole until the *Berganitan* comes back," Ressk reminded her. "Where are you going to spend it?"

"Maybe I'm saving it for my retirement, asshole."

"Maybe *cark*'ll fly, but I doubt it. Stop poking at the sealant or it won't heal clean."

"Stop telling me what to do."

Upper lip curled, he smacked her hand away from the wound. "Then stop poking."

"Private di'Stenjic Haysole, you may continue cleaning the sanitary facilities," Haysole snorted. "Guess Second Lieutenant di'Ka Jarret's too high class to call it a crapper like everyone else."

"Poor baby." Juan patted his cheek as he rose to take his turn with the doctor. "You think the lieutenant was too fukking hard on you?"

Haysole looked confused. "No. I just think he should've called it a crapper."

"He ought to thank us for dragging him out of whatever sexless diplomatic function he was at," Mysho grumbled. "But he won't."

By the time they got back to the barracks, the rest of the platoon was waiting only for specific details. Military structure inadvertently encouraged gossip and di'Taykans practically considered it a competitive sport. With the two combined, facts chased speculation through the troops at full speed.

Once the story had been told—and embellished—the unanimous belief, freely expressed, was that they'd gotten off easy.

"Then you can stand fukking night two for as long as we're on this rock," Juan muttered, checking the spare clip on his belt.

On station or on board ship, the second night watch, or night two, lasted from 2700 hours until

0430—a twenty-seven-hour day being the compromise among the three species who made up the military arm of the Confederation. No one liked it. Night one was at worst a late night. Night three was an early morning. Night two was a convenient punishment watch. On Silsviss it lasted four standard hours and twelve minutes.

"Too easy," Drake repeated, tossing a six-sided die from hand to hand. "Nothing on your record—clean a few toilets, help the doctor, lose some sleep, then finished and forgotten. If that's all you're getting, we can all go out the lock."

"Won't be as easy the next time," Hollice grunted, shrugging into his tunic. "They let us go. Haysole already went out that door once. You don't think they'd have taken care of a known weak spot in the perimeter?"

"Corporals." Ressk shook his head. "Paranoid."

Binti frowned. "No. He's got a point. Who told Staff where we were?"

"No mystery, the Silsviss who ran the *savara* obviously called someone when we arrived."

"Who? Who would a bartender call to report aliens walking in? The local cops?"

"The military cops."

"Yeah, right. Hello, Officer, I'd like to report aliens in my bar. They're not going to bother someone high enough to talk to our people until they know it's not a false alarm."

"Probably been a lot of them since we landed," Mysho said thoughtfully, fingering her masker.

"Right. So the MPs go to the bar, see us, then the

news starts heading up the chain of command until it gets to someone who can open a diplomatic channel."

"But the MPs were *at* the bar."

"Because of the fight. Staff showed up on the patio way, way too fukking fast unless she already knew we were there."

"Probably wanted to see us interacting with the Silsviss. There's been some concern about the lack of one-on-one unsupervised action."

Everyone turned to look at Haysole, who grinned. "Hey, you overhear a lot when you're always cleaning the crapper."

"All right, you want paranoid, think about this," Hollice suggested, taking his weapon down off its rack. "Staff and our assigned lizard were in a fight."

After a brief pause, where those who'd seen the staff sergeant filled in visuals for those who hadn't, Corporal Conn set aside his latest letter home, and said thoughtfully, "Maybe he didn't want her to take you guys away from Silsviss authorities."

"They weren't fighting with each other." Hollice checked his charge and hitched the strap up onto his shoulder. "Use your brains for more than insulation; they were coming to get us and they got jumped. I think there's some Silsviss who don't want us here."

Binti reached out and smacked his shoulder. "Hey! *We* got jumped in the bar."

"That was a bar fight, nothing more. But Staff wasn't with us when she got jumped." A jerk of Hollice's chin got his fireteam moving out the door.

The Marines still in the room passed confusion back and forth until, at the last minute, one of the di'Taykan called out, "Which means?"

"I think there's something going on here."

"I don't think so," Torin snorted. "Cri Sawyes says they were the type who keeps challenging and losing and are too stupid to stop challenging."

"I don't like it." Cradling a jar of beer between both hands, Mike frowned up at the senior NCO. "I don't like that they were in the same bar you were in. Too convenient."

"I got the impression that every bar has a few." She poked at the sealant on her thigh and did a few experimental deep knee bends.

Holding the destroyed uniform trousers between thumb and forefinger, Anne Chou snorted. "Gee, I can't wait until I'm a staff sergeant and I get to be beaten up by the locals in the name of cultural interaction."

"Yeah? Well, when you're a staff sergeant, you'll know that staff sergeants beat up the locals in the name of cultural interaction, not the other way around."

"So essentially what you're saying is, you should see the other guy?"

Torin grinned. "Essentially."

Cultural interaction had an immediate result.

"All right, people, lets get this place packed up, we're moving out!"

Jerked out of his bunk and onto his feet by Sergeant Glicksohn's bellow, Haysole grabbed for his pants. "I thought we were supposed to stay here for another three days."

"And that would be relevant, Private Haysole, if the Silsviss cared what you thought. Since they don't, get moving. Sleds are on the way in from the VTA."

"What about breakfast, Sarge?" Ressk asked as the room of Marines began resembling an anthill stirred with a stick. "Squad Three hasn't eaten yet."

"We pack the mess up last. You get in there as soon as Squad Two gets out." He paused and they could hear Sergeant Trey's voice rising and falling in the next room. "If I were you, I wouldn't worry about chewing everything a hundred times. Hollice, your team sees to it that the personal effects of Corporal Conn's team are packed up and put on the sleds."

"Come on, Sarge," Hollice protested, "we stood night two."

"And your point?"

"Get someone else to do it."

Sergeant Glicksohn stopped talking long enough to smile broadly. "No." Then he fell back into the familiar cadence. "Once our sled's loaded, we load the civilians', then the whole platoon forms up in the square. Lieutenant Jarret wants us leaving for the landing field at 0930."

Juan glanced down at the time on his slate. "Fuk."

"Well put. Fortunately, the Dornagain are already moving." His eyes unfocused for a moment. "Sleds are here. You can start humping gear outside any time."

"Hey, Sarge?"

He paused in the doorway.

"You know why we're leaving?"

"Yes, I do, Haysole. Because the lieutenant gave us an order."

The di'Taykan closed the distance between them. "Aw, come on, Sarge."

"Don't even try it, Haysole. And turn up your masker."

"He knows," Binti snorted as the sound of the sergeant's bootheels faded. "He's just not going to tell us."

"Ours is not to reason why," Hollice muttered.

"You think this has something to do with last night?"

The answering silence was a clear affirmative.

"You think the Silsviss are pissed?" Binti wondered.

This time the silence wasn't so sure.

"Do we fukking care?" Juan snarled under his breath.

As two billion Silsviss significantly outnumbered one lone platoon of Confederation Marines, everyone ignored him.

"I think they've come to a decision," Hollice answered at last.

Ressk picked up a game biscuit with his toes, checked the number, and tossed it at Binti. "Don't I keep saying he's too paranoid to be a corporal?"

* * *

As the VTA shuddered into the air, Torin watched Lieutenant Jarret unhook his harness and make his way to the front of the troop compartment. In spite of the uneven ride, he moved well, and she had to admit he looked good. Of course, from a Human perspective, it was difficult for a di'Taykan to look anything but.

I wonder what would happen if we did it again . . . .

Frowning, Torin denied ownership of the stray thought. They weren't going to do it again, end of discussion.

"The Silsviss have decided," the lieutenant began when he had everyone's attention, "to begin the final series of meetings intended to result in a decision about joining—or not joining—the Confederation two days early. We are therefore, moving to the location of these meetings, two days early. Unofficially, it seems very likely the Silsviss will join as I was approached this morning by one of their commanders and asked to develop a simulation that would begin integrating our fighting styles."

"Is this all 'cause we proved we could kick ass, sir?"

Although he looked a little startled by it, he took the interruption in stride. "In what way, Private Mashona?"

Binti smiled broadly, her teeth gleaming against the mahogany of her face. "Things are happening today, sir. Things weren't happening yesterday. The only difference seems to be what happened last night."

"I know this is hard for a Marine to believe, Private, but it isn't always about us." There were a few snickers, and he raised a hand to forestall any other interruptions. "That said, while we're traveling, Ambassador Krik'vir wants to speak, one on one with the six Marines who went out the lock. Sergeant Glicksohn . . ."

"Sir?

"Arrange an order and send the first person up now."

"Sir."

Which does make it seem, Torin thought, as Lieutenant Jarret walked to the door and motioned for her to join him, *that the events of last night gave diplomacy a boot in the ass.* Remembering the long, boring hours of ceremonial duties, of standing for hours in damp heat while cadres of dignitaries hissed speeches about historical importance, she snorted. "If I'd known how much it would move things along," she said, following the lieutenant out of the troop compartment, "I'd have smacked someone with a stool weeks ago."

"And I'd have ordered it." He paused to allow her to fall into step. "The Silsviss seem unduly impressed by a little force, don't they?"

"Alien species, sir. All things considered, I'm just glad we found them before the Others did."

"We have already interviewed the enlisted personnel who participated in yesterday's cultural interaction . . ."

Trying not to stare at her reflection in Ambassador Krik'vir's eyestalks, Torin wondered which of the enlisted personnel had used that particular phrase. Somehow, she doubted it had also been the diplomatic label for the exercise.

". . . and have heard a startling amount of minutia but very little of substance. As you are in possession of the overview, we would now like to hear from you, Staff Sergeant Kerr." The ambassador settled back on her lower four legs while behind her, taking up most of the remaining space in the large storage locker, one of her assistants stroked the controls of a Mictok recording device. At least that's what Torin assumed it was, although it might have been anything from a musical instrument to a sex aid for all she knew. "Please, Staff Sergeant, begin at the beginning."

"The beginning?" *My family were farmers and I hated farming . . .* "A combat unit deprived of stimulus creates its own . . ." She told the ambassador how she'd discussed the inevitability of the situation with Lieutenant Jarret, his decision to allow herself and Cri Sawyes to follow and observe rather than stop it from happening, the situation as she saw it down on the patio, the fight, what she'd observed as well as her personal battle, and finally the aftermath.

"You tell the story well, Staff Sergeant."

"I've given a lot of reports, ma'am."

"Until today we have found the Silsviss to be distant, putting on a—How did Corporal Hollice put it?—a dog and pony show for our benefit."

"A dog and pony show, ma'am?" Dogs had settled Paradise with Humans but Torin had never seen a pony.

"Apparently it is an old Human term." Her outer mandibles clicked together gently. "We understand that it refers to matters of no substance. Today, we touched on substance for the first time, and we are hurried toward greater substance still. We know that the leaders of the various factions have been meeting with each other as we were shown the dogs and ponies and perhaps the decisions they have come to are the only reason for our sudden movement. However, we cannot ignore that it may be because of the actions of last night."

"If I may, Ambassador, the Silsviss are a warrior species. General Morris made that very clear when he ordered a combat troop to a ceremonial post. Perhaps they were waiting to see some tangible indication they weren't about to hook up with a bunch of *paygari.*" It was a di'Taykan word meaning *mewling infants* and the least profane description Torin could come up with on the spur of the moment.

The clicking became louder and faster. "We can think of few things more tangible than a stool to the head, Staff Sergeant."

Given the alternative, Torin supposed she was glad Ambassador Krik'vir chose to find the situation amusing.

Except for the two Mictok using the dubious privacy of the storage locker, the civilians were in their seats when Torin finally walked into their compartment. Only Madam Britt, the Rakva Charge D'Affaires, was actually working, the rest seemed to be skirting sleep. Whether they were tired of the assignment, tired of each other, or merely conserving strength for the deliberations to come, she had no idea. Fortunately, Cri Sawyes stood at his usual place by the view screen.

"Another wilderness preserve?" she asked, rounding the bulk of a Dornagain and joining him.

"Not yet, but shortly. Thisss isss one of the leassst civilized areasss of my planet. To a certain extent, the challenge rulesss outside the pressserve as well. To sssurvive here . . ." He shook his head.

"We're over it now," he said a few moments later, although Torin couldn't see a change in the terrain. "I sssussspect your Captain Danielsss hasss been given thisss flight path in order to show the young malesss that timesss are changing. That we are not alone in the universsse."

"That must have been comforting. When you found out you weren't alone," she added in response to his murmured question.

"Not really, no."

"No?" Torin, fourth generation post-contact, couldn't imagine not knowing. As far as she was concerned, space was quite empty enough, even with seventy-two known species. "It was what, then? Disturbing?"

"For me perssonally?" Cri Sawyes kept his gaze on the screen but his inner eyelid slid shut then open again. "I wasss never one of thossse who asssumed that we were the only intelligent life, that the great biological accident of our creation had happened only the once. But yesss, it wasss. It is a great blow to the ego, Sssergeant, to dissscover that you are, after all, not unique." He looked up, his tongue flickering. "I am, however, mossstly recovered."

"Glad to hear it, sir." As she made her way up to the cockpit, Torin acknowledged that she had come to quite like the big lizard. She had no idea how representative he was of his species as a whole—his willingness to be thrust into close contact with so many alien races logically suggested he was culturally flexible—but based on their time together, she thought the Silsviss would function quite well within the structure of the Confederation Marine Corps. The whole lack of female things still weirded her out a little, but she supposed she'd get used to it in time.

The cockpit on the VTA had been designed for efficiency rather than comfort, and Captain Daniels, Lieutenant Ghard, and two members of their flight crew were just about a capacity crowd. Under the more normal circumstances of a drop from ship to ground Torin wouldn't have gone near it, but since the Silsviss continued to insist on atmospheric travel, she had time to kill. There was only so much ship to patrol and only so long she could spend in a pressurized chamber with four Dornagain.

The upper third of the front wall of the cockpit was made of the same clear silicon the Confederation used in the observatories on their deep space ships. According to the sales pitch the absolutely transparent material was stronger than the metals in the rest of the ship, and were it not for the vertigo many species were subject to—not to mention the price of production—it could have been the only material used to build the entire fleet. Advertisements insisted it could emerge unscathed from the heart of a star, but Torin suspected that claim had never actually been tested—not by the advertising department anyway.

Steadying herself against the back of Captain Daniels' chair, she squinted at the greenish-brown smear that obscured part of the view. "What happened there?"

"Bird." Both hands continuing to work the controls, the captain flashed a smile back over her shoulder. "Or something flying anyway."

"Something stupid," Lieutenant Ghard added. "I think it was challenging us."

Allowing for fluid dispersement, Torin put the bird at no more than half a meter from wingtip to wingtip. "Maybe it was depressed."

"Sir." One of the aircrew looked up from her instruments. "We are reaching the midpoint . . ." She paused, eyes unfocused. ". . . now . . ."

Torin's implant chimed midpoint.

". . . and our Silsviss escorts are peeling off. They say, good luck and that they'll be interested to see how it turns out."

"They did?"

"Well, that's more or less how it translated, sir."

Captain Daniels shook her head. "That's new. Usually they just wish us luck and clear skies."

"We're heading to the decision this time," Torin

reminded him. Leaning forward, she peered around at the crystal blue arc of sky. "Do we have no escort at all now?"

"Not for another few minutes, Staff," Lieutenant Ghard told her. "We're as far from the last place as our escort goes and not yet to the point where our new escort picks us up."

In the silence that followed, everyone turned to look at him.

Finally, Captain Daniels snickered. "Can we blame that on the translator, airman?"

She grinned at the back of the lieutenant's head. "No, sir."

"You know what I meant," Ghard muttered, slumping over his panel. Then, almost as a continuation of the same move, he straightened again. "Hey, there they are."

"I'm not picking them up on scanners, sir."

Torin turned to look at the other airman who was frowning down at his screen and turned back to the window again. Just at the edge of vision, she could see a pair of yellow/white flares. Sunlight reflecting from polished metal.

"All this atmospheric travel's gummed them up. We've probably got bird bits in the external sensors."

"That shouldn't make a difference, Captain."

The flares grew brighter, larger, and Torin felt the hair lift off the back of her neck. "Those aren't planes," she said softly.

"The Silsviss have some interesting design

specs," Lieutenant Ghard reassured her, sounding not entirely sure himself. "They're planes."

Torin tongued her implant. "Sir, we're under attack. Missiles approaching." She didn't bother to subvocalize.

"What?!"

Eyes locked on the sky, she tongued the implant again. "Sir, I repeat, we're under attack." And then more emphatically, to the cockpit crew, "Those are missiles."

"They're planes," Ghard repeated.

"No." The VTA slid sideways as Captain Daniels slapped the controls. "They're not." The *Secure All* sounded. "Where are you going, Staff?"

"Back to my platoon, sir."

She was through the hatch and had it dogged shut behind her before the captain could answer.

The civilian compartment was complete chaos. Only the Mictok seemed to have realized the gravity of the situation—all four were webbing themselves into their usual corner.

The ship twisted. A Rakva slammed into her, clutching desperately at her shoulders. "What is it? This one wants to know what is happening!" She threw him toward his seat, snapping, "Strap in, damn it!"

Another Rakva went flying by, avian bone structure providing little ballast. Torin ducked instinctively but saw Cri Sawyes grab Madame Britt's assistant and stuff her into a seat.

"Shit on a stick!" The three sergeants had keyed in an acknowledgment of the situation. There wasn't anything she could do for the platoon that they weren't doing. Someone had to take charge here.

"Staff?!"

Bone amplified or not, she could barely hear Lieutenant Jarret over the noise. Grabbing the safety strap from a Dornagain, she snapped it into place and turned to his companion who was moving with the same deliberate, slow speed. Winning the brief tug of war, she jerked the strap tight before tonguing her implant. "Sir, am securing civilians."

The VTA shuddered and she would have fallen had the Dornagain ambassador not wrapped one huge arm around her and pulled her against his stomach fur. "A noble attempt, Staff Sergeant," he said, hunkering down, his slow tones in direct contrast to the shrieking all around. "But now it ends."

Struggling to free herself, she saw his claws dig into the deck plating.

Impact.

I don't want to die with civilians. . . .

Seven

As near as Torin could tell from within the protective embrace of the Dornagain ambassador, only one of the two missiles hit the VTA. When, to her great surprise, she was still alive two heartbeats after impact, she began to hope.

Clamped tight against the ambassador's side, fingers hooked desperately into his safety straps, her world had been reduced to soft, pungent fur and the shriek of tortured metals laid over a thousand and one other unhappy sounds.

The world turned upside down.

One leg, flung free, tried to bend against the joint. The pain forced a gasp.

Then, miraculously, the ship leveled and the leg straightened.

Torin spat out a curse and with it a mouthful of fur.

She should be with her platoon. She should be *doing* something. Fighting something.

A slate biscuit bounced off her lower lip. She tasted blood.

A Rakva was screaming. The high-pitched sound

drilled into her head, singing a shrill descant to the sudden wail of the proximity sirens.

Proximity . . . ? Oh, no . . .

Her implant chimed.

Planetary surface in five, four, three, two, one . . .

The second impact was in every way worse than the first. Torin could feel the deck plates buckle, hear metal already twisted shriek a protest as new forces twisted it again, smell . . . she didn't know what she was smelling, but it grew stronger and stronger as the VTA finally shuddered itself still.

Compared to the chaos of an instant before, the civilian compartment had fallen silent enough for her to hear her pulse slamming against the sides of her skull.

Forcing reluctant fingers to release their grip, Torin shifted her weight onto her feet and pushed gently against the furry bulk of the ambassador. Just as panic began to chew at the edges of her control, the arm holding her sagged and she staggered back.

"Well." His ears slowly unfurled. "We seem to have survived." Blinking twice, he focused on her face. "Are you injured, Staff Sergeant?"

She coughed, dabbing crimson against the back of her hand. "Split lip. Wrenched knee. You?"

Two of the claws he'd driven into the deck had broken off leaving a ragged bloody edge at each fingertip. "I am bruised but, essentially, intact."

Her implant chimed. The lieutenant's implant, reading his vital signs, informed her he was unconscious but alive and in no immediate danger of dying. The weight of one in thirty-nine lives lifted off her shoulders.

"Thank you for securing me, sir. If you could see to your people . . . ?"

His whiskers fluffed forward. "Go where you're needed, Staff Sergeant."

The other three Dornagain were alive, but beyond that she couldn't tell; the emergency lighting threw shadows that masqueraded as injuries. Squeezing past them, sifting sounds into *deal with* and *ignore,* she tongued her implant.

Across the compartment, Cri Sawyes had unstrapped and was attempting to free the doctor from the ruins of his seat. Crest flat against his skull, Dr. Leor looked shaken but not visibly injured. The Rakva beside him, however, was clearly dead, head lolling on a broken neck. A closer look at the body and she recognized the young male who'd been learning to play poker. She knew his name, Aarik Slayir, but nothing else about him. And now, there was nothing more to know. . . .

Two of the sergeants keyed in. Glicksohn and Chou. Thirty-six lives to go.

All she could see of the Mictok was webbing, but as the structural integrity of their corner seemed intact, she could only assume they were alive.

Still no response from Sergeant Trey.

The controls of the hatch to the cockpit were out. Fighting with the manual override, she tongued her implant again and subvocalized, **Sergeant Glicksohn, report.**

**Staff, multiple casualties, three dead and Sergeant*

*Trey.** "Clear that space and set him down! Careful, watch his head!" The microphone in his jaw picked up the shouted order then he began subvocalizing again. **Sensors read half VTA under mud. Can't evac down here.**

Four dead. So far. But it could have been so much worse. It seemed that one of Silsvah's ubiquitous swamps had saved them. The hatch began to give. **Doctor's alive. Will send.** She wanted to send him immediately, but unless the universe had really buggered them, the *Berganitan*'s two corpsmen were in the troop compartment and she had no idea of what she'd find in the cockpit.

Levering the seals with a steady stream of profanity, she finally opened the hatch enough to squeeze through.

"Staff!" Lieutenant Ghard looked up from the captain's body, facial ridges almost white, both hands red. "I can't stop the bleeding!"

Torin turned her head. "Doctor Leor!"

To her surprise, he was at her side in a moment, and, after one look at the situation, at Captain Daniels' side a moment later. She'd expected him to protest, or hesitate, or have hysterics or do any of the other useless things civilians did in an emergency—that he hadn't was encouraging. Torin gratefully shifted him from "civilian" to a "will do his job so don't worry about him" category.

Moving back to let the doctor work, the lieutenant stared down at his hands, his mouth working but no sound emerging. Given the way that both control panels were flashing, they didn't have time for him to go into shock.

"Lieutenant Ghard!"

Her tone blew much of the confusion off his face. He blinked and swallowed, a little color coming back into his ridges as he scrubbed his palms against his flight suit. "Staff Sergeant?"

"The VTA needs seeing to, sir."

Facing forward, his shoulders stiffened. "The engines were hit . . ." Both hands and a foot began flying over the board. Torin didn't understand the steady stream of what sounded like prayer, but behind her the female Krai aircrew gasped.

Turning, she frowned. "You all right?"

"I guess . . ." Blood ran down the lower ridges of her nose, dripping onto her uniform. She stared wide-eyed up at Torin.

"You *guess?*"

Once again, the tone did its job. "I'm all right, Staff Sergeant." Straightening, she blotted the blood into her sleeve.

"Good. And him?"

Propped up against a canted wall, the other member of the bridge crew answered for himself. "Bumped head, Staff. Spinning . . ."

"Stay there. The doctor will take a look when he's done with the captain. You, Aircrew . . . ?"

"Trenkik, Staff."

"Aircrew Trenkik. Are the external scanners functioning?"

Stepping across her fallen comrade to the other

station, Trenkik scowled down at the board. "Topside bow seems fine, the rest . . ."

"Topside bow'll have to do, then. I need you to scan for enemy activity."

She dragged her thumb up a pressure bar. "Enemy, Staff?"

"Unless those missiles were launched accidentally."

"You don't think . . ." Then she caught sight of Torin's expression and flushed. "Oh. Right. There's nothing out there, Staff. Scanners show Silsviss life signs about thirty kilometers away. Our landing probably killed most of the local fauna."

They were right side up and essentially in one piece. Torin decided she'd count that as a landing, and the moment she got the chance she was buying Captain Daniels a beer. Deliberately looking past the doctor and the captain's prone body, she scowled at the mud covering the window. "Trenkik, are we still sinking?"

"Yes, but slowly."

The VTA was designed to withstand vacuum. With its physical integrity unbreached it could certainly handle a little mud. Unfortunately, the engine room had taken the brunt of the attack and the landing had pretty much finished it off.

"Fortunately, the mud seems to be containing most of the leakage."

"Fortunately," Torin agreed dryly. "Are the topside hatches usable?"

"Only the forward hatch."

"Then that'll have to do. Give me internal speakers." She glanced over at the lieutenant. "With your permission, sir?"

Ghard started, glanced down at the captain and suddenly realized what that meant. "Yes. Of course, Staff Sergeant."

". . . the situation as it stands. As Captain Daniels is badly injured and Lieutenant Ghard has his hands full with the VTA, until Lieutenant Jarret regains consciousness, you will be taking your orders from me."

"She had to tell us that?" Ressk snorted.

"Idiot." Binti smacked him on the back of the head. "She's telling the civilians. Now they know we know, they can't argue."

The staff sergeant's omnipresent voice continued. "When the doctor has done what he can for Captain Daniels, he'll come below. Sergeant Glicksohn, I want three fireteams, fully armed, at the forward hatch in ten. Once the area is secured, we'll begin evacuation. That is all."

In the moment's silence that followed, Mysho sighed deeply. "I don't know about the rest of you," she said in a voice that carried, "but I feel better knowing there's someone in charge."

"Someone who knows her fukking ass from a mudhole in the ground," Juan agreed.

Even the wounded laughed. It would clearly take more than a couple of missiles and a swamp to suck a VTA out from under Staff Sergeant Kerr.

Up in the cockpit, Torin stroked off the communication board with a steady hand. Later, once those she was responsible for were safe from both enemy action and their own damaged equipment, she'd allow herself the luxury of a reaction. Right now, she didn't have the time.

"The communications array is badly damaged, Staff, but I may be able to jury-rig something that'll enable us to send a . . ." The expression on her face cut Lieutenant Ghard off short. "What?"

"Send a message to who, sir? The *Berganitan* is not in orbit."

"We have to send a message to the Silsviss, let them know what happened and where we . . ." Once again he stopped without finishing. "There's only us and the Silsviss on this planet, isn't there, Staff?"

"As far as I know, sir."

The silence in the cockpit was so complete, Torin could hear the gentle hum of the doctor's bonder reattaching a piece of Captain Daniels' scalp.

"Why would the Silsviss shoot us down, Staff?"

"I don't know, sir. But I intend to find out." Reaching up over Trenkik's head, Torin pressed her right thumb into the dimple at the edge of the weapons locker.

"You're going to question Cri Sawyes?"

"Yes, sir." Wrapping her fingers around the familiar stock of a KC-7, she lifted it out and checked the clip.

"I'll go with you." He started to stand.

"Lieutenant!" Trenkik's voice held a touch of panic. "The rerouting you put in is failing! Leakage is rising!"

He hovered for a moment, clearly wanting to be a part of any questioning, then finally, he sat. "Be careful."

Torin felt her lip lift, then decided it was just one of those things officers said. "Yes, sir."

I should never have left that lizard alone in there. I should have got up and taken him out when he least expected it. If anything's happened . . . She'd got too used to thinking of Cri Sawyes as a friend.

The stink still lingered in the civilian compartment and her short absence made it quite clear that it lingered most strongly around the Dornagain. Breathing shallowly, as she squeezed through the partially open hatch, Torin had to admit that she wasn't surprised considering the way they smelled just generally.

She *was* surprised to find Cri Sawyes had already been taken care of. Curiosity replaced anger as she tried to take in this astonishing development.

The Silsviss had been barricaded into a corner behind several seats ripped out of the deck and webbed together. The largest of the Dornagain squatted on her haunches watching the barricade like an oversized cat watching a mouse hole. Resting her weapon on her hip, Torin cautiously approached. As no one seemed to have taken any injuries from tooth or claw, she could only assume the Silsviss was in there because he'd agreed to the captivity.

Why?

As a gesture of goodwill, obviously. Given that he was presently trapped in a VTA with a platoon of

Marines his people had just shot down, he was going to need all the goodwill he could get.

Halfway across the compartment, the Mictok ambassador scuttled out to meet her. "Staff Sergeant Kerr, is it safe to assume that our vehicle has been disabled and we are confined to the ground?"

"Yes, ma'am. It is." The ambassador seemed relatively calm about the whole thing. In fact, as Torin looked around, none of the civilians seemed to be panicking—at least not within species parameters she understood.

"We have assured the others that the military is in control of the situation."

"Thank you, ma'am." That explained it. They were used to being taken care of. If she could herd them like sheep, she had a chance of keeping them alive. Unfortunately, as sheep wouldn't have taken the initiative of confining Cri Sawyers, she suspected it wasn't going to be that easy. *More's the pity.*

"We hope you have sustained no serious injuries."

"Not personally, ma'am, but I have four dead including one of my sergeants. Both aircrew tending the engines were probably killed instantly. Lieutenant Jarret is unconscious. Captain Daniels is also unconscious and more seriously injured. I don't yet know the extent of the other injuries. You?"

"We have sustained no damage, Staff Sergeant. Our protection was sufficient."

Torin stopped at the barricade. "And this?"

"Upon emerging from our protection, we realized that, except for the Confederation members on board this vehicle, the Silsviss are the only missile-using species on this planet. Therefore it must have been Silsviss who shot us down and perhaps Cri Sawyes is not to be trusted." One eyestalk swayed from side to side. "Strength Of Arm volunteered to guard him."

They were so proud of themselves that, in spite of everything, Torin had to hide a smile.

The Dornagain's ears went up, feathery tips brushing the ceiling. "He gave us no trouble, Staff Sergeant."

"No reassson why I should," Cri Sawyes remarked dryly, framed in the triangular space between a seat top and bottom. "I am not your enemy. Thossse were not our misssilesss."

Torin snorted. "How do you know?"

His inner eyelids flicked closed and he pointed through the barricade toward the view screen. "I sssaw them approach."

"And a quick glimpse at a missile moving at just under supersonic speeds allowed you to make a positive identification?" It wasn't quite sarcasm.

"I wasss in the military for mossst of my adult life, Ssstaff Sssergeant, and at war for much of that time. Alliancesss change quickly on Sssilsssvah, an ability to make a fassst, posssitive identification of incoming ordinance isss necesssary for sssurvival."

From what little Silsvah history she'd learned, that was certainly true. Still . . . "I doubt you can identify every single missile on the entire planet. You'd know your own, and your closest allies' or enemies'."

His tongue flicked out. "You ssseem to be making my argument for me. If it was a Sssilsssvah misssile that I couldn't identify, it'sss clearly from a group I have no affiliation with. Will I be held ressponsssible for the actionsss of my entire planet?"

Son of a . . . He was making way too much sense. "For the moment," Torin began, then paused as her implant chimed.

Contamination levels now at 2.5 and rising.

Humans could stand a contamination level of 5.7, di'Taykan a little more, Krai a little less. An initial warning at 2.5 gave everyone time to get clear. At least that was the theory. She had no idea how much time the three species of civilians would need although the information was probably buried somewhere in her slate. *Best just to hurry.*

"You I'll deal with later." She nodded toward their captive, more than willing to let Cri Sawyes' loyalties slide for the moment. "Or the lieutenant will deal with you when he wakes up. The rest of you . . ." She found the massed attention of the civilians—particularly the massed attention of the Mictok—a little disconcerting and had to clear her throat before she could continue. ". . . get into your storage compartments and put together everything you'll need for personal and species survival in the wilds of Silsvah. We've only got one working exit and we can't get the sleds out of it, so you'll be carrying your gear over some rough terrain. Remember that when you put it together."

They wouldn't, but that could be dealt with later. It was more important now to get them moving, to give them enough to do that they wouldn't start thinking about the situation. Which, as far as she could tell, didn't bear thinking about.

"Staff Sergeant?"

Halfway out the hatch to the central axis, Torin turned. Grieving for her dead assistant, Madame Britt had broken the central feather in her crest. "Ma'am?"

"This one wonders if it wouldn't be safer to stay with the VTA?"

"No. The engines were hit. The mud is containing most of the leakage for the moment, but that won't last. We have to get clear."

"This one wonders if there is not enemy outside."

"Not according to the scanners, ma'am. But I'm heading out there now to check." She offered the only bit of comfort she had. "Don't worry. You're with the Marines."

The fireteams were waiting for her by the forward hatch. They'd managed to put together modified combat gear out of the limited supplies in the armory: helmets, vests, and belts over dress uniforms. The three heavy gunners were carrying KC-12s and, although the upper body exoskeletons they wore provided less than half of their usual amendments, they looked happier than they had since leaving the station.

Ressk stepped away from the panel as she approached. "Ship's scanners say there's nothing out there, Staff. Well, nothing alive bigger than two-and-a-half centimeters anyway."

"Right. Let's open it up and take a look."

Hollice tossed her a helmet, and she put it on as the hatch slid open.

The VTA's moving parts were not particularly thrilled to be moving. The reason became obvious as mud first trickled and then poured through the opening.

The Marines retreated.

"Topside's not supposed to be buried!"

"Get back here." Torin braced herself against the flood, and by the time she finished speaking it was over. Mud had filled the corridor ankle-deep, but the hatch was clear and the sky outside was a brilliant blue. "It was just debris from the landing." Ignoring the unpleasant sucking sounds, Torin stepped outside, flipping her helmet scanner down over her left eye. The grid remained empty. "Area's clear. Now let's find a way off this thing before that leakage gets worse and we run out of original chromosomes."

"This reminds me of a meal I had once," Binti muttered as they waded back to the hatch.

Ressk lifted his boot and stared down at the dripping, viscous brown mess ruining his shine. "I don't want to hear any more comments about what I eat if this reminds you of a meal."

"Specifically, it reminds me of a couple of hours after the meal."

"I needed to hear that?"

The area immediately around the VTA was a desolate, dripping mess. Beyond that was swamp. Torin sent teams out along both of the broad delta wings and up to the bow to scan for dry land. There wasn't much point in abandoning ship if it didn't improve the situation.

"All right, I'm getting something." Squinting through his helmet scanner, Hollice ran the terrain program through one more time with the magnification on full. "That way."

Squatting at the edge of the wing, Binti stared out at destruction that looked no different than any of the rest and then up at the corporal. "You're kidding, right?"

"No. That way. Twenty meters, then there's a ridge. We can follow it all the way to high ground."

"Your helmet's fukked, Hollice." Juan pointed his weapon along the line indicated. "I can see twenty meters and there's no ridge."

"There's a ridge, it's just covered in more *serley* mud." Ressk flipped his own scanner up and sighed. "And the way our day's been going, it'll be the only way out."

Mud lapped at the edge of the wing. Either they'd hit bottom or the broader surfaces were keeping them from sinking any deeper. Since the result was the same, it didn't matter much to Torin either way. The ridge would get them out of the swamp, but getting to the ridge . . .

"Never an engineer around when you need one," she muttered, glancing up at the sky. Just after noon. The sky was still clear, but at this time of the year in this part of the world, it usually rained after dark.

Traveling with wounded and civilians, they had to be able to put up shelters by then. "Aylex!"

Head turned into the breeze, the di'Taykan started. "Staff?"

"You're the closest thing to an engineer we've got."

"I am?"

"You came up with a way to get us over that canyon back on Junnas."

"Well, yeah, but I could see the other side. This stuff . . ." He waved out at the mud. "It all looks the same. The scanners are all that's telling us there's solid land out there. I can't even smell a difference."

"Your point?"

He stared at her for a moment, then he sighed. "I suppose I could shoot a cable across to those stumps and string a bridge off that."

"Do what you have to. Remember, we've got wounded to evac, and it's got to hold four Dornagain." His eyes widened, but Torin kept talking, preventing the protest. Protesting wouldn't change the fact that whatever he built had to stand up to the slow-moving weight of four very large responsibilities. "Corporal Ng, you're in charge of the work detail. Defer to Private Aylex when it comes to the actual construction." For a moment, she indulged baser instincts by wishing that one of the Dornagain had died instead of the birdboned Rakva and then reminded herself that the Dornagain could eat more of the local food and weren't likely to blow away in the first bad storm. Not to mention that one of them had just saved her life. "I'll send out as much help as I can. Corporal Hollice, as soon as there's a way across, I want your team on recon. Check back when you've gone a kilometer up the ridge. Let's go people, we're running out of time."

"Uh, Staff."

"What is it, Aylex?"

"What am I supposed to build a bridge of?"

Torin snorted and stamped one foot, her bootheel ringing against the metal skin of the VTA. "You're standing on a few tons of scrap. Improvise."

Her implant chimed as she stepped back into the muddy corridor.

Contamination levels now at 2.9 and rising.

"Oh, shut up."

"Staff?"

"Not you. Just go get the cables."

The civilian compartment had the appearance of a jumble sale with gear piled haphazardly on every conceivable surface and various arguments in progress. Captain Daniels lay on a stretcher by the door beside the covered body of the young Rakva—their island of quiet a foreboding contrast to the surrounding noise. Frowning, Torin knelt beside her and touched fingers to her throat. She was still alive. Torin straightened, feeling lighter by a life, then leaned forward again to examine the straps holding her in place. They almost looked like . . .

"Webbing. We felt it would better hold her without impairing her circulation. Dr. Leor is quite concerned about her," the ambassador continued, when Torin looked up. "We are watching her while the doctor sees to the other injured."

"Thank you." Webbing . . . Standing, she pulled her helmet off and tucked it under one arm. "Madame Ambassador, I apologize in advance if this is insulting, but I've got Marines out on the wing attempting to bridge twenty meters of essentially bottomless mud and . . ." All eight eyes were focused on her. She stared down the multiple reflections accusing her of breaking every rule of protocol in the book. ". . . a little webbing might help a whole lot."

"We don't see how."

Fortunately staff sergeants were stronger than a little embarrassment. If they weren't, that incredible night spent with Lieutenant Jarret would've been truly unfortunate. Torin gestured toward the improvised cell. "It holds things together."

Two eyestalks turned. "Yes, it does."

A few moments later, one of the ambassador's assistants was scurrying out to the wing followed by the slowly moving bulk of Strength of Arm. With the blessings of her ambassador, the Dornagain had volunteered her services. "If you think strength will be needed," she'd added shyly.

Torin stood once again by the hole in the barricade and watched Cri Sawyes watching her. "You're taking this very well," she said after a moment.

The tip of his tail drew a figure eight in the air. "Thisss isss no more than a temporary inconvenience. You will need me out there to sssurvive."

"I can survive without you." From the single flicker of his tongue, that seemed to amuse him. *Next time he sticks it out, I'm tying a knot in it.*

"I have no doubt you can sssurvive, Ssstaff Sssergeant, but you have wounded and civiliansss, and for them to sssurvive you'll need my help."

Torin glanced from Captain Daniels, lying too still by the hatch, to the Charge d'Affaires and her young assistant adding yet another container to their pile of gear and realized Cri Sawyes was not merely offering to help carry things through the mud. "We're still in the wilderness preserve, aren't we?"

"Yesss."

"Your wild boys will investigate the crash."

"Yesss."

"Will we be in any danger from them?"

"That dependsss on how you answer their challenge." He leaned forward, claws digging into a seat back, face so close to the hole that she thought she could feel the heat of his breath on her cheek. "I am not your enemy."

Not *her* enemy. Which didn't necessarily mean he wasn't the Confederation's enemy, did it? "Stay there for now. I've got enough to worry about."

Nostrils flared, he reared back, throat pouch expanding. "I have told you thossse were not our misssilesss, I have told you I am not your enemy, and ssstill you worry about what I may do? I tell you now for the lassst time that unless sssussspicion wearsss away my ssself-control, you and your people are in no danger from me!"

Half-turned away, Torin paused and came to a decision. "I believe you."

His throat pouch deflated so quickly he sneezed.

"Even if it *was* a Silsviss missile, you certainly didn't fire it. But there are another thirty-five Marines who may not see it that way," she continued, "and, right now, I don't have time to change their minds. You stay there, and I guarantee no one'll take a shot at you. You start wandering around . . ." She shrugged.

"I will ssstay here." His tongue flickered again and her hand rose; she forced it back down before anything came of it. "Thank you."

"You're welcome."

She taken two steps toward the argument in the middle of the room when her implant chimed.

Lieutenant Jarret has regained consciousness.

Contamination levels now at 3.1 and rising.

Torin stepped into the troop compartment and stopped dead. Outwardly, she was surveying the activity, inwardly she was drawing strength from being back where she belonged; no matter how bad it looked. *I should have been here . . .*

The right wall had buckled. Impact had loosened one of the sleds and it had slammed through from the vehicle bay. There were four body bags lying beside the wreckage and three stretchers beside them. Not exactly encouraging for the three injured but the best use of the available space. Two of the three were clearly sedated, the doctor was bending over the third. One of the two corpsmen was finishing a wrist-to-elbow field dressing on the arm of a corporal from Sergeant Chou's squad, and the other was putting together a second pack from the medical supply locker. There were field packs against the left wall and the armory hatch was open. She couldn't see the lieutenant.

She *could* see Corporal Conn, and she thanked any gods who were listening that she didn't have to tell a four-year-old why her daddy wasn't coming home.

"Staff."

She took another step into the compartment and turned. "Mike."

Sergeant Glicksohn held out his slate. "You want to download the full report?"

Reaching down she thumbed her input but didn't bother actually looking at the screen. "Highlights?"

"Sergeant Trey, Privates Drake . . ."

Did he die with his dice in his hand, she wondered.

". . . and Damon . . ."

Probably reading when it happened. Torin had approved extra memory for her slate so she could carry more books.

". . . and Corporal Sutton are dead."

She'd been planning on scheduling his sergeant's exam the day General Morris had given them their new orders. With Sergeant Trey dead, he'd have probably gotten a field promotion. Except that he was dead, too.

Torin added their names to the others she'd started carrying since she got her third hook. She knew there wasn't anything she could have done even if she'd been in the troop compartment, but that knowledge made her feel no less responsible.

"We had eight other injuries, three serious." His lips pressed into a thin line, then he snarled, "Haysole got both legs caught, the stupid bastard."

The doctor shifted position and Torin caught her first sight of turquoise hair lying still and unmoving. Before she could ask for an explanation, Mike spat it out, the words growing louder and crowding up against each other as he spoke.

"He was in the sled with Trey. They strapped in there, but that didn't do them any good when we hit ground." One fist slammed against the back of a seat. "Should have been in his seat. Goddamn di'Taykan, can't keep it in their pants . . ."

Torin laid her hand on his arm, and the diatribe cut off like she'd touched a switch.

The sergeant drew in a deep breath and let it out slowly. "Doc says he'll get new legs and a trip home." He lifted his head and met her gaze. "All we have to do is keep him alive until someone comes to get us. But the *Berganitan*'s gone and the Silsviss are shooting at us, so who the fuk is that going to be?"

"It's not our fault."

"He's in my squad. I should've tied him to his seat."

"We'll keep him alive."

"Goddamned right we will." He drew in another deep breath and seemed to exhale his anger with it, his voice sounding no more than weary when he added, "Ceremonial duties, my ass."

Contamination levels now at 3.5 and rising.

"You heard."

He nodded. "I heard."

"Get the stretchers topside before it gets any worse. Then I want half the able-bodied humping packs and the other half working on the bridge. Put the walking wounded on guard."

"The lieutenant's awake."

"I know."

"He seems to think it might be a better idea to stay with the VTA."

"Does he?" Torin spotted lilac hair coming into the troop compartment from behind the ruined wall. "I'll deal with him, you get moving on evac."

"Staff . . ."

She began threading her way between the remaining seats. "Don't worry. I'll be polite."

"Lieutenant Jarret." When he turned toward her, Torin could see that the side of his face was badly bruised and she was willing to bet that his cheekbone had been broken. "I'm glad to see you back on your feet, sir. Has the doctor taken a look at you?"

"No. I had the corpsman give me a pain block."

Only the unbruised side of his face moved when he spoke. If it was a side effect of the pain block, it was a new one. Given di'Taykan muscle control, Torin suspected he was still in pain and attempting to minimize it. "You should have the doctor rebond that bone, sir."

"There are Marines who need the doctor a lot more than I do, Staff Sergeant," Lieutenant Jarret told her stiffly. "He can take care of this . . ." His hand rose and two fingers lightly touched his cheek. ". . . when he's finished with them."

"Yes, sir." It was the textbook "good officer" response—*See to my men first.*—but there was a world of difference between those officers who made the declaration because they felt they should and those who meant it. The lieutenant seemed honestly insulted that she'd even made the suggestion, as though she should know him better than that. All things considered, she supposed he had grounds. "Sergeant Glicksohn has filled you in on the state of the platoon, sir?"

"Yes." He looked past her, eyes focused on the bodies across the room. "Four dead. Three badly injured. Seven others injured but mobile."

"Seven? I thought eight . . ."

As he turned toward her, she realized he hadn't counted himself among the injured, and she really hoped he wasn't so young that he'd consider *I'm fine* to be the last word on the subject. "Sir . . ."

"I'm fine."

Her expression provoked a smile on both sides of his mouth.

"For now," he added before she could speak. Then the smile vanished. "I hear you took command while I was unconscious."

"Yes, sir. Captain Daniels was badly injured and Lieutenant Ghard felt he should concentrate on the VTA. We lost one of the civilians, but the others have only minor injuries. Although contamination levels are rising quickly, we'll be able to get all personnel clear of the ship before any irreversible damage is done. There's a bridge being built from the ship to what passes for dry land in these parts, Hollice's team is scouting a route out of the swamp, and the wounded are being evacuated topside before the leakage gets any higher."

"What?"

She chose to misunderstand. "Topside, sir. We've settled so deeply into the mud that only the forward hatch topside is working."

"What I meant, Staff Sergeant, is *why* are you evacuating the wounded."

Under other circumstances she'd have admired the edge in his voice; under these circumstances she really hoped he wasn't about to pull rank. "Sir, as I said, contamination levels are rising quickly."

He shook his head and didn't quite manage to hide the pain the motion caused. "No. I've just had a look, and the engine room wall hasn't been breached. If we're under attack, the VTA is the safest place to be. The Silsviss haven't the technology to get us out."

"With all due respect sir, just because you can't see a breach, doesn't mean there isn't one." Her protest emerged as unchallenging as she could make it. The trick was not to sound as if she were talking to a three-year-old. "Your implant may not be functioning; we've been getting readings . . ."

"My implant is functioning fine, Sergeant. The last reading was at 3.5. That's still not enough of a threat for us to take civilians out into hostile territory." His gaze focused past her shoulder again. "Corporal Mysho! Leave that stretcher where it is!"

"Sir?"

So much for being polite, Torin decided. This had

to be stopped before it got messy. "Sir, the reading was 3.5 and *rising* . . ."

He cut her off. "Still well within species tolerances. The Mictok can take levels as high as 9.2."

"Good for them. I can't. Neither can you. Neither can any other Marine under your command." His mouth opened, but she continued in the same low voice before he could speak. "The engine *has* been breached, there's *no* telling how high the contamination will rise and, according to the ship's long-range scanner, the *only* hostiles are a primitive band of male adolescents thirty kilometers away. Sir."

In this particular instance, sir meant: *"These are the facts. I suggest you adjust your decision making accordingly."*

Torin could feel the corporal waiting for new orders. With any luck, she was the only witness to this standoff. With any luck, it wouldn't be the first of many.

"Primitive band of male adolescents?" the lieutenant repeated at last.

"We came down in a wilderness preserve." As understanding dawned, she added, "Sir, I realize that shepherding a group of mixed species diplomats through a swamp fills you with justifiable aversion, but killing them slowly isn't the answer."

For a moment she thought he wasn't going to see the humor in that last statement, but then the uninjured side of his mouth twisted up into a crooked smile. "It isn't?"

"No, sir, it isn't."

The smile twisted a little more. "You have everything under control, don't you?"

There were a number of ways to deal with that kind of incipient self-pity in a junior officer. "Thank you, sir," she said brightly.

"That wasn't . . ." He paused.

Torin met his gaze levelly. She could almost see the wheels turning behind his eyes.

His smile untwisted and turned to honest amusement. "All right, Staff Sergeant, you win. Upon considering all the options, I've decided to continue the evacuation. Corporal Mysho!"

"Sir?"

"Carry on."

"Yes, sir."

By a mutual, albeit silent, agreement they ignored the relief in the corporal's voice.

"All right . . ." Lieutenant Jarret gestured at the rapidly emptying compartment. "The Marines are taken care of. What about the civilians?"

"Two of them are helping build the bridge, the rest are packing."

"Packing? To march through a swamp?"

"Yes, sir."

"On their own?"

"Yes, sir."

He began to shake his head but stopped, hair flat, before the motion really got started. "Send one of the walking wounded up to supervise their choices, or the doctor will want to take along his specimens and the Mictok will be packing art supplies."

"Yes, sir." Half turning, she beckoned the last of

the minor casualties away from the corpsman and passed on the lieutenant's order. "Anything else, sir?"

"I think we'd better go have a look at that bridge." He swayed as he stepped forward, and without thinking, Torin reached out and slipped an arm around his waist, holding him until he steadied. When she released him, he stared at her for a heartbeat, eyes dark, and she wondered if she'd overstepped the line. It was one thing to keep him from making stupid mistakes—in fact, that was essentially her job description concerning second lieutenants—and another thing entirely to imply he couldn't stand on his own two feet. Young males of any species tended to be overly proud and young male officers . . . *Fuk it.* "Are you all right, sir?"

Twitching his tunic down into place, he pushed past her. "I'm fine."

Ready to catch him if it came to it, Torin fell into step behind him. "Yes, sir."

EIGHT

As they made their way up the central axis, Torin glanced over at the lieutenant and frowned thoughtfully. Although the bruising made it difficult to tell for certain, he seemed to be carrying what she called a "once more into the breach" expression on top of stiff shoulders and as close to a graceless walk as a di'Taykan could manage. From this point on, he'd do or die trying. And that had to be nipped in the bud before it was exactly what happened.

"Crisis of confidence, sir?"

Anyone but a di'Taykan would have tripped. "What?"

"You think you're off to a bad start. Through no fault of your own, you were unconscious when you should have taken command, and when you finally joined the party, you think you made the wrong decision." He *had* made the wrong decision, but reminding him of that wouldn't help. "You're determined to prove yourself because even though you're a trained combat officer and not a diplomatic baby-sitter—no matter how perfectly your background prepared you for the latter—you're afraid there's nothing you can do that I can't do better." She timed the pause so that he barely got his mouth open before she continued. "And you're beginning to wish that you'd had the doctor bond that bone because your head hurts like hell."

He'd stopped walking, so she stopped as well and turned to face him, counting silently to herself. If she got to twenty before he spoke, she'd begin an apology.

At nine, his eyes narrowed.

"There's a reason telepathic races are universally hated," he growled. "Do you always speak your mind so freely, Staff Sergeant Kerr? Because if this is some Human response to having sex . . ."

"Not at all, sir. It's part of my job description."

"Keeping me in my place?"

"No, sir. Keeping good officers alive by not letting them get trapped inside their own heads."

This time she only got to five.

"Good officers?"

"Yes, sir." She kept her answer matter-of-fact, as though he shouldn't have had to ask, and was rewarded by a long exhalation, a visible release of tension, and a grateful smile.

"Suck up."

"Yes, sir."

"Staff, why do you think the Silsviss shot us down?"

Torin shrugged. "They may not have, sir. Cri Sawyes was at the vid screen when it happened, and he says they weren't Silsviss missiles."

Jarret jerked to a stop and reached out to grab her

arm, only barely managing to keep his fingers from closing—the situation had not yet deteriorated to the point where he'd be excused for panic clutching his senior NCO. "Cri Sawyes!"

"Contained, sir."

"Contained?" When she nodded, he started breathing again. "I can't *believe* I forgot there was a Silsviss on board."

"Well, I wasn't the one who contained him," Torin admitted dryly, figuring one confession deserved another. "The Mictok ambassador arranged it while I was in the cockpit."

"Really?"

"Not something I'd be likely to make up, sir. And you, at least, had the excuse of having been knocked unconscious."

Fingertips lightly touched the bruise purpling his cheek. "Careless of us both, Staff Sergeant."

"Yes, sir."

He held her gaze for a moment, then started walking again. "Strangely enough," he said, his matter-of-fact tone an almost exact copy of her earlier one, "the discovery that you're not perfect is making me feel significantly more confident."

Unable to decide if she was insulted or amused, Torin fell back into step beside him. "I'm glad I could help, sir."

"Do you believe Cri Sawyes when he says the missiles weren't Silsviss?"

"I believe him when he says he doesn't recognize them, sir. As to whether or not they're Silsviss . . ." She shrugged. "I don't know. He also points out that we can't hold him responsible for the actions of the entire planet."

"We can," the lieutenant corrected wryly. "The question is whether or not we should."

"He says he isn't our enemy."

"And do you believe *that?*"

"Well, lying is in his best interests right now, but I don't think he was."

"Why not? Because you like him?"

"Essentially, sir, yes." When Lieutenant Jarret shot her a questioning glance, she shrugged again. "Not much to go on," she admitted, acknowledging his expression.

"I wouldn't say that." He nodded toward the rank insignia on her collar. "You didn't get those by being a bad judge of character."

Surprised at the depth of her reaction, Torin touched the stacked chevrons over the crossed KC silhouettes. "Thank you, sir." For no good reason, she found herself feeling better about the unmitigated mess they were all facing.

Contamination levels now 3.9 and rising.

A little better. Not a lot.

"Pontoons?"

"The empty storage units float, sir, and they'll hold the Dornagain."

Standing just behind the lieutenant's left shoulder, Torin leaned around him and glanced pointedly at Strength of Arm's muddy haunches.

"Well, they will now," Aylex amended, grinning. "As long as they cross one at a time."

Stepping onto the first of the completed sections, Lieutenant Jarret bounced thoughtfully. Dried mud flaked off the sides of the containers into slow moving ripples as the bridge undulated along its entire length. The omnipresent odor of rotting vegetation grew momentarily stronger. After one final bounce, he turned, stepped back onto the VTA, and yelled, "Well done!" over the sudden crash of two more units bouncing down the wing. "How soon can you have it finished?"

Aylex looked over at his crew and shrugged. "Well, sir, as long as Strength of Arm keeps tearing things apart and Gar'itac keep tying them together . . ."

The Mictok was actually tying the storage units together with cable but doing it with a speed and dexterity impossible to match with only two arms.

". . . it'll be done before it's time to leave."

"Talk about out of the frying pan into the fire," Hollice muttered. He squatted and stared into the water, but nothing had changed over the last fifteen seconds—suspended organic matter still made it impossible to see below the surface. "Damn."

Once they'd slogged their way out of the splatter zone, the ground, although not much higher than the swamp around it, had been relatively dry. Relative to the swamp. Given the unfamiliar terrain and the massed vegetation, they'd made slow but steady time.

Until now.

It looked as if something had taken a gigantic bite

out of the ridge they'd been following and the swamp had seeped into the hollow. There was no way around it that didn't involve a significantly worse scenario and the end of the kilometer they were scouting was on the other side.

"Ground gets a lot higher over there," Ressk assured him, squinting through his scanner and pointing at the opposite shore nearly six meters away.

"Yeah. But we're over here."

"My scanner says the bottom's solid."

"Yeah. So does mine."

"It's only just over a meter deep."

"Good. Then it won't be over your head."

Ressk snorted. "Oh, that makes sense, send the short guy."

Juan fanned a cloud of tiny insects away from his face and swiped at a dribble of sweat with the backstroke. "Would one of you just get your ass into the water! I killed the fukking snake and we haven't seen another one!"

"Haven't *seen* another one." Straightening, Hollice stepped back, staggering a little as the ground reluctantly released his boots. "Bin, take a look at those trees over there." They didn't look much like trees, more like giant sticks topped off with a tuft of fern, but they were the tallest vegetation in the area, and after a few planetfalls he'd learned to be flexible. At least they weren't moving under their own power. "Scanner says they're tall enough to bridge this—you think you can take them down from this side?"

"Sure." Weapon resting on her hip, Binti squinted across the gap. "But it'll attract attention."

"We're still showing no unfriendlies."

"Great. just one thing; I can't make them fall where you want them from here. It's got to be done from that side."

"You positive?"

"I'm positive. So, as much as I hate to agree with Juan, get your ass in the water."

"You should . . ."

"No, I shouldn't," she interrupted emphatically. "That's lumberjack work, and you want the best shot on guard in case that snake had friends."

He couldn't argue with that. Snapping his scanner down, Hollice took another look at the water. The organic soup remained too thick for a clear reading. "I ever mention how much I hate snakes?" he muttered, stepping back to the edge. "That whole legless thing they've got going just wigs me right out." Lifting his weapon over his head, he lurched forward, bumped into Ressk's arm, and stopped. "What?"

"I'll go."

"Oh, that makes sense," Hollice snorted. "Send the short guy. No, I'm in charge here, I'll do it. Just make sure you shoot anything that moves."

"But the snakes . . ."

"Especially shoot the fukking snakes!"

The water was warm, almost body temperature. Unfortunately, dress uniforms, while essentially waterproof, hadn't been designed for walking in a swamp. Combat gear presented one impermeable surface to the outside world. At the moment, his pack, vest, and helmet would stay dry, no matter what, but he could feel water seeping into his boots and pushing up under his tunic to pour down inside the waistband of his trousers. Placing one foot carefully in front of the other, he tried not to think of what might be seeping, pushing, and pouring in with it.

The moisture dribbling down his sides he at least knew the source of. If the brains at R&D had come up with an environmental control strong enough to handle fear sweat, he'd never worn it.

Halfway across. He was wet, and every ripple added another layer to the stink of the place that lined the inside of his nose, but so far so good.

Then something brushed against the back of his leg.

The next thing he knew, he was scrambling out on the opposite shore, heart beating so violently he couldn't believe it hadn't triggered his med-alert. Flopping over onto his back, he jerked up and pointed his weapon back along his path.

Nothing. His passage had whipped up a greenish-brown foam, but whatever had touched him was still below the surface.

"Hollice? You all right?"

"Did you see it?"

They hadn't. And nothing had shown up on Ressk's scanner.

"Are you all right?" Binti repeated.

"Yeah. Fine." Breathing beginning to calm, he stood, slowly, and watched a small orange blob slide off his legs to splat against the mud below. When it started to move away from him, he stepped on it. At the moment, building impossible bridges and humping gear back at the VTA held a definite attraction.

"Hey, Staff, you know what I heard?"

Torin dropped to one knee by Haysole's stretcher and linked her fingers through his. With their lower body temperature, di'Taykans usually felt cool to Humans, but his skin was warm. "What have you heard?"

"After I get my new legs, I can go home."

"Some people'll do anything to get out of cleaning toilets."

Haysole flashed her a fraction of his usual grin. "Cleaning the crappers wasn't so bad, but all that marching up and down in straight lines was really beginning to weigh."

They winced in unison as another supply container crashed against the wing.

"Staff, after I get my new legs, will I be able to dance?"

"Sure."

"That's great, 'cause I can't dance now."

Torin had always found it amazing how much bad humor transcended species parameters. She smiled even though Haysole's eyes were so pale she doubted he could see more than a silhouette of her against the sky. "I know a sergeant who got busted down a rank for that joke."

"Good thing I've got no rank to bust, then." He sucked at the straw the doctor had tucked into the corner of his mouth, and when he'd finished swallowing sighed deeply. "I never meant to be such a screwup."

"Yes, you did."

His eyes darkened as he forced himself to focus.

"And don't try to tell me you regret a thing because I won't believe it. You enjoyed bucking the system, even if it meant being a private for your entire time in. There're too many corporals around anyway. And way too many sergeants."

This time the grin lit up most of his face. "All after your job."

"Every damn one of them." She tightened her grip for a moment and then released his hand. "Speaking of my job, I should get back to it."

"Staff?"

She paused at the foot of his stretcher. "What?"

"If I die, take off the masker before you bag me."

"You're not going to die."

"Hey, even *you* can't guarantee that."

He laughed at her overly indignant reaction, and she carried the sound away with her, adding it to her armaments.

"How's Private Haysole?"

Torin shook her head, although she wasn't certain what she was denying. "His hair was so still . . ."

"It's the sedatives."

"The sedatives? Of course . . ." It wasn't like she'd never seen an injured di'Taykan before. She felt herself flush under Lieutenant Jarret's steady gaze. Every man and woman in the platoon was her responsibility. She wasn't supposed to have favorites.

And we weren't supposed to face any combat on this trip either. And generals aren't supposed to send their troops in unprepared. And . . . As the lieutenant's hair fanned out from his head—and she noticed he'd finally let the doctor attend to his face—she cut short her silent soliloquy and found a new subject. "They're securing the last floats to the bridge, sir."

"Good. Has Corporal Hollice's team reported back yet?"

"Not yet, sir." The communication system built into her helmet—into everyone's helmet—buzzed. "I expect this is them now."

"Not an especially fast kilometer."

Torin looked past the mud drying and cracking on everything in sight to the tangled mass of vegetation beyond. "Not especially," she agreed, thumbing the receive.

". . . last of the kilometer took us out of the swamp. We're sitting high, dry, and defensible."

"Unfriendlies?"

"Nothing on scanner, Staff."

Torin glanced at the sky. The sun had moved past its zenith some time before but was still a distance above the horizon. "Can we get there before dark? Carrying wounded?"

"Piece of cake."

"Corporal?"

"That's an affirmative on arriving before dark with wounded."

Lieutenant Jarret reached out and touched her arm.

"Sir?"

"Have them start back." The lieutenant's gaze swept over the VTA, over the civilians, over the wounded, over the dead. "We're going to need all hands."

"Back?" Ressk swallowed and wiped his mouth on the back of his hand. "Is she kidding?"

"Lieutenant's orders." Hollice told them, flipping the tiny microphone back up into its recess. "We're to set out a perimeter and leave the packs."

"We'll be walking it three fukking times while everyone else walks it once!" Juan protested loudly.

"Yeah, and back at the VTA they've been sitting on their collective ass while we've been working." Activating his perimeter pin, Hollice pushed it into the ground. "Set up and let's get moving."

Brows down and hair up, Lieutenant Jarret swept a questioning gaze up one side of the armory and down the other. "We seem to be exceptionally well armed for a ceremonial mission, Staff."

"Standard armory on a VTA this size, sir."

"But two extra lockers of KCs?"

Torin had wondered about that herself. The KC-7 was a Marine's personal weapon, and it made no sense that they were carrying enough to outfit a second platoon. "Supply back on the station told me they were part of the diplomatic mission and not our concern."

Jarret shot her an incredulous stare. "They were going to arm the Silsviss?"

"That's certainly what it looks like."

"Has the Parliament completely lost its collective mind?"

That was probably a rhetorical question, but Torin chose to answer it anyway. "I believe they thought the Silsviss were on our side."

"Still . . ." He sighed and stretched out a hand toward the closest locker. "Not a total loss, we can use them to arm the diplomats." Then he paused, thumb over the lock. "Why *haven't* you armed the diplomats, Staff?"

"The diplomats refused to be armed, sir."

His arm fell back to his side as he turned toward her. "Can't say as I'm surprised. What are we . . ."

Contamination now at 4.2 and rising.

". . . leaving behind?" he finished as their implants quieted.

Torin ran her hand along the edge of a weapons locker and sighed. "Everything here, sir. We're limited without the sleds."

"Everything? What about mortars?"

"I've sent two of the EM223s up, sir. Two ammo packs each."

"Two emmies? Is that all?"

"Even an emmy weighs in at 21 kilograms, sir, and we're already carrying food, water, and wounded."

"We're surrounded by water, Staff."

"Yes, sir, and we're carrying a purifier. Counting the two sergeants, we have fifteen uninjured Marines," she continued when he opened his mouth to protest further. "We'll need six to carry the three stretchers and four to carry the emmies. That leaves only five with their hands free for their weapons *if* Corporal Hollice's team makes it back before we leave. Granted, some of the injuries aren't serious—they'll be carrying the ammo packs and riding herd on the civilians."

"The aircrew . . ."

"The two surviving aircrew will be carrying Captain Daniels."

"Lieutenant Ghard . . ."

"Is not my responsibility, sir."

He drummed his fingertips against the curve of the helmet tucked into the crook of his elbow. Reading his mood in the rhythm, Torin decided not to remind him about fingerprints smudging the photoelectric receptors. Some things it was better just to let happen.

"All right." The drumming stopped. "Standard operating procedure has us making camp a minimum of three kilometers away from a downed VTA."

"Yes, sir."

"Once we've established a defensive position, we can send a team back to pick up more weapons."

She found that such an inane thing to say she had to step on the urge to ask him about his head injury. "First of all, sir, the contamination . . ."

"May never rise above the levels a di'Taykan can handle." His eyes narrowed. "And second?"

"Second, standing orders are to blow the armory." When she'd asked him to come down here with her, she'd said nothing to him but *"Sir, the armory."* and now she wondered what the hell he'd thought they were going to do. Given that he was di'Taykan, she decided not to speculate.

"When evacuating in territory held by the enemy."

"Sir?"

"I am familiar with standing orders, Staff Sergeant." His expression made it quite clear he found it insulting that she'd assumed he wasn't. "The armory is to be blown when evacuating in territory held by the enemy. We don't know who the enemy is, so we certainly don't know what territory they're holding. Do we?"

"No, sir," she admitted reluctantly, "we don't. But we are in a wilderness preserve, filled with hormonally hopped-up young males attempting to prove themselves by combat. If they get their hands on our weapons . . ."

"I think that Marine Corps security protocols are sufficient to keep out a boarding party of adolescent lizards, don't you?"

"With all due respect, sir, those sound like famous last words."

"Good." His tone drew a line and suggested she not step over it. "Because those were my last words on the subject. We *are* not losing a chance to add an SW46, and one of these sammies to our defenses." He stretched out a hand toward the locker holding the surface to air missile launcher and then, reluctantly, let it fall. "We don't know how long we'll be here or what we'll be up against."

For some reason the phrase, *hormonally hopped-up young males* kept repeating itself in Torin's head.

The lieutenant stepped out of the armory into the

empty crew compartment, motioning for her to follow. "Lock up behind us, Staff Sergeant." When she hesitated, he caught her gaze and held it. "You have your orders, Staff Sergeant Kerr."

The evacuation was a factual necessity. This was a difference of opinion, and he'd made it quite clear that she wasn't going to be able to change his mind.

"Locking up behind us, sir."

"Sergeant Glicksohn reports that everyone's topside, sir."

"Good."

As Torin followed the lieutenant into the civilian compartment, she frowned at a subtle difference in his gait. Was he strutting? And if so, was it because he felt he'd emerged triumphant from the armory? Or did he merely feel more confident because he'd given his senior NCO an order she'd disagreed with but she'd followed it anyway? The former meant he saw them in an adversarial position—either consciously or unconsciously—and that would be a bad thing. The latter was a part of the care and feeding of second lieutenants.

I think I've had as many bad things as I can cope with today. She decided to give him the benefit of the doubt.

"I wasss beginning to think you'd forgotten about me." Cri Sawyes peered through a hole in the barricade, the claws on his right hand embedded in the seat cushion that provided the bottom boundary of the space.

Lieutenant Jarret stopped well back out of arm's

reach. "I needed to get my people out and all in one place so that we can find out where you stand, together. If they're all clear on your status, there'll be no unhappy accidents."

"On my ssstatusss? The Ssstaff Sssergeant told you that the misssilesss weren't oursss?"

"She told me that you didn't recognize them as yours and that she believes you."

"And what do you believe, Lieutenant?"

"After considering all the information . . ."

Which, since we know squat, couldn't have taken more than about five seconds, Torin added silently.

". . . I have come to believe that you, personally, are not a threat and that nothing will be served by leaving you here. Although, just to be on the safe side, we will not be immediately issuing you with a weapon."

Cri Sawyes' tongue flickered out. "Not immediately?"

The lieutenant smiled—the expression charming in a di'Taykan way and therefore open to any number of interpretations. "The situation may change."

"Sssituationsss alwaysss do."

"Staff . . ."

Torin stepped forward, pulling the heavy bladed combat knife off her belt and hoping that it would actually cut through the Mictok webbing.

"Allow me, Ssstaff Sssergeant Kerr." Cri Sawyes bent out of view and a lower section of the barricade swung out into the room, using four thick strands of webbing as hinges. "I had plenty of time to ssstudy the consssstruction of my prissson," he explained, emerging out into the compartment. "And no intention of going down with the ship."

Sheathing her blade, Torin examined the exit. "You cut through the chairs."

"Yesss."

"With your clawsss?"

"Not entirely." As he straightened, he snapped open a piece of his harness and pulled out a slender knife.

The lieutenant shot an incredulous look at Torin. "No one searched him for weapons?"

"It'sss not a weapon, it'sss a tool."

Torin wasn't looking forward to taking it away from him.

"I see." Arms folded, the lieutenant swept an angry lilac gaze over the Silsviss. "Just so we're clear on it, what other tools are you carrying?"

Cri Sawyes patted a slender cylinder snapped into one the diagonal belts. "Jussst my cellular phone. But don't worry, it'sss ussselesss here; we're out of area."

Contamination level now 5.3 and rising.

Levels were at 4.2 moments before in the armory—they were rising faster.

"Sir."

"I heard." He started back toward the door, indicating that Cri Sawyes should fall in beside him. "Since we'll be spending some unexpected time on Silsvah, we'd appreciate any assistance you care to give."

"I would be more than happy to help out, Lieutenant."

Torin rolled her eyes at the quiet, conversational

exchange. Still, with Lieutenant Jarret now handling the big picture, she was free to remember that Cri Sawyes was weaker on his right. Just in case.

Taking a final look at the barricade, she followed the two males from the room—staying well back from the Silsviss' tail.

Given the patterns of the webbing over the stacked seats, she was afraid that the Mictok made better artists than engineers. Given that there was a Mictok working on the bridge, she hoped that observation was as inaccurate as most species generalizations tended to be.

As she stepped out onto the VTA, Torin put her helmet back on and flipped her scanner down. Thirty-four live Marines, four bodies, four Dornagain, four Mictok, three Rakva, one Rakva body. No unfriendlies in range, no sign of Corporal Hollice's team. She'd have been told if it was any different, but she liked to check for herself.

Picking up her pace, she moved out and drew even with Lieutenant Jarret.

"What's he doing here?"

Lieutenant Ghard's yell had a parade ground carry that drew every eye.

A number of Marines stood. A number of weapons were readied. Torin raised a hand, and that was as far as it went.

Lieutenant Jarret snorted quietly and murmured, "I'll handle this, Staff."

Torin answered in the same low voice. "Just making certain you don't get shot while you do, sir."

If he had a response, Lieutenant Ghard prevented him from making it.

"This," he snarled up at Cri Sawyes, "is the reason we're on the ground! His people shot us down! They killed two of my aircrew and almost killed Captain Daniels!"

The Silsviss' inner eyelid flickered out and in, but he made no other movement. Even his tail was completely still. Torin kept half an eye on his throat pouch.

"Yours weren't the only casualties," Lieutenant Jarret began.

"No, they weren't," Ghard interrupted, bare feet scuffing at the skin of the VTA as though he could barely hold himself back. "And his people are responsible for your dead as well!"

"Whatever his people may or may not be responsible for, Cri Sawyes is not responsible for them."

"Isn't he?" Ghard snarled. "Not everyone on Silsvah thought it was such a great idea to join the Confederation."

Which was the first Torin had heard of it, but she wasn't surprised.

"Not wanting to join the Confederation is one thing," Jarret pointed out evenly. "One lone planet starting a war with a sizable piece of the Galaxy is something else again."

"Maybe they're not one lone planet, did you ever think of that? Maybe the Others got farther into this sector than we knew!"

Torin felt her stomach muscles tighten. She hadn't considered that. Hadn't wanted to consider it. *Didn't* want to consider it. From the sudden, total silence, neither did anyone else.

"Maybe," Ghard continued driving the point home, "he was planted on board to ensure that any survivors of the crash died later, after we stupidly assumed he was on our side."

Jarret's expression suddenly cleared. "So he and all the Silsviss have been our enemy from the beginning?"

"Yes!"

"And I, being new, wouldn't have recognized this."

A little unsure if he was actually being asked a question, Ghard frowned. "Well, you . . ."

"And Staff Sergeant Kerr?"

"Wha . . ."

"And all three sergeants? And an entire platoon of combat-tested Marines; they wouldn't have recognized it either?"

Torin fought the urge to stare at the lieutenant in admiration as every listening Marine suddenly realized that *they* would have noticed something. And since they hadn't . . .

"I don't know who shot us down, or why." Jarret raised his voice slightly, ensuring everyone could hear. "But here and now, Cri Sawyes is not our enemy."

Because Staff Sergeant Kerr doesn't think he is. Torin finished the sentence in her head, sucked in a lungful of humid air, and exhaled sharply. *And I'm right. Because this would be a very bad time to be wrong.*

"So you're just going to let him walk around? Free?"

The lieutenant looked from the Krai to the Silsviss and back again. "Yes. Given the unfamiliar terrain, I expect we're going to need his help."

Ridges flushed, Ghard jerked around to face Torin. "Do you agree with this, Staff Sergeant Kerr?"

"I believe Lieutenant Jarret has made his position quite clear, sir."

"But do you agree?"

She gave him her best this-question-makes-no-sense look and threw enough of it into her voice that the listening Marines would have no doubt where her loyalties lay—which was also exactly what she would have done had she not agreed. If they were to get through this, there could be no question of who was in charge. "Yes, sir."

He stared at her for a moment, then nodded. "All right. Fine."

"If we might perhaps express an opinion . . ."

"No!" Ghard spun around to face Ambassador Krik'vir who'd moved silently closer during the argument. "This is military business now, Ambassador, and has been from the moment the Silsviss opened fire." Back facing Jarret, he threw his arms out from his body, hands open wide. "I didn't want to have to do this . . ."

Torin shifted her weight forward onto the balls of her feet. If he attacked, she'd take him out and worry about the consequences later.

". . . when did you receive your commission?"

She blinked. Not what she'd been expecting.

Not what Lieutenant Jarret had been expecting either. "You don't mean . . ." When it became quite clear that was exactly what Ghard meant, he sighed. "The sixth day of the fifth month, Confederation twelve thousand, five hundred, and four. It was also the second of *Mon gleen,* for what that's worth." He flashed a brilliant di'Taykan smile.

"You?"

"Later." Nose flaps opened and closed. "Which puts you in command." The pause spoke volumes. "Sir."

Gods save me from junior officers, Torin pleaded silently and decided it was time to step in. "Begging your pardon, sirs, but General Morris' orders put Lieutenant Jarret in command, regardless. Unless," she added as both men turned, "the VTA takes off again. In the air, as long as Captain Daniels is unavailable, Lieutenant Ghard will be in command."

It was an inarguable position. And there shouldn't have been an argument to start with. Torin only hoped that Ghard was still off-balance from the crash and the casualties and wasn't planning on being a commissioned pain in the ass until rescue arrived.

The next words out of his mouth didn't show much promise. It wasn't what he said, but how he said it.

"Then if Cri Sawyes isn't our enemy, who is?"

"You were probably on the right track when you mentioned the Others," Jarret told him. "They've been reported in this sector—the *Berganitan* is off chasing them. With our ship out of orbit, they could easily drop a small force through the Silsviss defenses."

"Not easssily," Cri Sawyes protested, throat pouch extending slightly.

"Easily," Jarret repeated.

Heads nodded up and down the surface of the VTA.

"And what better way to keep the Silsviss from signing the treaty," the lieutenant continued, "than by setting them up to take the blame for shooting us down. Had Cri Sawyes not seen the missiles, it might have worked."

It fit all the facts and most of the speculation, Torin reflected.

"Or a group of Silsviss from this part of the world, who would logically have weapons that Cri Sawyes from another part of the world wouldn't recognize, shot us down because they don't want their planet to join the Confederation. It won't work that way, but fanatics seldom realize they can't win."

So did that. *And where there's two viable theories,* Torin silently sighed, *there could easily be a third or a fourth.*

Lieutenant Ghard stared up at the di'Taykan lieutenant. "So which is it?"

Jarret snorted, a sound so unlike him it caught and held any wandering attention. "What difference does it make? We're ground combat troops and we're on the ground. We'll handle whatever the situation throws at us."

"Oorah," Torin agreed, just loud enough to be heard and ignored by both officers.

Ghard looked from the lieutenant to Torin and back again. "Good thing you'll have Staff Sergeant

Kerr to hold your *kayt*." he muttered softly as he turned away.

Which was an insult in Human or Krai, but he'd used the Taykan word and a di' phase Taykan would be quite happy to have anyone hold his *kayt* without it affecting anything but his *kayt*. On the other hand, Torin reasoned, intent had to count for something.

"Let it be, Staff."

She hadn't realized she'd stepped forward until the lieutenant's quiet command stopped her. "Yes, sir."

"And, Staff?" He'd moved up beside her, close enough to hold a private conversation while those who'd witnessed him taking command, dispersed.

"Sir?"

"Cri Sawyes may not be our enemy, but I'd appreciate it if you'd keep an eye on him anyway."

"I'd fully intended to, sir. And Lieutenant Ghard?"

"As you said earlier, not your problem."

A few moments later, she found herself beside Cri Sawyes as Lieutenant Jarret spoke with the civilians. The Silsviss' tail cut figure eight patterns through the humid air. "What?"

"Among my people, a challenge sssuch asss that would have drawn blood."

"Which should make it interesting to integrate your people into our military."

"Interesssting?" His tongue flickered out. "You have a way with undersssstatement, Ssstaff Ssser-geant."

"Just part of the job."

* * *

"How close is Hollice's team, Staff?"

"They'll be here in ten, sir."

The lieutenant glanced down at the bags lying on the highest curve of the VTA. "Then we'll wait."

Torin checked the seals and stepped back. Waiting for the absent fireteam had been a fine gesture, but if they were going to reach their first camp before dark—with the Dornagain—they'd have to hurry.

The Rakva had refused the use of a bag and moments before had slipped the weighted body of Aarik Slayir into the mud.

But the Marines didn't leave their people behind.

Lieutenant Jarret spoke the first acknowledgment of loss. *"Fraishin sha aren. Valynk sha haren."*

Beside him, Lieutenant Ghard bit a small piece from the back of his forearm. *"Kal danic dir kadir. Kri ta chrikdan."*

"We will not forget. We will not fail you." It wasn't the first time Torin had been the ranking Human. It never got easier.

"Staff."

But then it shouldn't get easier. She held out her slate and sent the command.

The bags stiffened, then flattened.

The ash fit into small cylinders that slid into measured spaces inside Torin's vest. The cylinders were virtually indestructible. Even if her body was destroyed in combat, the remains of these dead

Marines would still be recovered. She found that strangely comforting.

Calculating how much longer it would be until he could get his *serley* boots off, Kleers took three steps to the Dornagain's one. A collarbone broken in the crash had gotten him assigned to escort duty even though the doc had put things pretty much back together. Since the walking sucked just as much at the front of the column as at the rear, he didn't really mind.

"There are those who say you can judge a civilization by how much respect they grant their dead."

"Really?" He pulled a handful of soft fruit off a vine as big around as his wrist, wiped off a few splatters of mud against his vest, gave them a thorough sniff, and popped them into his mouth.

"If the dead has a large family, an internment on Dornage can take many days."

Kleers took another three steps and reached for some more fruit. "Can't say as I'm surprised."

"How do the Krai treat their dead?"

"We cook them and we eat them."

Thinks Deeply walked in silence for a moment or two. "And that is a sign of respect?" she asked at last.

"Well, I'd have to say that depends on who does the cooking."

NINE

"If the ridge joinsss up with higher ground here . . ." Cri Sawyes drew a curved line in the dirt and then crossed it, ". . . then the buildingsss I sssaw from the air are here." He drew a square toward the end of the crosspiece. "They could be asss near asss three kilometers or asss far asss five."

"If this is a wilderness preserve, why are there buildings at all?" The nose filters the di'Taykan had been forced to wear made Lieutenant Jarret's voice sound flat and angry.

It was a good question, though. Since the lines in the dirt were telling Torin nothing much, she looked up at Cri Sawyes.

"I have no idea."

The lieutenant's eyes narrowed. "Why not?"

"I'm not from around here." His tongue flicked out. When neither the two officers nor the three NCOs squatting around the crude map seemed to appreciate the humor, he expanded his explanation. "Sssome of what we Sssilsssvisss do isss bound by biology and therefore relatively ssstandard planetwide. All our young malesss are sssegregated until hormonal balance isss achieved and they—we—are able to control our aggresssion. Behavior within that sssegregation fallsss within biologically determined parametersss." He glanced around the circle of light, checking that his listeners understood. When no one indicated otherwise, he continued. "There are, asss I'm sure you're aware, many cultural differencesss even within a planet'sss dominant ssspeciesss and I believe that the buildingsss are one of thossse differencesss."

"A useful difference if we can get to them," Sergeant Chou muttered.

Heads nodded around the circle.

"The long-range scanner on the VTA placed the closest Silsviss at thirty kilometers to the northwest." Lieutenant Jarret jabbed a stick into the ground. "Approximately here. As the buildings are southeast of our position, we can assume they're empty." He frowned up at Cri Sawyes. "Could you tell if they were intact?"

"At that altitude and that ssspeed? No. I only sssaw them for a moment."

"But you're sure of where they are?"

"Within reason."

"Staff?"

Torin sat back on her heels and exhaled slowly. All things considered, it could have been worse. That she was fairly certain it was going to *get* worse didn't actually impact on the current decision. "We can't run away from a fight because of the wounded, so I'd prefer to have something solid between me and the enemy if we have to dig in."

"So would I. At first light, send a fireteam out to scout the position."

"Yes, sir." A sudden commotion in the darkness on the other side of the camp pulled Torin's attention.

"That sounds like Hollice," Mike muttered, head cocked to better separate the voices.

The unmistakable sound of a KC discharging brought everyone to their feet.

"Sergeant Glicksohn!"

"On my way, sir." He slapped down his helmet scanner and broke into a run.

Ghard shook off the lethargy he'd worn since abandoning the contaminated VTA to the swamp, dropped his weapon off his shoulder, and jerked the muzzle around toward Cri Sawyes. "Are they attacking?"

"Are who attacking?" Jarret demanded.

"His people!"

"It's not the Silsviss, sir." Torin turned slowly so as not to startle him into pulling the trigger. Tentative friendship aside, they needed Cri Sawyes alive—he'd already proved a valuable resource. "We're close enough to the VTA that all implants are still online and mine registered no perimeter violations."

"Nor did mine." Jarret stepped forward and gently pushed the other lieutenant's weapon down toward the ground. "And the sentry's helmet scanners are slaved to Staff Sergeant Kerr's. If there was anything, anyone advancing toward us, we'd know."

Ghard reluctantly moved his hand away from the

trigger. "Then what was Corporal Hollice shooting at?"

"A snake, Sarge."

"A snake?" Glicksohn repeated.

Hollice nodded and moved aside.

"Holy fuk."

"You know, Sarge, that's just about exactly what I said."

The snake was as big around as a man's arm and over three meters long. A tight beam of light played down its length picked out dull green diamonds bordered in mud brown. Difficult to spot in daylight, it would have been almost impossible to see at night. Almost. The tip of its tail was a brilliant orange, and it had two stubby orange legs a handspan back from the bloody stump where its head had been.

"It must've crawled up from the swamp, Sarge. I heard it slithering." Hollice kicked at the body and shivered when the dead weight merely rocked slightly, absorbing the blow. "I hate snakes."

"Was it poisonous?"

"What's left of it isn't," Ressk answered from the shadows.

There were a number of regulations pertaining to the use of weapons within a camp perimeter. Looking down at the snake, Sergeant Glicksohn considered and discarded all of them. "Nice shot," he said.

The night passed without further incident.

"Sleep well?" Mysho asked, passing a red-eyed

Hollice on her way from the di'Taykan's communal tent to the latrine.

Hollice shoved his fist up against a yawn. "I'm not sleeping until we're off this stinking planet," he snarled.

The Krai and Cri Sawyes had snake for breakfast.

It was midday by the time they finally got clear of the swamp. Torin didn't know who the morning had been harder on: the Dornagain, who'd struggled to keep moving at nearly twice their normal speed, or everyone else who'd had to fight the urge to leave all four of them behind. Even the stretcher bearers had been moving faster, and she'd be willing to swear they'd been passed by the local equivalent of a slug at least twice during the early part of the morning's march.

Having seen to the security of their makeshift camp, Torin stood and looked back down the ridge into the shallow valley that held the swamp. From her vantage point, she could see that dumb luck had dropped the VTA right next to one of only three fingers of higher land. Torin had never been a great believer in luck, preferring to trust in training, preparation, and strong artillery support, but it was impossible to deny the good fortune that had caused them to crash precisely where they had.

Good fortune and crash in the same sentence . . . that's something you don't hear every day.

Running her hand back through damp hair, she tried not to think of how wonderful a bath would feel or how badly they all needed one. Even one of the torrential downpours they'd been pummeled by at every *other* landing site on the planet would have helped, but the sky was almost painfully clear. Designed to repel dirt, the uniforms were surprisingly clean—the Marines wearing them were not. Even with an only Human sense of smell, Torin suspected the di'Taykan had removed their nose filters a little early.

Over the years she'd fought the Others on every sort of terrain imaginable, a number of them significantly more dangerous than the ground they'd just crossed, but she couldn't think of a battlefield that had smelled worse. Fortunately, as the land had risen, the ground had dried and thick stands of sharp-edged grasses had begun to take over from the multilayers of rotting vegetation. By the time they reached what turned out to be the edge of a low plateau, the ground cover had become nothing but grass and an occasional clump of low bushes. Nothing in the immediate area smelled worse than they did.

Which was a mixed blessing at best.

At least the lieutenant's scavenging parties won't have any trouble finding their way back to the VTA. She could see the muddy scar of their crash from where she stood.

And if she could see it, so could anyone else.

Reluctantly replacing her helmet, she flipped down the scanner and pivoted slowly a hundred and eighty degrees. There were no registered species—Confederation species or Other—within the five-kilometer range. Which had to be considered good news although Torin would have preferred to know exactly how close the young males of the preserve had come during the night. Only an idiot would assume they weren't planning to investigate the crash. *And I can guarantee they're making better time than we are.*

Glancing over at the Dornagain, she watched Strength of Arms lick up the last dregs of something they'd reconstituted the moment the lieutenant had called a rest. Finishing, she set the large bowl carefully aside and sagged almost instantly into sleep. From the state of her companions' bowls, it looked as though exhaustion had won out over hunger.

In contrast, the Mictok, affected by neither the mud, nor the heat, nor the distance were chittering cheerfully to themselves just out of range of her translator.

Well, it sounds cheerful anyway, Torin acknowledged. They could have been discussing ways to bisect the politician who'd sent them to Silsviss and was therefore responsible for getting them into this mess.

The Charge d'Affaires and her one surviving aide were grooming matted feathers. Dr. Leor was at the stretchers—every now and then Torin could hear Haysole's voice rising in a question. She hoped it was distance and position muting the doctor's answers and not the seriousness of Haysole's situation. Cri Sawyes had stretched out in the sun and, except for the team on watch, the Marines were stretched out by the stretchers, sharing a thin slice of shade. Lieutenant Jarret had given the di'Taykan specific orders not to wander off in search of a little privacy.

And considering how little privacy a di'Taykan needs . . . Torin cut off the thought before it took her places she didn't have time to go.

Thumbing a dribble of sweat out of her eyebrow, she decided that a few moments in the shade might be a good idea. As she walked past the piles of discarded gear, the pair of boxed emmies caught her attention. The targeting scanner on an EM223 covered between fifteen and twenty kilometers depending on conditions. Unfortunately, since the Silsviss had been considered an ally . . .

"Ressk."

The Krai lifted his head and blinked blearily at her. "Staff?"

"Can you download the data on the Silsviss from your slate into the emmy?"

"Sure." As he rolled up onto his feet, he pulled his slate from his belt. "But it's not targeting data."

"Can you reprogram the scanner to work with it?

That stopped him cold, and a number of the others raised their heads to better follow the exchange.

"You want me to reprogram the scanner?"

"That's right."

"To target an allied species?"

"Yes."

"It's against regs," Ressk reminded her gleefully.

"So's being overwhelmed by a pack of adolescent liz . . . Silsviss," she corrected quickly, "and being beaten to death with sticks. Do what you can and do it quickly. The lieutenant wants us to move out as soon as the report's in on those buildings."

"The lieutenant wants?"

Torin caught his gaze, held it, and slowly lifted a brow. It had taken an implanted learning program to teach her the trick, but she'd never regretted the lost sleep.

Ressk's ridges flushed. "Sorry, Staff. I'll, uh, start working on the emmy."

The fireteam sent out to recon Cri Sawyes' buildings reported both intact and one nearly filled with large cloth bags of grain.

"And water?" Torin asked.

"There's a well, of sorts. Not a lot of water, but what's there is clean. The Krai can probably drink it straight."

Jarret flipped down his own mike. "Is it a position we can defend if we have to?

"It's the best position I've seen since we grounded, sir."

Which wasn't saying much.

Before reprogramming, the targeting scanner found no enemies to lock onto. Had the Others shot down the VTA, they were apparently satisfied with the result and seemed uninterested in finishing the job.

That was the good news.

After reprogramming, it showed Silsviss only 7.3 kilometers away.

"Trouble is," Ressk admitted, around the disassembled piece of the emmy he had clamped between his teeth, "I can't get the program to tell me if that's one Silsviss or a hundred."

"Or if it's the local teenagers or the local army," Ghard added.

"I've already considered that, sir." Torin stepped between the lieutenant and Ressk before Ghard could make a grab for the targeting screen. "The Silsviss military knows what we're capable of; we've been doing demonstrations all over the planet. If that," she jerked her head toward the screen, "was an army, they'd be opening fire with artillery by now."

"You're sure?"

He needed her to be sure, so she showed him her lower teeth, as close to a Krai social cue as she could manage. "Yes, sir. The only thing we have to worry about is how many teenagers are approaching."

"Probably clossse to that hundred," Cri Sawyes announced. When both officers, Torin, and Ressk locked eyes on his face, he lightly tapped the ground with his tail. "The leader of the nearessst pack would never allow hisss sssubordinatesss to examine the crash without him for fear they'd find sssomething that would enable them to take power," he explained. "Nor would thossse sssubordinatesss allow the pack leader to invessstigate on hisss own. They're all coming."

"And quickly." Torin squinted toward the northwest wondering how much dust a hundred Silsviss would raise. "We'll never reach those buildings before they catch up. Are you sure they'll attack?"

"Yesss. As I told you, a good leader throwsss pack

againssst pack, keeping hisss followersss too preoccupied to take him down. However, I think you'll have time; they'll check out the crash sssite firssst."

"Are you sure?" Jarret demanded.

"Not one hundred percent sure, no, but clossse. We are on their ground, as sssoon ass they crosss our path—all eyes turned from Cri Sawyes to the broad, muddy trail that led back into the swamp—they'll know they outnumber usss. They'll believe they can take usss out any time, ssso firssst they'll sssatisssfy their curiosssity about the crash."

"Their weapons?"

"Pre-technology. Only what they can make from materialsss in the pressserve. Once at the buildingsss, we should be able to hold them off indefinitely."

"Then we have to reach the buildings. Staff."

"Listen up, people!" Her voice carried to the far edge of the camp, stopping both movement and conversations. "Pack up and get ready to move. If you brought it in, carry it out!"

"Hey, Staff! What about them?" Mysho pointed downwind at the four immobile heaps of multihued golden fur.

"I'll wake the Dornagain." They were large, they had claws, and for all Torin knew, they woke up cranky. She started toward them, deciding it might be safest to begin with Thinks Deeply.

"Wait!" Ghard blocked her way with an outstretched arm.

Rocking to a stop, she stared down at the Krai. She thought they'd settled that whole chain of command thing. Apparently, Lieutenant Ghard thought otherwise. While she had some sympathy for his insecurities—grounded pilots were all a bit squiggy having been forcibly ejected from their natural element—she had none whatsoever for his timing. Fortunately, the platoon continued readying themselves for the march, paying no attention. "Sir, I have my orders."

"But what if the Silsviss don't go to the crash site first?" he demanded. Without giving her a chance to answer, he jerked his head around to face Jarret and Cri Sawyes. "If they don't go to the crash site and we start for the buildings now, they'll catch us spread out and unable to defend ourselves. Maybe that's what *he* wants."

The emphasis aimed the pronoun directly at Cri Sawyes.

"If the march isss overrun, I alssso will be overrun," he pointed out, his voice as impatient as Torin had ever heard it.

"So? You're one of them!"

"No, I am not." His throat pouch swelled enough to flash a crescent of lighter skin and then deflated. "Firstly, I am an adult and secondly, I am not of their pack." One hand swept down the length of his torso, drawing attention to gray-on-gray markings. "And although I may be of the sssame ssspeciesss, I'm not of their race. I am in thisss with you, Lieutenant Ghard, whether you want me there or not."

"Lieutenant Jarret . . ."

"I've made my decision." Eyes dark, Jarret stared at Ghard a heartbeat longer. Then, without moving his head, he snapped his gaze over to Torin. "You have your orders, Staff Sergeant."

"Yes, sir."

"A word with you in private, Lieutenant Ghard."

Judging from his tone, Lieutenant Jarret was about to give his junior officer a well deserved reaming out.

"What're you looking so approving about?" Mike asked as she passed.

Torin paused and nodded back toward the two officers. Ghard's shoulders had slumped, but as Jarret continued talking, they began to straighten. "I like the way Lieutenant Jarret is taking command."

"As opposed to the way twoies usually take command?" He squeezed his voice into a shrill falsetto. "I'm an officer and I'm in charge, so you've got to do what I say, no matter what!" Then his voice dropped back down into its normal range. "And I'm inclined to think that's better than the overly earnest—if some idiot just out of the college is going to get me killed, I'd as soon not die thinking at least their intentions were good."

"So this time we got lucky."

"We've been lucky before."

"So this time let's keep him alive."

The sergeant sighed. "That's the trick, isn't it?" Head to one side, he looked up at Torin through thick lashes. "If I were a betting man . . ."

She snorted.

Grinning, he continued. ". . . I'd say you liked him."

Just for a moment, she wondered what he knew.

She hadn't given anything away. Had the lieutenant? Then the moment passed. If she wasn't hearing about her unfortunate indiscretion from the other di'Taykan, then no one knew. "I appreciate his ability as an officer . . ." Which she did. ". . . and I appreciate his appearance . . ." Safe enough, after all, she wasn't blind. ". . . but he's very young . . ." Not that age was relevant with a di'Taykan. ". . . and that's as far as it goes." Regardless of how far it had gone.

The grin broadened. "Yeah. That's what I meant. You like him."

Torin rolled her eyes. "I have an idea. Instead of making crude innuendoes . . ."

"You have a dirty mind, Staff.

". . . find us some stretcher bearers and four grunts to hump those emmies." Continuing toward the sleepers, she added, "I don't want to hear any complaints about who's had to carry what the whole way."

"Lieutenant, while my people are not in the habit of violence, we are more capable of defending ourselves than the wounded. If you hold the march to our speed, you delay getting them to safety. Four Marines, one Marine for each of us, will certainly be sufficient protection."

"I appreciate your offer, Ambassador, but it's just too dangerous."

The Dornagain ambassador stroked the back of one hand over his whiskers. "Come now, Lieutenant, it's only three kilometers to the buildings.

Even we can cover that much ground in the time it will take our young Silsviss friends to travel over twice that, pause to examine the VTA, and then come after us."

Jarret frowned. "What do you think, Staff?"

"The ambassador makes a good point, sir. It *is* only three kilometers."

"True. But I don't like dividing our march."

"We will fall behind regardless, Lieutenant, would it not be best to work with the inevitable?" The ambassador smiled down at the Marines, showing an impressive double ridge of teeth. "There is no need for everyone else to be made uncomfortable by the pace we set and no need for my people to be made guilty realizing that."

The lieutenant still looked unconvinced, and they were running out of time to convince him. From where Torin stood, the Dornagain were realists. She appreciated that in a species.

Dr. Leor, who'd been listening to the discussion, arms crossed and feathers flat, suddenly stepped forward. "This one would like the wounded under cover as soon as possible," he announced, "so that this one will be able to perform therapies impossible to attempt while on the move."

All eyes turned to the stretchers and quickly slid away again.

"All right." One hand raised, palm out, the lieutenant surrendered. "The Dornagain can set their own pace, but I'm sending Marines back to deepen your escort as soon they've dropped packs."

"I find that an acceptable compromise."

The doctor fixed the lieutenant with a gleaming black stare. "Then if the decision has been made, this one wonders why there is no forward movement."

"A good question, Doctor. Staff, assign a fireteam to the Dornagain and let's get this . . ."

Torin thought of several less than diplomatic descriptions.

". . . show on the road."

"Yes, sir."

With the stretcher bearers setting the pace, the column pulled rapidly away from the Dornagain and their escort. The ground was dry and firm and the vegetation short enough to make walking easy—especially compared to the mess they'd spent the morning in.

Walking near the front of the column, Jarret leaned down and plucked a stalk of Silsvah grass. "There's a lot of silicate in this," he said, rubbing it between thumb and forefinger.

Given the way it crunched, Torin acknowledged that seemed like a reasonable observation.

"But that doesn't explain why it's so short."

"Grazing, sir."

"Grazing?" he repeated, flicking the pulp away.

"Yes, sir. Pasture fields all over look pretty much like this. It's a dead giveaway when the only plants over a certain height are woody and too tough to chew."

"Too tough for *what* to chew, Staff?" His mouth

opened to check the scent on a breeze and closed again significantly faster. "What the *sanLit* is that?"

Torin grinned as her less efficient sense of smell picked up the only possible odor bad enough to make a di'Taykan who'd just crawled through a swamp, blaspheme. "I suspect your second question is about to answer your first."

As di'Taykan profanity moved down the line, she scanned the area upwind and finally pointed. "There. Under the cloud of insects."

Jarret's eyes darkened, but he shook his head. "I don't see . . ."

"It's a pile of shit, sir. If I can have a closer look, I'll be able to tell for certain if it's out of our grazer."

"How can you tell that from *shit?*"

"Herbivores are fairly distinctive. And if there's something walking around here big enough to drop that, I'd like to find out what I can about it."

"What about Cri Sawyes?"

They could hear the Silsviss behind them, arguing points of the Confederation treaty with the Charge d'Affaires.

"He's not from around here, sir. And he's a city boy, besides."

"Fine. Go." He waved her on, looking so appalled that she couldn't stop herself from snickering as she double-timed over to the pile, pack bouncing against the small of her back. As expected, the insects ignored her. Across the planet, Silsvah insects had ignored every species in the party except the Mictok. The non-Mictok carefully refused to speculate on a reason.

Almost two meters in diameter, the pile was half that high and had definitely come out of the back end of a single herbivore. In spite of the heat it had barely crusted, leaving Torin to believe said herbivore either hadn't gone far or had moved one hell of a lot faster than the cows back home.

Returning to the column, she filled in the lieutenant, adding, "It's heading off due west, about forty-five degrees to our line of march. I think we can safely ignore it for now."

"Well, I'm convinced; staff sergeants *do* know everything."

"You should never have doubted it, sir."

They walked in silence for a few moments.

"Staff . . ."

"I grew up on a farm, and farming and shit are pretty much synonymous."

"A farm?"

She nodded. His voice and expression suggested he'd never even seen a farm. Hardly surprising given his family's rank.

"So why did you leave?"

Torin grinned. "I just told you, sir."

It took him a moment to make the connection. He smiled when he did but refused to drop the subject. "All right, then, why did you join the Marines?"

Their shared past granted him an honest response. Torin wasn't sure why; it had, after all, lasted only one night and was never to be referred to again, but somehow it kept her from throwing out any number of the slick answers she kept ready. "I had a fight with my father, about crop rotations if you can believe it. I was sick of the farm, but it defined his whole life. Next thing I knew, I was standing in a recruiting office having a blood test, and twenty-four hours after that I shipped out. Crop rotations." She sighed. "A truly stupid reason to kill and be killed for."

"Then why do you stay? Why make it a career?"

Again, that shared past kept her from a glib response. And if it didn't entitle him to the part of the truth that involved love and honor, duty and sacrifice, it at least ensured that the truth be present. Because it sounded like he really wanted to know, she thought about it a moment. "Well, sir, it's a dirty job, but someone *has* to do it."

When he nodded, she knew he'd understood the emphasis. Unfortunately, understanding didn't stop the questions. "But why you?"

"Why me?" She considered saying, *Why not me?* and being done with it but found herself saying instead, "I'm good at it. In fact, I'm better at it than most. Parts of it I enjoy. All of it, I feel fulfilled by." This was getting perilously close to the line a single night's sex didn't get to cross. "There's a whole lot of people in this universe who wish they could say the same."

"And no one's shooting at them."

"Maybe that's their problem, sir," Torin said dryly.

"My whole family was career military," he told her after a dozen paces when it became clear she wasn't going to ask. "Every single di'Ka since contact has served the Confederation, and we served at home before that. It was a di'Ka who kept the military from shooting down the First Contact ship and the first di'Taykans to swear into both the Confederation Marine Corps and Navy were di'Ka. One of my progenitors even remained on the Admiralty staff in an advisory role after she shifted to qui'."

"So you're a professional soldier, sir."

"I suppose." He kicked at a purple bloom, beheading the flower and infuriating a large, yellow bug who spat, or possibly excreted something on his boot, and flew off. "All I know is that every time I give an order I can feel them all lined up behind me passing judgment."

"I wouldn't worry about them, sir."

Squinting slightly in the sunlight, the shadow of his hair not quite deep enough to block the glare, he snorted. "You don't have to worry about them. They're not your family."

"Very true, sir," she admitted so seriously he jerked around to face her. "But I don't think *you* should worry about them either."

"And why not, Staff?"

She smiled broadly at him. "Because *they're* not here."

Two paces later, he returned the smile. "And you are?"

"I certainly seem to be, sir."

"Why us? That's what I fukking want to know."

"Why not us?" Hollice shrugged. "Ours is not to question why."

Juan turned to stare at him, lip curled. "Why the

fuk not?" He turned a little farther, just far enough to watch the Dornagain lumbering slowly toward them, and sighed. "How's this for an idea—you bet your next pay packet that I can run around them three times before they make it to this spot."

"How's this for a better idea—you stay here and I'll move on to the next corner."

"Fukking corporals," Juan muttered, as Hollice moved away. He shoved his helmet to the back of his head and scratched at the damp line of exposed hair. "Rest of the platoon's probably nearly to the buildings by now." Squinting along the line of crushed vegetation they were following, he raised his voice as he added. "Probably sitting in the fukking shade."

Although he heard, Hollice didn't bother responding to the heavy gunner's observation. He didn't see the point, it wouldn't get them moving any faster, and it would only encourage more complaints. Given the difficulty of maintaining the same pace as the Dornagain, he kept his team rotating around the four corners of the march. After twenty paces, number one corner moved up to number two, two moved to three, three to four, four to one, and twenty paces later they did it all again. It not only gave them a chance to stretch their legs, but it helped stop terminal boredom from setting in.

"Binti."

She covered a yawn with the back of her fist as he fell into step beside her. "Is it that time again?"

"It is."

"You know Ressk's got his boots off."

Hollice flipped down his helmet scanner and glanced back at the Krai's position. "Can't hurt."

Binti snorted, turned around, and began walking backward. "The Dornagain aren't talking much today."

They both glanced over at their four charges, sunlit highlights rippling from shoulder to haunch as the huge bodies moved slowly forward.

"Maybe they're saving their breath to maintain this speed."

White teeth flashed in a sarcastic smile. "Oh, yeah, baby, *this* is speed."

"Staff Sergeant Kerr, we were wondering if we might ask you a question."

Torin thanked the training that had kept her from shrieking at the sudden, totally silent appearance of the Mictok and turned a polite smile toward the closest eyestalk. "Of course, Ambassador."

"We were wondering about the stretchers."

"The stretchers?"

"Yes. We cannot help but notice that they seem to be nothing more than a pair of lightweight poles with a piece of fabric stretched between."

"Essentially, ma'am, although there are legs snapped down against the underside of the poles and a certain amount of monitoring equipment built into both poles and fabric." More familiar than she wanted to be with the Corps stretchers, she glanced over at the four carried in the center of the column. Although she hadn't done it deliberately—or at least, consciously—she'd been flanking Haysole for most of the march. They had his environmental controls up as high as possible, but he still looked hot and uncomfortable. Shadows encircled his closed eyes, and his lips were so dark they were almost purple. If the ends of his hair hadn't been moving slowly, Torin would have feared the worst.

"We were wondering why."

A little confused, Torin brought her attention back to the ambassador. "Why what, ma'am."

"Why use such simple equipment? Hospitals throughout the Confederation use stretchers that operate by pushing against the planetary gravity. Granted, the Ghazix Generators making that possible would have to be calibrated for each planet you land on, but we're certain you would find them much more efficient than this." One foreleg gestured disdainfully toward the equipment under discussion. Had Mictok the features for it, Torin was certain the ambassador would have been frowning. "A modern stretcher would put none of your people at risk. Once up and running, it could be tethered, leaving all hands free."

"Unfortunately, ma'am, unless they're very large—VTA large—Ghazix Generators can be easily knocked out with a simple electromagnetic pulse, leaving us with an extremely heavy and completely useless piece of scrap."

"The Others would attack the wounded?" Her mandibles snapped together so hard heads up and down the line turned at the sound.

Torin decided not to get into that. Had the elder

races been able to understand war, they wouldn't have needed the Humans, the di'Taykan, and the Krai. And now the Silsviss. "They disable our equipment, ma'am. Just like we disable theirs. The more damage we can do from a distance, the less risk when we get up close and personal."

"So our forces also attack the wounded?"

Not for the first time, Torin realized she probably had more in common with the people she was fighting than the people she was fighting for. Dissembling seemed the order of the day. "The Others use something similar to a Ghazix Generator, ma'am, similar enough that they know how to disable one. We know they know that, so we use stretchers they can't affect because Marines don't leave Marines behind. We use primitive projectile weapons that have to be physically smashed to stop working for the same reason. So do they. Our helmets may contain complicated communication and surveillance equipment, but they're still fully functional as helmets should either or both be knocked out."

"We noticed that you did not answer our question, Staff Sergeant Kerr." She raised a foreleg to prevent an answer. "But we suspect we would be happier not knowing. We are diplomats and we spend much time dealing with the results of the war, but we have never spent so much time speaking to one actually within it." She paused. "Usually, we speak with officers."

"Lieutenant Jarret . . ."

"Is not near the rank we usually associate with."

Under those circumstances, Torin granted her the point.

"We must consider this conversation, but we would like to speak with you again, Staff Sergeant Kerr."

As the Mictok ambassador scuttled back to her companions, Mike moved up into the place she'd vacated, muttering, "Get it off me." And then a little louder. "What were you two talking about?"

Torin snorted. "Reality."

"Yours or hers?"

"Bit of both. Looks like we've arrived safely."

He squinted alone the line of her finger and shook his head. "I can barely see a roof. We've still got lots of time to be descended on and slaughtered."

"If you know something I don't, now would be the time to tell me."

"I don't like this shoot us down and ignore us crap. I keep waiting for the other shoe to drop."

"Did you hear something?"

"No, sir."

The Dornagain's ears swiveled, moving in progressively smaller arcs and, after a moment, he pointed almost due north. That way. I suggest you use your scanner, Corporal."

Hollice screwed the cap on his water bottle, sighed, and crammed his helmet back on. Intellectually, he knew that the environmental controls would keep his head a lot cooler than any breeze, but emotionally, if he was wearing a hat, he felt hot. Flicking down the scanner, he swung around toward the north and froze. "Shit on a stick."

"May I assume from your colloquial expression that there is something there?"

"Something?" He thumbed the controls, trying to bring in a more precise reading. "I bloody well wish it was just something! Unfriendlies! Thirty of them!"

"How far?" Ressk demanded, as the unwelcome information prodded the Marines up onto their feet.

"Between one and one and a half kilometers. Make that point eight and one point three of a kilometer."

Shoving one of the exoskeleton's pins in deeper, Juan muttered, "Fuk, they're fast."

"And we aren't." Raising his scanner, Hollice swept a practiced gaze over their surroundings. "There! Those rocks!" The planet's bones jutted up dark purple to pink out of the green, offering the only protection in the immediate area. Swinging his pack up on his back, he turned to the Dornagain ambassador. "Sir, can your people run?"

"For short distances only."

"To those rocks?"

"I am not certain . . ."

"Well, *I'm* certain we can't protect you against thirty unfriendlies on open ground."

"You make a convincing argument, Corporal. We will run."

To the Marine's surprise, he flung himself forward, body stretching in the air, long, muscular arms extending, knuckles hitting the ground, claws curled under. Then, with a shimmer of golden fur, his body seemed to fold in on itself until his feet dug in just behind his knuckles and he leaped forward again, heavy pack swinging and banging but somehow staying on.

"This is going to destroy my manicure," Thinks Deeply sighed as she followed the ambassador.

"They're not exactly running."

"Fuk it," Juan advised, swinging his weapon from side to side as he worked the kinks out of his shoulders. "It's getting the job done."

Hollice dragged his fascinated gaze off the Dornagain. "Binti, get to the rocks! Take the high ground!"

"On my way." The sharpshooter sped forward, her long legs making short work of the ground the Dornagain had already covered.

"And we're going to?" Ressk asked.

"Try not to get a pointy stick in the back," Hollice grunted as they started to jog after their charges.

"Be a lot fukking safer on the other side of the Dornagain."

"Yeah." Carrying his weapon one-handed, he reached up to flip down his microphone. "I've considered that . . ."

TEN

Only standing beside the buildings did it become obvious that they'd built in a shallow valley.

"An enemy on those hills would have the high ground," Torin muttered. "Not good."

"Not bad," Cri Sawyes corrected. "From here, those hillsss are in easssy range of your weaponsss, but on the hillsss your enemy hasss no weaponsss that will reach you. Againssst greater numbersss, it isss far better to have a wall at your back."

Torin couldn't argue with that.

Both buildings were a single story high. Rectangular, they were set so that the end of one angled off the side of the other with fifteen meters between them on the north and thirty on the south. If there was a reason for their placement, Torin couldn't see it. The walls were made of thick mud bricks coated in a facing layer of mud and were topped with shallow-angled thatch roofs. Inside they'd been divided into thirds, rooms closed off from each other by a surprisingly heavy wooden door. A narrow window high in each room's outside wall let in light. One building, as reported, was empty. The other was filled with large fabric sacks of grain.

In spite of their rustic setting, the waterproof, vermin-proof sacks were clearly the product of a technological society.

"I expect the grain isss brought in for the young malesss," Cri Sawyes explained to Torin, pouring a sample from one hand to the other. "We are, like all of you, omnivorousss."

An eyebrow rose of its own volition. "You intended for them to kill each other, but you don't want them to starve to death?"

"It isss more complicated than that, Ssstaff Sssergeant, but esssentially, yesss."

"So for the packs, this is neutral ground?" When he agreed that it was, Torin sighed. "And we've moved in. That's going to piss them off but good."

Chewing the grain he'd been examining, Cri Sawyes followed her out of the building. "If I underssstand your comment correctly, it does sssum up the problem."

"Maybe we should leave."

"That would be wissse—were there anywhere to go. Asss there isss not . . ."

They joined the lieutenant at the well just as Dr. Leor finished testing the grain.

"As usual, the Krai may eat it although they will need to supplement for the amino acids it lacks."

"And the rest of us?"

"This one thinks not. And now, this one has patients to settle. That building is empty? Then this one will use the farthest room for those already injured and the nearest room to treat those about to be injured."

"And the middle room?" Torin wondered.

"If there is to be fighting," the doctor pointed out disapprovingly, "the middle room will fill quickly enough." He minced off, shouting orders to the two corpsmen as he went.

Torin peered into the well. She could see her reflection shimmering in the darkness about six meters down. "Bad news about the grain, sir."

"We have food, Staff. The bags of grain are a lot more useful as part of our defenses."

"We'll use them to buy our way out of a fight?" she asked, straightening.

"Wouldn't work," Cri Sawyes said shortly. "They will attack regardless."

"We use the bags to build walls between the buildings." Jarret turned and pointed. "There and there. It'll give us one unbroken front with the well safely inside."

"There's certainly enough," Torin admitted, mentally converting the stored grain into walls. "An excellent idea, sir."

"I'm not totally helpless without you, Staff."

"Since you're smiling, sir, I'll accept that ludicrous observation in the spirit in which it was offered."

His smile began to broaden, then cut off completely at the unmistakable alarm sounding from the helmet tucked under his arm. "Staff!"

"On my way, sir. Mysho! Conn! Get your teams and follow me!" As she ran past her pack, she grabbed her own helmet and crammed it onto her head. Without turning, she raced back along the path of trampled vegetation, eight pairs of boots pounding the dry ground behind her.

"They're so fast!" Binti squeezed off another round prone from her vantage point on top of the largest boulder. It bit into the dirt directly behind where a Silsviss had been.

"Where are they fukking going?"

To everyone's surprise, the Dornagain ambassador answered. "They are using the contours of the land. Every hollow, every rise."

"But we went over that land! It's fukking flat!" The slightly louder whomp of the heavy gun sent every Silsviss in sight, out of sight.

"Apparently not so flat as you assume and, with their coloring, they lie like shadows on the ground."

"If they'd clump up a little more, I'd launch a fukking grenade or two at them. I don't need to see them to blow them up. And why do they keep yelling?"

"I believe they are issuing challenges."

"Well, they can just fukking stop."

Sitting back on his haunches behind the largest of the boulders, presenting the smallest target possible, the ambassador studied the Marine curiously. "Later, Private Checya, when we have time, I would like to discuss the psychological determinates in your use of copulative profanity."

Juan shot a short but incredulous glance back over his shoulder. "Yeah. Later. If we fukking survive." His eyes widened as he faced front again. "Incoming!"

Short arrows flung off the ends of whiplike branches filled the air on Juan's side of the boulders. Most fell short, but the rest rattled against the stone like hard rain.

"They gotta stop doing that soon!" Tucked as far into his crevasse as he could get, he winced as one of the arrows bounced off the protruding muzzle of his gun. "How many of those fukking things did they bring!"

"You want to know, you go count them," Binti advised, taking aim at the last of the archers to duck. "Got him!"

"I'm hit!"

The two statements came so close together that for a moment no one knew how to respond. Then Binti squirmed around to peer down the south side of her perch. "Ressk?"

The Krai said something in his own language that could have been either prayer or profanity and added, "A spear knocked my helmet off. My ears are ringing, but I'm all right." Gingerly replacing the helmet, he glanced up at the sharpshooter. "Binti, ignore the arrows from now on. The Silsviss are using them to draw your fire so they can get close enough to toss the heavy artillery at the other two sides."

"Ressk's right," Hollice called, hidden from view by the four Dornagain. "I had spear throwers this side as well."

"Then why didn't you fukking shoot him?"

"You try it, asshole. They throw and duck in the same motion." He wiped one sweaty palm after another against his thighs. "Okay, next time: arrow side ducks, spear sides will spray the whole area."

"Waste of ammunition," Binti cautioned.

Juan snorted. "Show of fukking force."

"I believe you are both correct," the ambassador offered. When the silence stretched, he added, "And what is Private Mashona to do?"

"Fire at anything that shows itself . . . Incoming!"

When the noise died and the varying projectiles had settled one way or another, three Silsviss were down and the rest had fallen completely silent.

"Well, that's a nice fukking change," Juan muttered, squinting out into the setting sun.

Ears ringing, Hollice risked a look back at their charges. "Everyone . . . oh, crap. You're hit."

"Who's hit?" Ressk demanded.

"One of the Dornagain. Uh . . ." He screwed up his face trying to remember the younger male's name. "It's Walks In Thought." He hadn't been able to see much beyond Thinks Deeply's bulk, but he had seen golden fur streaked with red and dark fluid glistening on a raised spear point. "Hey!"

Think Deeply turned at his nudge.

"Is he hurt badly?"

"No. It is a flesh wound only. I am sure it looks worse than it is."

"Speaking of flesh wounds," Binti called down from her vantage point. "One of those lizards just got winged and his buddy's crawling over to him. I've got a clear shot at the buddy."

"Leave it," Hollice told her. "We're not going to shoot them as they tend their wounded."

Moving frighteningly quickly in spite of his awkward position, the crawling Silsviss reached his wounded comrade, ripped out his throat with a vicious sweep of extended claws, and dove into the hollow the dying male no longer needed as bright red arterial blood arced up and sank down.

"I think tend *to* would be the more accurate phrase," Binti observed dryly. "The wounded Silsviss is now dead and buddy has his spot and his weapons."

"Odds are good they don't take prisoners either," Ressk noted.

Exhaling forcefully, Hollice sagged and banged his helmet lightly against the rock. "One more thing to worry about."

"Two more," Thinks Deeply corrected, extending her hand into the corporal's field of vision. Held pincerlike between her claws was one of the arrows. "Do you see this discoloration here?"

An orange/brown stain covered the pointed end.

"Don't tell me . . ."

"I believe the arrows are poisoned."

Her words carried clearly over the new challenges rising around them. "Poisoned?" Binti repeated. She laid her head down on her forearm. "Can this day *get* any worse?"

"Poisoned for lizards doesn't necessarily mean poisoned for us," Ressk reminded them.

"Do you wish to bet your life on that?" Thinks Deeply wondered. It sounded as though she actually wanted to know the answer, that she hadn't been asking a rhetorical question.

Ressk sighed, blowing out his cheeks until his ridges spread. "As long as we're having a lull, why don't I try running it through the sla . . ."

"Incoming!"

"Or not."

Lying prone just below the crest of a long, undulation in the ground—she couldn't bring herself to call it a hill—Torin stared down at the half-dozen boulders and the surrounding Silsviss. Her helmet scanner placed Privates Mashona and Checya and two of the Dornagain, but the rocks prevented her from reading the rest. She knew they were alive, but she'd have felt better had she been able to see them.

Early evening breezes brought with them the sounds of Silsviss shrieking. It might have helped had they known what was actually being said, but Torin's translator held only the common trade language and under these circumstances was completely useless.

"Sounds mocking," Conn observed thoughtfully beside her.

"Mocking?"

"Yeah, you know, *Come out here and try that, you big pissant, I just dare you!*"

On Torin's other side, Mysho snorted. "I think you've been spending too much time with four-year-olds."

"Hey, my daughter does not say pissant."

Torin raised a hand before the argument could escalate. "Taking into consideration all the warnings about not reading familiar motivations into an alien species, blah, blah, blah, I think Conn's right. It does sound like they're taunting."

"Trying to get them to come out from behind the rocks?"

"Very likely."

"So they think we're stupid."

"I suspect no one ever warned them about reading familiar motivations into an alien species."

Mysho and Conn exchanged an identical look over her back.

"So you're saying the Silsviss are stupid?" Mysho said after a moment.

"No. I'm saying that taunting must work on another Silsviss since they're putting so much effort into it."

"Unless it's a case of hope springing eternal," Conn offered.

"Unless," Torin agreed.

The ground between their hiding place and the rocks was superficially flat but actually pocketed with small irregularities into and behind which a single Silsviss could hide. Torin could see four of the enemy quite clearly—three were definitely hittable from where they were, and the fourth was about a fifty/fifty chance. Binti Mashona could have made it a sure thing, but she was currently perched on a boulder almost half a kilometer away. All four shots would have to be taken simultaneously so as not to give warning. And then what?

"Well, Staff, what do we do?" Mysho asked, as though she'd been reading Torin's mind.

"Hollice says they're surrounded and that of the original thirty unfriendlies, nine have been shot, leaving approximately twenty-one continuing to attack."

"Approximately twenty-one?" Conn shook his head in disbelief. "Even Myrna could do the math."

"They've spread out, and I expect they're moving too fast to get an exact count without actually having the Silsviss programmed into the scanners."

"If they've shot nine, it doesn't sound like they need us. At this rate they'll be able to walk out of there before dark."

"Unless this lot decides to stop showing themselves and just hold them there until their buddies arrive." Cri Sawyes had insisted that all the Silsviss would go first to the VTA. Torin couldn't help but wonder if that had been an innocent miscalculation or something more serious. Was he as much on their side as he argued he was?

Drop it. Just drop it. Her instincts said to trust him and she wasn't about to start questioning her instincts now. "All right, here's what we're going to do: we form a line, fire simultaneously at the four we can see, aiming as close as possible without hitting them. That'll get their attention in a big way and with any luck when they see a line of Marines coming over the hill, they'll run like hell."

"And if they don't? Or if they run like hell toward us?"

"Then we shoot them. According to Hollice, their

maximum range isn't much more than twenty meters—ours is considerably more than that. By the time we're close enough to be hit, they'll all be dead. Anchor both ends of the line with the heavy gunners; they can take care of any Silsviss who try to flank us."

"They're that fast?"

"Corporal Hollice's exact phrase was *like shit through a H'san.*"

Mysho pursed her lips, impressed. "That's fast."

"Just tell your heavies they're not to use the flamers under any circumstances." Torin tore a handful of dead grass out from under the living and waved it for emphasis. "I don't want this whole area on fire."

"But what happens if the Silsviss stay hidden?" Conn protested. "We can't hit them if we can't see them. If they lie still until we're close enough for their weapons, it becomes a crap shoot as to who gets their shot off first."

"There's two solutions to that," Torin told him. "First, everyone keeps their scanner down. I know it's a pain when you're moving, but it *will* see things your eyes won't. The closer we get, the harder it will be for the Silsviss to hide. Second, make sure you get your shot off first."

"Yeah, well that's the trick, isn't it," Conn muttered.

"Oh, come on, even Kleers can shoot faster than some primitive."

Torin glanced over her shoulder at the young Krai, who, hearing Mysho use his name, looked up and grinned. A sudden flurry of shots turned her attention back to the problem at hand. "Bottom line, we have to get our people and the civilians out of there before enough Silsviss show up to simply overwhelm them with numbers. Mysho, go left. Conn, go right. I'll hold the center. The two Marines to either side of me will be taking those first four shots across the bow, as it were, so place your people accordingly. Once the shooting starts, make every round count, we don't know how long we're going to have to make our ammunition last. Remember there's nine of us and only twenty-one . . ." Another shot rang out from the rocks. ". . . twenty of them." Reaching up, she snapped her helmet mike down against the corner of her mouth. "I'll let Corporal Hollice know we're on our way."

Rather than have her taken out by friendly fire, Hollice rearranged the Dornagain and had Binti relinquish her perch for a crevice by Juan. "When the Silsviss hear an attack on the south, they're liable to attack us on the north—they'll think our attention is fixed away from them, and if they've got any brains at all, they'll want into the shelter of these rocks."

"If they have any brains at all, they'll run away," Binti muttered, settling herself in her new position.

"Yeah?" Juan looked up from checking a wrist point and grinned. "If I'd had any brains, I'd have been a fukking beautician like my mama wanted."

"Look alive, people!" Hollice's voice bounced from boulder to boulder. "The cavalry's on its way in."

Binti shot a questioning glance toward the heavy gunner. "Cavalry?"

Juan shrugged, a minimalist movement to keep the exoskeleton from turning it into something more destructive. "I don't know what the fuk he's talkin' about most of the time either."

"All right, Marines, keep alert. If you spot an unfriendly running away from you, let him. Otherwise, shoot." Torin wanted to say shoot to wound but given Hollice's recent report of Silsviss first aid, she didn't see much point. While she had no desire to be a part of the Silsvah culling program, neither did she want to leave injured teenagers scattered about waiting in pain for their comrades to return and finish them off. Which meant they'd have to take care of the wounded. Since she had no idea of how they were supposed to manage that, better there weren't that many wounded to take care of.

If war was fun, everybody'd be doing it.

And this action was only a sidebar to the actual war. If they'd been shot down anywhere but over the preserve . . . For a moment, Torin wondered if maybe the whole incident *was* a part of the Silsvah culling program, then she dismissed the thought. Now wasn't the time.

"Keep your scanners down and watch out for Silsviss staying hidden until we're on them and they can use their spears," she continued, barely vocalizing into her helmet mike. "Remember that you're just as dead if they kill you with a pointy stick."

She felt a smile run both ways down the line of prone Marines—strange things were funny right before combat. "Rise on three. Make those first four close enough to scare the piss out of them. Wait for my command before moving ahead. One . . ." Knees brought up under the body.

"Two."

Weight back off her elbows, onto her legs.

"Three."

The nine Marines stood as one and took two long steps to the crest of the rise. Three of the warning shots sprayed dirt over wedge-shaped heads. The fourth went through a tail unexpectedly moved.

The enraged shriek of pain attracted the desired attention.

All four leaped up and raced toward the Marines.

They were just as fast as Hollice had described.

Like shit through a H'san.

They died long before they were close enough to do any return damage.

"Marines, at the walk, advance."

The line move forward.

When the second attempt to flank the line failed—the shot that stopped it coming from within the jumble of rock—the Silsviss began to realize they couldn't survive the fight. Instead of attacking, they stood and shrieked, banging their spear butts against the hard ground.

To Torin, it sounded as if they were shouting, *"Come on, I dare you!"*

"I could take them all out," Binti muttered, lifting her weapon and miming the shots. "Bang. Bang. Bang."

"Staff says to leave them alone," Hollice reminded her.

"I don't see why."

"Perhaps because the Silsviss are our allies," the Dornagain ambassador suggested calmly—in spite of the volume necessary to be heard above the surrounding shrieks of defiance. "Although," he admitted when heads craned and all eyes turned toward him, "the treaty is not yet signed."

The line moved closer to one of the standing Silsviss.

Still shrieking, he dropped the spear and slid a slender branch out of the open weave of his harness.

They've learned we won't shoot if they don't attack and they're using that to lure us into range of their arrows. Time for a new lesson. Torin put a shot into the ground between the archer's legs.

His tongue flicked out. He pulled an arrow out of the weave and set it in the end of the whip.

Wondering if he were brave or stupid, Torin shot him.

Two of the shriekers finally broke and ran.

When their companions saw they were allowed to retreat, five more joined them.

The Marines were now on the south side of the rocks, the Silsviss on the north.

"Listen up, everyone—we're going to form a large half circle around the north side of those rocks so that when the Dornagain break cover, they'll have as much protection as possible. We'll break the line to my right, outside positions move in, double time. Now."

As military maneuvers went, it could have gone better.

Moving in closer to the rocks, his eyes on the enemy, Kleers tripped over a dead Silsviss who turned out not to be. As he staggered, fighting to regain his balance, he took a tail blow across the backs of both knees. Falling, the Krai fired and missed and had no chance to get off a second shot before the Silsviss was on him, pinning him to the dirt with one set of claws, slashing with the other.

A moment later, Kleers kicked the headless corpse away and spat a mouthful of blood into the dirt.

"Any of that yours?" Torin asked, extending a hand. His med-alert hadn't gone off, but the chips had been set to trip only when they read too much damage to carry on. Combat soldiers learned early there was a whole lot of hurt between damage and *too much* damage.

"Some," Kleers admitted sounding more confused than in pain. "My shoulder . . ."

As he stood, the right sleeve of his dress uniform tunic fell away in three perfectly parallel lines that stopped at the edge of the combat vest. Three slices of shirt fell away under the tunic. It quickly became apparent that the blood soaking the remains of his sleeve was his.

Torin sat him back down again. "Get a field dressing on that! The rest of you, fill in the line."

Encouraged by the success of one of their number, another two Silsviss charged and died.

The remaining eight retreated . . .

. . . and then followed Marines and Dornagain all the long, slow way back to the buildings. Lightning-fast charges that ended before they came close enough to be considered an attack wore at the defenders' nerves. But worst of all, was the noise; singly and collectively, the shrieking never let up.

"Ssso. Sssuccesss."

"Did you do that on purpose," Torin muttered, as the extended sibilants cut a painful path from ear to ear.

Cri Sawyes stopped and looked around. When he saw there was no one else in the immediate area, he frowned. "Do what?"

"Never mind." Guards had been posted, the injured and the civilians were safely inside, and the grain-bag walls were going up as quickly as the Marines could build them. She winced as the background shrieking hit a new high note. "Do you think they'll stay out there all night?"

"No. I don't underssstand the actual language, but it'sss clear they're building up their courage for an attack."

"But there's only eight of them."

"I know."

Standing with one hand on the top of the northern barricade, she listened to the night and tried without much success, to think like a hormonally hopped up teenage lizard. "We have weapons on both roofs. We're covering all approaches."

"Yesss. But they are fasst and very hard to sssee in the dark. They don't know about your ssscanners, so they'll asssume they can ssslip in, ssslit a few throatsss, and ssslip out, none the wissser."

On cue, the lookout on the north end of the west roof shouted, "Lieutenant! There's a Silsviss approaching from the north. Damn, he's fast!"

Cri Sawyes' tongue flickered out at the suspicious expression on Torin's face. "It isss what I would have done," he explained. Then he sighed as her expression remained fixed. "Would I have sssaid anything if I'd wanted them to sssucceed?"

"I suppose not," Torin allowed.

"You could consssider it a lessson in our tacticsss."

"True."

"Or a warning."

"All right!" She raised her hand. "I get it. You've made your point."

Crossing the compound on the run, drawn by the lookout's shout, Jarret slid to a stop at Torin's side. "Can you stop him without killing him?" he called toward the roof.

"I can try, sir."

"Do it, then."

"Yes, sir!"

"Without killing him?" Torin asked softly.

"We're trying to make the Silsviss our allies, Staff Sergeant." He glanced over at Cri Sawyes as he spoke. "I'm not playing whatever game the Others think they set up when they brought us down in here."

"You believe it was the Others?"

"Don't you?"

She shrugged, unwilling to commit.

Two shots rang out, so close together the echoes back off the hill overlapped into one sound.

"He's down, sir! About fifteen meters off the end of the building."

"Corpsmen!"

"Sir?"

"Let's go!"

Jarret vaulted over the grain bags and paused on the other side. "You coming, Staff?"

"Yes, sir." She contemplated saying something like, *"You're in command, sir. You shouldn't be wandering around outside the perimeter in the dark with the enemy nearby."* but since he knew that and was out there anyway, there didn't seem to be much point. "Corporal Conn! Bring your team!"

"I don't think that's necessary, Staff."

"I don't want to lose you, sir. It'd look bad on my record."

They found the injured Silsviss without any difficulty but approaching him was another matter.

"Watch his tail! He's got some kind of thorny vine wrapped around it! Damn it, Conn! I said, watch his tail! Are you all right?"

"He caught my pants, Staff. Didn't break the skin."

Hissing through his teeth, one leg flopping uselessly by his side, the young Silsviss lashed out with the spear he still held, missed, and barely stopped himself from toppling over.

"Calm down, kid." Jarret held out his empty hands in a gesture common to all tool using species. "We want to help you. We'll patch you up and send you back to your friends, and you can tell them we're not the bad guys."

We'll send you back to your friends, and you can attack us again, Torin thought, but she didn't say it because it looked as if the lieutenant's approach was working.

His weight on the spear, the Silsviss sank slowly to the ground, staring up at the surrounding Marines through half-lidded eyes. He roused himself to make a couple more halfhearted feints but Lieutenant Jarret kept talking, quietly and calmly, and finally the spear slid from slack fingers.

"All right, corpsmen, move in."

Breathing rapidly, he ignored them as they put the stretcher down by his good side.

When they bent to lift him, he attacked.

One of the corpsmen was thrown like a rag doll into two of the Marines. The other screamed.

As Torin moved to get a clear shot, the lieutenant fired. The Silsviss flew back missing half his head, the corpsman still impaled on his claws.

Grabbing the cooling wrists, Torin yanked the claws straight out of their entry wounds, took a look at the extent of the abdominal damage and didn't like what she saw. "Get him in to the doctor. Now!"

With the other corpsman staggering alongside the

stretcher, Conn's team raced toward the nearer of the two buildings. The doctor met them at the door.

When it closed, and she could hear the sound of expletive-laced explanation rising in the compound, she turned to the lieutenant.

He was staring down at the body, still holding his sidearm. di'Taykan didn't have the best night sight, but there was starlight enough to for him to separate the shadows and the dead.

"I've never actually . . ." he began, then shook his head instead of finishing.

"I know." The troops knew as well. Torin could feel the weight of them watching, waiting to see how their young officer would handle his first kill, but they were far enough away that she could cover for him if she had to.

When he finally looked at her, his eyes were so dark she could see no color at all. "I had the only clear shot."

"Yes, sir. You did." And considering that it was a partially blocked, moving target, it had been one hell of a shot, too. But he wouldn't be ready to hear that for a while.

"Do you . . ." A deep breath and he tried again. "Do you ever get used to it?"

Torin looked down at the body, then up at the lieutenant. She could see that he half wanted her to lie, but this was part of the job also so she told him the truth. "Yes, sir, I'm afraid that you do."

He held her gaze with his for a long moment, drew in a deep breath, and let it out slowly, almost as if it was his first since pulling the trigger. "Let's get back inside, Staff. I have a feeling it's going to be a long night."

"Yes, sir."

Before going over the grain bags, he paused and turned to look down the way they'd come. The shrieking, silenced by the shots, had started up again.

Torin waited, wondering what he saw.

"Staff Sergeant Kerr."

"Sir."

"Tell the lookouts shoot to kill."

The lieutenant's feeling had been wrong. It was a short night. Before the first moon had risen a handspan above the horizon, all eight of the Silsviss who'd attacked the Dornagain's escort, were dead.

The grain-bag walls were finished at almost the same time the Silsviss were. Torin went over watch schedules with the sergeants, made sure everyone had taken the time to clean their weapons, sent all nonessential personnel to bed, then went for a walk around the perimeter.

She found herself standing at the same place at the north wall staring out into the now quiet night. She could almost understand about the attacks on the buildings. What she was having difficulty getting her head around, was the reaction to the overwhelming odds of the afternoon.

"You look troubled, Ssstaff Ssergeant."

One moment she was alone, the next Cri Sawyes was standing beside her.

"You're lucky I heard you coming," she growled.

She hadn't, but she wouldn't give him the satisfaction. "If you have a minute, I'd like to hear your take on what happened today."

"The attacksss?"

"No, during the rescue of the Dornagain."

"I sssee." He leaned against the wall and stared out into the darkness. "It hasss been a long time sssince I wasss that young, Ssstaff Sssergeant, but I will give you what enlightenment I can."

She mirrored his position. "When we fired those first four warning shots, we were giving them a chance to get away. Why did they charge us?"

"Becaussse they sssaw your arrival asss a challenge and a challenge mussst be anssswered."

"But by then they *knew* we could kill from a greater distance than they could. What were they thinking?"

"They weren't thinking." Cri Sawyes dug a thumb into the top bag of grain, pushing into the yielding surface. Torin watched him, and waited. "At that age," he said at last, "we merely react. A ssstrong leader can make usss do anything. I sssussspect that the attack this afternoon wasss a way for the local leader to get rid of hisss worssst troublemakersss."

"He was hoping they'd be killed?"

"Yesss. He probably goaded them into attacking what he knew to be a sssuperior force. He couldn't have known that a sssmall group would have ssseparated. Had my people won thisss afternoon, the ressstructuring of the pack would have kept them from attacking the ressst of usss for three or four daysss."

"A mixed blessing at best," Torin observed.

His tongue flickered out. "Yesss. Also, I ss-sussspect that the local leader wasss keeping the troublemakersss from sharing in whatever advantage he acquired at the VTA."

"There's no advantage he can acquire. Everything we left behind is locked up tighter than a H'san's grandmother."

"And that'sss tight?"

"Yeah. That's tight." She dug a hole of her own into the grain. "If a strong leader can make you do anything . . ."

"We'd be quite an addition to the Othersss' forcesss, wouldn't we? If the Othersss are asss unprincipled as your Confederation diplomatsss ss-suggessst . . .

"Trust me, they're the bad guys."

". . . imagine what they could do with an army of our young."

"Thanks, but I'd rather not." Out in the darkness, vegetation rustled, and a small something squeaked its last. "I take it this means you, your people, were definitely going to join up?"

"Trust *me*, Ssstaff Sssergeant . . ."

When she turned to face him, she could see the stars reflected in his eyes.

". . . we want our young to die no more than you do."

ELEVEN

Torin lay, barely breathing, wondering what had roused her. One moment she'd been dreaming about leading a charge on the Confederation's Parliament and replacing the politicians with the remarkably lively bodies of all the Marines who'd died under her care—her subconscious had never been particularly subtle—and the next she was wide awake. She could hear the quiet breathing of the surrounding sleepers and smell the faintest trace of the Dornagain, two rooms away. Opening her eyes, she stared up past the rafters into the thatch. A small, dusty green lizard, almost the exact same color as the Silsviss of the area, stared unblinkingly back.

After a moment, its tongue flickered and it scurried out of sight.

She wasted another moment working out the odds it might be spying for the Silsviss, and when they turned out to be too small to bother about, tongued her implant.

0513

It didn't seem worth going back to sleep for another seventeen minutes—not when she'd managed to grab nearly two full hours.

The morning had dawned surprisingly cold with a dense fog that hung close to the ground. Stroking her environmental controls to a warmer setting as she stepped outside, Torin made her way to the well where a di'Taykan, stripped to the waist, had his head in a bucket of water. As much as she appreciated the view, she couldn't prevent an involuntary shiver.

It wasn't until he emerged from the bucket, water dripping from lilac hair, that she realized it was the lieutenant—looking more cheerful than he had in days.

"Good morning, Staff. Looks like we finally got some decent weather."

"Yes, sir. You're up early."

"I thought the platoon would be impressed if I was already up and working when they woke."

"Really?"

"No, not really." He flashed her a smile. "I couldn't sleep." The smile faded. "I kept thinking about all the things I still have to do before we're attacked."

Since he'd probably been thinking about that as well, Torin let it go since he'd clearly come to terms with the order he'd had to give. *One down, and one to go.* And sending others out to die was the harder order of the two.

Knowing what she'd see, she glanced around the compound. There were two Marines stationed on the roof of each building and the walls between were waist-high and a half a meter thick. They had food, they had water, they certainly had more artillery than the enemy. They had a medical station set up, and an actual doctor on site. "There's nothing more you can do, sir. Nothing but wait."

"I know. And it's strange, in spite of what happened last night, waiting's still the hard part."

Torin found herself taking a step forward, aching to physically comfort him. Fortunately, she recognized the impetus. "Sir. Your masker."

It was lying on the side of the well.

"My . . ." He followed her line of sight. "Oh. Sorry, Staff."

He sounded more amused than sorry.

At least he's got his good mood back, Torin thought, waiting until the masker was safely hooked to the lieutenant's belt before she drew another breath.

"I thought there'd be no problem, what with being outside and the lower temperature and, well, being alone."

"Understandable, sir."

"Of course you'd be more susceptible, having been exposed . . . that time that didn't happen," he finished sheepishly, his original thought stopped cold by her expression. "So, according to the emmy's targeting scanner, the Silsviss are only just leaving the swamp. There's a chance that the authorities will find us first."

"The authorities?" Not the *Berganitan*. If the ship had returned to a planetary orbit, they'd have already been found.

"The Silsviss authorities." His hair emerged from its rubdown flying off in all directions, and it took him a moment to bring it under control. "Even if Captain Daniels didn't get off a message they could read, they certainly know we're missing and, as primitive as their planetary satellite system is, they must know where we are by now."

"Unless the Others drew the *Berganitan* off so that they could slip in and overthrow the planetary governments unopposed."

"I think the Silsviss would oppose, don't you?"

"Yes, sir." She firmly squelched an unvoiced offer to dry his back. "But that would leave them too busy to come for us. And if we were shot down by a non-Confederation faction within the Silsviss . . ." He shook his head, but she continued, still unwilling to elevate one theory over the others. ". . . there'll be fighting going on as well."

"So no matter how we look at it, no rescue."

"Not this morning, sir."

Draping his towel over the side of the well, he shrugged into his shirt and moved his masker from his belt back to his throat. "You know, Staff . . ." He shot her a sideways glance from under long lashes. ". . . I was actually enjoying the morning until you showed up."

"Sorry, sir."

"But I'm sure it's part of your job to keep my feet on the ground, to examine all possibilities, to keep me from unwarranted optimism."

A di'Taykan in a teasing mood was damned near impossible to resist. In spite of herself, she smiled. "Yes, sir."

"You're doing a good job."

"Thank you, sir." She fell into step beside him as he carried the bucket toward the north wall. "Uh, Lieutenant, where are we going?"

"I'm just dumping my wash water, Staff. There's no point in making mud inside the compound."

He had a point, Torin acknowledged, especially since anticipation of an attack would place a second latrine pit inside the barricades.

Angling away from the place he'd gone over the wall the night before, Jarret braced his legs against the grain bags and threw the water from his bucket.

It arced through the air, hit the ground, and . . .

A brilliant flash of light erupted into the northeastern sky, visible in spite of distance and in spite of fog. A few seconds later, a sharp crack of sound split the morning, then died to a low, lingering rumble felt in bones and teeth more than heard. The silence that followed came without any ambient noise at all. The dawn songs of birds and insects that had been providing a background so constant it could be ignored, were gone.

Drifting down from the roof of the west building came an incredulous, "What the fuk was that?"

"The self-destruct on the armory," Torin answered grimly.

Hair flat against his head, Jarret turned wide lilac eyes toward her. "Our armory? On the VTA?"

"Yes, sir." If there was another armory in the immediate area, no one had told her about it.

He stared into the distance, as though waiting for debris to come falling through the fog. "I guess we won't be making that supply run," he said at last.

Half expecting some kind of angry outburst, Torin was impressed by his calm. A calm officer was a good thing for a besieged Marine awakened by an explosion to see. "We'd have had to run *through* the Silsviss," she pointed out, her tone matching his.

"Very true." The ends of his hair started to lift. "Well, let's look at the bright side, shall we? At least we know they didn't get through the security protocols. And that explosion very likely took out a number of Silsviss. If it took out enough, they might think twice about attacking."

"You told me that the tracking scanner on the emmy put most of the Silsviss on their way out of the swamp," Torin reminded him. "The VTA would have contained all but the vertical blast, so I expect it deafened more than it killed."

A tentative birdcall broke the silence. And then another. A moment later, the morning refilled with sound. A moment after that, Torin winced as her implant went off-line. The techs insisted it wasn't supposed to hurt. What did they know?

"Did your . . . ?"

"Yes, sir."

"Do you think they left someone behind? Told him to keep trying while most of them started out after us?"

"No, sir." From what Torin understood about pack leadership, she didn't think that was likely. "Perhaps someone, thinking to challenge the leader, went back on his own. Even one of our weapons would significantly change the balance of power."

"Then it's a good thing they didn't get one, isn't

it?" As they turned together to face a compound full of questioning Marines, he added, "And you were right, Staff. We should have blown it ourselves."

"Thank you, sir."

Of course she'd been right. She only wished she felt better about hearing him admit it.

"They will try to draw you out into battle, to goad you into attacking them out where their numbersss will give them the advantage even over your weaponsss." Cri Sawyes stared out over the north wall, his head slightly cocked. Torin wondered what he could hear. Was he listening to the small clump of Marines grouped around the emmy or beyond that to the approaching battle?

"Cri Sawyes, regardless of who or what shot us down, these adolescents are not the enemy. We have every intention of fighting a purely defensive battle and causing as few casualties as possible."

Wearing her best noncommittal expression, Torin turned to face the lieutenant and realized he sincerely meant what he'd just said. The deaths of eight individual Silsviss didn't add up to actually being in combat and he still had no firsthand experience of how fast good intentions got blown to kingdom come. She kept her own opinion on the type of battle they'd be fighting locked firmly behind her lips. He'd learn soon enough; she had no desire to rush the lesson. Provided that they weren't endangering her Marines, she always found it a little sad when second lieutenants lost the last of their shiny, untried ideals.

Cri Sawyes had been a soldier. "Thossse are good

intentionsss, Lieutenant Jarret, but asss we sssay where I come from, it takesss two to *haylisss*, and I doubt the pack will cooperate." He continued watching the crest of the low purple hill to the north. "If you won't come out, they will come in after you."

"But we have an entrenched position . . ." Jarret's gesture took in the buildings, the compound, and the black-clad Marines filling it with shadow. ". . . and they have only primitive weapons."

"Yesss. Ssso?"

"And it's the same entrenched position they threw themselves at one at a time last night, isn't it?"

"Yesss."

"They won't be thinking, sir, they'll be reacting." Torin echoed Cri Sawyes' explanation for the lieutenant. "As far as they're concerned, we're another pack. The reaction to another pack is to defeat it. Our weapons alone are a prize worth the risk. If taken, they'd allow the pack to rule the preserve."

"Then we'll have to see they aren't taken."

All officers liked to state the obvious. In Torin's experience it was a habit they never outgrew. "Yes, sir."

His gaze shifted out to the Marines at the emmy, and Jarret exhaled loudly. "Looks like you were right again, Staff."

Again, he states the obvious.

"The sun's been up for three hours, and there's no sign of the authorities. Any authorities."

The fog had quickly burned off with the rising of the sun, and the temperature had begun to rise. The early damp had long since dried. There was already a promise of scorching heat in the still air. Torin suspected that as the day progressed, the di'Taykan would be pushing the limits of their environmental controls.

"The fact that we have not been ressscued . . ." When both Marines turned to glare, his tongue flicked out and he amended his statement. ". . . sssay rather dissscovered, leadsss me to believe it wasss not the Othersss who shot down the VTA but a disssident group of my own people. That would mossst certainly keep the variousss governmentsss at each othersss' throatsss for daysss."

"Based on what I've seen, I don't think your people have the technology to take us out."

The tongue flicked out again. "And you think you sssaw everything?" He raised a hand to cut off the lieutenant's answer. "Of courssse you don't. My apologiesss." When the lieutenant graciously allowed that the apology would be accepted, he continued. "I, perssonally, am more curiousss about why the pack hasssn't arrived. At that age, we *run* to a fight."

"Run to a *fight?*" Torin repeated, changing the emphasis. "Teenagers." She closed her teeth on what usually followed when sergeants got together to complain about new recruits. *Can't live with them, can't use them for target practice.* From the sound of it, they'd be using them for target practice today.

"Yesss. Teenagersss. Ssstill, they should be here by now."

"The explosion probably slowed them."

"Perhapsss." But he turned to stare over the north wall again.

"Sir! We have a reading!"

The ambient noise in the compound dropped as Binti yelled in the results from the emmy.

This was it. The beginning of it, at any rate. Torin felt her heart begin to beat a little faster as Lieutenant Jarret asked, "And?"

"The Silsviss are just under two kilometers away."

"How many of them?"

"Just a minute, sir." Binti reached down and gave Ressk a shove.

The Krai glared at her, then turned his attention back to the data in the emmy's targeting scanner. He frowned as he used his slate to work the program, shook his head, and stood. "I can't tell, sir. But since there's Silsviss reading at both two and three kilometers, I'd say there's more than a few."

"I'd say there's a whole fukking lot," Juan muttered.

Haysole was awake and smiling when Torin walked over to his corner of the infirmary although she suspected that had more to do with Corporal Mysho's having just left than with *her* arrival. According to one of the corpsmen, everything but the di'Taykan's legs worked fine.

"Morning, Staff. I hear about three million underaged liz . . . Silsviss are about to come bouncing down on our heads.

"That's an exaggeration, Private. No more than two million, tops."

"Is that all?" He snorted. "Well, you won't be needing me, then."

"Good thing, since the doctor seems to think I should give you another day off." She squatted down beside his stretcher, one hand on the metal edge for balance, the other resting lightly on the back of his wrist. His skin still felt warm even though the temperature within the thick-walled building was noticeably cooler than outside in the compound. When she checked his environmental controls, they'd been set almost as low as they'd go. "How are you feeling?"

His smile crumbled a little at the edges and long fingers plucked at the hem of his tunic. "Like I'd give almost anything to get up and clean a crapper." The pause wasn't quite long enough for Torin to reply, even if she'd known what to say. "Or these days I guess it'd be digging a latrine."

"I don't think so, Private. We need that latrine dug before the Silsviss attack, and you," she added wryly, "are a galaxy-class master in the fine art of looking like you're working when you're really doing piss all."

"It's a skill," he admitted smugly, looking pleased with himself.

Torin snorted and held her hand by his head. She didn't bother hiding her relief when the turquoise hair lifted and stroked gently across her palm.

"The lieutenant was in earlier."

"Was he?"

"Yeah." Turquoise eyes sparkled. "He's a cutie. Even if he is from a high family—talk about people doing piss all. He asked me what he could do to make me feel better."

Which, given the patient, was either very naive or very di'Taykan. "And you made an explicit suggestion."

"Oh, yeah."

"And he said?"

"Later." When Torin raised an eyebrow at him, Haysole gave her a look of wounded innocence. "I wouldn't lie to you, Staff." Wounded innocence became something more salacious. "Ask him yourself."

"I don't think so." She touched her slate to the stretcher, downloading the data on his condition. "And if the lieutenant is coming back later, I'd better go so you can rest up."

"You think I'll need it?"

He's only speculating, Torin reminded herself as she straightened. *He can't know.* She flashed him her best *staff sergeants know everything smile* as she moved away. "Not as much as *he* will."

Neither of the other Marines who'd been injured in the crash of the VTA were as coherent. Torin spent a moment with each, discovered the lieutenant had spoken to them as well, and then moved on to Captain Daniels. The pilot still hadn't regained consciousness and according to the stretcher, her vital signs were barely holding. If not for the near constant attention of her aircrew . . .

Torin chased the thought away. This was a diplomatic mission. No one was supposed to die. She thought about saying something to Aircrew Trenkik who was spooning a gruellike food into the captain's open mouth and then massaging her throat until she swallowed, but she'd long ago overcome the need to speak meaningless comfort in order not to feel helpless in the face of inevitability.

Her helmet chirped a summons, so she headed for the door.

"Staff?" When he saw he had her attention, Haysole touched the masker at his throat. "Remember your promise."

"If I die, take off the masker before you bag me."

She could have reminded him that she hadn't actually agreed. Instead, feeling the weight of the four cylinders over her heart, she said only, "I remember."

This time, she found the lieutenant standing with six or seven other Marines by the south wall near the site of the protected latrine.

"Make sure that dirt pile is away from the wall," she said, pausing. "Let's not be building access ramps for the enemy."

"How about I dump it there, Staff?" Stripped down to a sleeveless vest over her exoskeleton, Chandra Dar pointed a heavily laden shovel back into the compound.

"There's fine."

"How deep do you want it?" the heavy gunner asked, dumping her load and driving the blade in for another.

Torin glanced over her shoulder, but the lieutenant had his attention firmly fixed on something outside the wall. "How deep were you told to dig it?"

"Not as deep as the water table."

"Then I suggest you follow the lieutenant's orders."

Dar looked down at dirt so dry she couldn't have got the blade into it without her augmentation and then up at the staff sergeant. "Well, yeah, but he's . . ."

"Your commanding officer."

Golden-brown skin blanched at Torin's tone. "I didn't mean anything against him, Staff."

"Good." A gesture suggested the heavy gunner return to work. Torin watched another shovel load removed, then continued toward Lieutenant Jarret. It wasn't difficult to fill in the end of Dar's protest.

Yeah, but he's never done this before and you have.

Heading into combat, that sort of attitude was going to crop up a lot more often. With some justification. It hadn't mattered while they were marching up and down before various governments but no one wanted to die because a brand new second lieutenant gave the wrong order. *So I'll just have to see that he gives the right orders. After all, if the job was easy, everybody'd be doing it.* "You wanted to see me, si . . ."

The ground under her boots trembled.

"What was that?"

"That," Jarret told her, smiling, "was what I wanted you to see."

She followed his pointing finger, moving close enough to the wall so that the eastern building didn't cut off her line of sight. "That's . . ."

"Your herbivore. I apologize for ever doubting your ability to correctly identify a pile of shit."

"Thank you, sir," she answered absently, her gaze locked on the creature chewing a path through the vegetation. From the lines of drying mud high on its haunches, it had recently came up out of the swamp. "That thing's bigger than our sleds."

"It'sss a *ghartivatrampasss*." Cri Sawyes announced, joining them. "I've heard of them, but thisss isss the firssst I've ever ssseen. Video doesssn't do it jussstice."

"Couldn't possibly," Torin agreed.

A glistening purple tongue emerged from a lipless mouth, wrapped around a square meter or so of stems, and scooped the grasses up into its mouth. The background rasp Torin had assumed was insects moved to the foreground and was identified as the sound of the silicates being ground between whatever served the creature for teeth. The ground trembled as it took another step, then it continued to placidly feed, ignoring its audience. In spite of its size, it was a performance that could only hold the attention for so long.

"All right." Torin turned to the cluster of Marines. "Who told you lot to stop working?"

By the time the *ghartivatrampas* had moved out of sight behind the west building, only Cri Sawyes was still watching it. "I've been told they're extremely tasssty," he explained, when Lieutenant Jarret asked him why.

"Tasty?" Lieutenant Ghard looked intrigued. "I'll just go have another look, then." He glanced over at Jarret who waved him off.

"That's the most enthusiasm he's shown about anything since Captain Daniels was wounded," Jarret murmured as they watched the Krai run into the building where a window would give him a framed view.

"I believe he wasss jussst asss enthussssiassstic about taking me apart," Cri Sawyes mentioned offhandedly.

"Staff Sergeant Kerr, have you a moment?"

"Of course, Ambassador Krik'vir." Torin stood and snapped her slate back onto her belt. She'd made her preparations. If the Silsviss didn't attack, soon she'd have moved right through anticipation and into annoyance. *And an annoyed staff sergeant is an ugly thing.* "How can I help you?"

"Actually, we wished to know how we could help you. We have never been in a battle before and we are uncertain of how to behave."

"The best thing a noncombatant can do in a battle is to stay out of the way."

"We were actually thinking more of transporting your wounded to the doctor's position. Using one of the wounded in the infirmary, we have determined we are strong enough working together to lift a stretcher and a Marine as well. We are capable of great speed and our movements are not restricted by bilateral symmetry."

It took Torin a moment to work out which "we" involved all four Mictok and which were merely part of a communal speech pattern. "It sounds like you've really thought this through."

"We have." The ambassador paused, left antennae running up and down the right. "We did not agree with this battle," she said at last. "As we are here, we will be of use."

Did not agree? *Diplomats,* Torin thought. *Can't*

have a battle without filling in the paperwork. "You should speak with the lieutenant, ma'am."

"Lieutenant Jarret is concerned with keeping us safe, Staff Sergeant. We find that admirable . . ." Her mandibles clicked a time or two. ". . . but stifling. We are civilians, yes, but we are also adults and able to make our own decisions. We understand you have survived many battles."

"Yes, ma'am. But it wouldn't be wise to remind the lieutenant that he hasn't."

"Of course not, but we hoped you would be willing to use that experience to put our offer in its best light."

If the Silsviss ever arrived, they'd be vastly outnumbered.

If there were enough Silsviss, some of them would get through.

If some of them got through, Marines would be wounded.

If the Mictok acted as stretcher bearers, the one remaining corpsman could assist the doctor and she could keep all her Marines in the fight.

"I'll speak to the lieutenant."

"Thank you, Staff Serg . . ."

"Oh, yeah? You wanna fukking make something of it!"

"Tough guy! You weren't plugged in, I'd flatten your ass!"

"Well, if that's all that's fukking stopping you!" Juan shrugged out of his vest and tunic in the same motion and was working on the fasteners of his shirt when he went down.

"If you'll excuse me, Ambassador." A dozen steps took Torin to the fight. Leaning away from a wild swing, she grabbed first Juan's upper arm between two of the exoskeleton's contact points and then mirrored the grip on the other Marine. Using their own momentum, she slammed their bodies together. "That will be quite enough of that."

More surprised than stunned by the impact, they staggered apart, turned toward her, and began to simultaneously yell out their reasons for the fight.

Torin raised her hand and the yelling stopped. "I don't care why," she said. "If you two want to beat the snot out of each other on your own time, well, you're adults, feel free. But, in case you hadn't noticed, we're at combat readiness right now, which puts you on my time. You start up again and I will personally throw your sorry butts over the wall at the first Silsviss I see. Do you understand me, Private Checya?"

"Yes, Staff Sergeant." He fiddled with his wrist point, looked as though he wanted to add something, and clearly thought better of it.

"Do you understand me, Private Anderson?"

"Yes, Staff Sergeant."

"Good. Now, since you're clearly bored, I can always find something for you to do. . . ."

To no one's surprise, they both suddenly remembered urgent preparations they needed to make.

"All right, you lot, show's over." Sergeant Glicksohn's voice scattered the small audience. "You enjoyed that too much," he said to Torin when they were alone.

"Nothing breaks up the morning like banging a couple of heads together."

He nodded toward the place where Torin had been standing. "What did the sp . . ." When that raised an eyebrow, he finished, ". . . speaking Mictok want."

"Oh, nice recovery."

"Best you'll get."

"The ambassador was offering her party's services as stretcher bearers."

"And you said . . ."

"It's not up to me, it's up to the lieutenant."

"Yeah, right."

"I said I'd present their offer in the best possible light."

"Well, here's your chance. I think our fearless leader wants to know what all the shouting was about." He sighed. "God save me from twoie looies who need to be kept informed about every little detail."

"Give him a break, Mike. He's not doing too badly."

"He's doing what you tell him."

"No. He's making his own decisions, but he's listening to what I tell him."

"It's a start. Hey, Torin." He stopped her as she turned away. "If I get hit, I don't want a Mictok to be the last thing I see."

"Easy solution. Don't get hit." She couldn't make out the words, but from the tone his response was decidedly insulting. She was still smiling when she reached Lieutenant Jarret. "Yes, sir?"

"There was a fight . . . ?"

"Not really, sir. Just a disagreement brought on by the waiting."

"It does feel like we've been waiting forever, doesn't it? Half the platoon's asleep."

A quick glance around the compound showed slightly more than half the platoon with their helmets pulled forward to shade their eyes. Corporal Conn appeared to be writing home—again—and from the faint sound of dramatic music, Binti Mashona had a game biscuit in her slate. Strictly speaking, during combat readiness the slates were for military use only, but Torin trusted her people to be ready when the fighting started.

"Old soldier's trick, sir. Sleep when you can."

"You're not sleeping, Staff."

"Staff sergeants never sleep, sir."

"Ever vigilant?"

"You've been reading the brochure."

He smiled, and she had a sudden memory of those incredible lips tracing a cool, moist line from her throat to her navel.

"Staff?"

It had to have been triggered by the heat. Or the waiting. Or that hit of pheromone she'd taken at dawn was still working on her. She buried the memory before the lips moved any lower and she embarrassed herself. *And none too soon. My heart's pounding like a . . . wait a minute.* "Can you hear that?"

Jarret nodded, head cocked, hair fluffed fully out. "It sounds like an engine of some kind. An old one. Maybe internal combustion."

It was a steady, regular thrum that seemed to thicken the air. The sleepers woke. The lookouts up on the roofs began twisting around, trying to pinpoint the direction. There *was* no direction. It came from all around them.

Weapon ready, Torin slowly turned in place. The civilians had spilled out of their building and stood in the compound, unmoving. Listening. Cri Sawyes, still unarmed, was standing by the well, tail lashing from side to side, throat pouch fully extended.

When she faced the north again, she understood.

Throat pouch fully extended . . .

"I don't think it's an engine, sir."

"Then what else could it . . ."

One moment the surrounding low hills were merely an empty, purple horizon. The next, they were crowned with Silsviss. The thrumming from a thousand throats grew louder and ended in a bass note so deep, it continued to buzz through the silence that followed.

"Holy fuk."

Lieutenant Jarret snorted. "Private Checya, I think you've just expressed the official reaction."

Laughter banished the last of the buzz, and Torin threw a silent *well done* to the lieutenant. His ear points flushed slightly.

"Thisss explainsss why they took ssso long to arrive."

"And if you could share that explanation," Jarret suggested pointedly.

Cri Sawyes' pouch had deflated by half but was still a pale circle at his throat. "They were waiting for the ressst. Thisss," he scanned the horizon, "hasss to be every male in the pressserve."

"Drawn by our crash?"

"I don't know. Doesss it really matter *why* they're here?"

"No. I guess not."

"Why were they thrumming?" Torin wanted to know. "The Silsviss we fought yesterday shrieked."

"Thossse you fought yesssterday were having fun. Thisss lot, however, meansss busssinesss."

As the thrumming started up again, Lieutenant Jarret's eyes darkened and his lips moved silently. Counting or praying, Torin figured, and given the situation, the later would probably be more useful. "Everyone's in position, sir."

"Good. Get Cri Sawyes a weapon."

"Thank you." He slapped his tail against the ground. "Although, ultimately I doubt it will make much difference."

"Maybe not," Jarret agreed, gaze locked on the surrounding Silsviss. "But it certainly can't hurt."

TWELVE

"Why are they just standing there?"

"I believe they're making a point, sir."

"A point?"

"That there's more of them than there are of us."

"Point taken." Jarret flipped up his scanner and slid his helmet off so that his hair could move.

"Sir . . ."

"I know. Setting a bad example." Sighing, he put it back on. "May I ask you a personal question, Staff?"

That was enough to move Torin's gaze from the surrounding Silsviss to the lieutenant. At some point in their working relationship, usually while the shit was hitting the afterburners, junior officers always wanted to get to *know* their senior NCOs. She didn't understand it, but she'd come to accept the inevitability. Unfortunately, Lieutenant Jarret had a better base to ask questions from than most. "You can *ask*, sir."

"Are you afraid?"

And that moved her gaze back to the Silsviss again. Hundreds, maybe thousands of them; they couldn't get a clear reading. Granted, they were attacking an entrenched position with primitive weapons, but the numbers . . .

"I'd be a fool if I wasn't, sir."

"And as you're not . . ." He smiled. "Neither am I."

"Glad to hear it." More for something to do than because it had changed, she checked the tiny line of data running across the bottom of her scanner. "They're well within range of the emmies, sir."

"I know." He rocked forward onto the balls of his feet and then back again. "But as Cri Sawyes insists it won't scare them off, I'd just as soon keep the slaughter to a minimum. We still need the Silsviss to sign that treaty when this is all over."

Whatever this *is*, Torin added silently. She'd seen enough combat to know that there were a limited number of reasons why sentient species killed each other en masse; patterns always evolved. The pattern currently evolving was so blatant, so slap-in-the-face obvious that she couldn't help think it was hiding something. Eyes narrowed, she stared out at the enemy. Unfortunately, an awareness that there were a thousand or more eyes staring back kept the analysis from progressing very far.

"Why aren't they making any noise?"

Torin and Lieutenant Jarret turned together to watch Lieutenant Ghard crossing the compound.

"I don't get it," he continued as he reached them. "Why are they just standing there? It's unnerving."

"I think that's the idea, sir. Is this your first ground combat?"

Ghard looked sheepish. "Is it that noticeable? I don't mind admitting I'd feel better if I was just a little more mobile and about thirty thousand feet up."

"Look at the bright side, sir. If you get shot down here, it'll hurt a lot less when you hit the ground."

After a startled moment, he found a smile. "Thank you, Staff Sergeant."

"You're welcome, sir."

"And thank you." He turned toward the other lieutenant. "Firing from the infirmary windows will allow us to keep an eye on Captain Daniels."

"Is she . . . ?"

"No change."

A sudden clatter from inside the building sheltering the civilians spun him around with enough force to drop his weapon strap off his shoulder. Torin caught it before it hit the ground.

"Thanks again, Staff. You know . . ." Both hands closed tightly around the grips. ". . . I'll be fine once something starts. Why don't we nail them with the emmy? Surely we're in range."

Excusing herself, Torin left for a walk around the perimeter as Lieutenant Jarret began explaining his first strike policy.

Halfway along the south wall, she paused.

"Aylex."

The di'Taykan glanced up from his position, looking guilty.

"Put your helmet on."

"But, Staff, my hair . . ."

It was standing straight out, a pale pink aurora.

"Your hair won't protect your head. Put the helmet on."

"But . . ."

"Now. And keep it on," she added, continuing around the compound.

A heat shimmer made the distant Silsviss seem vaguely unreal. Facing them, the waiting Marines looked like the toy soldiers she'd played with as a child. They looked confident in their abilities, certain they could do what was necessary. No one fidgeted, no one spoke. She'd built this platoon out of the best Sh'quo Company had to offer—this was where it showed.

At the north wall, she paused again and peered toward the highest of the hills. There was something . . . Swarming up the grain bags stair-stepped by the side of the eastern building, she crawled over the thick thatch and stretched out belly-down on the roof. In a perfect world she'd have been able to exploit the advantage of height with more than just one fireteam per building, but she didn't think the thatch would safely hold more than four bodies. *Just hold me. That's all I ask.* "Mashona, get over here."

Binti exchanged a speaking glance with the rest of her team—she'd been waiting for the summons ever since the four of them had been sent up.

"What's the word, Staff?"

"Mashona, can you see that group, there, on the high point."

Binti squirmed into place on the northeast corner of the building, squinted, and shrugged. "Sure."

"What's the guy in the middle holding?"

"Looks like—wait a minute, he's moving—like a staff with a skull on it."

"Silsviss skull?"

"Could be."

"Can you take him out?"

Raising her weapon, Binti squinted through the scope. "This is just a standard KC," she murmured, adjusting her sights. "I don't even have a sniper scope on this thing."

"If you'd had the scope, I wouldn't have asked if you could take him out. I'd have assumed you could."

"Thank you for that . . ." She dug her elbows further into the thatch. ". . . vote of confidence, Staff. Yeah, I think I can hit him." Maintaining the position of the gun, she flashed a dazzling white smile back over her shoulder. "Do you want me to try?"

"I'll let you know in a minute." Crawling back to the side of the building, Torin spit out a mouthful of chaff, and called for the lieutenant. She could have used her helmet mike, but since he was barely ten meters away, there didn't seem to be much point.

"What is it, Staff?"

"Excuse me, sir, but I think we've pinpointed the pack leader." She dropped her voice as he came closer. "Mashona says he's hittable. What do you want to do?"

"How do you know he's the leader."

"Just a guess—he's holding a staff with a skull on it."

"Yesss." Cri Sawyes came up behind Lieutenant

Jarret and flipped his head back almost ninety degrees to look up at Torin. "That isss the leader. Although, how it wasss decided with ssso many . . ." His voice trailed off as he lost himself in silent speculation.

"What would happen if he were killed?"

"Under normal circumssstancesss, it would throw a *carreg* in the nessst . . ."

If they got out of this alive, Torin planned on asking just what the hell that meant.

". . . but thessse are not normal circumssstancesss." He shrugged. "At bessst, they'll fight amongssst themssselvesss and forget usss. At worssst, we'll have one lesss enemy and our action will be taken asss a challenge and will prod them to attack."

Torin watched the lieutenant weighing the odds. She could almost read his mind. *One death now could save the platoon. But the longer they delayed attacking, the greater the chance the* Berganitan *would return and pull them out without a battle ever occurring at all. There was no point in provoking an attack and losing that chance. On the other hand, one death now could save the platoon.*

She watched the thoughts chasing each other around on his face and knew which one he kept returning to. Had she been on the ground beside him, she might have said something to help him decide, she might have said, *One way or another, they're going to attack and one death now could save the platoon.* But she wasn't on the ground and she couldn't very well shout advice to the commanding officer in front of his command. He was on his own.

"Do it," he said, at last.

"Yes, sir." Flipping over, Torin crawled back to the peak and repeated the order. "Head shot if you're sure," she added, "but if not, their hearts are pretty much dead center." Scanner at maximum magnification, she waited.

Binti drew in a deep breath, held it, and squeezed the trigger.

An instant later the Silsviss' head exploded, spraying everyone within three or four meters with brain, bone, and blood. He stood there for a moment, headless, then slowly collapsed backward.

"She's got him, sir." And moving her mouth away from the mike. "What have you got in your clip?"

"Impact boomers, Staff Sergeant."

"The 462s?"

"Yep."

"That explains it."

The skull-topped staff remained upright for a moment longer, the bone gleaming in the bright sunlight, then it too crashed to the ground. Unfortunately, it didn't stay there long. The battle for possession was brief, but bloody.

"Did that guy just lose a leg?"

"I think so, Staff."

There were two more bodies when the skull was raised again, but the vast majority of the Silsviss didn't even seem to notice. The whole thing, from shot to recovery, took less than four minutes.

"Well, bugger that," Torin muttered.

"I could take him out, too," Binti offered, taking aim.

"Doesn't seem like it would do any good," Torin told her. "Watch the sun on your scope and scanner," she said, crawling away in a cloud of dust rising up out of the crushed thatch. "It wouldn't take much to set this stuff alight."

"We may not have stopped anything, but at least we didn't set anything off," Jarret observed as she dropped off the wall at his feet.

"Sir!" Mysho's voice caroled over the compound from the west building. "There's something happening!"

One after another, sections of the line boomed from expanded throat pouches, ran about ten meters forward, stopped, and boomed again.

"You were saying, sir?"

For the first time it became obvious that the line of Silsviss was four or five bodies deep. Six deep on the more uneven ground.

"Do the ones in front look smaller to you?" Torin asked quietly.

Cri Sawyes nodded. "They're probably the youngessst, the mossst rash. The mossst eager to show their courage."

Boom. Run. Boom.

Eventually, all the layers of the entire circle had moved in.

"Enough of this," Hollice muttered. "Shit or get off the pot!"

The booming stopped and the shrieking started as the inner ring of the circle charged forward.

"I think they heard you." Juan swung the heavy

gun around and slipped his finger over the trigger. "Now, try telling them to go fuk themselves."

Down on the ground, Torin moved to the north wall.

"In the middle of the compound, Jarret drew in a deep breath. "Marines, ready!"

His helmet modified the volume and made sure that every other helmet got the message, but Torin was pleased that the mechanical assistance hadn't been necessary. It took some new officers a while to realize that in combat the equipment backed up the verbal order and not the other way around.

"Mark your targets," she said quietly, walking behind the line of kneeling Marines. "We haven't got the ammo to waste on wild firing."

The ring of shrieking Silsviss charged closer.

"Aim!"

And closer.

"Fire!"

Technology had made the KC essentially noiseless when fired. R&D had been thrilled but the people actually using the weapons had been less than happy. They'd compromised somewhere between a good old bang and ear protection.

Thirty-six of them going off at once made satisfactory noise.

Silsviss began to fall.

"Heavy gunners! Switch to grenades!"

Up on the roof, Juan snapped his upper receiver into a new position. "Fukking A."

Clusters of Silsviss were blown into pieces.

The shrieking changed in pitch.

Leaving the fallen, the ring pulled back until it rejoined the rest of the circle.

"Cease firing!"

They were surrounded by the dead, but there didn't seem to be many wounded. A ragged keening drew Torin's attention to a Silsviss thrashing from side to side in a bloody froth. She turned to the lieutenant.

His eyes so dark they held almost no color, he nodded.

"Mashona!"

When Binti looked over the edge of the roof, Torin pointed.

A single shot.

The thrashing stopped.

"With any luck," Lieutenant Jarret said as she reached his side, "that was enough to discourage them."

Torin understood how he felt—it hadn't been a fight, it had been a slaughter—but it didn't feel over to her. "Sir, I'd like to check out the reaction of that command group." When he nodded, she ran for the roof.

They were crouched down, drawing in the dirt, the skull keeping watch overhead. One of them looked up, pointed toward the buildings, then began to draw again.

Feeling a little sick, she realized what they were doing. What they'd done.

"I don't know what they're planning to do next, sir," she said, joining the two lieutenants and Cri

Sawyes at the well. "But I think I know what that charge was for. They were mapping our weapons. Looking for weak spots in the defense."

"They were sending kids out to be shot?" Jarret shook his head in mute denial—not of her theory, she was pleased to note, but of the very idea. "They were deliberately using the deaths of their own to plan their offense?"

She kept her tone matter-of-fact to better absorb the pain in his. "It's just a guess, sir."

"But an accurate guesss." Cri Sawyes whistled his approval. "The lowessst membersss in a pack hierarchy have little worth."

His ridges white, Ghard took a step away. "I can't believe you people! You're savages!"

The Silsviss shrugged, his tail moving from side to side. "And thisss isss why you need usss on your ssside."

"We don't *need* you!"

"No?" His voice was calm, but the movement of his tail sped up. "Then why are you here?"

"Enough!" Jarret threw the word between them. "Our fight is out there!"

"And he should be out there with them, not in here with us," Ghard snarled, his upper lip pulled back off large, ivory teeth.

"Lieutenant . . ."

Torin was impressed by the amount of quiet warning in that single word.

". . . you are so far out of line that if we didn't need every weapon for our defense, I'd relieve you of yours. For the last time, Cri Sawyes is our ally."

He took a step toward the Krai, using the difference in their height to his advantage. "And I mean it, Ghard; that *was* the last ti—"

Torin knocked Lieutenant Jarret flat a second before the well exploded. Their faces were inches apart as small bits of debris rained down around them and the proximity made her head swim. Before the lieutenant had quite recovered from his surprise, she cranked his masker up another notch.

What the . . . !"

"I heard it coming in, sir." She rolled off him and stood, half expecting a salacious comment to ignore. Most di'Taykan wouldn't have been able to resist, regardless of circumstances, but the lieutenant got quickly and quietly to his feet.

The well had contained most of the blast. One of the head-sized rocks had been flung inches into the mud brick of the western building but the rest hadn't traveled far. Torin picked her way to the edge of the blast zone, retreating quickly when the ground shifted underfoot. "The good news, a foot in either direction and we'd have had casualties. The bad news, we won't be using that well again."

"That was one of our weapons."

"Yes, sir. It was. An emmy if I'm not mistaken." Tone and expression made it quite clear that she wasn't. Which was when the next logical assumption occurred to them both.

Jarret straightened, dropping the pieces of rock he'd just picked up. "Marines! Off those roofs! Now!"

Training put eight bodies in motion before the emphasis was added.

Not fast enough.

Hollice cried out, spun sideways, landed flat against the thatch, and slid.

Torin caught him before he hit the ground, ignoring the background warning from her slate that his med-alert had gone off. She didn't need a computer implant to tell her that his right shoulder would probably need to be replaced—would definitely need to be rebuilt.

"Nice catch . . . Staff." His voice was surprisingly strong, but his eyes were glassy as she lowered him to the ground.

"I try not to let my people bounce, Corporal. Stretcher!"

To give the Mictok credit, they arrived with admirable speed. In spite of everything, Torin's mouth twitched at the pattern of crimson crosses painted onto their carapaces and she wondered whose idea that had been.

Not until Hollice gasped, "Mine." did she realize she'd asked the question out loud. "From the medics of old Earth," he added weakly. "They were . . . bored."

Torin assumed he meant the Mictok, not the medics of old Earth.

Another explosion pounded them with dirt clods as she helped lift him onto the stretcher.

"Our own . . . weapons?" he asked, sucking air through his teeth.

"Our own weapons," Torin told him.

"Adding insult to . . . injury," he muttered as the Mictok carried him away.

The third explosion fell short and hit a cluster of Silsviss bodies. From the sudden screaming, one of them hadn't been dead.

With no order given, three shots rang out and the screaming stopped.

Wiping her hands against her thighs, Torin crossed the compound to the lieutenant, wondering idly how much blood a pair of dress uniform trousers could absorb.

"Everyone keep your head down!" he shouted as she stopped beside him. "Staff, with the roofs denied us, we've got to open firing holes in those walls."

"Yes, sir. If I could suggest we send the di'Taykan inside; without water, we're going to have to keep them cool."

"Them?"

"Are you willing to go inside, sir?"

"No."

Torin shrugged, silently but eloquently saying, *"I thought not."* and began barking orders. She sent fourteen of the fifteen di'Taykan inside and set a twenty-minute chime into her slate to rotate the fifteenth. Lieutenant Ghard and his two aircrew moved reluctantly to crouch behind the south barricade.

Sporadic KC fire tore chunks out of the walls without penetrating the building, a few slammed into the grain bags, and some whistled by overhead.

"Staff?"

She frowned and held up a hand. A moment later she lowered it. "Sorry, sir, I was counting. I think the Silsviss only got the one locker open. That would make twenty-eight KCs spread pretty much all around us, but no heavy guns and no sidearms."

"How can you tell?"

"There's no heavies firing because they'd be going right through both the walls and the grain bags. I'm assuming there's no sidearms because they were in the locker with the heavies."

"But they have an emmy."

"Yes, sir. The evidence certainly points that way."

She heard him sigh, the sound eerily audible even over all the surrounding noise.

"Go ahead, Staff," he said without looking at her. "Say it."

"Say what, sir." Attempting unsuccessfully to work out the actual position of the guns, she was only half paying attention.

"That you were right and I was wrong." His hands curled into fists at his sides. "We should have blown the locker."

That brought her back to the moment. Torin looked from the clenched hands to the muscle jumping in his jaw and pitched her voice for his ears alone. "Sir, I will give you my opinion—occasionally, whether you want it or not—before you give an order, but after, I will support you, totally. *We* should have blown the locker. *We* didn't. So now *we* deal."

He turned to face her, and she saw the knowledge that he was responsible for Hollice's injury in his expression. Well, he was. But if he was going to be a combat officer, he'd be responsible for a whole lot more soon enough.

"Looking at the bright side, sir—they could have grabbed a box of impact boomers instead of standard ammo."

They both flattened as a shell whistled overhead but blew thirty meters on the other side of the south wall.

"And," she added as they stood again, "they're lousy shots."

"I expect that they'll get better," Jarret observed dryly, dusting himself off. "We've got to take that thing out."

"From the trajectory, I'd say that they're moving it between shots and pretty damned quickly, too. If we can't pick it up on a targeting scanner . . . Ressk!"

The Krai ran in from his position at the north wall. "Staff?"

"Can we target one of our own pieces?"

"Our own . . . ?" Understanding dawned. "I don't think so. The specs aren't in the scanner, Staff. We don't usually shoot at ourselves."

"Can you reprogram it?"

He shook his head. "That's not exactly how it works."

"I don't care *how* it works, as long as it works."

"Okay . . ." Shoving his helmet back on his head, he thought for a moment, then he smiled. "If I convince it that the other emmy is a captured piece, it can input the specs from that." The smile faded. "But that'll mean we'll have one less weapon because the second emmy can't be fired or the first'll lock on."

"It'll also mean they'll have one less weapon out there," Lieutenant Jarret reminded him. "Do it."

"Yes, sir!"

The next shell exploded just outside the south wall, the concussion knocking several grain bags into the compound.

"Ressk! Hurry up!" Ears ringing, Torin raced for the wall, grabbed one end of a grain bag and together with Cri Sawyes, swung it off a downed Marine. "Are you all right?"

"Bruised, but I think so . . ." She blinked as a round from a KC whistled past her nose then managed a strained smile. "I guess that one wasn't for me."

"Good." Torin clapped her on the shoulder as she stood, then jumped as the lieutenant's voice rang out behind her.

"Cover that south hill with fire. I want their heads kept down while we rebuild this wall!"

"Sir, you should be back in the center of the compound. It's too dangerous out here."

"Stop arguing and start stacking, Staff. This wall has to be repaired before the dust settles and they can see to aim."

And if you take a random shot in the head, you'll be just as dead, Torin thought, wrestling one of the bags back into position.

Hurriedly repaired, the wall was neither as straight, nor as secure, but it was a solid barrier again and that was what mattered. The lieutenant was sweating freely by the time they were done. Torin racked her brains for a way to get him inside and out of the worst of the day's heat.

"Should I go check on the civilians, sir?"

He glanced toward the western building and squared his shoulders. "No, thank you, Staff. I'd better do it. There's going to be a lot of explaining to do when this is over, and I'd like us all to be telling the same story."

"Well done," Cri Sawyes murmured as they watched the lieutenant walk away. "If you'd sssuggesssted he go inssside, he'd have thought you were trying to coddle him and never agreed."

Torin shot him a look from the under the edge of her helmet and led the way back into the center of the compound. "I don't know what you're talking about."

"No. Of coursssе not. He'sss coming along very nicely, Ssstaff Sssergeant. He isss learning to take command, and your Marinesss will notice that he wasss willing to put himssself at risssk to sssee that the wall protecting them wasss rebuilt."

Another shell whistled by overhead, very nearly exploding within the opposite curve of the Silsviss circle. Torin shook her head ruefully at the miss. It'd make the day so much easier if they'd just start killing each other and leave her Marines alone.

"One would almossst think that thisss whole incident had been ssset up."

"Set up for what?"

"A training exercissse, Ssstaff Sssergeant. Diplomacy, then combat. Show, then sssubssstance. Who could ask for more?"

That sort of accusation was just what she needed. She glared at him through narrowed eyes. "I don't know how your people train, Cri Sawyes, but Marines do *not* set up training exercises where other Marines get shot."

"Of courssse not." He bowed, his tail rising. "I apologissse."

"Good."

After a moment's silence, he said, "Ssspeaking of Marinesss being shot, I wasss impresssed with the way you caught Corporal Hollice. And with the way you handled thossse grain bagsss jussst now. You're much ssstronger than you look."

The last was said in such a hopefully speculative tone that Torin reluctantly replied. "It's an easy answer—Paradise, where I was born, is 1.14 Earth gravity. Silsvah, is .92 Earth gravity. It's a small difference, but it comes in handy."

He looked around the compound. With all but one of the di'Taykan inside and only two Krai in the platoon, the Marines looked as though they were a single species force once again. "Ssso all the Humansss have at leassst the advantage of that .08 difference?"

"Well, yes . . ." She started moving toward Ressk and the emmy. ". . . but I'm also much stronger than I look."

Out on the low ring of hills, any Silsviss who showed his head for long enough—whether he was rising up to take aim or just having a look around, died. And for every Silsviss who died, there seemed to be an infinite number to take his place. Not exactly infinite, but . . .

"Any sufficiently large number might as well be infinite," Torin muttered.

"What was that, Staff?"

"Just talking to myself, Ressk."

"The only way you can have an intelligent conversation?"

"Don't step on my lines, Private," she advised with mock severity. "It makes me cranky. We're under fire and no one would ever notice another casualty." Then in her normal tone, she added, "How's it coming?"

He steadied the cover with his left foot. "Almost done."

"Good. Because . . ." A faint whistle drew her eyes upward. Time slowed to a crawl. Impossibly, she could see the shell arcing down from a painfully bright sky directly at . . .

Time regained its proper pace.

"MARINES, DOWN!" One arm grabbing for Ressk, the other for the emmy, Torin managed four, five, six long strides, before the explosion threw her to the ground, her body half covering both the weapon and the Krai. Something smashed into the back of her helmet. Something else drew a line of pain across the top of her right shoulder. Something else dug into her right thigh.

Under her, the ground shook.

Above her, hundreds of deadly pieces of shrapnel filled the air sounding like a swarm of angry wasps.

Someone screamed, the sound strangely blunted.

It couldn't have lasted even a full minute, but Torin felt as though she'd been lying there for at least an hour when she finally lifted her head.

Distant figures moved through a nearly impenetrable cloud of dust.

A touch on her arm brought her attention down to the Marine beneath her and she shifted until he could free himself. His mouth moved, she could hear sound but not content. From the panicked expression on his face, he couldn't hear himself at all.

Her hand closed around his chin and she turned his head until he was looking directly at her.

"We were very close," she said, forming each word carefully. "Don't worry." She left him to draw his own conclusions from that. As much as she wanted to give him more comfort, there wasn't much point. Her hearing would return. But he was Krai, and she couldn't be positive about his.

Favoring her right side, she slowly stood and held out her hand. Ressk took it, and when he was standing, they turned together.

The shell had hit the second emmy and both ammo cases. Had the ammunition actually detonated instead of merely blowing to pieces, Torin doubted anyone in the compound would have survived. As it was . . .

The Mictok appeared for a moment, carrying a stretcher between them. Then two Marines, one supporting the other. Then the Mictok again.

They really are fast.

She heard Sergeant Glicksohn shouting orders,

his voice sounding as though it had been squeezed into her head through a small hole. Other voices followed growing clearer and louder as the hole stretched.

"Staff!"

A hand grabbed her right shoulder and turned her around.

The sudden pain snapped the world back into focus.

"Sir."

"You're alive!" Jarret looked down at his hand covered in her blood and his eyes darkened. "You're wounded!"

She poked a finger through the hole in her uniform sleeve, dragging the edges of the fabric apart. "It's nothing much, sir. It's a clean slice."

"It needs taping."

Sucking air through her teeth, she agreed.

"Is that the only place you were hit?" he asked as though he couldn't believe that was possible.

It wasn't.

They both looked down at the four inches of metal fragment sticking out of the back of her upper thigh.

"Good thing I was lying so that it hit the vest," Torin grunted. "Slowed it enough to keep it from going right through me."

"There's another in the back of your helmet." Jarret reached up and tugged it free then stood staring down at a shard of an ammo box. "This could have killed you."

It wasn't the first time Torin had seen her own

death. Familiarity had bred, if not contempt, a certain fatalism. "Point is, sir, it didn't." Twisting around, careful of the edges, she grabbed the piece in her hip and yanked it free. "Son of a fukking bitch!" Breathing heavily, she threw the triangular bit of metal on the ground, and pressed the heel of her hand against the wound.

"You need to see the doctor!"

"Or the corpsman, but not right now." Her other hand on his shoulder, she turned him to face the chaos around them. "Right now, we have work to do."

"Yes . . ." He visibly gathered himself, then nodded once, determinedly, and strode off. "Sergeant Glicksohn, report!"

Ressk had escaped without a scratch although by the time Torin turned her attention back to him, his hearing had only partially returned. "STAFF! YOU SAVED MY LIFE!"

"You're shouting, Ressk."

"SORry."

Frowning, Ressk's fingers danced over the screen of the surviving emmy. "IT SHOULD fire, STAff, and the tarGET lock shoULD WORK."

Torin glanced over at the hole where the ammunition had been and snorted. "It doesn't matter."

Following her gaze, Ressk smiled and flipped open the cover of the chamber.

All things considered, she decided not to give him the standard chew out on reprogramming a loaded weapon. Running her tongue over the front of her teeth and tasting grit, she nodded. "Make it count."

The explosion in the ranks of the Silsviss was very nearly as large the explosion in the compound had been.

Torin didn't know about anyone else, but it made her feel better.

THIRTEEN

Another Marine was dead. Two more badly wounded. Half a dozen others had taken injuries similar to Torin's—not bad enough to be disabling but bad enough to need help. Walking into the med station out of the heat and the dust, she found the building cool enough inside that the familiar smell of blood wasn't entirely overwhelming. Mictok webbing crossed and recrossed the ceiling holding a quartet of mirrors in such a way that light angled in from the windows and bounced between them, illuminating the bodies below.

Only the Mictok would pack mirrors during an emergency evacuation.

Doctor Leor, his feathers matted together, worked long fingers within the belly of one of the wounded Marines. Beside him, the unwounded corpsman worked a jagged hunk of metal out of the shoulder and past the exoskeleton of a heavy gunner while one of the Mictok held her forelegs down on the pressure points. Both stretchers were balanced on a rectangular pile of grain bags stacked high enough to ease access.

One hand still pressed against the hole in her

thigh, Torin's eyes narrowed. She had half a dozen Marines who needed nothing more than a patch job, who were needed back on the walls, able to fight.

A commotion at the doorway into the middle room, drew her attention in time for her to see the other corpsman, the one who'd taken the brunt of the injured Silsviss' attack, slide to the floor. Before she could move, one of the di'Taykan she'd sent inside to shoot through the walls, scooped him up.

When he straightened, staggering a little under his burden, she saw a pale fringe of pink under the helmet's edge.

Becoming aware of her scrutiny, Aylex met her gaze. "He said he wanted to help, Staff. Stupid *ablin gon savit* can hardly stand."

"Get him back to bed." Ignoring the only possible di'Taykan's response, Torin flipped down her helmet mike. "Sergeant Chou!"

"Staff?"

"Bring the Charge d'Affaires and her assistant to the med station on the double."

"I thought Lieutenant Jarret wanted the civilians safely tucked away."

"I'll deal with the lieutenant." She bent carefully and picked up a med kit. "You just get their tail feathers in here."

"On my way."

She took another look at the situation. "Anderson!"

The Marine, sitting on a bag by the wall, looked up, tossing light hair back off her face. "Staff Sergeant?"

"You still got one working hand?"

Anderson looked down at the long gash along her left forearm barely held together by the grip of her right fingers. She opened and closed her left hand. "Sort of."

"Good." Torin set the kit down beside her on the bag and bent awkwardly forward. "You twist, I'll pull." Someday, with any luck, she'd find the stupid son of a bitch who'd designed a latch on a med kit that needed to be opened with two hands and be able to give their ass the kicking it deserved.

By the time they'd fought it open, she could hear the two Rakva approaching. And from the sound of it, they weren't alone.

"Your staff sergeant has no authority to have this one dragged out of the dubious security of that hovel, Lieutenant. This one is not in a uniform and this one is not hers to order around. Neither is Purain."

"I'm sure she has a good reason for sending for you both. Why don't we hear what she has to say?"

"All this one wishes to hear," the Rakva insisted, stepping into the room and halting just over the threshold, "is you ordering her to apologize."

Lieutenant Jarret slid past the indignant civilian and turned to Torin, looking significantly unimpressed. "Staff Sergeant Kerr, Sergeant Chou says you directed her to bring Madam Britt and her assistant to the med station."

The assistant looked frightened, but whether of Madame Britt or the situation, Torin couldn't tell. "Yes, sir, I did. We have Marines that need a minimum of attention so they can get back to their positions, but our medical personnel have serious injuries to deal with. Madame Britt and her assistant each have two working hands the right size to handle the equipment and should both be capable of operating an aid station."

"Capable is not at question, Staff Sergeant," Madame Britt snapped. "If you need an aid station, this one suggests you use a Dornagain—from what this one has heard, they wish to help but are unable to see a way they can."

"The Dornagain's fingers are too big."

"Then use a Marine."

"All able-bodied Marines are needed to defend the compound." Torin narrowed her eyes and swept both Rakva with a speculative look. "If you'd rather pick up a weapon . . ."

Her crest rose, the stub of the broken feather jutting straight up. "This one does *not* become involved in the business of the military. Lieutenant!"

Jarret nodded. "An aid station is a good idea, Staff Sergeant. Carry on." As the astounded Charge d'Affaires stared after him, he walked out of the building calling for Sergeant Chou.

"All right." Torin showed the open med kit to the two Rakva. "It's not hard. Use one of these to wipe the edges of the wound clean, lay down a line of bonder, pinch the edges together, then spray on a coat of sealant."

Madame Britt took a step back, vestigal beak snapping open and shut a time or two before she could find a suitable protest. "This one does not . . ."

A torrent of high-pitched, fingernails-on-slate sound cut her off. It wasn't necessary to understand

Rakva to catch the point of the doctor's tirade. When he finished, young Purain was looking appalled and Madame Britt, slightly stunned.

"Fine," she said, taking the kit from Torin's hand. "This one will help."

"Good." Torin undid her dress pants and dropped them down around her knees, ripping fabric out of the line of blood that had dried down the back of her leg. "You can practice on me."

Still favoring her right leg, Torin stepped back out into the compound and realized the environmental unit in her tunic had shut down—probably because of the slice in the sleeve. As the afternoon heat wrapped around her, insinuating dry fingers in under her clothes, she added the name of the idiot who hadn't included combat backup systems in the dress uniforms to her hit list—currently consisting of the med-kit designer and General Morris. The latter was there mostly on principle; he *had* given the order that had sent the platoon to Silsvah.

And the way things have turned out, it's a good thing he didn't let us wait for those new recruits. They were in a tough enough fight for seasoned combat troops. Green Marines would have turned a bad situation into a nightmare.

Glancing around the perimeter as she crossed to her lieutenant's side, she realized that the atmosphere had darkened since the explosion. The easy confidence had been replaced by an edged intensity acknowledging the deaths that had already occurred as well as those that were likely to and, on an individual basis said, *I, at least, am not leaving here bagged.*

By the time she reached the shade of the other building, where Lieutenant Jarret and the Dornagain ambassador were talking, Torin could feel warm lines of sweat running down her sides, her shirt clinging to her damp back. Glancing over at the slate-gray clouds piling up in the west, she sighed. From the look of things, she was going to get wetter still.

". . . very sorry, Ambassador, but your hands are simply too large to deal easily with our medical supplies."

"And we are too slow to carry stretchers as the Mictok do."

"Yes, sir. I'm afraid so." It hadn't been a question, but Lieutenant Jarret answered it anyway. "Stretcher bearers are very vulnerable. I wouldn't have allowed the Mictok to assist were they not so very fast. It is our job to keep you—all of you—safe."

"Yes." The ambassador sighed. "All of us. An entire Confederation of ancient cultures hides behind the deaths of its youngest members." Stroking back his whiskers with his broken claw, he stared out over the lieutenant's head at the surrounding litter of reptilian bodies. "We are like the Silsviss in this, I fear, only we are old enough to know better." He sighed again, and turned his bulk toward the building that sheltered his people. "You will tell us if there is anything we can do, Lieutenant Jarret?"

"Yes, sir, I will."

"Good. Staff Sergeant Kerr." He nodded in Torin's direction and disappeared inside.

Jarret's gaze flicked to her shoulder and hip. "Are you all right?"

"Yes sir, I'm fine. Thank you."

"You'll have a little trouble sitting."

Torin waited for the echoes of a sudden flurry of shots to die down. "I don't think I'll have much chance to sit for a while, sir."

Sunset painted bands of orange and gold across the bottom of the clouds in such brilliant hues that only the di'Taykan could look to the west without their scanners. When the Silsviss charged out of the sunset, the di'Taykan stopped them.

"The lieutenant took a chance, not moving some of the others over," Mike murmured as he passed Torin a pouch of food. "You should've said something."

She broke the self-heating unit across the bottom of the bag and waited, tossing it from hand to hand. "No di'Taykan were injured in the explosion or the first charge. They felt like they weren't doing their share."

"That's ridiculous."

"Still, that's how they felt."

"Trey's dead and Haysole's legs are paralyzed."

Torin waited, she could feel the weight of more words that needed to be said filling the space between them.

"He always hated not being able to move his legs. He hated it when he had to be secured during a drop. He gave me more damn trouble than everyone else in the squad combined, but put him in combat and he settled right down." The sergeant stared into his food, not seeing it. "I should have tied him into his seat."

Torin reached out and lightly clasped his arm. When he lifted his head, she tightened her grip. "It wasn't your fault."

"I know."

"Really?"

"Yeah." His pause suggested Torin not push. So she didn't. "I could really use a beer."

Torin stared up at a cloud covered sky, willing one of the hidden points of light to be the *Berganitan* returning before anyone else got bagged. "Me, too."

"Hey, what've you got?"

"Same fukking thing as you," Juan grunted. "Hot bag of balanced nutrients in a tasty fukking paste."

Binti snorted, eyes and teeth alone visible in the darkness. "I meant, what flavor have you got, asshole."

"What flavor asshole?"

"Don't go there," she warned. "Just answer my question—dark or light."

"Dark."

"Figures. I pulled a light; you want to trade?"

Juan sucked paste out of the pouch, swallowed and smiled. "Are you fukking nuts? Nobody likes the light ones."

"I don't mind them," Ressk offered from Juan's other side.

"Big surprise." Leaning out from the grain bags, Binti tossed the pouch past the heavy gunner toward the outline of the Krai as showing on her scanner. "Go ahead and suck it back, Ressk. I'm not going to eat it."

"I can't trade, I've already finished mine."

"Again, big surprise." Adjusting an already perfectly adjusted sight, Binti flinched when a huge drop of water splashed against the back of her hand. "Oh, that's the perfect end to a perfect day."

"We need the water, the fucking liz . . . Silsviss blew the well."

"We need a lot of things," Binti snorted. "We need the rest of the company, including full artillery and air support. We need the luck of the H'san. We need to defeat the Others once and for all. We don't need to get wet."

Less than a minute later, scattered drops had turned into a steady downpour.

"And," she sighed, "I think it's getting colder, too."

"It's not gettin' fukking colder, it's just less warm."

"The Silsviss aren't going to attack in this," Ressk declared as water ran off the curve of his helmet and down the back of his neck. "I think the lieutenant should call it a night."

"Oh, yeah. And everyone who thinks that's going to fukking happen, don't speak up all at once."

Ressk turned a worried frown on the heavy gunner. "So you think they're going to attack?"

"No, I think we should all curl up in our little beds and be buddies until morning. How the fuk should I know?"

Sighing heavily, Ressk stared out into the night. "This is beginning to remind me of Hallack IV. You remember; we got pinned down covering the *serley* evacuation of those H'san colonists?"

"I remember. I was trying not to fukking think about it."

They listened to the rain for a while.

"You guys think Hollice is going to make it?" Binti asked at last.

"We've all seen worse," Ressk reminded them. There was no need for him to go into more detail; some things couldn't be forgotten.

Juan sighed. "Yeah, and some them didn't fukking . . . did you hear that?"

"There's nothing out there but dead Silsviss, Juan."

"Fuk you, too. Something out there is alive. And moving."

Peering through his scanner, Ressk muttered, "Got it. I hate it when you're right."

Binti snapped down her helmet mike. "Staff? There's something happening over here."

"Sir? Private Mashona reports movement to the north about halfway between us and the hills."

Jarret resealed the top of his food pouch and stuffed it in his pocket as he stood. "Could the Silsviss have moved up without our scanners seeing them?" he asked, picking up his helmet and tucking it under his arm.

"I don't think so, sir." Torin kept her voice as low as the pounding rain allowed as together they hurried toward the north wall. "We couldn't have missed seeing them come down those hills.

"There's a lot of bodies out there, maybe it's scavengers."

"That's the most likely explanation, sir."

"Staff? This is Conn at the south wall. We've got movement."

Torin passed the new message on to the lieutenant, mentioned that his helmet would be of more use on his head, then asked Conn, "Are they at about the halfway point?"

"About that, Staff. Between the speed they're moving at and the rain, it's hard to get a solid fix. Whatever they are, they're staying awful close to the ground."

Torin checked that the lieutenant had heard just as her scanner picked up movement no more than five meters from the north wall. From Jarret's expression, he'd seen it as well.

Frowning, he stared into the darkness. "I think I'd like some light on this."

"Yes, sir. Heavy gunners! By number, illuminate!"

From the westernmost end of the south wall, a voice bellowed, "One!" then, from high above, the compound was lit by brilliant while light.

"Don't stare directly at the flare!" Torin warned, turning slowly in place so that she could examine all approaches. "And remember to . . . son of a . . . !"

One moment, the night had been a solid presence on the other side of the wall, the next, a Silsviss leaped into the light, landing on top of the grain bags howling at full voice and brandishing a short spear in one rain-slick hand.

Ressk threw himself backward into the mud and fired.

The howl lingered for a moment after the body fell.

"You're lucky the stupid fuk paused to pose," Juan noted, ignoring the spray of blood dribbling down his cheek as he snapped his upper receiver over to flares. "If these kids were real soldiers, you'd be fukking dead." He took a step back from the wall. "Cover." When the Marines to either side shifted position slightly, he aimed at the sky. "Two!"

The second flare.

Another six Silsviss.

None of them made it to the top of the wall."

"They spent the day hiding behind their dead." Jarret yelled over the mixed sound of challenge and gunfire and pounding rain. "We were scanning the hill for them, and they were already halfway here."

"Smart kids," Torin acknowledged.

The third flare.

Only Cri Sawyes saw the arrows arching over the south wall. Grabbing Torin's arm, he swung her around.

Her eyes widened and her reaction changed from enraged snarl to, "Arrows incoming!"

Most buried their points in the ground. A few skidded off the impenetrable curve of a helmet. Only one Marine was hit.

When Torin reached his side, Aylex had his hand pressed to his forehead. At sunset she'd started cycling the di'Taykan out to positions on the wall—maybe she should have been keeping a better eye on them. "Where's your helmet?"

"There." di'Taykan hair shed water as though it were made of plastic instead of protein, but pain had clamped Aylex's tightly to his head.

Squatting by his side, Torin softened her voice. "Let me see."

He slowly moved his hand away.

Another flare went up, illuminating an ugly red line running diagonally from the inside corner of his right eyebrow up into his hairline, blood running in unbroken watered lines down his face.

"Looks like it hit the bone and skidded. It's nothing serious."

Aylex's eyes lightened. "di'Taykan have hard heads."

"I am *fully* aware of that, Private. Now pick up your damned helmet and go get that cut sealed." She backed out of his way. "And I want the helmet on your head when you come out of the med station."

"Yes, Staff." Looking considerably less stunned now that someone had taken charge of the situation, he dumped the water out of his helmet, hung it from his belt, and began to move away from the wall.

Torin paralleled him for a moment, both of them bending low. *Which'll get us an arrow in the ass,* Torin thought, *but does bugger all otherwise.* Still, instincts insisted that when under fire the only intelligent response was to duck.

When she was satisfied he could make it on his own, she began to angle away. She could hear shouting from the south, Mike's distinctive parade ground bellow bludgeoning back the Silsviss challenges. Aylex didn't need her any longer, but there were others who . . .

She saw him fall from the corner of her eye, the brilliant pink hair drawing an almost visible arc through the night as he pitched forward and landed facedown in the mud. By the time she had him rolled over on his back, the Mictok were there.

"Allow us, Staff Sergeant Kerr."

Eight forelegs slid under the fallen di'Taykan and in spite of the tremors beginning to rack his body, lifted him easily onto the stretcher. Torin had to run full out to keep up.

After picking off a Silsviss archer too slow to drop back down behind his shielding corpse, Binti stared at the arrow buried deep in the mud by her leg. "You guys think Hollice told anyone about what the Dornagain believed?"

"What? That traveling faster than fukking snails is impossible?"

"No, asshole, that these arrows might be poisoned."

Juan and Ressk exchanged worried frowns.

"If the brass knew, they'd have told the platoon," Ressk said at last. "We'd have got some kind of warning."

"You better fukking tell somebody," Juan pointed out, firing twice at a suspicious break in the rain.

There wasn't any point in asking why *she* should tell, Binti realized. With Hollice wounded, she was next senior, so the shit jobs came automatically to her. Beginning to rethink her desire to get her corporal's hook, she flipped down her mike. "Sergeant Glicksohn?"

Torin paused dripping inside the door of the med station while the Mictok slid the now thrashing Aylex onto Dr. Leor's table and answered her helmet's insistent call. "What is it, Mike?"

"Mashona says the Dornagain think the arrows might be poisoned."

Back arced, Aylex began to fling his arms from side to side. A loop of webbing gently restrained him.

Torin's stomach clenched. "Tell the lieutenant." Spinning around, she raced back out into the rain. The north wall was closest, but the few arrows that had made it over, were buried point down in mud. She didn't even slow. Ignoring the lieutenant's voice in her helmet ordering the Marines to treat the arrows like the death threats they were, she placed her left hand flat on the top bag propelling herself up and over. She grabbed the first two arrows she saw sticking into the grain, and, fully aware of the sudden flurry of shots her activity had provoked, jumped back.

She had the slate off her belt before she'd taken two steps. The first arrow had only traces of toxins too small to read, but the second . . .

"Doctor! It's poison!"

Dr. Leor kept his eyes on the needle going into Aylex's throat. "This one is aware of that, Staff Sergeant."

"I've done an analysis."

"And you want this one to do what?" He removed the needle and closed his fist around the body of the syringe. "Create an antidote? With what?" He turned to face her then, fist raised. "With these primitive tools? This one is not a miracle worker, Staff Sergeant!" His voice rose with every word. "This one has no proper equipment! No proper light! This one has patients dying!"

Torin took another look at the body on the table and realized it was just that—a body on the table. "He's dead."

"Yes! Dead! This one does not have patients die!" All at once, his crest fell and he sagged. "This one," he said softly, laying one hand against Aylex's cheek, "is an environmental physician. This one does the research that allows members of the Confederation to live safely on new planets."

"Then do it." Torin held out her slate. "If I understand this stuff correctly, it can kill every Marine in the compound with a scratch. Humans, Krai . . ." The pause was barely noticeable. ". . . and di'Taykan. I can't worry about scratches, not and keep my people alive."

"But you are not keeping your people alive, are you, Staff Sergeant? You can perform miracles no more than this one can."

"Performing miracles is part of my job, Doctor." She understood his distress, she didn't give a damn about it, not if it was putting her people in danger, but she understood. "And whether you like it or not, it's part of your job, too."

He stared down at the slate, then slowly pulled it

out of her hand. "This one will try to find an antidote."

"No. Trying isn't good enough. Find one."

"And if this one doesn't have the right drugs?"

"Then find another. Find one that uses the drugs you have."

"Ah." He glanced down at Aylex and over at her again. "It will not bring the dead back to life."

Torin drew in a deep breath and let it out slowly. "It never does," she said, and walked out into the rain, rubbing the falling water off her face with the palm of one hand.

"You hear that?" Hollice asked, head turned toward the next stretcher.

"My ears still work," Haysole muttered.

"Sounded like Staff ripped a few feathers out of the doctor."

"Sounded like someone just died."

Hollice sighed. "Yeah, that, too."

The stretchers had been moved to the center of the room. A Marine stood on a grain bag against each wall, weapon resting on the thick lower edge of the window, attention fixed on any movement in the night. The room behind them could have been empty for all the attention they paid it.

"You know why they won't look at us?" Haysole asked suddenly. "They're afraid that our bad luck will rub off on them. See the dying, become the dying."

"I'm not dying," Hollice snapped. "I'm just missing a shoulder." Under a thick layer of sealant, blood vessels had been stretched across the damaged area in an attempt to save the arm. He felt nothing at all since the corpsmen had numbed the part of his brain that would have acknowledged the pain, and if he had his way, it would stay numb until they slipped him into a tank back on the *Berganitan*. Actually, he felt pretty good—which, all things considered, was just a little too weird.

On the other side of his injury, Haysole sighed.

The only light in the room came from the two corpsmen who were tending to one of the Marines unconscious since the crash, but it was enough for him to see the di'Taykan's hair had flattened tightly to his skull. "And you're not dying either," he added sharply.

"I'm not living."

"Oh, for fuksake, Haysole, it's just your legs. They're easy enough to rebuild."

"If the *Berganitan* comes back."

"If it doesn't, another ship will, Marines don't abandon their own. And I'll tell you something," he continued quickly before Haysole could make another melancholy objection, "if no one comes back for us soon, Staff'll build a ship out of lizard shit and . . . and . . ."

"And bones."

"Yeah, and bones. Sounds like there's enough of them piling up out there. She'll build a ship and kick it off this planet with her own dainty foot before she lets us rot here."

"You're probably right." The di'Taykan sighed again, and his hair began to make a few tentative movements.

"No probably about it." Hollice firmly believed that after a point living and dying was as much a state of mind as anything and no one was dying right next to him. Not if he had anything to say about it. "You feeling better?"

"Why not try groping it and find out?"

"Oh, yeah, you're feeling better. My work here is done."

"Does that mean you're not going to . . ."

"Yes."

"You are?"

"No."

"But . . ."

"Get some sleep, Haysole." A grenade exploded not far from the building and bits of chaff drifted down from the thatched roof, lightly dusting both men. "Or not."

By the time Torin reached Lieutenant Jarret, grenades were exploding all around the compound.

"I ordered the heavies to blow up the closest bodies," he told her. "Everything within the illumination of the flares. If we can keep them back out of arrow range, we don't have a lot to worry about." Then he caught sight of her expression. "What is it?"

"Aylex is dead. Poisoned. The doctor's working on an antidote."

"Too late."

"Yes, sir, for Aylex, but there are plenty more Marines in this compound."

Jarret looked around, squinting as the rain drove

up under the edge of his helmet and into his face. "We can only react, can't we?"

"It *is* the problem with a defensive position, sir."

He nodded and waited for the sounds of another grenade to fade before saying solemnly, "I never expected my first command to be like this."

Torin reached out and lightly grasped his arm. The di'Taykan needed touch for comfort. Humans kept insisting they didn't. They were wrong. "No one ever does, sir."

The rain stopped shortly after midnight. The Silsviss didn't.

An arrow, its forward momentum almost spent, scraped across the abraded knuckles of a Human Marine. Humans proved to be significantly more susceptible than the di'Taykan. She died instantly, looking surprised.

About to fire a flare into the air, the heavy gunner by her side fired at the Silsviss archer instead. He also died instantly, but the smoke rising up from the burning hole in his chest made it impossible to see his expression before he fell.

Torin snuggled down into the clean sheets with a contented sigh. The feeling defined safety for her and had her whole life. As a child, it meant she was free of her father's expectation that she'd take over the stupefying drudgery of the farm. As an adult, it meant she'd survived the filth and horror of combat once again, that *she* at least had survived. By then, she wasn't always alone between the sheets because there was no point in survival unshared by those she cared for. Or was responsible for. Or, bottom line, both.

Sometimes it got a little crowded.

Today she was alone. She stretched out, thankful for the space, and smiled as the cool fabric slid across her skin.

"Staff Sergeant Kerr?"

"Sir!" Forcing her eyes to focus on the concerned gaze of Lieutenant Jarret, she realized to her intense embarrassment that she'd been asleep. "I'm sorry, sir. I just closed my eyes for a moment."

"It's all right, Staff. No harm done. It's not like you were awake for the last thirty-two hours or anything." Smiling, he handed her a pouch of coffee, already warmed. "Sun's rising, the Silsviss seem to be having a lie in, and an old friend's back."

"An old friend?" She sucked at the spout as she stood, sliding the webbed strap of her KC up onto her shoulder. About to ask him what he was talking about, and hoping she could be polite about it, she felt the ground vibrate slightly. "Ah."

The *ghartivatrampas* stood looking confused, forelegs shifting from one massive foot to the other, tail sweeping back and forth.

The wispy remains of an early morning fog laid a surreal perspective over the ring of carnage around the compound. The grenades had torn up the ground and scattered Silsviss body parts far and wide. One or two whole bodies, missed in the darkness and rain, punctuated the scene, beginning to bloat in the rising heat of the morning. Small scavengers scuttled about feasting on bits of flesh, occasionally squabbling over choice chunks although there was certainly enough for all. Hundred of thousands of carrion flies provided a constant background buzz.

"Why did it come back?" Jarret wondered as they watched the giant creature's distress.

"This is probably a regular trail. I'm guessing it sleeps in the swamp at night where the water can support some of its bulk and heads out every morning to its grazing ground. At night it goes back to the swamp by a different route."

"But why stay on a trail that leads through this?"

"It's operating on instinct, sir. Look at the size of its brain case compared to its body. These things were designed to be eaten."

Jarret swept a lilac gaze over the huge creature and whistled softly. "Eaten by what?"

"Once there were carnivoresss on Sssilsssvah of equal ssstature to a *ghartivatrampasss.*"

Jarret jumped, flushed, and tried to look as though he hadn't reacted. Torin turned a bland gaze on the Silsviss, secure in the knowledge that no one could hear her heart slamming against her ribs. "What happened to them?" she asked.

Cri Sawyes shrugged. "A few ssstill exissst in zoosss. There'sss been much dissscussion lately about whether or not there should be a breeding program in place aimed at releasssing them back into the wild."

"I can see how releasing something big enough to eat *that* might cause a few second thoughts."

"Well, yesss, but the problem isss more one of ssspace. They'd need large pressservesss of their own. If they were released in with the young malesss they wouldn't lassst a week." His inner eyelids flicked across. "Defeating the *ravatarasss* was historically the choice way to prove manhood. Which, incidentally, isss why they're very nearly extinct."

"The young males killed them?"

"It took sssome time, of courssse, but, yesss."

Jarret sucked thoughtfully on his coffee for a moment. "Could they kill that?"

"For food, yesss. A ssstrong leader could organize a hunt, but . . ."

"There's a strong leader out there."

All three heads turned toward the surrounding hills.

"Unless they've gone," Torin offered, more because someone had to than because she believed it.

"No. They're ssstill out there. Once the challenge hasss been given, they will not, can not, back down."

Torin snorted. "I'm amazed the *Silsviss* aren't extinct."

"We have a better breeding program," Cri Sawyes explained dryly.

"All right." Jarret tossed his hair back, spreading it out like a lilac corona around his head. "We need time to regroup. If we frighten that thing up into the hills, they'll have to kill it to keep it from trampling them. Once dead, it becomes food and they'll all want some. Sharing it out will take some time."

"And caussse a few fightsss asss well."

"Which will buy us some more time."

Torin nodded, understanding where the lieutenant was going. "Enough time and you never know, the horse may talk."

"What?"

"Sorry, sir, an old Terran expression I picked up from Hollice. It means that given enough time, anything could happen. The *Berganitan* could return."

"Exactly." He frowned. "I thought Humans were the only verbal species on your home world?"

"Yes, sir."

"Then horses don't . . ."

"No, sir."

Surrendering for the moment, he flashed her a brilliant smile. "Once we're clear of this situation, will you explain it to me?"

"Sir, once we're clear of this . . . situation . . ." And only an officer would use so politely nondescript a word for the carnage they found themselves at the center of. ". . . I will happily deliver Corporal Hollice to you and he can explain not only that expression but a thousand more."

"A thousand?"

"And he knows all the lyrics to something called ALW."

"Thank you for the offer, Staff, but I'll pass."

"Look at those two," Ressk grumbled, sucking vigorously at a bag of rations. "Sun's barely up and they're cheerfully planning the day. Don't they ever sleep?"

"They can't," Binti yawned, trying scratch an itch in the center of her back. "He's an officer and has to be an example to us all. And do you have to look like you're enjoying that stuff?"

Ressk shrugged. "*Chrick's chrick.* She's not an officer."

"Yeah, but it's worse for her. She has to be an example to him. Fortunately, by the time you make staff, you're so evolved you can piss into the wind and not get wet."

"Mashona!"

Binti turned to see the staff sergeant beckoning her over.

"Looks like you're wanted."

"Looks like."

"You want me to hit it where, sir?"

"Just under the base of its tail. It'll be sensitive there and that should send it stampeding up into the hills. What?"

"Sorry, sir." She took a deep breath and managed to stop laughing. Then she caught the staff sergeant's eye and it almost sent her off again. "I didn't get much sleep."

"That's all right, Private, none of us did. Can you do it?"

"Yes, sir." The big thing carried its tail out from its body—not very far but far enough. "Now?"

"Now."

She knelt in the angle of the building and the wall and rested her weapon on the grain bags. *Officers. The lizards spend all day and part of the night trying to kill us, and we send them breakfast. . . .*

Fourteen

The *ghartivatrampas* took a while to die although the delay was in no way due to a lack of enthusiasm on the part of the young Silsviss. Torin suspected that after failing to take the compound, their level of frustration was so high they were happy to kill anything. Although the smoke from a number of small fires had begun to smudge the sky, butchering the carcass and distributing the meat had barely begun.

Lieutenant Jarret's idea had indeed bought them some time.

Time enough for the navy to return and pull them out? All Torin's instincts said probably not.

She turned so she could watch the lieutenant talking to the Dornagain ambassador by the remains of the well, and smiled.

"You like him, don't you?"

"Morning, Mike. Platoon taken care of?"

Sergeant Glicksohn leaned against the building beside her. "Everyone's had their piss and porridge, and odd numbers along both walls are catching thirty. Except, of course, those who in the face of imminent death have to get it off one more time. You didn't answer my question."

"Do I like Lieutenant Jarret?" She shrugged. "Well, I haven't had to shoot him yet. For an untried second suddenly commanding in combat, that's saying *something.*"

He scratched at the quarter inch of dark hair filling in the area between collar and cheekbones. "Say more."

"More?" Rolling up an empty food pouch, she shoved it in her pocket. "I think he's handled everything that's been thrown at him with remarkable aplomb. He gives orders like he means them, but he's been willing to try new things. He honestly cares about his people, but he doesn't let that paralyze him. He listens to those with more experience, then makes up his own . . . what?"

"You're gushing."

"I am not."

"Yes, you are. You don't think he's enjoying all this . . ." One hand swept out in an arc around his body. ". . . a little too much?"

"He's not enjoying the combat, but I'll give you that he's enjoying his chance to command."

"And?"

"And he's little more than a kid, Mike. He's getting a chance to prove himself, and he's doing a good job. Let him enjoy it."

"You like him."

Torin surrendered. "Yes, all right. Are you happy now? I like him. Given a little time, he'll be an officer worth serving under." It wasn't until Mike's brows rose to meet his hairline that she realized she was smiling again. "Never mind."

"Do I look like the sort to speculate on a friend's facial expressions? No."

Torin banished the memory and dimmed the smile. "What do *you* think of him?"

"The platoon's stopped glancing over at you when he gives them an order. That's good enough for me."

"Well, I'm happy if you're happy."

"I'd be happier if I had a couple of beers, twelve hours' sleep, and a chance to get Ressk in a game of five card draw."

"Why Ressk?"

"The Krai can't bluff for shit."

"Probably why they don't play."

"Odds are." Covering a yawn with the back of one hand, he gestured toward the center of the compound with the other. "Looks like you're wanted. Wonder why he's looking so cheerful."

"He's a morning person. It's one of his least endearing traits. If it turns out to be more than that, I'll let you know." Torin reluctantly pushed herself off the wall and limped out of the sliver of shade into the sun. The fine patina of sweat that covered her entire body by her second step reminded her to find a moment and have Juan Checya look at her environmental controls. Collapsing from heat stroke came under *setting a very bad example.*

"Staff Sergeant, the Dornagain think they can repair the well."

Torin looked down at the rubble-strewn, unstable piece of ground then back up at her lieutenant. "With what, sir? Spit and luck?"

"With brute strength engineering, to hear the ambassador tell it. Point is, we're going to need that water." He glanced up at the section of sky that held the yellow-white circle of sun. "And soon."

"Yes, sir. What did you want me to do?"

"See that the Dornagain get all the materials they need. They can have everything excepting weapons, helmets, and vests."

"Stretchers?"

"Not all of them, but it won't hurt if they use a few. We're not going anywhere," he added in response to her silent question. "Win or lose."

She watched a muscle jump along the line of his jaw and knew exactly what he was thinking. "Win, sir."

It took him a moment and then he smiled. "You're sure?"

"Yes, sir. It's my job to be sure."

"Conn, what are you doing?"

"I'm looking at a vid of my daughter, what's it look like I'm doing?" The corporal snorted and settled back against the grain bags, his slate propped up on his knee. "I took it just before we left the station; she's showing me some kind of weird dance she made up."

The Marine on his other side glanced down and grinned. "Hey, cute. Let me see."

As Conn held out the slate, strong fingers closed

around his wrist and augmented muscles dragged arm and slate back to his lap.

"Are you out of your mind?" the heavy gunner snarled. "Don't you ever watch war vids?"

"The what?"

She rolled her eyes. "Some poor sap shows off a picture of his darling family back on station, and the next thing you know his brains have been spattered all over his buddies and they have to pry the picture from rigor mortis fingers. It's guaranteed to get you bagged!"

"Guaranteed?"

"Yeah. It's got the same bag rate as announcing to the world that you're short. Gosh, fellas . . ." She plastered on a goofy grin. ". . . just three more months and I'm a civilian again and I know exactly what I'm going to do. I'm going to go into partnership with my dad. He's old and he needs me." The grin disappeared and she drew a line across her throat. "Speech like that and next thing you know, bagged."

"But I am short."

She blinked. "What?"

"Two more months and I'm a civ . . ." It was Conn's turn to blink as her hand clamped over his mouth.

"I don't know why I even bother talking to you," she sighed.

"Staff? You've got to do something about Mysho."

"Do what?" Torin asked, looking up from an ammunition list. Then she took a closer look at the way the two men facing her were standing. That couldn't be comfortable. "Oh. I see."

"We didn't want to say anything, but she's got her masker turned up as high as it'll go, and it's still not helping. Even when we . . ." He met Torin's eyes, turned very red, and rushed on. ". . . you know, take care of it. It just comes right back and it's . . ."

He paused to search for a word and Torin hid a smile. "Distracting?" she offered at last.

"Yeah, distracting."

"And embarrassing," the other man muttered.

"I'll deal with it," she told them.

"But, Staff, why my tunic?" Binti asked a moment later.

"Because Humans can deal with this heat better than the di'Taykan can. Mysho's environmental controls are operating at no better than half capacity."

"But why *mine?*"

"Because mine's not working at all and yours will fit her."

"Oh. Do I get hers in return?" she asked, unfastening her vest. "I mean, half capacity's better than nothing."

"Do you really want to wear a tunic a di'Taykan's been pumping pheromones into all morning?"

"Uh . . ." She considered it.

"*And* deal with the next Silsviss attack?"

"I think I'll just sweat."

"Smart."

* * *

Sometimes, Torin said to herself as she came back from burying Mysho's tunic in the latrine, *I forget how young most of this lot is.*

"Staff Sergeant Kerr?"

"Dr. Leor." She turned to face him, noting how dull his eyes had become. "Are you all right?"

He raised a long-fingered hand as if to block her concern. "This one is merely tired." Unclipping her slate from his belt, he passed it over. "This one has found an antidote to the poison although the Humans may die too quickly for it to do any good. And also, this one regrets to inform you that one of the Marines injured in the crash died in the night."

And sometimes you can only get through it by forgetting how young they are.

"Fraishin sha aren. Valynk sha haren."

"Kal danic dir kadir. Kri ta chrikdan."

"We will not forget. We will not fail you."

The bags flattened, and Torin added four more cylinders to the three she already carried. And all the others that she'd never entirely put down.

"Sir! Movement on the hill!"

Jarret hurried out into the compound and scanned the horizon, one hand shading his eyes from the noon sun. "Where?"

"Everywhere, sir!"

"Get off the roof, then: both of you! Before they start shooting."

"It's showtime, people!" Stopping by the lieutenant's side, Torin handed him his helmet.

He put it on without comment. "What's that coming over the hill to the north?"

Flipping down her scanner, she frowned. "I believe it's a rock, sir."

"Big rock."

"Yes, sir. I believe the word we're looking for is boulder."

Boulders, most taller than the Silsviss moving them, crested the hills to east, west, and south.

Jarret shook his head in disbelief. "How far did they have to go to get all those? That many boulders don't just happen to be lying around on top of the ground, ready to be moved."

"Yesss, they do," Cri Sawyes told him, arriving in time to hear the lieutenant's protest. "The area to the northeassst isss a glacial plain."

"Next to a swamp!"

"The swamp isss to the wesst, Lieutenant Jarret. And it hasss been a very long time sssince the glaciersss rolled through."

"Still . . ."

"There are a great many bodiesss out there, Lieutenant."

"I'm aware of that, Cri Sawyes."

"We have a sssaying, many handsss can move a mountain."

"And apparently did," Torin muttered.

"Yesss."

"With two more dead, there's going to be holes in the line," Hollice mused.

"Yeah, holes. Nice to have an effect. My death'll have no effect at all."

Hollice sighed. "If you're back in the depths of despair, I don't want to hear about it. In fact, I'm sick of hearing about it and . . ." He turned to glare at the di'Taykan. ". . . if I hear one melancholy comment out of you, I'll kill you myself."

The turquoise eyes blinked. "That's not . . ."

"I mean it, Haysole. I've had it with you. And I've had it with lying around here, too."

"You're in pieces."

"So?" His right arm had been taped tightly against his side to keep it from losing its tenuous hold on his shoulder, the remains of the shoulder had been packed in under sealant, and thanks to the pain blockers, he still didn't feel a thing. Dropping his left leg off the stretcher, he grabbed the edge with his left hand and hauled himself up into a sitting position. The world wobbled for a moment, then settled more or less level.

Reaching out cautiously, he scooped his helmet up off the floor and dropped it onto his head. "Staff Sergeant Kerr, Corporal Hollice. I have an idea that can free up two more Marines for the walls."

"Two more?" Haysole asked when he flipped away the mike.

"Why not? You're not holding your weapon with your toes."

"I can't *stand*."

"Can you sit?"

"I don't know."

"So try."

"What if I can't?"

"We'll flip you over on your stomach, and you can fire prone."

The di'Taykan suddenly smiled. "It is a position I'm familiar with."

"Is there a position you *aren't* familiar with?" Hollice asked him wearily.

"This one does not believe it is a good idea."

"It's not my idea," Torin reminded him. "It's theirs. They seem to know what they're capable of."

"Do they? Do they know how movement and gravity acts on their injuries? They think because they feel no pain they are not as damaged as they are. If the di'Taykan is not taken out of here soon, he will die of the injuries that keep his legs from working. Move him around, and he will die sooner rather than later." Dr. Leor ran both hands up and over his crest, smoothing the feathers down tight against his skull. "If you wish this one to continue doctoring your people, Staff Sergeant, you will not fight this one on this matter."

"Lieutenant Jarret . . ."

"Neither of you will fight." His shoulders sagged. "This one thinks there is fighting enough going on."

Torin looked past the doctor into the room where the two Marines were waiting for her word. *If the di'Taykan is not taken out of here soon, he will die of the injuries that keep his legs from working.*

"What about Corporal Hollice?"

"This one would prefer he remain on the

stretcher; however, if you truly need him . . ." The shrug spoke volumes.

"We could certainly use him."

"Then you may. Do you want this one to tell the di'Taykan?"

Yes. "No, thank you, Doctor, it's part of my job."

"Corporal Hollice, I want you sitting, not standing, your weapon is to rest on the edge of the window, and the moment you feel you can't contribute to our defense you are to let me know immediately. I don't want any heroics, and I don't want any crap. Am I understood?"

"Yes, Staff."

"Good. North side window. Corporal Ng, outside on the south barricade."

"Yes, Staff."

"But before you go, Ng, give me a hand with this." Together, they lifted the grain bag under the window up on its end. "Now, go. Hollice, sit. They're caught in a crossfire on the north, so it won't matter much if your aim's a bit off. Haysole . . ." The look on his face stopped her cold. If she told him he had to just lie there, he'd be dead before sunset.

Fine. She bent and pulled his weapon out from under his stretcher and tossed it to him. "Hollice can't reload one-handed, and you can't get up or the doctor'll have my ass in a sling, so you'll be reloading for him."

"Wha . . ."

Both combat vests landed close by Haysole's stretcher. "Can you reach them here?"

"Well, yeah, but . . ."

"Good. Hollice needs a reload, he passes his weapon to you, you pass yours—with a full clip—to him, and reload his. Hang on." She dragged stretcher, di'Taykan, and vests closer to the window. "There." Arms folded, she stepped back and studied the two of them. Then she smiled. "I guess together you'll make one half-assed Marine."

For a moment she thought it wasn't going to work. The two able-bodied Marines on the east and south walls had turned to stare at her in astonishment. She glared their gaze back out the windows. The corpsman, trying to spoon some nourishment into a face ruined by the emmy's explosion, was not looking at her so intently that he might as well have been staring. They weren't the ones who mattered.

Hollice's expression she couldn't read, not with the light pouring in the window behind him, but he hadn't said anything, so he must've understood.

Haysole closed the fingers of one hand around the stock of his KC and lifted Hollice's vest by its ruined shoulder with the other. "I've got more clips left than he does, Staff. What happens when he runs out?"

Torin started breathing again. "Use yours."

"In his weapon?"

"The clips are interchangeable, Haysole. Or were you paying less attention in basic than I thought?"

He grinned up at her, and it almost masked the gray shadows on his face. "I don't think that's possible, Staff."

* * *

When she explained what she'd done to the doctor, more so he wouldn't undo it than because she felt he deserved an explanation, he shook his head.

"This one understands about the will to live, Staff Sergeant. You have devised an elegant solution."

"Thank you."

He stopped her before she made it out the door. "But what this one does not understand is why you seem to think you have—how do you Humans say?—put one over on the di'Taykan. He performs a necessary function."

Torin sighed. "No, he doesn't. If any of my people couldn't reload one-handed, either hand, I'd kick their butts back to basic training myself."

"But he accepted the function."

"No, Doctor. He accepted the hope."

"Settled?" Lieutenant Jarret asked when she returned to his side.

"Yes, sir."

"Good, nothing happened while you were . . ."

All around the hills the boulders began to roll forward, two or three Silsviss behind each keeping it moving down the slopes.

"Nice of them to wait for me," Torin muttered.

The lieutenant flipped his helmet mike down. "Fire at will but only if you've got a clear target. Don't waste ammo. What's the situation with the grenades?" he asked, turning to Torin.

"Insufficient quantity, sir, and they wouldn't stop those rocks anyway."

"Why not?"

"Well, they're rocks, sir."

As they watched, a Silsviss stumbled and was crushed by an errant bounce, his scream of pain lost in the shrieking of his companions.

"They're crazy!"

"They're only crazy if it doesn't work, sir."

"If *what* doesn't work?"

"I expect we'll find out in a minute, sir."

The first of the boulders reached the flat and slowed considerably, the heavy rain of the night before not yet baked out of the ground. Then the first stopped, captured by the soft ground. A second slammed into it, the impact moving them both only another few feet.

"Follow the fukking bouncing ball," Juan snarled, the muzzle of his weapon moving through jerky four-inch arcs. "Who can hit something moving that fast when you can't see anything but fukking bouncing boulders."

Beside him, sunlight gleaming darkly on her bare arms, Binti squinted through her sights and pulled the trigger.

Two hundred meters out, momentum moved a Silsviss through another three steps before he crumpled, a bloody hole where his chest had been.

The heavy gunner shook his head in admiration and grumbled, "Fukking show-off."

"They're not trying to get to us. They're building a barricade."

Torin watched the impact of another two boulders throw shards of rock up into the air and swore softly under her breath. The Silsviss now had shelter at the halfway mark. Race down from the top of the hills, charge in from the rocks. It would become a two part attack and the part from rock to compound a fast dash instead of the end of a long run.

"That should mean we have twice as many chances to stop them," Jarret muttered.

"And wouldn't it be nice if it worked that way, sir."

There were gaps in the ring of boulders. Some of the smaller ones had rolled closer to the compound, some of the larger had bogged down farther back. Most of the Silsviss running with the rocks had survived.

"If it was me," Lieutenant Jarret murmured, almost to himself, "I'd have moved the guns they took from the VTA down the hill with the boulders. Then I'd run as many people as possible to the rocks while the guns lay down a covering fire."

"And now they'll be close enough to hit us deliberately, instead of only by accident," Torin observed, flipping up her scanner. She couldn't see anything useful, and the glare had started a pounding headache. Just what she needed.

"You're not helping, Staff."

"Sorry, sir." Tone and delivery, that comment could have come from Captain Rose. Somewhat taken aback, she rubbed at a dribble of sweat running between her breasts and remembered how concerned she'd been that the polished diplomat working the *Berganitan* cocktail party wouldn't be able to handle combat. Her lips twitched. *They grow up so fast.*

"Once the Silsviss reach their barricade, can the heavies drop a grenade in behind?"

So much for the defensive battle he'd told Cri Sawyes they were fighting. Although, at this point, anything that helped keep them alive could pretty much be defined as defensive. They certainly weren't charging out anywhere.

Torin traced the trajectory from the piled grain bags to the boulders. "It might take them a shot to establish the angle, the heavies aren't exactly precision shooters, but it can be done."

"Are you sure?"

"It's my job to be sure, sir."

"Good. Tell them."

"Yes, sir."

The surrounding Silsviss started thrumming again before she finished speaking with Sergeants Glicksohn and Chou. By the time she got back to the lieutenant's side, they were at full volume and she could feel her teeth vibrating right out of her jaw.

"Another challenge?" Jarret was demanding of Cri Sawyes as she joined them.

"The sssame challenge, part two." His throat pouch had half inflated. "They're telling you they aren't going away."

"Really. Well, neither are we." To Torin's surprise, he took his slate off his belt and thrust it toward the Silsviss. "Tell them."

"Lieutenant, the dialect . . ."

"They aren't using words just sounds, emotions given voice. You don't need to speak the language."

His inner lids flicked across, and he shook his head. "They won't be able to hear me, Lieutenant."

"Oh, they'll hear you."

After a quick glance at Torin, who kept her expression absolutely neutral, Cri Sawyes took the slate.

Heads turned as the Silsviss challenge boomed out in the compound. Under helmet rims, eyes were wide and hands moved nervously up and down the length of weapons.

The lieutenant scanned his perimeter, pointed and beckoned. As Ressk ran toward them, Torin flipped down her mike. "Eyes front, Marines!" Barely able to hear herself over the noise, she nodded in satisfaction as the gawkers spun back around.

Ridges flushed, Ressk skidded to a halt. "Yes, sir?"

"Can you take out the background noise so we just have Cri Sawyes' voice on the slate?"

"Yes, sir."

"Do it. Then use my code to transfer a copy of the recording to everyone in the platoon."

"Your code, sir?"

Jarret's eyes lightened. "Are you telling me you don't know it yet?"

"Uh, no, sir."

As Ressk's fingers danced over the lieutenant's slate, Torin took a step closer so she could be heard without shouting. "May I ask what you're doing, sir?"

"Certainly, Staff. We're about to tell the Silsviss that *we* aren't going away either."

Both older and larger, Cri Sawyes' voice had a deeper tone than the massed voices of the surrounding Silsviss. Booming out of every slate in the compound, it laid a bass line under their challenge that spoke not so much defiance as contempt.

Half a dozen Silsviss broke cover and died, one of them hit nine or ten times.

"Let's be a little more frugal with the ammo," Torin advised sharply. "That's six down and two thousand, nine hundred, and ninety-four still out there."

"You counted?" Jarret asked as she flipped her mike back.

"Ballpark, sir."

Lilac brows drew in. "What?"

"An approximation," she corrected, making a mental note to smack Corporal Hollice upside the head if they both survived the day.

"I wonder what we're saying."

"Fuk you!" Haysole grinned as Hollice turned to scowl at him. "No, really, that's what we're saying!"

Weapon butt tucked under his good arm, he lifted his slate off the windowsill, listened for a minute, then nodded. "I think you're right."

"Not a phrase I'm usually wrong about."

* * *

The tempo of the thrumming changed.

Shots rang out from behind the boulders.

Torin glanced down at the new hole in the wall beside her, then up at the lieutenant, knowing he hadn't dropped only because she hadn't. "Good call, sir."

"Thank you, Staff. Tell them to turn off our reply and get ready."

"Yes, sir."

"You two are both crazy," Cri Sawyes hissed from the ground.

"Most of the targets will be coming down from the top of the hill. Some won't. Those are the ones not to miss." Torin rested her weapon on grain bags—once used for access to the roof, now built into a sort of command center. Given the angle of the buildings, they had as close to a full field of view as was possible. "Mark your targets and remember that they're shooting at us from a lot closer now."

"Here they come!"

No Silsviss reached the compound.

A great many reached the boulders.

As the first of the grenades arced up and over, Torin scanned the perimeter. No casualties, but that wasn't likely to last. She finished the circle and realized that all four Dornagain continued to work calmly at the side of the well.

How did we miss something that big?

"Sir! The Dornagain!"

Another grenade arced up and over.

"Get them under cover, Staff!"
"Yes, sir."

Juan stared out at the almost solid mass of bodies running for the south wall. He'd just dropped his last grenade behind the boulders. "I don't fukking believe it."

"You don't have to believe it," Binti snarled. "Just shoot!"

"Ambassador!" Torin had to grab at a fur-covered arm and pull to get his attention. "Get your people inside!"

"We are almost finished, Staff Sergeant." He effortlessly tugged his arm free. "We choose to continue working for the few moments more it will take. If we are injured, we absolve you from any blame."

"And if you're all dead, who's going to tell that to my superiors? Get your people inside. Now!"

His sigh fluffed out his whiskers. "A compromise, then. Strength of Arms will work from within the well, placing the last few pieces."

"She'll be within the well?"

"Yes."

All things considered, that didn't seem exactly safe, but at least it would move the others out of danger. "Fine. Do that. Just get inside!"

Biting her lower lip to prevent an undiplomatic outburst, she waited while the ambassador passed on his decision to his people. Shifted her weight from foot to foot, while they gathered up makeshift tools. Muttered under her breath while Strength of Arms climbed into the well, her movements surprisingly graceful although no faster than usual. And finally gave thanks to whatever gods were listening when all four Dornagain were safely under cover.

The lieutenant had moved to a position by the south wall while she was gone.

"Sir!" She had to shout to make herself heard. "The attack is strongest here!"

"I *had* noticed that, Staff Sergeant." He fired, adjusted his aim, and fired again.

Torin snapped off two quick shots of her own. While she admired the lieutenant's enthusiasm, leading from the front was not a good idea. If he died, she'd be stuck with Lieutenant Ghard—and she'd have to shoot him. "Sir! You're in command! We can't afford to lose you!"

"If the Silsviss get over this wall, there'll be nothing left for me to command!"

Dropping one of the front runners, she had to admit he had a point.

"What's happening on the north?"

One of the last grenades landed short of the rocks, but since there had to be more Silsviss in front than behind, it didn't much matter.

"There's a lot less of them on the north. They know they don't stand a chance running into the crossfire between the buildings, so they aren't. They're only trying to keep us busy enough that we can't reinforce the south."

Snapping another clip into his weapon, Jarret shot Cri Sawyes a tight glare. "Considering that until we arrived they'd been fighting with pointy sticks, they learn fast."

"For the sssake of my ssspeciesss, I accept the compliment. For the sssake of the sssituation, I apologissse."

"Apology accepted." He fired point-blank at a Silsviss, nearly to the wall, and took out the runner behind him as well. "Staff! Pull every third Marine off the north wall and send them to reinforce the south!"

"Yes, sir!"

The reinforcements weren't enough. The first Silsviss came over the wall.

Then the second . . .

Torin spun around as a Silsviss launched itself over her head and barely managed to block a spear thrust. Ducking under the point, she slammed the metal-reinforced butt of her KC up into an unprotected elbow and when the arm flew wide got the muzzle in under the chin and pulled the trigger.

A weight landed on her back.

She let it take her to the ground, rolled, and watched a spear point drive into the earth inches from her shoulder.

Not good.

Standing over her, the Silsviss paused to scream a challenge, and the center of his chest exploded with a soft, incongruous phut. Torin blinked away a spray of blood and rolled again as he toppled forward.

Up on one knee she fired twice more over the wall and without even the seconds necessary to change the clip, swung the KC like a club, smashing in the head of a Silsviss about to stab Cri Sawyes in the back.

That seemed to clear the immediate area.

Breathing heavily, adrenaline sizzling along every nerve, she slapped in a new clip and looked around.

There were more Marines than the enemy standing.

Always a good thing.

Then she saw Ressk take a spear in the leg. He screamed, fell, and bit down on a tail that just happened to be too close to his mouth. The Silsviss seemed more surprised than hurt, but it delayed the second blow long enough for Torin to fire.

Chewing and swallowing the mouthful of flesh, Ressk shoved aside the dead Silsviss, got his good leg under him and tried to stand without much success. Frowning, he glared down at the wound.

Most of the muscle had been carved off the side of his thigh and he could see bone.

It hadn't actually hurt until then.

The world became pain.

Blood welling up through his fingers, he squeezed everything back more or less where it went and curled protectively around it. He'd have screamed except he couldn't catch his breath.

When, inexplicably, he began to rise into the air, he whimpered.

"We do not wish to hurt you, Private Ressk, but we must move you."

He opened his eyes to see a Mictok eyestalk bent down by his face. "G'head," he gasped at his reflection as multiple forelegs laid him on the stretcher. "Get me out of here."

The eyestalk suddenly disappeared.

That was strange enough he found the strength to lift his head.

One of the Mictok—he didn't know which one, they all looked the same to him—had been flipped over on its back, all eight appendages in the air. No, seven. One was in the hand of the Silsviss standing over it. Given time, the Mictok could have righted itself, but a second Silsviss smacked it with its tail and sent it skidding across the compound.

The other three stood motionless around him.

"My weapon!" He swung at one, imprinting the mark of a bloody fist next to the red enamel cross. "Give me my weapon!"

No reaction.

The underside of a Mictok looked a lot softer than the top.

One of the Silsviss smacked it again.

Mandibles clacking, it bumped hard against the back of Sergeant Glicksohn's leg.

Half off the stretcher, fingers still inches from his weapon strap, Ressk watched Glicksohn turn.

Nearly trip over the Mictok.

Deflect the first spear thrust with the barrel of his KC.

Bend, get both hands under the body of the giant spider.

"Every time I see one, this little voice inside my head keeps screaming, Get it off me! Get it off me!"

Flip it back onto its feet.

Straighten.

Die.

The second spear went up in under the edge of his combat vest, slicing through soft tissue, up under the ribs, and into the heart.

He looked down at the rough wooden shaft angling out of his body.

His weapon fell from nerveless fingers.

His knees buckled, and he hit the ground.

"MIKE!"

Halfway across the compound, Torin saw him fall. Her first shot took out the Silsviss who'd speared him. The second Silsviss fell before she could get off her second shot.

As the world went black, Ressk closed his fingers around the KC. This time, he wasn't letting go.

By the time, Torin reached Glicksohn's side, the Mictok were clustered together and beginning to spin webbing around themselves. She didn't need his med-alert to tell her he was dead. Only the dead fell with that boneless disregard for gravity. She dropped to one knee and laid two fingers against his throat anyway.

No pulse.

But Ressk was still alive.

Lifting his upper body back onto the stretcher, she pulled her knife from her boot. Mictok webbing was supposed to be uncuttable. Torin got through it.

"You!" She grabbed an eyestalk below the bulge and turned it to face her. "Get the ambassador inside to the doctor. Now!" The loss of the leg had sent the whole collective into shock. She used her voice to bludgeon it aside. "And you!" Releasing the first eyestalk, she grabbed another. "Pick up that end of the stretcher!"

"We don't think . . ."

"Don't think! Do what you're told!"

Once they started moving, they moved fast. Even with only seven limbs. Torin had to run full out to keep up. Ressk wasn't getting the smoothest ride in, but at least he wasn't lying bleeding to death on the ground beside the dead sergeant.

They were almost to the med station when the largest Silsviss Torin had seen landed in front of them.

Landed?

He came off the roof!

The Mictok froze again. The end of the stretcher caught Torin in the stomach but she managed to get stopped. Unfortunately, the immobile Mictok on the other end continued to hold Ressk's feet up in the air.

The Silsviss throbbed out a challenge, throat

pouch fully inflated. Torin was about ready to drop Ressk on his head and bring her weapon around when Strength of Arm rose up from the depths of the well. And kept rising.

At her full height, she towered over the Silsviss.

Her fur gleamed brilliantly gold in the sun.

A sharp, musky smell bludgeoned aside the smells of the battle.

Long, muscular arms spread out to their full extension, making her look even larger. Then she roared.

The sound echoed off the surrounding hills.

A moment of stunned silence followed from Marines and Silsviss both. Someone sneezed. Before the Silsviss in front of her could turn, Strength of Arm reached down, grabbed his tail, and flung him nearly six meters over the north wall.

Roaring again, she started for the next closest tail.

For a nonviolent species, she seemed to have caught on quickly.

A third Silsviss flew past about four meters off the ground.

Torin appreciated the help, but they had bigger problems.

There were Silsviss on the roof of the eastern building, the building holding the med station and the injured. And the thatch was on fire.

FIFTEEN

"There's hundreds of them out there!"

Haysole tossed him his reload and caught the empty KC one-handed, labored breathing rising and falling around every movement. "You hitting . . . any of them?"

"A few." Blinking sweat out of his eyes, Hollice squeezed off three more rounds. "Doesn't seem to be making any difference, though. Hit one and two more take his place."

A deep breath in and out; Haysole's voice steadied as he snapped in a new clip. "Sooner or later one'll get through."

"Not on my watch."

"Oh, yeah, I forgot. You're Corporal Hollice, super Mar . . ." He broke off and stared up at the line of falling dust, gleaming in a stray ray of light. His eyes darkened. "Hear that?"

Hollice snorted. They were less than a meter apart and shouting to hear each other. "You mean the shrieking?" he asked sarcastically.

"No." The line of dust broadened. Thickened. His hair spread, each end straining up toward the thatch. He drew air in slowly through his open mouth. "I smell smoke."

"I don't."

"Useless Human noses." The di'Taykan changed his grip on the KC, sliding a finger in through the guard. "I hear something on the roof."

"The pitter and patter of each tiny hoof?"

"What?"

"Never mind."

"You're weird, Hollice, even for a Human."

A spear point drove through the thatch, and the line of dust became a sudden fall of debris. Haysole smiled, and fired nearly straight up.

The Silsviss that landed beside him, narrowly missing the stretcher, was dead.

The two who followed, were uninjured.

Haysole shot one as he drove his spear into the back of the Marine on the east wall and winged the other as he turned. The thrown spear took him in the leg. Unable to do more than point the KC in the right direction, he fired again and again until the Silsviss danced backward and died.

Knocking the spear free of nerve-dead muscle, he had a whole heartbeat to enjoy his victory when the northeast corner of the roof fell in, spraying the room with pieces of burning thatch.

"Bloody great!" Hollice spun around and wished he hadn't as the world tilted. Teeth clenched, he forced it straight. "The roof! It's on fire!"

Haysole used the KC to knock an ember off his ankle. "No shit!"

"The wounded!" Including the di'Taykan, there were six occupied stretchers in the room. "We've got to get the wounded out!"

Haysole fired two short bursts as a Silsviss came up the unguarded east wall and in through the hole in the roof. "So do it! I'll cover you!"

"Dream on." Remembering how Staff Sergeant Kerr had moved both stretcher and occupant, Hollice reached for the same grip with his good hand but had it knocked aside. "Don't argue! Your legs . . ."

Another Silsviss appeared, wreathed in more burning thatch.

"Get the others out first!" Haysole fired two quick rounds and then a third for insurance as the body pitched forward. "You said it yourself, I don't need my legs to shoot!"

Given that the others couldn't shoot at all, couldn't do anything but lie there and die, it was a convincing argument. Coughing in the rising smoke, Hollice tossed his weapon onto Captain Daniels, grabbed the end of her stretcher and began dragging her toward the door, yelling at the Marine on the south wall to help.

"But my post . . ."

"Is on fire, jackass!"

At the door to the second room, someone grabbed the stretcher from him, but before they could grab him, he dove back into the smoke. There were four more stretchers in there. And Haysole. And the Silsviss were still attacking the compound. He'd have fallen over and let someone else deal with it, but there wasn't anyone else available.

A quick look around showed the corpsman dragging his injured partner clear and no sign of the Marine from the south wall, but as only two of the wounded remained, he hadn't gone empty-handed. Both stretchers were closer to the door than Haysole.

"What are you doing?"

"Moving you!" The protests wouldn't have stopped him, but as he got the di'Taykan even with the others, a Silsviss emerged suddenly out of the smoke at the far end of the room. "Have it your way! Shoot from here!" He transferred his grip to the next stretcher without actually stopping his backward shuffle toward the door, sucking air heavy with smoke in through his teeth. His chest felt as though it were being ripped apart by jagged lines of pain. Apparently the blockers extended only to the edge of his injured shoulder. Eyes streaming, he got the stretcher to the door, but this time the waiting hands grabbed him first.

"Are you insane?" the corpsman yelled, trying to hold him without doing more damage to his injured side. "The whole end of the roof's about to go!"

On cue, chunks of falling thatch drew lines of flame though the smoke.

Coughing too hard to argue, Hollice ripped himself free of the corpsman's grip and threw himself down on the floor. Where it wasn't a whole lot better.

Either the pain blockers had given up or his brain

had figured out a way around them, but since everything hurt with equal intensity, he figured it couldn't get any worse. On his knees and good elbow, he scuttled forward, aiming for the sounds of di'Taykan profanity he could hear coming out of the smoke.

Hands closed around both his ankles.

He sprawled, full length, arm stretched out. As he began moving backward, his outstretched hand touched fingers. Then the fingers closed around his.

"Taking . . . too long," Haysole gasped. "Thought I'd . . . meet you . . . halfway."

Blood dribbled in two dark lines from the corners of his eyes, and his lips were nearly blue. Whatever he'd done to get this far had clearly added to the damage he'd taken in the crash.

Hollice felt as though his arm was about to come out of his socket when Haysole started moving as well. He couldn't have crawled more than three meters from the door; they'd be out of it soon.

The sudden stop forced a cry out through cracked lips. He'd been wrong about the pain not getting any worse. The pull intensified. Haysole didn't move.

"Something . . . on my legs." A falling line of sparks raised a blister along one cheek. He looked up. Looked down and smiled a charming di'Taykan smile. "Fuk it," he said clearly. Then he let go.

Hollice couldn't maintain the grip alone. His fingers were ripped free and he was hauled backward so fast only his outstretched hand was burned by the collapse of the roof.

* * *

The thatch had been over a meter thick on closely laid wooden beams. It burned with an intensity that ignited the fibers used as binding within the thick mud walls.

Perhaps the fire had been more than the Silsviss had bargained for.

Or perhaps Strength of Arm's sudden decision to get involved in the battle had turned the tide.

Torin didn't know and she didn't care. The Silsviss had withdrawn behind their boulders and that was good enough for her. As the fire roared unchecked and Strength of Arm returned, shaking and whimpering, to the astounded Dornagain, she started a bucket brigade to soak the western wall of the burning building, the wall that she needed to keep her perimeter whole. She made sure the med station got set up again, that the injured were tended. That the rest of her people got fed and watered and that they remained alert. That the bodies, Mike's and two others, were bagged and reduced. She was the calm that anchored every other emotion in the compound—regardless of how she herself felt—because that, too, was part of her job.

When the sun went down, the fire . . .

The pyre.

. . . was still so high there was no need to send up any of the few remaining flares.

As the sun rose, Torin splashed water on her face and bit into the second of the three stims all ranks above sergeant carried. Three, because they only delayed the need for sleep, they didn't replace it and someone who'd never spent their nights trying to keep the remnants of a platoon alive against overwhelming odds had determined three was all that was safe.

Safe was a relative term.

She swallowed the bitter gel—purposefully bitter to keep them from becoming a habit—and walked dripping over to the remains of the eastern building. They'd saved the bottom three feet of the wall and rubble enough had fallen into the doorway to keep the line more or less unbroken. The grain bags the doctor had been using in the first room had exploded in the heat, leaving behind a smell reminiscent of burned toast. Compared to the stink of rotting bodies that surrounded them, it was almost pleasant.

Her stomach growled, and she ripped the strip off a food pouch, pushing the contents up into her mouth and swallowing without actually tasting.

"How many?"

"Three. Privates Eislor, Stovak, and Haysole. Two di'Taykan and a Human if you're keeping score."

"Staff."

She swallowed the last of the paste. "I'm sorry, sir. That was completely uncalled for."

Lieutenant Jarret tested the temperature of the wall with the palm of his hand, then leaned his forearms on it. "It's all right," he said after a long moment. "I understand where it's coming from."

It had come from places he'd never been, from battles he'd never fought. Torin turned, ready to challenge his assumptions, but his profile—carved out of the morning, too tight, too unmoving to be flesh—convinced her to hold her tongue. He couldn't understand it all, not at his age, not his first time out, but, unfortunately, he was on his way.

"Twenty-eight of us left; plus Lieutenant Ghard, two aircrew, and an unconscious Captain Daniels, and still hundreds of them." He sounded as though he were discussing the weather. Not good weather perhaps, but his voice held neither the self-pity nor the despair that Torin expected. That anyone might expect under the circumstances. "If we don't get out of here, do you think this'll be considered one of those legendary last stands like Carajys or Dalfour?" he wondered, crushing a rough pellet of baked mud under his thumb.

"Very probably, sir." Every military organization needed heroes; tragic heroes if they were the only type available. "But if it's all the same to you, I'd rather this became one of those amazing last-minute rescues, like Laysalifis."

"You were there."

She'd been on her first combat drop and so scared she'd tested just how waterproof combat uniforms were. "You checked my records."

"I checked everyone's records, Staff. General Morris insisted this mission was vital to signing the Silsviss, and I wanted everything to go well, to justify his trust in me." Without moving his head more than a fraction of an inch, he indicated the ring of bodies. "If the Silsviss aren't impressed, they should be." Then, pausing no more than a heartbeat, he added, "I don't want to die here."

"I don't want to die anywhere, sir."

The corner of his mouth moved toward a smile. "That's the trick, isn't it, Staff? Do you ever regret leaving the farm?"

She stared down into the ashes. "Every now and then, sir. Every now and . . ." Squinting into the rising sun, she let the words trail off. Something glittered out by the outline of the doorway that had led to the third room.

Something glittered.

Heart pounding, she took a step back and vaulted over the wall.

"Staff!"

Her boots and legs were covered in a fine coat of gray by the time she reached it.

A masker. Partially melted, covered in char but unmistakable for all that.

Eislor had died by the far wall. It couldn't have been hers.

"If I die, take off the masker before you bag me."

She weighed it on her palm for a moment, then turned and threw it as hard as she could toward the Silsviss. It very nearly reached the rocks. Breathing heavily through her nose, she wiped her face clear before she turned back toward the perimeter.

Lieutenant Jarret said nothing until she was back on the other side of the wall. Then, as if she were another di'Taykan, he touched her lightly on the back of the wrist, fingers cool against her skin, and said, "Don't ever do that again."

"I won't, sir."

"If you died . . ."

"You'd manage without me, sir." She took a deep breath and straightened. "And it isn't every second lieutenant, I'd say that of."

He was young enough that he couldn't help looking pleased, but he quickly sobered. "We won't survive another attack like yesterday's, will me?"

Mike Glicksohn was dead, so was Haysole. Ressk had taken a blow that would have removed the leg of anyone but a Krai. There couldn't *be* another attack like yesterday's. But that wasn't what he meant. "No, sir."

"They could have overwhelmed us then, but they didn't. Why?"

They turned together toward the ruin, and when he met her eyes a moment later, Torin knew they were thinking the same thing.

"Survival at what cost?" Jarret murmured.

She had no answer. She wouldn't be the one giving the order.

He looked away first. "Come on, we'll talk to the Dornagain."

"No."

"But, Ambassador, yesterday . . ."

"Yesterday was a terrible and unique situation, Lieutenant. Terrible and unique."

"And that same situation is likely to be repeated today."

The Dornagain ambassador cocked his head, a

gentle breeze ruffling the fringe of fur along the curve of each ear. "I hear nothing from the Silsviss."

"Yet," Torin told him, shortly.

"Ah. Yes. Yet. And if they come, you would like the Dornagain to join your Marines in defense, Staff Sergeant?"

"In answer, Ambassador, I ask you what you once asked me, do you not think it would be better if you learned to fight your own battles?"

He sighed. "And I must answer what you answered me; it is a little late for that."

"So you won't help?"

He raised a hand and she noticed that the pad under the broken claw was red and inflamed. "Not won't, I'm afraid, can't." When he saw where her scowl was directed, he used the hand to brush his whiskers back. "No, not because of so minor an injury; we would literally not be able. Strength of Arm reacted without thought, impulsively if you would, and that is not a reaction we can replicate on command. As a species, we weigh everything we do, considering all possibilities. If we were to weigh our own death against the taking of another sentient life, I'm afraid we would die."

"But Strength of Arm . . ."

He glanced back over one massive shoulder to the building that sheltered the other three Dornagain. "Strength of Arm is now thinking, and her impulsiveness is causing her a great deal of pain. She is the first Dornagain in centuries to take a life. We fear for her sanity." He looked down at them both and spread his hands in surrender. "I am sorry, but if it comes to it, all we can do is die beside you." Rising up off his haunches, he turned and walked back to his people.

"Given their size, they'd be a lot more useful if they died in front of us," Torin muttered.

"Staff."

"Sorry, sir." She fell into step beside him, wondering why she was having so much trouble maintaining her detachment. *Maybe because this wasn't supposed to be a combat mission. Maybe . . .* She touched the cylinders she carried. *. . . because no one was supposed to die.*

They'd barely gone three meters when the Silsviss began to thrum.

"Seems like we're out of options, Staff." He sounded calm, but the end of his hair had begun to flip about. "Get Sergeants Chou and Gli . . . sorry, get Sergeant Chou and the heavies. We haven't much time."

Frowning, Juan scratched at his wrist point. "You want us to fukking flame them, sir?"

"Yes."

"But we don't flame people, sir."

Standing just behind the lieutenant's left shoulder, Torin wasn't certain she'd ever heard Juan Checya complete a response without a profanity before.

Lieutenant Jarret managed to maintain an outward calm but they could all see the struggle under the surface. "It's all we have left," he said at last. "If any of you have a better idea . . ." He paused so they could hear the Silsviss gaining volume. ". . . now would be the time."

Only the Silsviss answered.

"I'm issuing the orders. I take full responsibility."

Juan glanced around at the other eight heavies grouped in a loose half circle in front of the lieutenant. Over half of them were fighting injured. Then he looked from the lieutenant to Torin. Then he sighed. "Just followin' orders has never been much of a fukking defense, sir. We'll take our own responsibility, if you don't mind." Leveling his weapon, he reached out and twisted the front receiver around so that the pressurized gas cartridge clicked into place. "We've only got two of these each," he said over the sound of eight other cartridges, "so it had better be enough."

They couldn't use the flamethrowers from the remaining building, so Torin doubled the number of KCs shooting through the walls. If the Silsviss moved toward the buildings to get away from the fire, they'd move into a fire of a different type.

"Here they come!"

"Steady." Torin dropped into position behind the wall and raised her weapon. "Wait for the lieutenant's order."

They'd distributed the ammo from the dead and from those too injured to contribute to the defense. It had to be enough.

Other days, other attacks, they'd started shooting by now. Torin squinted into her scanner. Did the Silsviss look confused? Were there moments of hesitation in the shrieked challenges? And since they kept coming closer, did it matter?

"Marines!"

Lieutenant Jarret's voice in her helmet sounded completely confident. If he had any doubts at all, she couldn't hear them. And if she couldn't hear them, no one could. Which was exactly how it should be. She drew in a deep breath and held it.

"Fire!"

A three-round burst slammed into the Silsviss from every KC in the compound. They rocked back but didn't stop.

"Fire!"

Another three-round burst.

"Heavies!"

She felt rather than heard the nine ready themselves to stand.

"Flame!"

The Silsviss were so close to the perimeter, they were almost shoulder to shoulder, too tightly packed for the sort of erratic defensive maneuvers they excelled at. The flame swept over them and back, and over and back, each of the heavies roasting their own arc of the circle.

The screaming didn't differ that much from the shrieking, but the smell . . .

Torin clenched her teeth and ignored it.

"Marines on the walls, fire at will!"

The Silsviss who broke forward died.

"Marines, in the building, fire!"

The Silsviss who broke away from the flames died.

"Fire!"

And kept dying.

"Fire!"

The smoke had begun to make it difficult to find a target. Sighting through her scanner, Torin kept firing.

A burning Silsviss crashed into the grain bags and died. The closest Marine reached over and pushed the body off the barricade.

An arrow rattled off her helmet, bounced off her shoulder, and hit the ground. Beyond hoping that the doctor had the antidote ready, Torin ignored it.

Then the first of the flamethrowers ran out of fuel. The rest lasted only a second longer.

The only Silsviss moving on the other side of the perimeter were writhing on the ground, keeping the smoke from settling. Wondering why the lieutenant hadn't called a cease fire, Torin turned. She knew exactly where he was supposed to be, but it took her a moment to find him. She hadn't expected him to be lying on the ground.

By the time she reached his side, his muscles had begun to tremble.

"Corpsman!"

He'd been on one knee to shoot and the arrow had gone almost an inch into the back of his left calf.

His eyes were half open and the palest lilac she'd ever seen.

"Corpsman!"

Hollice fell to his knees on the other side of the lieutenant's body and held out a small, snub-nosed syringe on a wrapped hand. "Legs work, not much else," he panted. "Doc says . . . wham it into one of the big blood vessels in the neck."

Pushing the lieutenant's chin up with one hand, Torin took the syringe with the other. Below the surface, Human and di'Taykan physiognomy was not exactly the same and the tremors weren't helping. If she injected the antidote into the wrong place . . .

He'll be as dead as if I don't inject it at all.

She ran her thumb along the column of his throat, found a pulse, and drove the syringe home.

Lieutenant Jarret jerked once, his eyes dilated almost black, and he went totally limp.

Ripping her slate free, Torin checked his medalert, breathing as heavily as if she were running full out. "It says he's stable. This is stable?" A short nudge showed no response at all. "He's unconscious!" Glaring up at Hollice she snapped, "This is an antidote?"

Sitting back on his heels, Hollice sighed wearily, cradling his burned hand in his lap. "At least he's not dead."

And the world came rushing back.

Breathe, Torin. She filled her lungs with smoky air and found calm. Or possibly denial, but at this point either would work. "You're right." Mirroring Hollice's position, she hooked her slate back on her belt. "Aren't you supposed to be lying down?"

"Corpsman needed help. The spi . . . Mictok webbed themselves into a corner."

"And the Dornagain?"

The disgusted expression answered for him.

Torin shook her head, not exactly in disbelief because this information only reinforced something she'd believed all along. "Let's try and look at it like job security, Corporal. If it wasn't for us, the Others would overrun the Confederation in twenty minutes."

Hollice snorted. "Fifteen."

"Very likely. Can you stay with him?"

"Yes, Staff."

"Good." She flipped her helmet mike down as she rolled up onto her feet. "Cease fire! Let's have a look around."

Greasy smoke rose up from every point on the compass, drawing inky lines across a blue-white sky. There were Silsviss bodies everywhere, most stopped by fire, then shot. Against the south wall of the remaining building were places where the bodies were piled three deep. The smell of burning flesh could be ignored, but the smell of burning blood was very nearly overwhelming.

In the heavy silence, Torin could hear someone vomiting behind her but she didn't turn to see who. It wasn't important, and it wouldn't be the last. All along the inside of the perimeter, Marines knelt facing the enemy, duty and adrenaline together overcoming exhaustion to hold them in place. In a few minutes, if nothing happened, they'd start to sag. The corpsman knelt by another casualty. It looked as though a Silsviss had made it over the wall and had fallen, burning on a Marine. The Marine was alive. The Silsviss was dead.

The only living Silsviss in sight was Cri Sawyes,

standing motionless by the well, a KC hanging limply from his hands.

Torin sent out a team to deal with any possible wounded, watched as Lieutenant Jarret was moved to a stretcher and inside, then, finally, walked over to Cri Sawyes.

"Are you all right?"

He shook his head. "Ssso many dead. I have ssseen battlesss before, Ssstaff Sssergeant. I have marched into citiesss after the bombersss have been there, but thisss . . . That ssso few of you could dessstroy ssso many of usss."

"For what it's worth, I'd have preferred it if the platoon could have survived another way."

"At the moment, that isss worth very little. Later, perhapsss . . ."

She didn't insult him by saying she understood. He either knew she did, or he didn't want to hear it. "I suppose this'll pretty much close the door on the Silsviss signing that treaty with the Confederation."

His tongue flicked out, just once. "On the contrary, it will ssseal it. Thisss isss the sssort of thing our governmentsss ressspect."

"And you . . ."

"Me?" He turned slowly in place, his eyes never leaving the circle of bodies and the Marines now walking among them. He flinched as a single shot rang out. "I am here, Ssstaff Sssergeant, the government is not. Lieutenant Jarret was injured?"

"An arrow. Dr. Leor's antidote stopped the poison, but he's unconscious." *At least he's not dead.*

Torin shifted her weight onto her good leg. "I'd better go tell Lieutenant Ghard that he's in command."

"Should I be worried?"

She snorted. "I can handle him."

"Me?"

"Yes, sir." If there was another functional officer around, Torin had no idea where she or he was hiding. "Lieutenant Jarret was hit by an arrow."

"A poisoned arrow?"

"Yes, sir." By the time she finished explaining, Lieutenant Ghard's facial ridges had returned to their normal color.

"I wanted this command you know, back on the VTA." He turned, much as Cri Sawyes had. "I don't now."

Torin swallowed her first response. And her second, which was considerably longer and just as inappropriate. "The hard part's over, sir. It's only mopping up and waiting now."

"You think the Silsviss won't attack again?"

"There's no way of knowing, sir."

"Then what are we waiting for, Staff?"

"Whatever happens, sir. A Marine's expected to improvise."

Ghard stared up at her, eyes wide. "We're almost out of ammo, there's only a handful of us uninjured, we still don't know who shot us down or why, and you're saying we're expected to improvise!" His volume had risen with every word, and the surrounding Marines were turning to listen.

"Do you have a better idea, Lieutenant?" She held his gaze with hers and locked it down.

"No, no better ideas."

"Orders, sir?"

"Orders?"

Torin raised a single brow.

Ghard swallowed. "I, uh, guess you'd better get me a list of, uh, personnel and supplies."

"Yes, sir." She would, of course, obey every order he gave, but until he convinced her he knew what he was doing, he'd give the orders she *intended* to obey. Releasing him, Torin turned and walked away.

"What the fuk was that about?"

Binti tossed him a pouch of water, then dropped down with her back to the grain bags and laid her KC across her knees. "Staff was just telling Lieutenant Ghard he's in command."

"So we're down to that, are we? Fukking air support in command."

"Don't sweat it, Juan." Eyes closed, she let her head fall back. "Staff won't let him screw us over. Keeping twoie looies in line is what she does best."

"Good fukking point. She did a nice job on Jarret."

"Yeah, he's been doing okay. Nice buns, too."

Juan snorted. "Hadn't noticed. You think it's over?"

"I'm too tired to think."

"You see Ressk and Hollice when you went for the water?"

"Hollice looks like death warmed over, but he's going to make it. Ressk's got so much sealant holding him together he can't bend his leg."

"That's no fukking reason to leave us out here all alone."

Binti opened her eyes and stared up at the heavy gunner. "He can't bend his leg, how's he supposed to kneel behind these bags?"

"Let him stand," Juan snickered. "He's short."

A sigh followed close on the heels of her answering chuckle. "I must be tired, that wasn't funny. Anyway, Staff had him shooting from inside, propped up against the wall. And he says the smell of all this cooked meat is making him hungry."

"Fuk!"

"That's what he said you'd say."

They'd left the station with forty-one Marines plus six—the two pilots and four aircrew, forty-seven Marines altogether. There were fifteen dead—thirteen in cylinders and two aircrew in the VTA's engine room. Thirty-two live Marines. Of that thirty-two, nine were too badly injured to do anything but wait for rescue—and at least three of those had better not be kept waiting for long.

"We have twenty-three Marines able to stand the perimeter, sir." Although Ressk wasn't so much standing as propped. "Including you and me. The heavies have three flares left between them, nothing else. Combining all remaining ammo, we can give each of the twenty-three a little better than half a clip."

Lieutenant Ghard rubbed so hard at his lower ridge it paled. Torin barely managed to resist grabbing his wrist and pulling his hand away from his face. "And the good news?" he demanded, clearly expecting there to be none.

"We have plenty of rations still and the Dornagain did fix the well."

"So we won't starve while we're waiting to be slaughtered."

"Apparently not, sir." She hooked her slate back onto her belt. "Also, the Silsviss have retreated all the way to the top of the hill. The teams sent out to deal with the wounded report no one alive behind the boulders."

"How do you send people out to *deal* with the wounded, Staff Sergeant?"

"Without hesitating, sir, when the only other option was to let them die slowly in great pain."

He shuddered. "Better you than me, Staff."

"Yes, sir."

"They're not done with us. I can feel it. They're up there regrouping."

"Lieutenant, I don't think . . ."

From the top of the hill, the Silsviss started to thrum.

Torin turned away before she smacked the "I told you so" expression right off Lieutenant Ghard's face.

SIXTEEN

"What are they doing?" Torin curled both hands into fists to stop herself from grabbing Cri Sawyes by the shoulders and shaking him until he answered. "Why haven't they had enough?"

Cri Sawyes turned a dull, defeated gaze toward her. "Why should they? Becaussse you have?" Then he snorted and smacked his tail against the ground. "But you haven't, have you? You'll keep fighting until there'sss no one left ssstanding."

Arriving in time to hear that last bleak observation, Lieutenant Ghard stumbled to a stop and panted, "Would they give us an opportunity to surrender?"

"No."

"Then this is it. It's over." He swung his KC up, stared at it as if he'd never seen it before, and let it swing back against his side on its strap. "They'll show no mercy; we've been killing their wounded."

"They've been killing their own wounded, sir. A mercy death from us changes nothing." Torin found herself almost reluctantly pushed back into pragmatism by the lieutenant's reaction. A little hysteria would've felt good.

"But we won't survive another attack!"

"Begging your pardon, sir, but how the hell do you know?"

Looking confused, he opened and closed his mouth but was unable to find an answer.

"We survived the last attack. And all the attacks before that. We survived a crash landing, weeks of diplomatic posturing, and the incredible tedium of marching in straight lines. Why should we quit now?"

He stared up at her and, after a long moment when the only sound in the compound was the thrumming of the Silsviss, he sighed. "Marines don't quit, Staff Sergeant. We may retreat on occasion, but we don't quit. Was that the answer you were looking for?"

"It was the only answer, sir."

"You're a *serley* pain in the ass, you know that, Staff?"

"Just part of the job, sir."

The corners of his mouth curled up into a reluctant smile. He flipped down his mike. "Heads up, Marines, they're coming back for more. If you need me, Staff, I'll be in position on the perimeter."

"Sir."

"Do you really believe that you can sssurvive another attack?" Cri Sawyes asked quietly when Lieutenant Ghard was out of earshot.

"Not for a minute."

"But you convinced the lieutenant."

"I doubt it; he's a pilot, not a fool. Attitude, Cri Sawyes, is all we have left." She glared out at the surrounding hills, teeth clenched together so tightly her temples ached. Attitude wouldn't be enough. Then she frowned. But it might be the answer. "What if we decided to play it their way?"

"Their way?" Cri Sawyes repeated.

"I challenge their leader, one on one. Winner takes all." Her heart began to beat harder, faster.

"Do you think you could beat a young male in hisss prime? One whossse only thought isss to win?"

"Yes."

"Thessse young malesss are not like that pitiful creature you fought in the bar."

"That doesn't matter."

It was his turn to stare. "Perhapsss you could win, Ssstaff Sssergeant, but you are not the leader here. Lieutenant Ghard isss."

"Oh, yeah." It was a stupid idea anyway. She was a Confederation Marine, not some hormonally hopped-up teenager. Stupid, stupid idea. Her nails dug painful half moons into her palms. But it might have worked. . . .

The thrumming changed suddenly, picking up a new rhythm and rising in pitch.

Torin swung her KC up and slid a finger behind the trigger guard. "You know, dying like this really annoys me."

"Dying like what, Ssstaff Sssergeant?"

"Dying for no good reason."

"It may not come to that."

Her first step back to the perimeter became her only step. Cri Sawyes had sounded almost as though he were in shock. "What?"

"That isss not a challenge. Look."

She looked out along the indicated path and saw three Silsviss coming down the hill, one carrying the bleached skull on the pole, one of the others carrying a wrapped object held out on both hands. "If it's not a challenge, what is it?"

"I think it'sss a sssurrender."

"I can take all three of them," Binti said softly, squinting through her sight and targeting each in turn.

"No." Standing behind the north wall, in line with the descending Silsviss, Lieutenant Ghard wiped his palms on his vest. "Let them come."

Barely turning her head, Binti glanced up at Torin, who nodded.

"They must know we can drop them," she murmured. "They've got balls, I'll give them that."

"Their ballsss are what got usss all into thisss messs," Cri Sawyes observed dryly.

Binti snickered. "Ain't that usually the case."

The three Silsviss split up to move through the boulders, then re-formed on the other side. Where they waited.

"Now what?" Ghard demanded.

"I suspect they want us to go out and meet them, sir."

"I don't trust them."

"Cri Sawyes and I will go if you want."

"Oh, yeah," he snorted. "Like it would be better to lose you than me. No chance of Lieutenant Jarret regaining consciousness in the next couple of seconds?"

If only. "No, sir."

"Pity." He shoved his feet into his boots and straight-armed himself over the grain bags. "Private Mashona."

"Sir?"

"If we fall, see that they fall right after us."

"Yes, sir!"

I notice you didn't check with me on that *order,* Torin thought, following the lieutenant.

"Keep your mike on, Staff. I want everyone to hear what's happening."

"Yes, sir."

Clouds of carrion flies rose up as they walked, settling almost immediately behind them. They had little enough time to feed before the sun baked all moisture out of the dead.

It took Torin a moment to realize that the faint hissing she could hear was Lieutenant Ghard sucking air through his teeth. The Krai sense of smell wasn't as acute as a di'Taykan's, but it beat out a Human's three to one. And his nose was about half a meter closer to the ground than hers was.

As the two Marines and Cri Sawyes stopped about nine meters from the three Silsviss, the thrumming from the hills softened until Torin could barely hear it. *Now what?*

Their backs against one of the boulders, the

Silsviss stared, throat pouches inflating and deflating slightly with every breath.

Just kids, Torin realized. Next to Cri Sawyes, their physical immaturity was obvious. They were smaller, their faces were sharper, and they fidgeted constantly, tails jerking through agitated figure eights.

This is the first time they've gotten a good look at us. Probably the first time they've seen mammals our size. She remembered the first time she'd seen a Mictok and wondered at the lack of reaction. *Still, we've been killing each other for days now, I guess they feel like they know us.*

The Silsviss holding the skull stepped forward, shifted his grip, half turned, and smashed the bone against the rock.

Torin's finger was on the trigger by the time the shards settled. She couldn't hear the thrumming over the pounding of her heart.

No one moved.

Then the Silsviss holding the wrapped object stepped forward. Moving slowly, submissively, the third Silsviss unwrapped it.

Torin stared down at the bloody head and thought she'd never seen anything quite so pathetic.

"Their leader," Cri Sawyes murmured. "He dissshonored hisss pack by losssing—asss you hadn't killed him, they did. You're to mount hisss ssskull asss a sssymbol of your victory."

"We are?" Lieutenant Ghard sounded dubious about the honor. "Could you get that, Staff Sergeant Kerr."

"Yes, sir."

It was surprisingly heavy.

The walk back to the perimeter seemed to take longer than the walk out. Carrying the rewrapped head in outstretched hands, Torin listened to Sergeant Chou's voice describe the Silsviss returning to the top of the hill and tried not to think about what she was stepping in. At the grain bags, she waited until both Lieutenant Ghard and Cri Sawyes were over, then she set the head down and followed.

She could feel every eye in the compound on her as she picked it up again. *If that was a trick, now would be the time to attack.*

"They're back at the top of the hill," Sergeant Chou announced over the helmet relay. "Nothing seems to be happening."

The thrumming grew louder.

"Fuk!"

Torin had no idea which Marine had said it, but it seemed to sum up the situation.

Then the thrumming stopped.

"They're gone." Cri Sawyes blew out his throat pouch, then deflated it completely. "All of them."

Although he could no more see beyond the hills than any of them, there was something in his voice Torin had to believe. When there was no reaction, she remembered that only Sergeant Chou, Lieutenant Ghard, and herself had understood. She waited a moment, scanning the empty horizon, willing it to remain empty, then she translated Cri Sawyes' observation.

"They're gone. All of them."

The cheers and whistles were fifteen voices short, but they sounded good regardless.

"What are you going to do with the head?" Lieutenant Ghard demanded. When the noise in the compound suddenly stopped, he snatched off his helmet and scowled into it, muttering, "Forgot the *serley* thing was on."

Technically, the question should have been what was *he* going to do with the head, but since he seemed to be leaving it up to her . . . Torin grinned and, lifting the bloody package high into the air, raised her voice. Staff sergeants did not need microphones to make themselves heard. "I'm going to mount the skull as a symbol of our victory!"

This time, the cheers and whistles were loud enough that she could almost believe she didn't carry thirteen small metal cylinders in her vest. Conscious of Cri Sawyes' gaze, she lowered her arms and turned to face him.

"Will your Confederation allow you to hold sssuch a battle honor?" he asked.

"I'd like to see them try and stop me." The blood that had run down her wrists was beginning to itch as it dried.

Cri Sawyes' tongue flicked out. "Asss a matter of fact, Ssstaff Sssergeant, ssso would I."

Torin slipped the head inside the doctor's largest specimen bag, sealed it, and activated the charge. In a matter of hours, there'd be nothing left of the soft tissue but a full molecular survey. *Time enough then to go looking for a stick to mount it on,* she reasoned, crossing to Lieutenant Jarret's stretcher. He was still stable and still unconscious, although Dr. Leor was working on an antidote to the antidote.

She squatted beside him and laid her hand over his. After a moment of watching his chest rise and fall, she sighed and stood. Nothing had occurred to her except half a dozen well-worn clichés.

One good thing about the kind of battle they'd just been through together; it put that unfortunate night into the proper perspective. In comparison, it meant nothing at all. Which was exactly how it had to be.

In the next room, the Dornagain ambassador had somehow convinced the Mictok to emerge from their protective cocoon. Remaining seven limbs held tight to her body, Ambassador Krik'vir lay cradled in a nest of webbing, her companions protectively grouped to either side and above her. As Torin approached, she swiveled an eyestalk around and broke off her conversation with the Dornagain.

"Staff Sergeant Kerr, the Human who saved us; he has died?"

"Yes, Ambassador."

"We are sorry to hear that. We are sorry to hear of any death, but this one we feel responsible for."

"You're not. Sergeant Glicksohn chose to save you."

"Knowing that it put him at risk?"

"Yes, ma'am."

"We find it strange," the ambassador murmured, almost to herself, "how a species can be able to make such a sacrifice one moment and can kill another sentient being the next. This mix of caring and violence is most confusing—it must be a factor of bisymmetrical species." Then realizing whom she could count in her audience, she swiveled an eyestalk up toward the Dornagain. "We mean no offense."

He smiled. "We take none."

"Staff Sergeant Kerr, will you see to it that we receive the details of Sergeant Glicksohn's life? We will ensure that he is never forgotten and will live forever in Mictok memory."

"Every time I see one, this little voice inside my head keeps screaming, Get it off me! Get it off me!"

"You'll have the download as soon as possible," Torin assured her, thinking that Mike would appreciate the irony.

"We thank you for your assistance in this matter." Ambassador Krik'vir shifted position slightly, causing a ripple effect through her companions. "We understand the Silsviss have offered you the victory and retreated."

"Yes, ma'am."

"So it has ended. What happens now?"

Torin actually had her mouth open to answer when her implant chimed, letting her know she was back on-line.

"Staff!" Ressk hobbled in from the front room. "Lieutenant Ghard says the *Berganitan* is back! They're sending another VTA to evac!"

Feeling somehow separate from the nearly hysterical reaction of Marines and civilians alike, Torin found herself wondering why she wasn't more surprised by the Navy's sudden reappearance.

Med-op stripped the old sealant off Torin's arm and leg, pronounced the healing well under way, resealed only the leg wound, and released her. Scratching at the dry skin on her arm, she made her way through the crowded outpatient area to the quieter section reserved for those who'd need bed rest to recover.

"Hey, Staff! What's the word on the lieutenant?"

She stopped at the end of Hollice's bed. "He'll make a full recovery. They're bringing him up slowly, but he should be conscious by 1500."

"And Captain Daniels?"

"Tanked. But they're still running tests to determine the full extent of the damage."

"Maybe now Lieutenant Ghard'll stop acting like a hen with one chick."

"Maybe."

"You think they're getting it on?"

"I try not to think about the sex life of officers, thank you, Corporal. But since you ask, no. The lieutenant clearly worships the ground the captain flies over. If she should lose her mind and agree, he'd never be able to get it up." She nodded toward Hollice's heavily sealed shoulder. "I expect they'll be tanking you, too."

"Yeah. Full body immersion." He shuddered dramatically. "I hate it. You come out with your fingers and toes all wrinkled, and while you're in there, it's like returning to the womb without the room service."

"The what?"

"Not important. Hey, Staff?" Eyes narrowed, Hollice lifted his head off the pillow, as though he had words for her ears alone. "Is it just me or is there one hell of a lot of medical personnel here? I mean, this is twice the size of what we usually get, they've added six med-op modules to the ship."

"It isn't just you," Torin told him shortly. No one had been able, or willing, to tell her why the remnants of a single platoon were getting so much grade-A attention. It wasn't that she was complaining, and it wasn't any more than her people deserved, but the whole thing added to the nebulous feeling she'd had since pickup that something wasn't exactly level.

Not, not just since pickup . . .

Circling the room, she spent a moment with everyone else, advising Ressk not to get any of the KC's cleaning solution on his bad leg. "That stuff'll dissolve the sealant, you know."

"I know." He showed her a missing patch about two centimeters square. "But it's the first chance I've had to strip it down, Staff. First time in days I haven't been actually using it. Although," he added, "if that chirpy Human medic says *'And how are we feeling?'* one more *serley* time . . ."

"You'll grin and bear it."

"Not my first choice," Ressk grumbled as she walked away.

Stepping outside the medical module, Torin noticed a lock that led out of the Marines' section of the ship. Not entirely certain why, she walked over to it and hit the release. Her implant chimed.

Access denied without proper clearances.

That was new. But somehow not unexpected.

Seemed like the brass didn't want word of their experience on Silsvah reaching unauthorized ears. Didn't want it discussed over a jar of beer in the Chief's and PO's mess. Interesting.

Rolling various bits of memory over to see the other side, she turned and made her way to the ladder leading down to the platoon's quarters. Those Marines who'd either come through miraculously unscathed or, like her, able to be patched and released, had cleaned their weapons, eaten a huge meal, and with only two exceptions, crawled into their bunks. Kleers was still eating, and Corporal Conn was deeply immersed in the vid from his wife and daughter he'd found waiting for him.

Torin took the report from Sergeant Chou, told her to get some sleep, and went into her own quarters where she methodically wrote up the casualty reports, entered a recommendation that Corporal Adrian Hollice and Private First Class di'Stenjic Haysole receive the Medal of Honor, then sat and stared at her reflection on the desktop screen. When no answers were forthcoming from her other self, she called up the military news channel, half-expecting it to be blocked.

There were no reports of the *Berganitan* being in a battle although the Others were moving quickly toward the sector. The Silsviss hadn't yet signed the treaty, and time was running out. The phrase *vitally important* was used seven times in a ten-minute report. It was vitally important the work on the defense grid begin immediately or it wouldn't be ready to activate in time. It was, therefore, vitally important the Silsviss sign the treaty. The remaining five occurrences were variations on the theme.

She keyed in the code for Ressk's slate and, when he responded, sent him an encoded text-only message.

At 1430 Torin's implant chimed.

General Morris would like to see you in his office at 1530.

So. General Morris was on board. Another nonsurprise.

She showered, changed into her service uniform, downloaded the reports into her slate, and paused at 1455, one hand raised to activate the door. If she was about to hear her suspicions confirmed, there were others who deserved to be there.

With the familiar weight of her combat vest resting on her shoulders, Torin made her way back to the med-op modules.

"The lieutenant is awake, Staff Sergeant. However, I don't feel that it's in his best interests to have visitors at this time."

"Sir, I am on my way to speak with General Morris about a . . ." The pause was deliberate and went on just long enough for the captain to begin frowning. ". . . situation where the lieutenant was in command. The general will want to know his condition."

"The general will find out Lieutenant Jarret's condition from me, Staff Sergeant."

"Yes, sir," Torin acknowledged. "But I also have casualty reports the lieutenant will need to see, and . . ."

"Let me speak plainly, Staff Sergeant. I have been given orders that no one is to talk to the lieutenant *before* the general debriefs him." The fuchsia gaze flickered around the room, alighting everywhere but on Torin. "That will be all, Staff Sergeant."

"Yes, sir." Wondering why the doctor should be feeling guilty about following what was, after all, a fairly common order, Torin made a quick visit to the general ward.

"Medical data now?" Ressk snorted. "Oh, come on, Staff, even you could hack into *those* files. But," he added quickly, as she caught his eye, "since I'm stuck in this bed with nothing to do, I'd be happy to do it for you. Can I ask why?"

"You've got all the pieces I have. Just put them together."

"Will I like what I find?"

"Probably not."

General Morris was not alone in his office module.

"Staff Sergeant Kerr, this is Cri Srah," he announced, nodding to the Silsviss standing by his desk after the barest of military formalities had been observed. "He represents the Silsvah World Council."

If the Silsvah had a functioning World Council, this was the first Torin had heard about it. As she understood it, their final destination had been intended to assist in the creation of such a body.

The Silsviss misunderstood her expression. "Cri Sssawyesss, who I believe you know, isss of the sssame firssst egg."

Wishing she'd taken a moment to have the sibilants in her translation program repaired, Torin nodded.

General Morris cleared his throat, reestablishing himself as the center of attention. "In light of what your platoon went through, Staff Sergeant Kerr . . ." His gaze dropped down to her combat vest. Although his eyes narrowed slightly, he continued without mentioning her peculiar combination of uniforms. ". . . I thought you should know that the Silsviss have decided to join the Confederation."

He thought she should know? A general thought a staff sergeant should know? *Nice to be thought of, but that's not how it works.* Not usually anyway.

Cri Sawyes had said that the Silsviss governments would be impressed.

She looked from Cri Srah to General Morris and back again, and she remembered what Haysole had told her about the general after her first meeting with him. *I've heard the general's looking for a chance to be more than he is.* He had to have set things up so that he was certain the Silsviss would sign. But the only significant thing he'd actually done was to send the remnants of Sh'quo Company down to the planet.

"This was a test, wasn't it, sir?" The silence waited for her to continue. "The entire battle was a setup from the beginning. The Silsviss are a . . ." Cri Srah shifted position and Torin made a diplomatic edit. ". . . have a warrior culture and wanted to be certain that they weren't aligning themselves with the weak. That was the real reason why you sent a combat platoon on a ceremonial mission. The Silsviss decision to join was based on the way we performed when under attack."

"I'd be interested to know how you arrived at that theory, Staff Sergeant." The general leaned back in his chair, confirming her suspicions by not denying them.

"It was all just a little too convenient, sir." Although the muscles of her shoulders and back were rigid, training kept her growing anger from showing as she outlined all the little coincidences that could be piled into something that stank of a setup. Their Silsviss escort had gone back to base just before the missile shot them down, but the escort from their destination had never shown up. They'd been shot down not only over a wilderness preserve but over a swamp that would cushion the crash. The various small packs of Silsviss adolescents in the preserve had come together into what amounted to an army far, far too quickly. There had been a full platoon's worth of extra weapons on the VTA for no good reason.

A frown cracked the expressionless facade. "Was

Lieutenant Jarret aware of the true nature of our mission, sir?"

"No. But his psychological profile was such that the odds were very high he'd not blow the armory. Or allow himself to be overruled by his NCOs." The general's tone was light, conversational, almost amused. "If you figured this out in the midst of that battle, I'm very impressed."

"No need to be, sir." And her inflection added, *because your opinion means less than nothing to me.* "Although I'd begun to doubt the string of coincidences early on . . ."

Where there're two viable theories, there could easily be a third or a fourth.

". . . my suspicions were fully aroused when the Silsviss in the reserve had no reaction to our appearance. The largest mammal on Silsvah is about the size of a Human infant and yet they showed no curiosity about us. They had to have seen, if not live mammals, some sort of representation previously." She remembered Cri Sawyes mentioning his fear of how an unscrupulous power could use the teenage males. General Morris had certainly proved his point. "My suspicions were strengthened when the *Berganitan* showed up so quickly after the battle was over. They solidified when I saw the medical facilities that had been added to the ship."

"The medical facilities?" For the first time the general looked surprised.

"Far too great a commitment of equipment and personnel for a single platoon, and the only possible reason for it could be guilt—at a very high level. So

I did some checking." Technically, Ressk did the checking, but working on the military's need to know basis, that was something the general didn't need to know. "You ordered the *Berganitan* away from Silsviss and instructed the captain to lie." Which made General Morris not only responsible for the deaths of good people but for ensuring they died without knowing why. The first was something officers had to do every day, and the strength that took was one of the few things Torin respected them for as a group. The second was unforgivable.

The weight of Cri Srah's regard pulled her gaze from the general's face.

The Silsviss leaned forward, almost in anticipation. "Your general dissshonored your warriorsss by deliberately sssending them into an ambush."

No. Not almost in anticipation. Very definitely in anticipation.

Which was when Torin understood why she hadn't been allowed to see Lieutenant Jarret. According to his medical data, once the antidote had been neutralized, he'd made a nearly instantaneous recovery. He should be standing here, not her. He was the commanding officer.

But they needed her.

Because General Morris believed a mere second lieutenant wouldn't be able to do what needed to be done and she would.

What had they planned on doing to him had he not been injured? At least she knew why the doctor looked so guilty. Didn't they take oaths about that sort of thing?

Cri Srah was waiting for her reaction.

As Torin understood the Silsviss, it was unimportant that the general did not, could not, have made the original decision to sacrifice the platoon, that it had to have been made at the parliamentary level. For the Silsviss, it was enough that he had been responsible for giving the order to those actually doing the fighting and, as essential as the order may have been to keep the Others out of this sector, he had dishonored the platoon by doing so.

She had a skull in her quarters that defined the Silsviss' response to dishonor.

It was vitally important that the Silsviss sign the treaty.

This time, when Torin looked to the general, he met her eyes. What she saw there didn't surprise her. She'd begun to suspect that she was forever beyond surprise.

General Morris was prepared to die. He expected to die. She'd seen the same dark expression too many times over the years to mistake it now.

Whoever had decided that Lieutenant Jarret would be incapable of the necessary ending had been right. Could she end it? Yes. Would she?

She could see Cri Srah's tail beginning to lash back and forth, but all she could think of was an old joke.

Back before the Confederation combined their three newest members into one military organization, three officers, a Human, a di'Taykan, and a Krai are standing in a shuttle bay, at the edge of a stasis field discussing the courage of their troops. To prove the courage of their race, the Krai officer calls over a Krai samal *and gives the order to jump through the stasis field. The* samal *snaps off a salute and leaps into space, decompressing messily.*

The di'Taykan sneers, and to prove the courage of the di'Taykan, calls over a di'Taykan fe'harr *and gives the same order. The* fe'harr *snaps off a salute and leaps into space, also decompressing messily.*

The Human raises a brow and calls over a Human private, giving the same order.

The private snaps off a salute and says, "Fuk you, sir."

"Now that,*" says the Human officer, turning to the others, "is courage."*

Torin had no trouble following orders, but she really hated being manipulated.

General Morris' lip curled and she could hear him say, *Would you get on with it!* just as clearly as if he'd spoken out loud. He'd screwed his courage to the sticking point, and he clearly didn't know how much longer it would stick.

It was by no means a truism that insight into a species could be gained by wholesale slaughter, but Torin was willing to bet that, right at this particular point in time, no one in the Confederation knew the Silsviss as well as she did.

Her right foot caught Cri Srah solidly in the stomach. As he folded forward, gasping for breath, she dove onto his shoulders, slamming him down to the floor.

"Have you gone crazy?"

General Morris sounded a little shrill, but preoccupied with maintaining her hold on a remarkably flexible lizard without being either brained by the tail or shredded by the claws, Torin ignored him.

Cri Srah got one arm around at an impossible angle and raked his claws across her back.

The combat vest took most of the damage. If she survived the fight, Torin figured there was more than enough room in med-op to take care of the rest.

"Staff Sergeant Kerr! Stop it immediately! That's an order, Staff Sergeant!"

The shouted, almost hysterical orders weren't a problem, but when the general grabbed her uninjured arm and tried to yank her away from Cri Srah's throat, she moved her leg just enough to release the tail on a narrow trajectory. She didn't see it hit, but the general grunted and staggered back, not so much releasing her arm as no longer being able to control his hand. *If he was ready to die,* Torin reasoned, struggling to trap the tail again before it broke bones, *he shouldn't complain about a slight concussion.*

She could feel Cri Srah struggling to inflate his throat pouch and she tightened her hold.

Fortunately, when he began to claw at her arm, fighting for air, he didn't have strength enough to do much more than shred skin.

"How dare you imply that we were dishonored," she shrieked, pain lending volume. "We were vastly outnumbered! We were under fire from our own weapons! And we fukking won!" If this worked, history could edit out the profanity. If not, it didn't much matter.

Gasping, Cri Srah clutched her arm and tried impotently to pull it away.

She eased up slightly—if he passed out, they'd have to do it all again. "You know the importance of this treaty! By sending us unknowing into battle, our general tells us that we're expected to win whatever the odds! That he believes us to be the best warriors of the Confederation!" Using her knee, with all her weight behind it, Torin threw the Silsviss away from her and then loomed over his prone body, dripping blood onto the floor. "You dishonor my general by suggesting he dishonors us! I demand that you yield!"

One hand clutching his bruised throat, Cri Srah began to yield.

Torin kicked him in the thigh. "Not to me! To my general!"

Cri Srah rose as the general staggered out from behind his desk, nose bleeding and no longer exactly straight. Still holding his throat, he bowed, "General Morris, I yield." Then turning to Torin, he bowed again, whistling his approval. "We insssissssted on the ambush and that you be so dramatically outnumbered. The packsss demanded accesss to at leassst a few of your weaponsss before they'd cooperate."

"You could have judged our skill from our history."

"Yesss," he admitted. "But it wasss more important we judge thossse usssing the ssskillllsss."

"Did Cri Sawyes know?"

"No. He doesss now." His tongue flicked out. "Hisss reaction wasss sssimilar to yoursss although he actually killed the government member who informed him. He'll be promoted."

Good for him, Torin thought.

"Now, General . . ." As he turned, Cri Srah smacked his tail against the floor. "I believe I have a treaty to sign."

Torin decided to take that as her dismissal.

"So we were judged worthy, and they're going to sign."

"Yes, sir." This time, Torin hadn't asked to see the lieutenant. She'd used the code Ressk had given her to his room and walked right in. The doctor had taken his masker in order to keep him isolated, so she sucked air through her teeth and tried not to bleed on the bed.

"And the Others?"

"Not even in the neighborhood, sir."

Lieutenant Jarret's eyes were as dark as she'd ever seen them and his hair stood out like a lilac fringe around his head. "I don't like being used, Staff. And I don't like the Marines under my command being used to make a point."

And the politicians will note your protest, and it won't make a damned bit of difference.

He must have read the thought off her face; his hair suddenly flattened. "Was it worth it, Staff?"

Was it ever? Was it worth the loss of Haysole and Mike and all the dead Marines in all the different battles on all the different worlds? She had to believe that it was or what was the point in continuing. She had to believe. "We needed the Silsviss to sign, sir."

"That doesn't answer my question, Staff."

"Best I can do, sir."

After a long moment, he nodded. "Go get yourself patched up, Staff Sergeant. I'd hate for you to bleed to death now it's all over."

She looked down at the thick crimson stains that all but glued her left hand to her right arm and frowned. "Actually, sir, I'd hate to bleed to death at any point in the proceedings."

The doctor had just finished sealing her arm when General Morris walked into med-op. The two black eyes and the broken nose attracted the attention of everyone in the room, but he waved them all away.

"I need to speak with Staff Sergeant Kerr. Alone."

The room emptied. The general waited until both hatches had swung shut, then he walked over to stand by Torin's examining table. She sat up. She should have stood and come to attention, but she didn't much feel like it.

He didn't seem to notice. "I was supposed to die. I was never actually in combat, you know, but I *was* willing to die. My not very notable career had come to a full stop, but this, this would have ensured I was remembered. It would have given me a place in Confederation history."

"A noble sacrifice for the good of the many, sir?"

"Yes, exactly."

"And the Marines who died on Silsvah?"

He tried to frown, but the swelling had gotten too bad. "They were Marines, Staff Sergeant, and they died in battle like hundreds of Marines before them."

Torin weighed her options and decided it wasn't worth it. "Yes, sir."

The general visibly relaxed. "How did you know?"

"Sir?"

"How did you know I wasn't supposed to die? Why did you choose to attack Cri Srah?"

"The Silsviss have a pack mentality, sir. Each Silsviss knows where he fits into the pack, and the strong fight to rise. They've just joined our pack, and they wanted to see how much they could push us around. If we'd fulfilled their expectations, they'd be running the Confederation by the end of the century."

His expression almost made the whole thing worthwhile. "They're not going to be an easy species to coexist with," he said after a long moment, trying to sound as though she didn't know he'd agreed to die for nothing.

"Yes, sir." Torin slid to the edge of the table and stood. "But that's not my problem."

"No," the general agreed stepping back, "I don't suppose it is. Still," he added calculatingly, "it could be. If you wanted to apply for officer's training, I'd support your application." He chuckled encouragingly. "After what you did today, half of Parliament would support your application."

"Officer's training?" Torin lifted her combat vest off the chair where the medic had placed it.

"That's right."

"Thank you, sir, but no." One by one, she slid the cylinders out of her vest and indicated that the general should hold out his hands. "There's two very good reasons that I'd make a lousy officer." She dropped the thirteen Marines who'd paid for his place in history into his cupped palms. "First of all, I work for a living."

Stepping back, she gestured at his face. "You should have a doctor see to that, sir." The gesture snapped into a perfect salute that he was unable to return; there were too many cylinders for him to hold them with only one hand. Then she turned on her heel and walked toward the hatch.

"Staff Sergeant Kerr."

One hand on the hatch release, she paused.

"You said there were two reasons. What was the second?"

"The second reason, sir?"

"Yes."

"My parents were married."

AUTHOR'S END NOTE

Hands up everyone who recognized that battle.

Yes, it *was* loosely based on the battle of Rorke's Drift, one of the early battles of the Zulu War. (January 22nd and 23rd, 1879). In this battle, a hundred and thirty-nine men and officers of the British Army, thirty-five of whom were sick or injured, held off what was later estimated to be a force of 4,000 Zulus. The movie *Zulu*, staring Michael Caine, was a fairly accurate dramatization of the battle although none of the many historical records mention competitive singing.

For their efforts in saving the Rorke's Drift post, a total of eleven men were awarded with the Victoria Cross for conspicuous bravery, making this the highest number ever awarded for a single engagement in British Military History.

Color-Sergeant F. Bourne, the senior NCO, was not among those eleven. He received instead a Distinguished Conduct Medal.

Why, although his bravery and courage under fire

were unquestioned and he was instrumental in turning a number of the Zulu attacks, didn't Color-Sergeant Bourne receive the Victoria Cross?

Because he was only doing his job.